Praise for *The Iron Rose*
A *Publishers Weekly* Best Book of the Year

"A swashbuckling tale."   —*Booklist*

"Canham spins a terrific yarn, complete with vivid historical detail, humor, and characters that will touch the mind and heart. . . . Xena the Warrior Princess has nothing on Juliet, who's as proficient with her biting wit as she is with a blade. . . . Readers who are tired of the traditional romance formulas, characters, and conflicts will find this little treasure a welcome escape."

—*Publishers Weekly* (starred review)

"The key to the brisk plot besides the action is Juliet, a strong independent leader whose lust for life grips the audience. Fans of the genre will take great pleasure in this vividly strong seventeenth-century tale."
—*Midwest Book Review*

"A colorful historical backdrop, believable and memorable characters, and a love story to dream about— all in one book. This one's a keeper for those who love the sea and wild adventure rides."

—*Romantic Times*

continued . . .

My
Forever Love

Marsha Canham

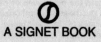

A SIGNET BOOK

SIGNET
Published by New American Library, a division of
Penguin Group (USA) Inc., 375 Hudson Street,
New York, New York 10014, U.S.A.
Penguin Books Ltd, 80 Strand,
London WC2R 0RL, England
Penguin Books Australia Ltd, 250 Camberwell Road,
Camberwell, Victoria 3124, Australia
Penguin Books Canada Ltd, 10 Alcorn Avenue,
Toronto, Ontario, Canada M4V 3B2
Penguin Books (NZ), cnr Airborne and Rosedale Roads,
Albany, Auckland 1310, New Zealand

Penguin Books Ltd, Registered Offices:
80 Strand, London WC2R 0RL, England

First published by Signet, an imprint of New American Library,
a division of Penguin Group (USA) Inc.

First Printing, July 2004
10 9 8 7 6 5 4 3 2 1

This one is for my longtime agent, Aaron Priest, who has always been my champion, despite the grief and aggravation I give him.

For my family, Peter, Jeffrey, Michelle, Austin and Payton, who bring sunshine to all my days.

For the Intrepids, who have never flagged in their support and friendship.

For the Loopies, who share the days of ranting as well as those of utter fun and laughter.

Lastly, to my inner muse, who keeps whispering over my shoulder and has led me down such a wonderful path.

Prologue

The sound was like that of tearing silk. Tamberlane did not see the arrow coming, but he heard it and ducked to the side, avoiding the barbed tip by such a small allowance that he felt the hot lick of air singe his cheek. He swung around, his sword raised before him, long threads of blood spinning off the tip in strings of red pearls. His mantle, once white, was as crimson as the croiserie that marked him as a Crusader. His armor was rent in a dozen places. The links were split and broken by blows that brought his blood forth to mingle with that of the countless Saracens who harried and attacked the Christian army every inch of the way along the sun-baked road to Jerusalem. They were less than twelve miles from the city gates, and despite the Saracen army being scattered across the desert, their leader, Saladin, refused to relent. Word had reached the English camp only yesterday that fresh reinforcements from Egypt had arrived to bolster the infidel's numbers as well as fortify the Holy City's defenses.

There was fighting every day. Bloody, violent, pitched battles that started when the boiling yellow eye of the sun rose over the sand dunes and ended when it sank red and vaporous into the desert night. King Richard, called Lionheart by his men, had been determined to reclaim Jerusalem and had marched his army through the August heat in miserable conditions, but even his seemingly boundless strength was beginning to flag. He woke with fevers and putrid bowels nearly every morning, yet he was always the first to appear in armor, his leonine mane burnished gold by the hot sun.

Tamberlane had been in Outremer two years longer than his king. He knew the merciless heat of the desert. He knew the unrelenting hatred of the Saracens who lauded those among them who were killed in battle as martyrs for the faith. Fanatics, all, they fought hard and they fought well. They crept through the desert like an army of black ants, able to vanish down hidey-holes in the sand without a trace and to move like the wind on magnificent horses bred for speed and endurance.

On this particular day, the attack had been launched on a hail of arrows that had rained down upon the tiny coastal village where Richard had set up camp, killing soldiers and townspeople alike.

Tamberlane found himself standing in the midst of chaos. The sun had turned the fine desert sand into shimmering clouds of dust. There was panic in the village as the people flew in all directions. Some ran with their hands over their heads as if that would shield them from the arrows that continued to fall

all around them. Some merely stood and screamed and waited for death.

Out of the corner of his eye, Tamberlane saw a woman dart out from behind a mud hut, a babe swathed in blue blankets clutched in her arms, the only thread of bright color in the otherwise dun and gray chaos. An arrow jutted out from her cheek, pinning the cloth of her veil to her face.

The next instant, he was swinging his blade again, his attention diverted by an enormous Saracen wielding a starburst—a spiked iron ball tethered to a length of chain. The ball streaked across his chest, narrowly missing the bulk of wool and armor. The look of a zealot's hatred was in the Saracen's eyes as he lunged forward a pace and wielded the chain in another lethal circle.

Tamberlane's own faith had once been equally pure and uncompromising, his obedience blind, his convictions unshakable. He had been knighted on the eve of his twenty-first birthday, and by nightfall the following day, he had knelt before a tribunal of warrior monks and pledged his sword, his life to the Order of Knights Templar. He had forsworn all material possessions, forfeited all earthly desires and ambitions, and pledged his service to God, vowing— earnestly and eagerly so—to become a lifelong servant and slave to the Holy Order.

"Do you swear to God and to our dear Lady Mary to be, all your life long, obedient to the Master of the Temple and to the Prior who shall be set over you?"

"Yea, with the help of Almighty God, I do swear it."

"Do you swear to God and to our dear Lady Mary to observe, all your life long, the manners and customs of our Order without question, doubt, or reservation?"

"Yea, with the help of Almighty God, I do swear it."

"Do you swear to God and to our dear Lady Mary that you will, with the utmost strength and powers that God hath bestowed upon you, help as long as you shall live to conquer the Holy Land of Jerusalem; and that you will, with all your strength, will, and honor, aid to keep guard all that which the Kingdom of Christ possesses?"

"Yea, with the help of Almighty God, I do swear it."

Two months later, he had been on a ship bound for Cyprus, his white mantle as unspoiled as his confidence, for he had yearned since he was a stripling boy of twelve to one day wield a mighty sword in God's name. His faith was like an intense light, as searing and hot as his first glimpse of the fierce desert sun.

During the intervening four years, however, the brilliance of that light had begun to fade. His unshakable faith had been eroded by doubts and misgivings. Unquestioning obedience had been tested by the laughter of the Brothers who watched while ragged, beggarly Muslims were chased down for sport and their heads mounted on pikes like trophies. It was tested each and every time he witnessed the murder and slaughter committed in the name of Christianity. And it was strained nearly to the edge of breaking after the Lionheart ordered the execution of two thousand seven hundred prisoners—many of them women and children—after the months-long siege of Acre had ended in a negotiated surrender. The prisoners had submitted themselves as hostages, trusting the English king's promise to set them free, but a week after Richard had taken control of the city, he had ordered them all dragged outside the city gates and executed.

The Templars had been in the forefront, carrying out the butchery without reservations. It had taken a full day to complete the slaughter, a day throughout which Tamberlane kept his back turned and his rage focused on the many attempts the Muslims made to rescue their people. That night when he returned to the city, he could barely bring himself to look at the bloody horror strewn outside the gates. Nor could he, for the first time since taking his vows as a knight and a Templar, bring himself to give thanks in prayer to a God who commanded such a terrible price for His love.

Yet here, months later, he was still fighting under the black and white silk Beauseant, still rallying to the Crusaders' battle cry: Remember the Holy Sepulchre.

Tamberlane bared his teeth and braced himself as the Saracen warrior windmilled the chain and starburst in a great hissing circle overhead. His gaze flickered for a split second—it followed the woman with the arrow in her cheek who was running a gauntlet of clashing soldiers and rearing warhorses. The bundle in her arms was nearly knocked free, but she stumbled to keep her balance and kept running away from the burning village toward the open sand of the desert.

The ball swished close enough to scrape the steel of his helm and brought Tamberlane's concentration sharply back into focus. The Saracen was a big bastard, and there was too much power in his trunklike arm for the English knight to hold off a direct blow with his sword; the blade would likely snap like kindling.

Taking a calculated risk, he waited for the next sweeping revolution and stepped swiftly into the circle carved by the arcing ball. The chain caught him high on the arm, driving the links of his mail into his flesh, but the ball whipped around and lashed the Saracen in his own back, the three-inch spikes driving deep into his body and shattering his spine.

The Saracen screamed, spraying Tamberlane's face with bloody spittle as he fell forward. The knight shoved the sagging body aside and, once again, his gaze was lured away by a flash of bright blue wool.

The woman and babe had reached the far side of the road and were stumbling out into the soft sand. She looked weak and dazed, for her footsteps staggered side to side and she went down twice, hard onto her knees.

Tamberlane's sea-green eyes narrowed.

A pair of mounted Templars had seen her and had broken away from the mêlée to give chase, their swords drawn. While they were as filthy and crusted with dust and blood as Tamberlane, he thought he recognized one of them by the configuration of dents in his helm.

Hugh de Bergerette. He had been first to offer his sword at Acre and last to walk off the bloody killing field, covered head to toe in gore and seeming to revel in it.

Tamberlane stepped hastily over the body of the dead Saracen and broke toward the open sand, intent on cutting across the path of the two Templars. He had been fighting all morning in the oppressive heat and wore seventy pounds of heavy mail armor, but he reached the woman's side just as the knights reined their horses to a halt beside her.

Without thinking about what he was doing, Tamberlane lifted her up from where she had fallen and placed her behind him, using his big body as a shield.

"Stand aside, Brother. We do God's work here."

"God's work is over there," Tamberlane said in a low voice, "where men fight back with swords and pikes. This is but a woman, sorely wounded, with a babe in arms."

"Babes in arms grow to become men at arms," one of the Templars snarled. "Now stand aside, in the name of God."

Tamberlane heaved a breath from his lungs. He startled the knight by reaching up and grabbing the outthrust sword by the blade. Taking it in both fists, he brought it down hard over his knee, snapping the steel at the hilt.

"I have seen enough senseless slaughter committed

in the name of God to last me a thousand lifetimes."
He threw the broken halves of the sword onto the
ground in disgust. "I'll not bear witness to another."

The Templar whose sword lay in pieces on the
ground was so shocked he jerked back on the reins,
which set his horse to skittering sideways on the
sand.

"She is a filthy paynim," he hissed. "Whore to an
even filthier infidel. You would break your sacred
covenant with God in order to defend *this*?"

Tamberlane gave no response other than the one
they could see blazing in the cold green eyes. Because
his features were obscured by grime, shadowed by
his helm and camail, it was that selfsame eerie color
that brought a flash of sudden recognition to de Bergerette's ugly face.

"Tamberlane. By God's holy order, it is Ciaran
Tamberlane who lusts after the foul-smelling whore.
Is the babe yours, then? Is that why you place your-
self and your oath to God before them?"

The first knight brought his horse back under control and scowled. "Methinks you may be right, Hugh.
Shall we have a look? Shall we see if the babe has
fair coloring and the devil's own green eyes?"

Tamberlane felt an odd heaviness settle over his
body, then spread to encompass the very air around
him. He heard the two knights baiting him, but their
voices became muffled and the words indistinct. The
sounds of clashing steel and the screams of men and
animals dying faded and grew dim, replaced by the
very acute sound of a single pendant of blood dripping off Tamberlane's fingertip and landing in the

sand below. The next thing he knew, the panting of the horses' breaths were blowing like an armorer's bellows, and he was using that to time his motions as he swung upward with his sword and smashed the first knight across the face with the flat of the blade.

Spurred on by the sound of his Brother's jawbone cracking and the screams that sent him staggering out of the saddle, de Bergerette's instincts prompted him to raise his blade in defense against a second strike. But he was too slow. The movement put his arm directly into the path of Tamberlane's blade, which took away de Bergerette's sword along with half of his arm in a gout of blood.

Tamberlane had no pity to spare on either one of them as he reached back and took the woman by the arm. He started leading her across the sand toward the safety of the high dunes that ringed the village, but she was already beyond feeling normal terror. She squealed and dug her heels into the sand; she clawed at his hand, tearing her nails on the iron scales that were fitted like a layer of snakeskin over his gloves. He kept walking, kept dragging her behind him.

Only when he reached the top of the first dune did he pause on the crest a moment and look down over the sparkling expanse of the Mediterranean that stretched out before them. As far as the eye could see, the calm blue waters glittered under an even bluer sky, the waves showing pale foamy heads where they washed up on the shore. They had been doing so for centuries, and would continue to do so despite the horror, the turmoil, the war and bloodshed behind him.

Walking again, he stripped off his gauntlets and threw them away. He unhooked the pennyplate camail from under his chin and removed his helm, discarding that in the sand as well. His hair, tonsured in the style the monks favored, was stuck flat to his head with sweat; droplets slid down his neck and under his tunic as he worked to rid himself of the blood-soaked mantle, the underlying layer of mail, the padded leather gambeson. By the time he had stripped himself of everything but the sweat-soaked woolen shirt and leggings, he had reached the shoreline. He turned and started following the beach west, walking away from the sounds of fighting, away from the road to Jerusalem.

He walked for an hour, perhaps more, his boots leaving indents in the wet sand behind him. A stand of palm trees far in the distance held his focus, and he kept walking toward it, accompanied only by his shadow. He had no idea where the woman had gone, had no recollection of when he had let go of her hand or when she had scrambled away.

When Tamberlane reached the trees, he just stood there a moment, staring at them. The sun was low enough in the sky that the air had cooled and a light scrift of sand was blowing down the dunes toward the water. The bushy tops of the palms were bending, bowing like the heads of old men, slicing the sharp beams of the setting sun into blades that cut through his lethargy and forced him to look around. He was miles from camp. He had no weapons, no armor. The cut of his hair marked him as a Templar, and the irony was not lost on him. He had shed all his worldly possessions once to give himself to God, but there had still been a trace of something human left inside that marked him as a mortal man. Now he wanted nothing more than to shed himself of all things to do with war and killing, yet he still bore the outward vestiges of men who thought of themselves as the true warriors of God.

He knew the consequences of his actions would be far-reaching. It was a crime worthy of expulsion from the Order to raise a sword against another Brother, regardless of the reason. And if the reason was to defend an infidel, it would mean excommunication and disgrace.

Oddly enough, he did not care about the Order itself; he was obviously no longer fit to be a monk or a Templar if he found himself questioning every command issued by the Master. He did care about the men he had fought beside for so long. Templars would be forbidden to speak to him, and the king's knights would turn their backs, shunning him for a coward, possibly even a traitor.

Tamberlane sat heavily on a piece of driftwood and bowed his head, cradling it in his hands. The watery heat in his eyes he blamed on exhaustion— the same exhaustion that made him slow to react when he saw two elongated shadows stretching up into the sand in front of him. They were wearing long robes and banded burnouses, that much he could tell from their silhouettes. Arabs. Saracens. Possibly fighters from Saladin's camp, probably returning from the very village where they had witnessed yet another massacre by the tonsured warrior monks who called themselves knights of God.

And now they had found one wandering alone, unarmed, miles from anyone who could hear his screams.

Tamberlane closed his eyes.

In truth, when he heard the unmistakable sound of a curved scimitar being slowly drawn from its scabbard, he was not too proud to whisper a faint prayer of relief, for a beheading would be fast and painless. Without even turning to see who was delivering him from one hell to the next, he bowed his head lower, exposing more of the back of his neck for the cold kiss of steel.

Chapter One

England, 1194

A split second before the arrow struck, the girl's
instinct sent her ducking back into the shadow
of the cottage door.

The shot had come from one of the half dozen
crossbowmen who stood at the edge of the clearing.
With lethal calm, their eyes stalked fresh victims,
and as soon as one was found, they raised their
weapons, steadied aim, and fired the stubby eight-
inch quarrel. Behind them, laughing and shouting
encouragement, were four mounted knights, their
gray wool gambesons devoid of any distinguishing
crest or blazon. The sleepy village, innocent and unaware only moments before, was under attack by
men who did not want their identity known and for
good reason. An ambush on unarmed villagers broke
every law, defiled every precept of the knighthood's
code of honor.

The first flight of quarrels had been wrapped in

pitch-soaked rags and set alight before being dispatched. The mists at dawn had been thick enough to conceal the raiders' approach, but the wind had passed through the clearing like an errant hand, sweeping the fog away. That same wind fanned the sparks, sending flames leaping across the roofs, and within seconds, columns of coiling black smoke were rising from the cluster of mud-and-wattle cottages.

The three swaybacked asses in the village were too old, too work-worn to even bleat an alarm as the flames licked across the thatch and ran down the walls. They were also dead on the second flight of crossbow bolts, as was the solitary milk cow and the brace of fat hogs.

As the roofs burst into flame above them, the men ran out of the cottages in a panic, snatching up pitchforks and scythes as if the handmade tools could afford protection against the deadly arrows. They were followed by their women, who pushed and dragged children behind them, urging them to run for the perceived safety of the woods. Goats and chickens added to the confusion, for most were too insignificant a target for the archers—seasoned marksmen who wound their bows taut and fired with unrelenting accuracy, choosing the husbands, fathers, sons first.

They were patient killers. They tracked a man as he ran behind the wall of a burning hovel, then waited for the heat and smoke to drive him out into the open again. The women fared no better. Several were sprawled on the ground already, arrows jutting from their backs.

Amie remained crouched in the doorway of the smithy's cottage, her eyes watering from the smoke, her nose burning from the waves of heat that were sucking the air out of her lungs. Her back and shoulders were being scorched through the threadbare cloth, and her only choice was to break for the forest or be enveloped by the roaring flames overhead. The trees were fifty paces away, but there was nothing between them and the cottage save for a miserly vegetable patch scratched into the earth.

Clenching her teeth around a half-sobbed prayer, she darted through the door and ran as fast as she could to the feeble protection afforded by a low mound of hay. Over the sound of her heart pounding in her chest, she heard the telltale *thunk* of an iron quarrel furrowing into the earth a few inches from her foot, but she was already running again, weaving this way and that in an attempt to elude the archer's aim. She was slight of build and wiry. The only softness on her body was in the vicinity of her breasts, which were pressed almost flat inside a tunic that was two sizes too small. Her hair was braided and hung in a long brown tail down her back; the hem of her skirt was pulled up between her legs and tucked into her belt so that, from a distance, it was possible she had been mistaken for a lad in an ill-fitted jerkin.

She heard a shout, followed by two more sharp *thunks* as arrows kicked up clods of dirt close on her heels. She felt the spray of pebbles against her bared calves but did not once look away from the bed of ferns that grew in the shadow of the trees. They were thick and high as her waist, covering the ground in a canopy of green, and she knew if she could just make it that far, she might have a chance . . .

She heard another *whoosht* and dove for the undergrowth. Something punched her in the back of the shoulder and helped propel her forward, but she barely skidded to her knees on the spongy loam before she was on her feet again, scrambling deeper into the sea of ferns. She ran one way for a dozen paces, then veered sharply to the left for a dozen more. She kept running, changing direction every few wild moments, trying to ignore the shouts and screams that filled the clearing behind her. The wind was a blessing now, keeping the tops of the ferns swaying and dipping in constant motion, helping to conceal the direction of her flight.

Another sound brought her briefly to a halt. She risked a glance behind her and confirmed the dreaded *thud* of horses hooves scything through the saplings and underbrush. One of the knights had left the scene of slaughter and was pursuing her— with almost lazy confidence—into the greenwood. Even at a hundred paces, she could see that he was huge, his destrier enormous as it trampled an indiscriminate swath through the ferns. The knight had his visor lowered, and there was not much to see between the iron grating that covered his eyes, but while she doubted his face would be familiar to her, she knew why he had come. He and others like him had been hunting her for more than a week, and now the villagers were paying the price for sheltering her.

Biting back a sob, she ducked again and lunged deeper into the woods. The main vein of the creek that ran past the village was somewhere close by, but she had spent most of the past seven days in a fever and was not familiar with all the paths and turns. She was running blind, disoriented by all the green, the shadows, the new and excruciating pain in her shoulder that was forcing her to hold her arm in a hard curl against her chest.

Without warning, the saplings thinned, and the ground took a sheer plunge downward. She had found the creek, but it was at the bottom of a steep embankment. Driven by another brief glance behind her, she grabbed an exposed root and started to ease herself over the edge. The lip of earth crumbled under her weight and she slipped, only managing to break her fall by clutching at a second root. The action jerked her injured arm, and she felt the iron arrowhead grind against bone. Barely able to bite back a scream, she let go and dropped straight down, landing on a bed of decades-old decayed leaves. The momentum of her fall sent her rolling onto the shaft of the arrow, and she gasped with agony as the iron tip was pushed all the way through the flesh of her shoulder, tearing through the coarsely woven wool in front.

Nearly blinded by the pain, she dragged herself under the tangle of roots that overhung the bank. She made a last, feeble attempt to rake some of the decayed leaves over her legs to conceal them, but a chill unlike anything she had ever felt slithered across the base of her neck and began to spiral down through her belly, numbing her all the way to the tips of her toes.

He was there. He was above her on the embankment, his laughter coming to her softly over the creak of saddle leather as he guided his horse down onto the lower bank. A moment later, the jangle of his spurs told her he was dismounting, and through her own sobs and pleas, she heard the sinister whisper of a sword being drawn from its sheath.

"My lord . . . over there."

The knight followed the direction indicated by his squire's finger to the treetops where a rolling spiral of black smoke rose above the green. There was a village beneath the smoke, a small vill that he was aware existed in the heart of the forest but had never felt the need or curiosity to visit.

One of the other lackeys suggested, "A fire in the woods, perhaps?"

The knight studied the smoke through narrowed green eyes and drew a deep breath. He suspected it was no ordinary forest fire, and his doubts were confirmed as yet another of the woodsmen came running out of the thicket, winded and sweating.

"My lord Tamberlane! The village is under attack. More than a score of men. Knights. Foot soldiers . . ." He stopped, out of breath and words. Behind him, the three other yeomen dropped the stag they carried slung between them and instantly unslung their bows from their shoulders. The squire, Roland, spurred his horse closer and frowned.

"Why would knights be attacking a poor village, my lord?"

Tamberlane started to shake his head but stopped when the faint sound of screams reached them through the lifting mist. Even at a distance, the cries were full of terror and fear, a sound that had haunted him nearly every night for the past three years. Beside him, Roland instinctively drew his sword, still young enough and eager enough to be ignorant of his own mortality. Tamberlane supposed it would do no good to point out the fact that they were at a weighty disadvantage against armed knights. The yeomen were armed with falchions and hunting bows, with perhaps two dozen slender ashwood arrows between them, and while the young squire was on the cusp of full manhood, approaching his year of majority, he had not gained much fighting experience in the two years he had been bound to Tamberlane. Moreover, they were dressed for hunting, with nothing to protect them other than soft leather jerkins and doeskin leggings.

It was, however, as good a way to die as any, he supposed.

Armor of another sort rippled along Tamberlane's arms and bulged across his chest as he adjusted his sword belt and withdrew his own bow from the sling that hung across the saddle horn. It was a Welsh weapon, twice as long as an English bow, capable of flinging arrows two hundred yards with enough accuracy and weight to pierce chain mail. Having only recently given in to his curiosity over the unknightly weapon, his proficiency left a great deal to

be desired, but he could hit a tree trunk at fifty paces
if it was wide enough. And if it did not jump out of
the way.

Disdaining the eagerness in Roland's eyes, he
spurred his stallion in the direction of the columns
of smoke. As chance would have it, he had chosen
to ride his piebald that morning to give the beast
exercise, and he could feel the excitement rippling
through the warhorse's powerful flanks as they cut
through the ferns and saplings. Similarly, the two
wolfhounds that were Tamberlane's constant companions responded to a softly whistled command
and streaked cleanly—and silently—between the
trees, leading the way straight and true to the small
hamlet.

Within minutes, Tamberlane and Roland had ridden close enough to the village to smell more than
just the burning cottages. The stench of scorched
flesh was something the knight could not mistake for
anything else, and he raised a hand for caution, slow-
ing their approach, waiting for the rest of the woodsmen to run up and fan out behind them.

After a brief, muffled conferment, they split into
two groups, Tamberlane taking the wolfhounds—
Maude and Hugo—and circling to the east, while Roland led the five huntsmen around to the west. The
screams had ended, but there was shouting now and
the occasional robust laugh to indicate that the vic-
tors were celebrating their success. They were arro-
gant in their triumph, and there were no sentries left
to guard their backs. Roland was easily able to creep

within a few broad paces of the cornfield without being seen.

He deployed the huntsmen with a keen eye for defense and waited until each had taken cover behind the stout trunk of a tree. From his own position he could see the charred ribs of the cottages, the smoke thinning now as most of the huts fell to ruin. He could also see the men-at-arms starting to move among the dead and dying, kicking bodies onto their backs, searching for signs of life, cutting into still-warm flesh to retrieve the valuable tips of their arrows.

The squire waited an impatient three minutes. He raked a hand through the loose golden waves of his hair and glanced repeatedly at the far side of the clearing, expecting his overlord to thunder out at any moment.

"Roland! There!"

One of the foresters stabbed a finger in the direction of one of the burned huts. Two of the soldiers had found a woman who was still alive and, without paying heed to her cries for mercy, drew their daggers. While one knelt down to slit her throat, the other started to cut into living flesh to recover the spent arrowhead.

Roland drew two arrows from his quiver. With one clenched between his teeth, he stepped out from behind the tree, raised his bow, and struck the first soldier down with a clean shot to the heart. The second was dead before he even knew the cause for his comrade's shocked cry.

Just as death had come swift and unseen to the villagers, it streaked out of the forest now and took the raiders unawares. They too were caught out in the open, and after the first flush of arrows found their marks, most of them stumbled back in confusion, unable to immediately grasp the sudden turn of events. The knights drew their swords and lowered their visors but by then they had in turn become targets. One screamed as an arrow caught him high on the thickest meat of the thigh.

Well away from the clearing, Tamberlane cursed when he heard the change in pitch and timbre of the shouts coming from the burning village. He had followed the riverbank, intending to circle around the village and attack from the far side, but there in front of him was one of the knights, dismounted, standing over the body of a young peasant girl stretched out on the ground. It was obvious he had chased her to ground after she fled the village. It was equally obvious that he was not content to merely finish his work quickly and return to the others, for his sword was drawn, and he had used the point to ruck the maid's skirts up above her waist. Where the steel had touched her skin with ungentle purpose, it had scored a bright red line of blood to mark its path.

At the sound of shouts and more fighting, the knight had given pause, his blade poised over the cleft between the maid's thighs.

He had not yet seen Tamberlane, though that was about to change as an arrow cut swiftly across his path and thudded into the soft earth of the embankment.

Swearing at his own ineptness, Tamberlane nocked a second arrow and drew the fletching back to his cheek. The two fingers that were curled around the resined string snapped free and sent the arrow *shoosh*ing across the fifty yards that separated him from the startled knight, who was now spinning around, searching for his unseen foe. The knave's chest was surely as broad as any thousand-year-old tree trunk, but the shadows were distorting and the inexperience in Tamberlane's hand made his aim unfaithful. The arrowhead missed the rightful target by a foot or more, but in doing so, struck the knight's left arm at the narrowest part of the wrist. The iron head shattered the bones, tearing through the tendons and tissue in a bloody red spray.

Tamberlane dropped the bow and drew his sword. He held the blade upright before him, barely aware of paying homage to old habits as he mouthed a single word and spurred his horse forward.

It was over on the first pass. Tamberlane's blade swept down in a lethal flash of steel, catching the knight high on the chest where the links of his camail joined the lower edge of his helm. So great was the power unleashed behind the stroke that the head was almost fully severed from the trunk. The knight spun away, his body falling with a heavy splash into the muddy riverbed, his sword clattering away on the pebbles.

Tamberlane reined his horse to a halt and wheeled about. When he saw that another rout was not required, he trotted slowly back to the embankment, his sword still held at the ready.

The knight was dead, no question. The girl's condition was not so certain, but he had no time to check. Maude and Hugo, responding to a shrill whistle, were told to "stay" and to "guard" while Tamberlane urged his horse up the bank and rode hard toward the clearing.

Roland had managed to drive the attackers back toward the verge of the woods, but when they saw that their adversary was a mere squire in hunters green, they had formed up in a solid line and armed their bows again. Two of the unwounded knights even managed a laugh, although that sound faded too, as Tamberlane's enormous destrier emerged from the greenwood behind them.

Once again the line of marauders scattered, half of them casting their cumbersome crossbows aside in their haste to avoid the thundering hooves. Several who stood their ground paid dearly for their stubbornness. One of the knights sallied forth, his visor dropped in place, his shield and sword raised in readiness. When the distance between Tamberlane and the knight closed, they both swung their blades in a vicious swath, the combined force of their blows ringing out with the strength of a church bell. Steel scraped along steel before the momentum of their horses tore them apart. Without the cumbersome bulk of armor to hinder his balance, Tamberlane was first to swing around and spur his steed into another strike. This time his blade struck heavy armor across the chest, denting the mail and banging the knight's air out of his lungs in a harsh grunt. The links did not give, and Tamberlane had to recover quickly to block the counterthrust that would find nothing but linsey-woolsey and flesh to resist the blow.

Roland charged valiantly forward to defend his lord's back, but the second unwounded knight made no chivalrous distinction between squire and master. He bore in for the kill, his sword aiming to cut Roland from the saddle—an effort that would have succeeded but for the twin ashwood arrows that flew through the air and thudded into his body like cleavers striking meat, one taking him under the arm and one cleanly through the throat.

The two archers, aptly named Quill and Fletcher, took a moment to congratulate each other's aim while the third knight, his thigh still pinned to the saddle with an arrow, saw how the tide had turned and screamed for the remnants of the raiding party to retreat into the woods. He led the flight, kicking his horse into a full gallop that soon lost him to the trees and shadows.

Tamberlane, meanwhile, was still locked in mortal combat, still slashing and hacking at an opponent who was not lacking in either courage or fortitude. He fought, in fact, like a man accustomed to killing in God's name, and the realization startled Tamberlane enough that he froze for a precariously long moment—a moment that allowed his adversary to open a stripe of flesh along his arm.

Recovering his shock, Tamberlane brought his sword down with both fists clamped around the hilt. The blow caught his opponent under the left ear. Even though the steel-pot helm was shielding the point of contact, the sheer fury behind the strike caused the knight's neck to snap violently from the spine. Horse and rider spun for a turn, the latter slumping forward with all substance suddenly drained from arms and legs. He reeled to one side, and if not for a spur hooking in the stirrup, the weight of his body armor would have carried him straight to the ground. As it was, it kept him canted at an odd angle as his horse galloped away into the woods.

Tamberlane stared, his brow gleaming with sweat.

He squeezed his eyes shut and heard a great roaring in his ears. It was the roaring of a thousand voices, the screams shrill with religious fervor. The sun was beating down; the heat was rising in waves off the desert sand. The steel of his sword was so hot the blood bubbled and sizzled along its length and the palms of his hands were scorched raw.

"Are you all right, my lord?" Roland rode up beside him. "Have you been struck? Are you injured?"

Tamberlane gasped and blinked his eyes open. The visions faded along with the shivering echos of the screams, and he wiped a hand across his brow, damning the oily wetness he found there. There was blood on his sleeve where the knight's blade had slashed him, but the cut was a trifling thing, scarcely worthy of the concern on his squire's face.

"No. No, I have not been struck. And you?"

"I—I think I have broken a finger, but I give thanks to God that it was not my sword hand."

Tamberlane looked grimly around the clearing, sincerely doubting God had been present overmuch that day. There were thirty, perhaps as many as forty bodies strewn amid the smoldering wreckage of the village, many of them—as if his memory needed more provocation—women and children.

"Who do you suppose they were, my lord? Why did they do this?"

Tamberlane clenched his jaw. He did not dare give voice to any suspicions; instead, he dispatched Quill and Fletcher to follow the scattered raiders at a cautious distance and to give warning if they appeared to be regrouping for a counterattack.

Apart from that, he made no comment as he dismounted and walked slowly over to the body of the dead knight. It lay facedown in the crush of ferns, and he nudged it onto its back with the toe of his boot. There were no markings on the tunic, no clues as to whom the dead knight owed his allegiance. He was dressed in drab from his tunic to his gloves and bore no crest or blazons on his gambeson.

A mercenary?

A quick search beneath the dead knight's mail was rewarded with the clinking discovery of a small leather pouch filled with solid gold coins.

Tamberlane closed his fist around the pouch and pursed his lips in thought. No question, then, that they were paid assassins, yet the weight of gold did not match the weight of sin for committing mass murder. Moreover, mercenaries would expect something more than a few coins—plunder or loot at the very least. Again, it was a poor village. What little of worth they had was in their livestock and in the crops they harvested to pay their rents and tithes— a pittance to men accustomed to the wages of war.

Aware of Roland and the others watching him, Tamberlane tugged at the leather gauntlets, difficult to remove from limp fingers, but when he pushed the sleeves of the mail coat above the wrist, there were no markings on the skin.

He refrained from glancing at his own wrist, at the patch of shiny scar tissue that marked where he had taken a red-hot iron and seared away the faint tattoo of a five-pointed star. At the time, he had come perilously close to burning through to the veins that would have ended all the nightmares once and for all. Only the slimmest of threads that still bound him to his faith had prevented him from doing so.

He pushed to his feet and glanced at Roland. "Have the men checked for survivors?"

Roland shook his head. "They are all dead, my lord. We caught them while they were searching the bodies and finishing any who might have had a heartbeat."

"You did not think to try to take one of them alive?"

"We had too few arrows to dwell on courtesy. Their men shot to kill. We did the same."

Tamberlane wiped the blade of his sword clean on the knight's jerkin then resheathed the weapon in his belt. He frowned at the slight stinging sensation in his hand and noticed for the first time the layers of skin that had been peeled from his fore and middle fingers when he fired the longbow.

"There is one other," he said. "A young girl. She was sorely wounded, and I doubt if she lives still, but I left Maude and Hugo to stand guard."

"Shall I send a man to check?"

Tamberlane thought it a useless gesture, but he curled his tongue against his lower lip and issued forth a piercing whistle. The sound shivered around the clearing a moment before fading, and when there was no immediate response from the dogs, he scowled and strode back to his horse. "I will see what holds their attention while the rest of you collect your wits and make for the north road."

"The road, my lord?" Roland looked shocked again. "Are we not even going to bury these good people?"

"There are too many graves to be dug. We will send word to the abbey and advise the monks to dispense their shovels and prayers."

"But, sire—"

"You have already disobeyed me once today by charging into a fight without waiting for my signal," Tamberlane said quietly. "Are you spoiling to do so again?"

"No, my lord. I just thought—"

"There is naught to think about," Tamberlane said bluntly. "We have no way of knowing if this was their full force of men or if those who ran so nimbly into the greenwood ran toward a larger compliment. If so, they will not be pleased with the turn of events. Take the men. Go to the north road."

Roland's shoulders squared, and his lips pressed into a flat line. He had served as squire to Lord Tamberlane for two years, and in all that time he had not once glimpsed a single morsel of warmth or compassion in the cold green eyes. He had not seen

Tamberlane smile or laugh, had not heard a sentence delivered with ten words when one, harshened by a miser's contempt, would do.

Tamberlane saw contempt of another kind reflected in the squire's hardened gaze, but he had no time to coddle the boy's illusions. He had not wanted a squire, had not needed one in his self-imposed isolation, and the only reason he tolerated the responsibility at all was because it was a condition of his being left alone by the outside world.

Upon his return to England, his uncle had dredged up some distant memory of the valiant, eager young knight who had left to go on Crusade. In his misguided hopes of resurrecting that knight, he had assigned Roland into Tamberlane's care. A foolish mistake, for even though the boy had come willingly into his service—undoubtedly deceived by those same tales of heroism and derring-do—the reality of the ruin Tamberlane had become had long since tarnished the gleam in the young man's eyes.

No matter. Another few months, the lad would turn twenty-and-one, old enough to wear his own spurs, and Tamberlane would be rid of the unwanted obligation. For both, he suspected, the time could not pass quickly enough.

His mouth twisted in a grimace, he swung onto his destrier's back and took up the reins. A few paces into the woods he gave another short, shrill whistle, and moments later Maude came bounding up to lead him back to the riverbed. Hugo was still standing guard, his massive front paws planted firmly apart, his eyes fixed threateningly on the dead knight, ready to attack if the corpse should suddenly spring to life.

Tamberlane called him off with a quiet word and knelt beside the body, searching for clues as to why mercenaries would be hired to attack and slaughter the unarmed inhabitants of an entire village.

The head, half submerged in the stream, had been severed enough that it lay at an odd angle to the torso. Tamberlane was able to unfasten the ruined pennyplate camail and remove the helm without having to roll the body onto its back, but the face— if he was expecting to find some revelation there— was unfamiliar.

The village was on his land, and it did not take a great leap in reasoning to surmise that the attack had been launched against *him*. He had striven to spend the last two years in the shadows of obscurity, yet if someone wanted to find him, he did not suppose it would take more than a question whispered in the right ear.

Perhaps he should have shed his name along with his Crusader's mantle.

The sound of Maude's heavy panting beside him made him turn his head. The girl lay a few feet away, her face paler than any living thing could be. Her skirt was still rucked above the top of her thighs, her legs crudely splayed where the knight had kicked them apart. The sword had sliced a red ribbon from her ankle to her groin, and where the point had come to rest, it had drawn a bright bead of blood that had run down into the cleft of her sex like jagged streaks of lightning.

Against the whiteness of her skin it had been easy to miss seeing the silky bush of yellow hair that grew there. It put the lie to his initial assumption that she was a child, as did the plump mounds that rose over her chest.

Whether it was his own monkish discomfort that prompted him to cover her or the thought that it was no way for a maid to lie, even in death, he unstuck his boots from the muck beside the stream and dropped down on one knee beside her. He was about to smooth the skirts of her tunic back down to her ankles when he heard a faint rattle in her throat. He looked at her face again, and although her skin was as translucent as old wax, he noticed what he had missed before: a thin blue vein in her temple throbbed erratically; another fluttered in the slender column of her neck.

She was alive.

An arrowhead was protruding from her shoulder. There was blood staining her gown from neck to waist, and she had lost enough to soak the leaves beneath her red. Already there was a small army of ants gathering to feast on the fresh bounty.

When his gaze returned to her face, he was surprised again to see that her eyes had flickered open. They seemed to roam without purpose or focus for a long moment before fixing on the shadow that knelt beside her. Blue as the waters of the Mediterranean, they widened in terror as her lips trembled apart on a broken cry.

Tamberlane remembered the sword poised over her cleft. The mercenary had been on the verge of impaling her, of tearing into her sex to mutilate her in a final act of disdain, and he realized at once that she feared he was that same brutish knight.

"Easy, girl, easy. The cur who did this to you is dead. The one who meant to harm you is dead. You have nothing to fear from me."

"Dead?" she gasped. Her eyes rolled once side to side, then came to a halt on Tamberlane's face again. "As am I?"

Tamberlane had seen enough mortal wounds to know that the likelihood of her surviving out the day was slim. He'd had to lean forward to catch the faintly whispered question, and it was just as well, for the act of straightening allowed him a moment to decide whether it was kinder to lie or tell the truth.

She saved him the need to decide by moving her hand and curling her cold fingers around his wrist. "Please. End it. End it now."

Tamberlane drew farther back. On a field of battle, to find a comrade-in-arms so gravely wounded, he would not have thought twice of obliging, of ending the pain quickly and cleanly. The fact that she was begging him to show her an equal mercy should not have unsettled him, and yet it did. Enough that he stared, and continued to stare as a clear, fat tear swelled at the corner of her eye and trickled down her temple.

Despite scratches on her cheek and grime on her face, she had a sweet countenance, with softly sculpted features and a delicate tenderness. He surprised himself by thinking of her as pretty. Pretty and undeserving of such a fate.

"It is not your time to die just yet," he said—and from whence the words or the falsely offered hope behind them came, he knew not. In any case, she was not fooled. Her lashes, long and honey gold, fluttered again, and the grip on his wrist tightened.

"Please . . ."

The single word, uttered with desperate futility, stabbed his chest like the point of a dagger and, for reasons he could not explain, opened such a well of anger and rage that it spilled through his body like acid.

"You do not have my leave to die," he said gruffly. "Do not even think to do it."

With a flush rising in his face, he blew out half an oath and bowed over her again, sliding one arm beneath her shoulders, the other beneath her knees. Without stopping to acknowledge the foolishness of what he was doing, he lifted her off the bed of leaves. A gasp escaped the blue-gray lips as her wound was jarred; another brought her head rolling against his chest as he grasped the horn of his saddle and pulled himself up onto his horse. The action was awkward, undoubtedly an agony for the maid, and by the time he was settled with her cradled before him, he could feel fresh blood from her wound soaking warmly into his sleeve. He whistled once for the dogs, then picked his way carefully but quickly back through the woods in the direction of the north road.

Roland was already there with the woodsmen, and to judge by the look on his face, he would not have been more surprised had his lord emerged from the greensward carrying the body of Richard the Lionheart in his arms.

Jaw slack, mouth gaping, he stared at the girl.

"She is still alive," Tamberlane said, forestalling the question.

"Alive, my lord? Did she know who attacked the village?"

"We had no time for idle chatter. Here, take her from me. You likely have a gentler touch."

Roland moved his horse closer, but one look at the arrowhead jutting from the girl's shoulder made his frown deepen.

"The arrow is acting as a stopper, my lord. Jostle her too much and the bung may pop free."

"The bung will pop free if I throw her to the ground."

The squire's gaze rose sharply, and Tamberlane swore under his breath. "Very well. She will likely be dead long ere we reach the castle anyway. Where is the stag? You have not left it to rot in the woods, have you?"

"We thought . . . that is to say, my lord, I thought—"

"Well, you thought wrong. We came out to put meat on the board tonight, and by God, there will be meat. Send two men back to fetch the stag and another two to the abbey to fetch the monks. Will that act as a sop for your conscience?"

Tamberlane took up the reins and spurred his destrier onto the road. The girl's head bounced a moment, but then she settled back into the crook of his shoulder with such a soft sigh he looked down, expecting to see her eyes open and staring up at him again.

They were not, and his own gaze slipped unwittingly to where her breasts were pillowed against his chest. A ragged tear in the bodice gave him a shadowy view beneath the cloth, and he glimpsed a flash of silver cut in the shape of an ornate crucifix.

The sight of it set his jaw, for here again was proof that faith was no protection against evil.

It had taken him many long and bloody years to learn that. The girl had discovered it in less than a day.

Chapter Two

Taniere Castle was perched at the tip of what had at one time been a finger of land that jutted out into the silky smooth waters of a lake so small it bore no name. When the Normans had conquered England and replaced the Saxons' mud and timber keeps with stone fortifications, a small army of men had labored for months to dig an aqueduct fifty feet wide and equally as deep to completely surround the castle with water. The crumbling breastworks were replaced with rock and mortar walls twenty feet high and twelve feet thick. The wooden enclosure was razed, and in its place grew a massive stronghold consisting of a stone keep three stories high, with a slanted base measuring five hundred long paces down each side of the square. Each corner was surmounted by a tower extending out over the crenellated walls. The parapets that spanned the distances between these four towers provided a breathtaking command of the view for miles in every direction.

The only way into the newly formed island fortress

was across a drawbridge guarded at one end by a
gatehouse, on the other by an arched portal flanked
by ominously unwelcoming barbican towers. The
walls of the barbicans were slit with cross-shaped
meurtriers through which archers could fire at anyone trying to gain entry uninvited. The gate itself
was built of solid oak timbers a foot thick and
banded with strips of iron worked by a master into
a depiction of coiled dragons guarding the entrance.
This gate was recessed beneath a stone arch pierced
with murder holes that allowed defenders to drop
flaming pitch or rocks on the heads of attackers.

A large grassed common formed the outer ward
and was ringed with stone outbuildings that contained, among other things, the stables and smithy.
Entry to the inner ward was through a curtain wall
that divided the grounds in half, requiring visitors to
pass through yet another arched gateway.

Oddly enough, despite the strength and extent of
the fortifications, the castle was not located in a stra-
tegically important area. The vast forests of Lincoln
were to the north, the sea to the east, the richest
baronies in England to the south and west. The lake
was small, surrounded by an outer ring of greenwood so dense it would take an army months to
hack its way through.

Taniere's existence had never appeared as anything
more than a passing notation in the crown's registry.
No king had ever visited. No rival baron had ever
vied for its possession. It stood empty more often
than not, and over time had became overgrown with
brambles and lichen. The vaulted passageways and

chambers became home for invading hordes of birds and spiders, the latter spinning huge blankets of white filaments from beam to beam, door to sill.

The inhabitants of the village that had sprung up along the shore of the lake waited expectantly for new overlords to arrive, but none ever did. The usual stories of ghosts and dragons and unsettled spirits were told to discourage children from crossing the draw and possibly tumbling to their deaths from the high stone walls. Those children grew into the men and women who cautioned their own offspring to stay well away from the hulking ramparts. Several of the village men went so far as to raise the drawbridge and bolt it to the wall, ensuring that whatever demons dwelling within the walls remained there.

So it had remained, silent and steeped in shadow, until one spring day the villagers awoke to the sound of grinding chains and groaning timbers. The drawbridge was being lowered, and waiting patiently on shore was a knight dressed in plain armor. He had arrived with a small caravan of four wagons, a meager handful of servants, and a strange assortment of retainers, one of whom proved to be a dark-skinned woman whose cheek was horribly disfigured by a puckered scar. Clutched in her arms was a small child barely a year old, his eyes wide with awe as he watched the huge draw being lowered.

Standing beside the knight was a tall figure completely swathed head to toe in flowing black robes. Even his face was shielded by an elongated hood, and it was not until later that the villagers learned he was completely devoid of any coloring. His hair and skin were pale as bone; his eyes were a transparent gray rimmed in pink and shielded by white lashes.

The simple villagers who had never seen such a sight whispered among themselves that he was surely a demon, a satyr, an incubus. They refused to venture near the castle walls, fearing he might steal their souls and barter them to the devil. When it was further discovered that he practised the art of alchemy, many bundled the few belongings they possessed and fled the village, leaving Taniere Castle to the dragons and demons.

Those who remained did so because they had nowhere else to go. By twos and threes they grudgingly took up residence inside the towering castle walls, and when none were seen to grow horns or exhale forks of fire from their nostrils, the others returned—wary, but obliged to give their three days a week in service due their liege.

To the puzzlement of many, the new lord had no pressing desire to scrape the walls clean of moss or cut down the tangled thickets grown like a ring of thorns around the island. Only the barest of necessities inside the domicile were restored. The great hall was swept clean of rot and filth, the tower rooms were made habitable, the cookhouse was restocked with ironware and clay pots. And wine. The alehouse was pressed into service almost at once, for it was a rare night that passed when the lord of the keep did not drink himself into a stupor and have to be carried to his bedchamber by the tall, hooded seneschal.

No one knew for certain what the woman's role

was. She was not a wife, nor was she a leman. The child was dark-haired and dark-eyed like the mother, and was almost as terrified of the broodingly silent knight as the rest of the household. The only cheerful face among the new residents was the squire, Roland, who went to great pains to assure the villagers that his lord was not the devil and that the cowled Marak was not Beelzebub's incubus. Roland himself was a distant cousin to Lord Tamberlane, who was in turn the nephew of William de Glanville, brother to the late chief justiciar of England, Ranulf de Glanville, who had died while fighting alongside his king at the siege of Acre.

Once Lord Tamberlane's name was revealed, it was whispered with awe and reverence by the villagers who, even though they abided in the farthest corner of God's green earth, had heard the tales and feats attributed to one of Christendom's mightiest Crusaders. It was said the Lionheart had once called him Dragon Slayer for his ferocity in battle, and that he was one of only two knights who had survived the slaughter at the Battle of Hattin, where more than two thousand Christian soldiers had been captured and beheaded. It was said he fought later at Richard's right-hand side. That he had saved the king's life when Saladin had sent his assassins into the Christian camp in the dead of night.

But then there were the other whispered tales. Rumors of cowardice, of disobeying orders, of spitting on the Beauseant—the holy banner of the Templars— came back to England on the tongues of returning Crusaders. They told of a trial of inquisition held by

the Grand Master of the warrior monks, wherein the
vaunted Tamberlane had been stripped of his secular
mantle, excommunicated for his sins, and cast from
the Holy Order with nary a penance harsh enough
to redeem his soul.

Defrocked and disgraced, he had returned quietly
to England. His presence had been commanded before his uncle, and while the meeting was held in
private, with not the keenest of ears able to hear what
was said, a month later he had arrived at Taniere
Castle to take up residence with little fanfare. Villeins
who had lived their entire lives without an overlord
suddenly found themselves bound by feudal law to
the infamous Dragon Slayer.

Over the ensuing months, it was not just the villagers who returned to Taniere to take up service but
soldiers and men-at-arms. Knights who had served
with Tamberlane in Outremer and distained the
charges of cowardice appeared at the gates, kissing
a ring he did not offer willingly, pledging loyalty
with vows he did not actively seek. Some came
marked by a weariness of bloodshed and war. Others
simply carried too many nightmares in their heads
and needed the peace and tranquillity of Taniere's
isolation to grapple their demons to ground.

The villagers who worked inside the castle eventually overcame their fear of the tall, robed seneschal
who, while still able to chill blood on a mere turning
of his cowled head, proved to be efficient and fair.
He also had a gifted hand with medicines. A maid
who had burned her arm horribly with a spill of
boiling oil was treated with a thick unguent that not

only took away the pain upon the instant but within days had soothed the blisters and encouraged fresh new skin to grow over the wound. Similarly, a young boy with a caul over his eye was made to see again. A miller with a scrofulous boil on his neck was healed after wearing one of the albino's poultices, and a woman who had labored in childbirth for three days, and would surely have bled to death following the breech delivery, allowed him to pack her womb with special herbs and was working in the castle a month later, her babe comfortably asleep in a sling across her back.

As for the knight who now called Taniere Castle home, he remained silent and withdrawn. An occasional hunt would lure him across the draw, but he favored his own company, rarely went to the village, and never held mass in the castle chapel. His chambers occupied the entire north tower, and some swore to have heard frightened cries and whimperings coming from behind the locked doors each night. Others claimed to have seen, on dark nights when the threat of lightning was in the air, a strange greenish glow emanating from the solitary high window.

So it was that when Tamberlane returned from the ill-fated hunt that day, the men working in the wards stopped what they were doing to turn and stare at their overlord as he rode past, plainly startled to see an injured maid cradled in his arms.

While Roland held the reins of his horse steady, Tamberlane threw a leg over the front of his saddle and landed on the ground with the surety of a big cat. The wolfhounds close on his heels, he carried the unconscious girl inside the keep, his boot heels ringing off the stone floor as he traversed the great hall and climbed the narrow corkscrew staircase into the east tower. Roland was a step behind and opened the heavy door before Tamberlane could kick his way through.

As usual, the chamber was dark, the shadows as thick as mist. There was a solitary candle flickering insipidly in the far corner of the chamber, a low fire glowing red in the hearth that provided barely enough light to discern one shadow from the next. Marak was there, dressed in his long black robes. He sat in the far corner grinding some herbs together with a mortar and pestle, but at the sound of the door swinging open, he looked over.

While Tamberlane and Roland waited for their eyes to adjust to the gloom, Marak calmly set his pestle aside and raised the hood of his robe to shield his face as he came into the stronger light.

"You mentioned you might be going hunting this morning. You did not say your game would be two-legged."

"She has an arrow in the shoulder," Tamberlane said. "Can you help her?"

"One of your arrows?" Marak inquired, looking down.

"Would that my aim was that good."

The seneschal's eyes, unseen beneath the hood, studied the girl's limp body, while a pale hand touched the side of her neck to search for evidence that the blood still pulsed through her veins. Tamberlane was unsure himself, for he had not felt her move, had not heard a breath or a whimper over the last half hour.

With a gesture that did not promise much hope, Marak skimmed his fingers over the blood-soaked tunic. "She is almost bled dry."

"Can you help her?"

"If I say not, will you toss her over the rampart and go about the rest of your day?"

Tamberlane looked startled for as long as it took the seneschal to sigh and point a long finger at a table close to the fire. While Roland cleared the board of assorted bottles and pots, Marak lit several more candles from a taper, all of them fitted with special metal shields that would shine the light downward. Stray beams bounced off the rows upon rows of clay vessels and pots that crowded the many shelves along the walls. Mysterious powders from Africa sat beside those brought at great cost from the Orient. Wings of small creatures sat in bottles neatly marked with Latin script. Next to them were pots of dried eyeballs and venom from a dozen variety of snakes.

As soon as Tamberlane laid the girl out on the table, the senechal adjusted the light and pushed his sleeves above his wrists.

"The arrow," he murmured, leaning over the object in question to inspect it more closely. "You have not disturbed it?"

"No more so than was necessary to bring her to the castle."

The hooded figure grunted. His fingers rested over the girl's brow a moment, and he ordered Roland to add several dried pieces of wood to the fire, bringing it to a blaze again. With his hood pulled even lower over his face to protect him from the glare, he gently took a knife to the girl's tunic, nicking the cloth at her neck first and cutting his way across her shoulder and down her arm. The threadbare fabric, once blue, was dark as ink where the blood had begun to dry, still shiny and wet and red where the jostling had kept the wound leaking. With the tunic now peeled back, Marak could see that the quarrel had gone straight through the meaty part of her chest, just above the left breast.

"She has lost a deal of blood, my friend. She may lose a deal more if the arrow has cut through the heart vein."

"How will you know if it has?"

The seneschal glanced up. "If you see a gout of red when I take the bolt out . . . you will know. Who is she? Her face is not familiar."

"Her village was raided this morning. She was the only one we found alive, and may be the only one able to tell us why the vill was attacked and all in it slaughtered."

Marak stopped what he was doing and glanced up. "All?"

"To the last child."

The albino's eyes were shadowed by the hood, but Tamberlane could sense them searching his face, then dropping lower to stare at the slash in his shirtsleeve.

"You might have had a better chance questioning one of the killers had you let him live."

"They were mercenaries. They did not look the type who would betray their secrets too easily."

"You show a marked lack of faith in my skills," Marak said dryly. Turning back to the maid and using the veriest tip of his finger, he touched the arrowhead where it protruded through the front of her tunic, carefully watching her face for any flicker of reaction. There was none. Muttering softly to himself, he fetched up a small black kettle and wandered along the wall of shelves, taking a leaf here, a pinch of powder there, a few drops of some viscous liquid from a stoppered bottle, and adding them all to the pot. He added water and hung it over the fire, pointing a bony finger at Roland as he made his way back to the pallet.

"Guard that it does not boil." And to Tamberlane, he asked, "Has she wakened at all?"

"Once. Back at the river."

"Was she able to speak?"

Tamberlane nodded. "Briefly. But her words were tumbled and made no sense."

Marak fetched a large square of linen from one of the shelves and tore it into two equal strips. Folding them into two thick wads, he sprinkled more herbs and powders between each layer. By the time he finished, steam was rising off the surface of the posset. He removed the kettle from the fire, dividing the contents evenly between the two poultices.

As carefully as he could, Marak cut away the tethers binding the iron arrowhead to the shaft. He felt gingerly beneath the girl's shoulder and found the splintered bits of wood where the bolt had snapped in her fall over the river embankment. Straightening again, and without further ado, he used his forefinger to push the shaft quickly through the flesh and pull it out the other side. Both ends of the wound filled instantly with fresh blood, but there was no gushing. He then took one of the herb-soaked poultices and laid it beneath her shoulder, the other one on top, and pressed down with much of his weight for several counts of ten before easing off and peering under the corner of the uppermost wadding.

Satisfied that the heart vein had not been severed, he finished cutting away the shreds of her tunic.

Roland, who had seen many a naked maid in his lifetime, scarcely followed the proceedings. He was anxious to be away, to join the hunters in regaling the castle minions with tales of the attack and their bravery in foiling it.

Tamberlane, whose experience with nudity of any kind had been severely limited by his vows of chastity, found that it would be too easy to stare at the pale white body if he allowed himself to do so. To avoid any temptation, he moved back to stand beside the hearth, and after unbuckling his belt and pulling his tunic over his head, he tossed the bloodied garments at Roland with a nod that indicated the squire could leave. He then leaned over a large bowl of water and used another scrap of cloth to wash the girl's blood off his chest and shoulders. The gash on his arm was neither deep nor debilitating, but the skin would require a few knots of thread to hold the edges together while it healed.

The newly kindled flames in the hearth bathed his

upper body in red and orange light, sparkling off the beads of water that clung to his skin. The long, flame-burnished waves of his hair—grown in thick and dense over his once-tonsured pate—curled over shoulders that had been strengthened over the years to carry a hundredweight of mail and armor. Shorter, curlier hairs covered his chest like a dark breastplate, while smoother, silkier down darkened his forearms. He was a tall man, solid in the waist and hip. His legs were long and tautly thewed, his hands square and hard, the palms thickened with callouses.

No one who saw him doubted that he could slay dragons. Only Marak knew the mighty knight could be unraveled, undone, and brought to ground by a single touch from a lady's soft hand.

"Whoever cut this girl had no love of women," the seneschal remarked, frowning over the slash that ran from the girl's ankle up to the juncture of her thighs.

Tamberlane was drawn reluctantly into the circle of light again, and when he followed Marak's pointed finger to the cut above the golden thatch of pubic hair, he recalled seeing the tip of the mercenary's blade stabbing into the tender flesh. The yellow curls were still pink with blood, bringing forth another memory of a painting he had been shown during his induction as a Templar, when it was declared that all women were the daughters of Eve. The monks were told that a woman's sex was constantly bloody from their roles as whores and temptresses for Satan. They were also told that good men, devout men, had lost their wits, their souls, their very lives worshiping at the bloodied altar of carnal sin.

The green eyes traveled higher, touching on the girl's face.

She did not look like Satan's whore. She looked fragile, broken. The wound in her shoulder was brutally grotesque, the flesh torn so cruelly it made him curious enough to pluck the arrowhead off the table and examine it.

The points were hooked and jagged, the iron meant to tear the flesh rather than simply pierce it, thereby ensuring that whoever bore the wound would likely die from mortification regardless of where it entered, for it would do more damage being pulled free. The girl was lucky insofar as it had been driven straight through.

Tamberlane curled his fist around the arrowhead. His eyes, glowing an eerie green in the muted light, rose, and he was not surprised to find Marak watching him.

With the hearth behind him, the seneschal had lowered his hood, the better to work without encumbrances. Hair as white as sun-bleached parchment surrounded a face that was long and thin, the skin devoid of color even to the lips that were lacking the smallest hint of definition. His eyes were clear as water, rimmed in pink, shielded by lashes that were fine and white.

Anything stronger than muted candlelight caused excruciating pain to those sensitive eyes, and a beam of unfiltered sunlight could scorch his skin red after a few moments' exposure. All of his vast knowledge, his experiments with alchemy and herbal medicines, could gain him little relief from his own curse, condemning him to a world of shadows and heavy woolen garments.

"The peasants committed no crime," Tamberlane said, his eyes searching Marak's for an explanation. "It was just a poor village with nothing to hide."

"Nothing that you could see, perhaps," Marak amended carefully.

"Nothing worth searching for. They burned the huts without a care to what was inside. They slaughtered the people without pausing to ask any questions."

"And you are thinking that perhaps they were not merely attacking the village."

"The vill is on my land."

"Who knows you are here?"

"There are a host of secrets better kept."

"Surely the man you are thinking of would have come straight to the castle gates."

Tamberlane closed his fingers around the arrowhead and squeezed. Hugh de Bergerette. He had lost an arm that day on the road to Jerusalem; he would want a greater revenge than merely seeing Tamberlane humbled before the tribunal and stripped of his ranking with the Templars.

"It does not make sense that he should come now," Tamberlane admitted softly. "Not after all this time."

"Some men have longer memories than others." Marak started to draw a sheet of linen over the girl's naked body but stopped. He looked at the golden triangle at her thighs, then tipped his head to cast a curious look at the dull brown plait that lay beside her head.

"We have been in this fog-ridden England of yours for two years now," he murmured, "and I have determined that your countrymen will attack almost anything or anyone without much provocation. That aside"—he dropped the sheet in place and turned to rinse his hands in the barrel—"you did not make many friends when you refused to show remorse over your actions, even less when you scorned the penance dictated by your brother knights. The fact that you live and breathe solely because your veins flow with Granville blood would surely be more than enough cause for some to burn you to the ground as a heretic."

"Then they should attack me, not innocent peasants."

"What better way to attack you than strike out at innocents? Or do you forget it was because of the innocents that you found yourself questioning your purpose in Outremer?"

The knight gave a derisive snort and tossed the arrowhead aside. Yet something inside him had been admitted aroused by the weight and feel of a sword being wielded in combat again. He punished his body daily in the practice yards, killing burlap sacks by the score and beheading cabbages by the hundreds, but it was not the same. His blood was still running rich through his veins from the morning's confrontation. Even the lingering smell of the mercenary's death on his skin caused his nostrils to flare with relish.

"I care only that someone thinks they can attack what is mine with impunity." He glanced down at the girl, aware that the declaration he just made included her, for by law she was his chattel, and as such, he was responsible for her now.

"Will she live?"

The seneschal shrugged. "I can do nothing but ply my simple medicines and hope it is enough to let her breathe one more day."

"If she wakens, send for me, no matter it should be day or night."

Marak nodded, knowing full well the Dragon Slayer never slept. He knew the warrior, no longer a monk, paced most nights away, reluctant to close his eyes, unwilling to lay himself bare to the nightmares that continued to haunt him.

A lesser man would likely have flung himself from one of the castle turrets by now, and in truth, there were times Marak hid in the shadows on the wall walk watching the troubled knight stare out over the parapets, his hands gripping the stone, his face turned into the night wind. A simple matter to climb onto one of the crenellated teeth and cast off the mortal world. As someone confined to perpetual darkness, Marak had considered it many times himself, and his torment was not half so great as that of the Dragon Slayer.

To that end, after studying the deep circles beneath Tamberlane's eyes, he set about steeping another brew that would not only dull the pain of having a needle and thread drawn through the wounded arm but would provide a few hours of dreamless sleep. He was not hopeful of success. He doubted there were possets strong enough in all the land that would be able to burn the nightmares out of Tamberlane's soul.

Chapter Three

Amie rose out of the depths of darkness like a bubble of air rising to the surface of thick oil. She regained consciousness through fragments of sensation, the first being heat and pain, the second being the pungent sting of incense in her nostrils. The closer she rose to the light, the stronger the taint became until the smell became a taste at the back of her throat, acrid and bitter, begging for water to ease it.

Her body ached everywhere. Fever raged in her blood, coursing through a body that shivered uncontrollably despite the flames that consumed her.

The blackness behind her closed eyelids took on a reddish hue, hinting at a source of light somewhere beyond her grasp. Sounds began to emerge from the void as well, muffled and terrifying at first, for the last thing she remembered was the prick of a sword between her thighs. Was she now lying somewhere impaled and helpless, kept alive on the whims of her tormentor?

Amie rolled her head to the side and tried to focus on the light. Seen through the crusted spikes of her lashes, it was no more than a blurred glow, a distorted splotch of red and orange that emanated from a fire blazing in a nearby grate. Like a moth, her gaze was drawn achingly toward it. She stared until her eyes felt scalded, until her vision drowned in a stinging liquid that made seeing anything impossible.

Something in the shadows moved. It detached itself from darker shadows beside the fire and approached the pallet on which she lay. She could not move her head, could not see who or what stood over her, but a whimper shivered in her throat as a cool, wet cloth was pressed over her cracked lips. It dabbed her cheeks and blotted the heat off her neck and chest. Dipped in cool water again, it stroked gently down between her breasts, then ran the length of each arm, each leg. A hand cradled the back of her head and raised her up enough to tip a cup against her mouth, but she was shaking too hard and the liquid spilled down the sides of her chin and puddled at the base of her throat.

"Drink, Little One, drink. It will ease the pain, I promise."

Amie rolled her eyes open, but the voice had no face. It was just a shadow blocking out the light.

"You are safe. You have nothing to fear. There are strong walls around you now and many men with swords to guard you against further harm. Believe what I say, for I speak only the truth."

The shadow leaned forward again, and the cup was tipped to her mouth a second time. She managed to swallow a few drops, then a few drops more, but the effort took most of her strength.

"You have done well, Little One. Better this time than the last. A moment, no more, and the pain will fade. By all my skill, it will fade."

He reinforced his soothing words with gentle strokes of the cooling cloth, and Amie spiraled slowly, gratefully back into the darkness.

But despite the voice's reassurances, the terror and despair, having been the first sensations to emerge from the pain, were also the last to fade.

"She is still alive?"

"It would seem as though she does not want to leave this life so easily. The maggots have done their work at last, and the wound is clean. The fever, also, has finally broken."

"Has she wakened at all?"

"A moment here or there, no more."

"Has she spoken?"

"The fever talked, but said very little that made sense."

Amie detected movement beside her. She had come awake at the sound of voices but had not moved or made a sound to betray that fact. There was still pain in her body, but the worst of it seemed to be concentrated in her left shoulder . . .

The arrow. Jesu, she remembered now. She had been running, trying to reach the safety of the forest, and the arrow had struck her in the back. She had found the river . . . but a fall . . . then more pain . . . then the figure of a knight standing over her, his sword drawn, his eyes blazing with bloodlust behind the hammered iron nasal of his helm. He had been grinning as he drew the blade up her thigh, grinning and murmuring promises of worse pain to come.

Was it he who stood over her now, waiting for her to show signs of waking so that the torment could continue?

She remembered nothing. Nothing aside from white-hot pain and dark, misshapen images. If she had indeed wakened, she had no recollection. If she had spoken . . . what might she have said?

Something else stirred at the edge of her mind, but she was having difficulty concentrating. Whoever was standing beside the pallet was very close and very still, as if he was trying to detect whether she was awake or asleep. She could feel his shadow blotting out the warmth of the fire, miserly as it was.

Were her hands bound? Her feet? Was she pinned there while irons were being heated to further her torture? For surely she would be tortured. Odo de Langois's punishment would be neither swift nor merciful.

A soft, involuntary moan escaped her throat. The sudden sound must have startled whoever was hovering over her, for the shadow moved back and called to another.

"Marak? She stirred."

A second shadow came up beside the first. A cool, dry hand was laid across her brow, and when she whimpered again, she heard a faint shuffling of robes and sleeves and felt the corner of a blanket being lifted off her arm and shoulder.

The gentle sliding of the wool against her skin made her realize she was naked beneath the blanket. Naked, stretched out flat on a table with nothing to shield her from the probing eyes of her captors.

"Have you decided to come back to us, Little One?"

The voice. It was soothing and soft, and she knew instinctively she had heard it many times already, through the pain, the fever, the brief periods when the darkness gave way to light and awareness. It did not sound like the voice of a tormentor, although she had been duped before by silky words and a glib tongue.

She attempted to turn her wrist, testing to see if there were bindings. Her hand came up freely, and despite the fact that it felt like a deadweight, she dragged her fingers upward to search for the crucifix that lay between her breasts.

It was not there.

Amie opened her eyes. The first, the only thing she saw was the silhouette of a hooded man standing beside her. The room was so dark, the shadows so thick that she feared perhaps her eyes had been partially scorched by the fires in the village.

But then the shadow of the second man moved, and her gaze was drawn to him. He stood closer to the fire, and she could see the blurred lines of his profile, the rim of brighter light around his hair, the glow that outlined his shoulders and chest.

The hooded figure moved, and Amie's gaze flicked sharply back.

"Wh-who are you?" Her voice was barely a whisper, emitted from a throat that was so dry the words cracked and broke. "Wh-where am I?"

"You are safe, child. There is no one here who wishes you harm."

Here? she thought wildly. *Where is here? Where am I? Who are you, and why have you brought me here?*

"My name is Marak," the stranger continued, "and this"—he turned slightly—"is Lord Tamberlane. He was the one who found you in the woods and brought you here, to his castle. I have been tending your wounds these past six days."

Amie released another small whimper. Six days? She had been lying here fevered and oblivious to all for six days?

"Where is F-Friar Guilford?" The rasp that came out of her throat contained more pain than sound, and it was just as well, for she had blurted the question and the name without thought.

"Wait, child, wait." She must also have tried another abortive movement, for the pale hand moved from her brow to her arm as if to keep her from leaping off the table. The one called Marak murmured something over his shoulder, and when he turned back, there was a cup in his hand. He slid an arm gently beneath her shoulders and raised her head enough to tip the rim of the cup to her lips.

"It is only wine and water," he assured her, "mixed with a little honey to help restore your strength."

Amie looked from the elongated black shadow where his face should be . . . to the cup . . . back to the hidden face. If it was true he had been tending her wounds for six days, it was not likely he would poison her on the seventh. Bolstered by the thought, she parted her lips and let some of the liquid trickle into her mouth. It was warm and sweet, and she took a second sip, then a third. When she had emptied the cup, he lowered her head carefully back onto the pallet with a promise to bring more.

The other shadow, Lord Tamberlane, had not moved. His profile revealed a jaw that seemed carved from a square ridge of granite, a nose that was long and Romanesque, a mouth formed with an utter lack of compromise or compassion. Certes, he was no man's lackey, for Amie had seen enough knights to recognize the musculature and bearing of a man accustomed to wearing armor. He stood with his hands clasped behind his back, but as if *he* was now sensing *her* eyes fixed upon him, he shifted his weight from one foot to the other and brought his arms up, crossing them over his chest.

You still have the advantage, sirrah, she thought. *You are not lying naked and helpless on a tabletop.*

Amie moved her hand again—the left, this time— and the effort brought forth such a bolt of pain that she dropped it back with a stifled gasp.

"The arrow struck you in the shoulder," Marak explained. "These past six days, while you burned with fever, I have given you herbs to keep you from moving too much. I can give you more if you wish it."

Amie released a pent-up breath, feeling it take the rush of pain with it. Herbs to keep her from moving too much . . . was that why her arms and legs felt

weighted down by stones? No, she did not want to
have her wits dulled by potions and possets. She
needed her strength back, and she needed it soon.

Her thoughts tumbled to a standstill as Marak offered her a second cup of the sweetened wine.

"You must be hungry. Drink this, then we will try
some broth."

The wine tasted different. There was a slightly bitter edge to it, and she refused to take more than a
few drops on her tongue before pushing it away.

"Willow bark," he assured her at once. "Only for
the pain. Ciaran"—he turned and held the goblet out
to the knight—"drink some and show her that no
harm is intended."

"Me? Why not show her yourself?"

"Because a clever poisoner would know how to
protect himself."

The knight stared at the cup a moment but took it
and indulged in a long, deep swallow—more than
was necessary for a simple demonstration against
poison—then handed it back. Briefly, his gaze locked
with Amie's, and the effect of those eyes burning into
her was instant and powerful, stripping her of the
ability to do aught but stare back. They were a clear
crystalline green, rendered strangely luminous by the
shadows and scant light. They were also cold and
expressionless, and after a few moments, the sheer
intensity of his stare caused the skin across the nape
of her neck to tighten.

She had seen a wolf once, wounded and lying by
the side of the road. Not only had the beast's eyes
been equally sinister; it had regarded her with the

same shuttered watchfulness. Despite a mangled leg and a hip ripped open to the bone, the wolf had risen and braced itself to attack, its teeth bared in a snarl, its eyes flashing with a thousand years of predatory hatred.

"Are you well enough to answer a few questions?"

His voice matched his eyes: impersonal and detached, no hint of compassion nor any pretense of possessing any.

Instinctively, she knew that to lie to this man, like approaching a wounded wolf, was to invite unparalleled danger.

"Can you tell us what happened at your village? Do you know who the men were who attacked you, or *why* they attacked?"

"Must you do this now?" Marak asked in a murmur. "Can you not see the child is frightened beyond clear thought?"

"Frightened or not, the questions need answering, and she is the only survivor."

Amie's eyes rounded and rose to the knight's face again. *The only survivor? Dear God!*

"Did you know the men who attacked your village?"

The tightness she was already feeling in her throat and chest spread, sending chilling little pinpricks of sensation rippling the length of her spine, making her heart beat faster, her breath come quick and shallow.

Shocked into speechlessness by those luminous eyes, she could do nothing but shake her head.

"Do you know why they attacked or who sent them?"

She shook her head again and prayed that God would forgive the lie, for it was almost a certainty this cold, uncompromising knight would not. The healer reassured her with words of safety and protection, and in her weakened state, she might almost have surrendered to the promissory lure of the very things that had eluded her for so long. But there were no such promises in the knight's eyes. Nothing that suggested he would not send a messenger to her husband upon the instant simply to avoid any further infringements on his time.

Moreover, if he knew, if he even suspected he harbored a would-be murderess under his roof . . .

Her hands curled into small fists beneath the linen sheet. A wave of unbidden images filled her head, not of the attack on the village this time but of a man's hairy, muscular body sprawled facedown on a blood-soaked mattress beside her, and of her kneeling over him, the weight of a heavy candlestick gripped in her hand. She had wanted to hit him a thousand times. She had wanted to kill him a thousand times over, and then to kill him again just for spite. His whore, he had called her. His broodmare. It had been their wedding night, and he had taken her with a brutality that promised more and worse to come.

"What is it? Are you remembering something about the attack?"

The sound of the knight's voice intruded, and Amie blurted an answer without thought. "No. No, I cannot remember what happened. I w-was asleep and heard him scream, then . . ."

"Him?"

Shocked by the blunder, she focused stupidly on the knight's face.

"You said you heard *him* scream."

"M-my uncle. I heard my uncle scream."

"You lived with your uncle?"

She nodded, scarcely able to breathe through the incredible pressure in her chest. She drew a shaky breath, hoping to pull her thoughts into line, then added what she prayed was an adequate explanation. "The bothies were on fire, and everyone was running, everyone was confused and trying to escape. I . . . ran into the forest, but I was followed." She paused again and attempted to moisten her lips with a dry tongue. "Did you say . . . I was the only one who survived?"

"We found no one else alive."

"Not even the children?"

The sheer depth of horror in her voice made the healer reach out and touch her arm.

"Enough questions for today," he told the knight quietly. "She needs to rest and build her strength, or all my work will have been for naught. Tomorrow she will be stronger, and stronger the day after that."

It was hardly a comforting thought, and Amie felt an unbidden tear slide from the corner of her eye and trickle down her temple. She turned her face away from both men and let the resentment flow unchecked alongside the tears. It was her fault. Her fault that they were all dead. They had been good, simple people who had believed her story, and now they had suffered the ultimate consequence for their kindness.

Odo de Langois was a black-souled devil, and God only knew what he would do when he discovered that his bride had escaped the raid on the village. Certes, he would send more men to hunt for her—men who would not be so foolish as to attack a whole village before knowing for sure their quarry was trapped inside.

Amie knew he would not rest until he found her. And this time, to be sure there were no more mistakes, he would kill her with his own bare hands.

Chapter Four

Odo de Langois took great pleasure in killing. He was kneeling beside a thin bright stream of water and washing smears of blood from his hands. The deer he had just gutted hung from a nearby tree. The carcass was still steaming in the cool air; the entrails were lying in a pile to one side being fought over by a pack of long-nosed hounds.

He had made camp by the stream four days ago, and the portable trappings of thirty men and horses were everywhere. Several small fires sent columns of smoke into the leafy growth overhead. There were blankets and saddles, bundles of armor and weaponry scattered throughout the clearing. Several canvas tents had been pitched among the trees, most of them small and practical only for keeping the rain at bay during the night.

His own pavilion was somewhat larger, for Odo was not a man who liked to travel without certain necessities. Aside from the nearly three dozen men-at-arms who accompanied him, he had two squires, several lackeys, and an armorer in his retinue; the latter traveled with all the tools of his trade packed into a large, square wagon. Odo also had a full string of horses, two suits of armor—one of chain mail and thick plated iron, the other of molded bullhide. His swords, shield, lances, and glaives were carried in a warwagon along with items of a more personal nature—clothes, cooking utensils, tables and chairs that could be broken apart and moved with ease, as well as a cot for sleeping.

He had not departed his castle at Belmane expecting to need more than a paring knife and a long length of rope to hang his wife when he was finished with her. Two days into the hunt, however, she had seemed to simply vanish into the dark forest mists. He had dispatched men back to the castle for supplies and more men, and now, two weeks later, they seemed no closer to finding the murderous bitch. A sennight ago they seemed to have success within their grasp. An almoner had mentioned seeing a woman and a priest on the road to London. A storm had kept Odo and his men huddled in caves for a full day, but when it passed and scouts were sent out, a second report identified those same two travelers taking refuge in a small village.

With his head still bound in bandages and his balance affected by the blow he had suffered to his skull, Odo had bowed to his brother's insistence that Rolf be the one to approach the village and determine if the pair were indeed Elizabeth and the poxy priest, and to bring them both back to camp if it proved true. But something had gone wrong. Rolf had returned with an arrow lodged in his thigh. The three paid assassins who had accompanied him to the village were dead along with nearly two dozen armed retainers.

While a man cut the arrowhead out of his thigh, Rolf related how he had given the archers free rein to raid the village and take away whatever they could find of value. He said it had begun as cleanly and neatly as any surprise attack could, but that out of nowhere, men had appeared to defend the village, foresters by the look of it, whose arrows cut them down with the precision of outlaws. Rolf had regrouped and sent men back within the hour. They had searched among the bodies but the corpse of Elizabeth de Langois was not among them.

Odo's rage had very nearly accomplished what Elizabeth's aim with the heavy pewter candlestick had not. His blood rose in such a fury that the pressure in his head came close to bursting. His face boiled as red as his hair, and the pain became so great he eventually had to be held down by six men just to keep him from smashing his skull against a tree trunk. It took four days for the agony in his brain to subside, for the pressure to ease, for the fury to cool into a icy, deadly calm.

His whore-wife was missing; his men were dead. And now there were witnesses to the unwarranted slaughter of an entire village. Adding to his aggravations, he discovered that the vill belonged to the demesne of Taniere Castle. While he was not acquainted personally with the Dragon Slayer, the reputation of Ciaran Tamberlane, former Knight

Templar, former champion of Richard the Lionheart, was more than enough to make him treble the guards around the camp and to set the men to sharpening every sword and blade in their arsenal.

A man like that did not take kindly to having his villages raided, regardless of the provocation. A man like Tamberlane, with family ties to the king's royal court and enough personal confidence to scorn the penance of excommunication would not simply stand by and do nothing to avenge an insult to his property.

When several days passed without the sound of warhorses and armor approaching their camp, Odo had sent men to make discreet inquiries at other villages and hamlets. They had returned bearing the same rumors: that the knight lived in near seclusion at Taniere Castle; that there were powerful black forces at work there; that the former priest and servant of God was now a follower of Lucifer and counted among his retainers a hideous creature who could alter his shape at will and change men to stone at a glance.

Odo had discounted the tales of necromancy as just that: rumors fostered by peasants whose lives were governed by superstition and fear. He did, however, give a measure of truth to the tales of seclusion. The Glanvilles were a prominent family in royal circles, and because Taniere Castle was owned by his uncle, Tamberlane had probably been directed to remain there in permanent exile until his name was forgotten, his hair turned gray, and his skin turned to parchment.

Even so, it was difficult to imagine such a knight,

blooded on the battlefields of Outremer, content to relegate himself to a chair by the hearth.

When Rolf had gone back to search through the bodies, he had not found Elizabeth's body among the dead, but he had found blood in the woods—a great deal of blood that did not all belong to the dead mercenary lying alongside the creek bed. Moreover, a wound such as that which had felled the experienced soldier was not the work of a common forester. A wound like that required the power of a trained sword arm, and who but another knight, skilled in the art of wielding a sword with such power and finality could affect such a blow?

Had Tamberlane himself been present at the vill that day?

Had he found Elizabeth lying wounded in the forest?

Had he carried her back to Taniere Castle to recover from her wounds?

This last fevered suspicion was what had fueled Odo's hand as he gutted and carved the deer. He had imagined the ropes were tied around Elizabeth's wrists and that she, not the deer, had been hauled upright to hang before him. He had slit the skin with care and deliberation, peeling it back strip by strip as if he could hear and savor her screams. When the knife had sunk into the deer's breast, he had actually felt his head swim with pleasure, and by the time he had finished removing the entrails by dripping handfuls, his body had grown so hard with bloodlust it was all he could do not to ride straight to Taniere upon the instant and search for his wife.

When he did catch her, she would be held to account for more than just the insult of running away. She had fought him, scratched him, lashed out with the intent to murder him on their wedding night, an offense that would not go unanswered. She could not even scream for the loss of her virginity for she had been the wife of a gifted whoremaster before he died of debauchery. She should have been eager to regain the mantle of respectability. She should have fallen onto her knees and shown her gratitude before the ceremony was even completed.

The deer was lucky, Odo mused. It had been dead before he skinned it. The lovely Elizabeth de Langois would not fare half so well.

He stared down at his hands, still running pink with blood. The front of his clothes looked like a butcher's apron, and he knew from his reflection in the pond that there were streaks of it splattered across his face and hair. He cupped his hands in the water again and started to scoop some out to rinse it off . . . but stopped. The blood made him feel strong. It made him feel powerful. Invincible.

Pushing to his feet, he turned and glared around the campsite. He was a handsome man, broad-built, with shoulders chiseled from rock, legs thewed with iron. The color of his hair combined with the quantity that grew across his shoulders and back had earned him the byname Red Boar, and he had incorporated a depiction of the snarling beast into his coat of arms. He had run the lists many a time and never been unhorsed, never been defeated. At twenty-and-six, he was in his prime, unafraid of an aging, disgraced, banished, and defrocked warrior monk.

His brother was leaning against a tree a few feet away, and when Odo caught his eye, Rolf de Langois limped over.

"Your leg troubles you?"

Rolf shrugged. He was tall and lean, his attitude far less imposing than his older brother's. His hair was dark mahogany; his face had left handsome well behind and verged on beautiful. His voice was a soft, melodic contrast to the lethal, cold-blooded instincts of the killer that he possessed. "It is tolerable."

"Good. For I was thinking if this Dragon Slayer is reluctant to come to us, perhaps we should go to him."

"From all accounts, he does not welcome visitors."

"I have no wish to beg his hospitality."

"You think he may have Elizabeth?"

"I think she did not get up and walk out of the forest on her own."

Rolf nodded. "We cannot be sure it was even her."

"It was her," Odo said through a snarl. "And if she thinks to hide from me at Taniere Castle, I will know. I will know, and I will have her out."

"Tamberlane is still the king's man. What if she . . ."

"She will say nothing; she will do nothing. She gives her trust as readily as a fox to a hound."

"She apparently trusted Friar Guilford."

"Yes." Odo's eyes narrowed and he glanced across the clearing to where a slender figure in the brown robes of a mendicant sat slumped at the base of a tree. Several loops of rope had been circled around his chest, binding him to the trunk; his hands and feet were tied as well, though it was more for the pain and discomfort the ropes inflicted than an additional safeguard against escape.

They had caught the friar walking alone, out on the open road, not far from a broken cart they had found hidden in the forest. He had pleaded ignorance, of course, declaring he knew nothing about Odo's missing wife, denying he had helped her escape Belmane. But the purse he wore at his waist contained too many coins for a priest to explain away on happenstance. And his eyes, when questioned about his destination, had flicked away from Odo's and refused to rise again.

As an ally and fellow conspirator, he made for a miserable liar.

"How many men have we in camp?"

"Thirty. Six of them mounted."

Odo pursed his lips. "When we approach Taniere Castle, we would do well to do so with a show of force."

"We are going to Taniere Castle?"

"Would you rather sit here in the woods and roast squirrels?"

"I only meant—"

"I know what you meant. And we will send an envoy first. He is still a knight and as such cannot refuse his hospitality to a brother knight."

"Not even if that brother knight has slaughtered an entire village on his demesne?"

Odo smiled wanly. "We will offer our most sincere and humble apologies and explain that we were mistaken in our information that this village harbored a dangerous band of outlaws that has been raiding our lands. We will even offer compensation for his loss. Indeed, how much can he demand for a score of worthless peasants?"

"And if your wife has taken sanctuary inside the castle walls?"

Odo's smile thinned. "If she is there, I will feel her presence and smell the odor of treachery between her thighs."

"Perhaps we should have with us some bait to draw her out?"

Odo followed the tip of his brother's head to where Friar Guilford was slumped against the tree. "He is almost dead now. As bait, he would not be of much value."

"He has breath left in him still. Enough for our purposes at any rate, even if we have to spike him on a lance to make him sit straight."

With thoughtful steps, Odo strode across the clearing and lowered himself into a squat before the priest, his forearms resting on his knees, his hands clasped together in front. He stared at the top of the tonsured pate a moment, then turned his head slightly and sucked a scrap of food from between his teeth.

"Truly, it would have gone easier for you, Priest, if you had simply told us where she was."

Friar Guilford's head came up slowly. His face was puffed and swollen under the bruises that marked his cheeks and jaw. One eye was closed to a slit. The other, despite his exhaustion, despite the cramps that racked his body, was a sharp and clear blue.

"I have told you a hundred times," he said through scabbed lips. "I do not know where the Lady Elizabeth is, and I cannot tell you what I do not know."

"You expect me to believe you, Priest? You expect me to simply say, 'Ah, yes, good fellow, and so be on your way'? And this even though you can see for yourself that God himself has judged you false."

The priest's gaze flickered down to his hand . . . a hand so swollen and inflamed it was distorted beyond recognition as a human appendage. He had endured Odo de Langois's questions; he had endured the slaps, the blows, even the clawed fingers that had nearly burst his testicles like grapes. All of that he had endured with prayers on his lips and faith in his God.

The last test had come with Odo's amused insistence that he prove his ignorance of the Lady Elizabeth's whereabouts by undergoing an ordeal by fire. A heavy iron bar was produced and heated red-hot in the coals of the fire. As a test of purity, the accused person had to hold the bar and walk three paces. The hand was then bandaged and left for three days. When the bandages were removed and if the wound was seen to be healing, then the accused's innocence was proclaimed. If the wound was not healed, if it was festering and growing worse, then obviously God had abandoned the accused and declared him guilty of the charge.

Half the skin on Friar Guilford's hand had come

off with the filthy rags. The scorching was to the bone, and he knew, by the fevers and aches in his body, that there was poison in his veins.

Wearily, he looked back up at Odo de Langois. "I expect you will believe only what you wish to believe, and therein lies the cause for pity."

"You pity me, do you, Priest?"

"You could have had her love."

"Her *love*? The love of a *whore*? You countenance this as being something I should have sought?"

"She was not a whore until her uncle sold her in marriage to the first man who waved a purse of gold coins under his beak. Even then, she accepted her fate with a sweetness that only needed someone to see it, to coax it forth, to nurture it into loyalty and love. You could have done this. Instead you chose to treat her no better than the man who had to beat her nearly every night before she would comply with his demands."

"She did not give me the chance to treat her any differently, nor did she give me cause. She spread herself for every man who walked the halls of Belmane Castle."

"You know this as fact, do you?"

"I saw with mine own eyes," Odo roared. "I caught her with her legs spread and her skirts shoved above her waist."

"With your brother Rolf? And did he tell you she begged him for it? Begged him to drag her into the woods where her screams would not be heard, then begged him to squeeze his hands around her throat until her lungs were starved for air?"

"Such a crushing would leave bruises. There were none. And there were five other men present who said she lay beneath him willingly. Are you saying they all lied?"

"They were Rolf's men," the priest said simply. "They would say what he told them to say."

Odo sucked in a deep breath and hawked noisily into the soft earth. "Maybe it is you who would say whatever she asked you to say. Maybe you are more man than priest and would beg a little surcease of your own? She has the face of an angel, does she not? The body of a nymph with a well of nectar so sweet it makes your tongue ache from the pleasure." Odo leaned in closer and lowered his voice to a conspiratory whisper. "Is that why you defend her, Priest? Because you have tasted her nectar yourself?"

Friar Guilford leaned his head back against the tree trunk. Neither food nor water had passed his lips in more than ten days, and he was weak enough, feverish enough, that he had begun to fear he might say or do anything to gain relief for his thirst, if nothing else. Somewhere he had heard that it took a healthy man more than three weeks to die by starvation, but that madness, brought on by ravening thirst, came much sooner.

He could smell the water on Odo's skin, see it glistening on the fine red hairs that coated the freckled hands. He prayed day and night to keep his mind off the sound of the stream burbling by only a few dozen paces away. During the night it had rained, but he had been too far under the trees to catch more than a few drops on his tongue. In the end, that had been worse than nothing at all.

When he was not praying, he was thinking of Amaranth. He had been utterly convinced he would see Rolf de Langois returning to camp that day dragging Amie behind him, and he had scarcely been able to believe his own eyes when the men came back from the raid bleeding and empty-handed.

His relief had quickly turned to fear. If she was not in the village, where he had left her, then where was she? Surely she would not have wandered off on her own?

Their escape from Belmane had been hasty and ill-planned at best. Friar Guilford had accompanied Amie there as her confessor. He had remained steadfast by her side through the week of feasting and jousting that led to the nuptials. He had felt her hands shaking, seen her lips trembling all through the ceremony, and could scarcely bear to see his bright little butterfly—already so sadly disabused by her first marriage—led away to the bridal chamber by the roisterous, bawdy throng.

Her face had been pale, her eyes huge, and he had wept and prayed and wept some more until he had fallen into an exhausted sleep, slumped over the prayer stool.

A frantic knocking on his door hours later had wakened him. Amie was standing there, her night sheath splattered in blood, her teeth chattering so badly she could not speak. A cup of wine heated with a fire tong had loosened her tongue enough to set the hairs on the friar's neck standing on end.

She had bludgeoned her new husband to death. She had crushed his skull with a candlestick and left him soaked in blood on their bed. He had been drunk. With the guests standing outside the door cheering and goading him on, he had torn into her like a ravening beast. He had called her a whore and a bitch and a dozen other filthy names even as he tugged on her hair and howled out his pleasure.

When he was spent, he collapsed beside her still groaning promises of carnal horrors yet to come. Blinded by disgust and rage, she had grabbed the closest thing to hand—a candlestick—and brought it smashing down across his head once, twice, three times.

Amaranth assumed she had killed him. She had not fled to the chapel seeking help to escape. Rather, she had come in search of absolution, to confess her sins and wait for the dawn to bring the sound of the alarm bells. Despite her noble blood, she would be punished as harshly as any peasant for her crime.

Women who committed murder were strangled then burned.

But sweet death, she declared, was preferable to spending another day trapped inside Belmane Castle, and strangulation would be a merciful relief.

Friar Guilford, while unable to condone what she had done, could not just sit by and wait for the guards. A quick look into the newlywed's chamber assured him that the bridegroom yet breathed, for now. He was well aware of Odo de Langois's brutish ways and suspected her death would not be as swift or as merciful as she imagined.

Without thinking of the consequences, the friar had hastily outfitted Amie in boy's clothing, tucked her hair under a worn felt hat and, after pausing in the chapel and praying for forgiveness, had removed the coins from the bishop's box.

Bundling Amie in a cloak, he had taken her out of the castle through the postern gate, not winning more than a grunt and a sleepy nod from the guard. They had made their way south through the forest, heading in the direction of Kent and the abbey at Maidstone. The prioress there was Guilford's sister, and he knew the holy mother would shield Elizabeth Amaranth de Langois with the last breath in her body if need be. Moreover, Maidstone was nearly a hundred leagues away, far enough that whispers of Amaranth's whereabouts might not reach the ears of her hunters.

The first night they had stopped to beg respite at a small cottage. Upon seeing the dazzled look in the peasant's eye when he beheld Amie's silvery yellow mane, the friar had mixed a paste of burned acorns, coal dust, and lard and applied it thickly to her hair. Darkened to a dull brown, the disguise took them anonymously through two more days of hard walking before a storm drove them to seek shelter. Amie had wakened with a chill, so stiff she could hardly stand, leaving Guilford no choice but to beg shelter for her in the humble vill.

Odo de Langois, very much alive and burning with vengeance, came upon him the next day.

"I defend her," Friar Guilford said, looking Odo calmly in the eye, "because no one else will. Because her uncle cared little for her and sought to relieve himself of a burden by selling her first to a lecher three times her age, then to you."

Odo tipped his head, his eyes narrowing with the curiosity of a hawk tracking a mouse. "You cast insults, Priest, like a man who is not afraid to die."

"Do your best," Guilford said wearily. "And cease your tiresome threats."

"My best?" Odo's mouth spread in a grin. "Ah, Priest, you have not seen my best. Not by half. My little whore-wife will, however. She will live long enough to rue the day she ever lifted a hand against me. But I am a generous man and make you a final offer: Tell me where she is, and I will let you go. I will let you walk away from here unmolested."

Friar Guilford frowned and tasted fresh blood from a new crack in his lip. He suspected he would never be walking anywhere ever again. "I will do nothing to help you find Lady Elizabeth. I pray to God that she runs fast, runs far, and that she never needs to lay eyes upon you again in this or any other lifetime."

Odo's gray eyes kindled with sharp points of light, and he pushed to his feet.

"His usefulness is at an end," he said quietly to his brother. "Kill him."

Rolf, as hardened as any nail that ever came out of a smithy's forge, pursed his lips a moment and frowned. It was one thing to put a man of the cloth through a trial by ordeal and leave him to his own fate; it was quite another to run him through in cold blood. Odo saw his hesitation and swore. Quicker than the eye could follow the motion, he drew his dagger, leaned down, and slashed it across the friar's neck from ear to ear. He watched the blood bubble out and spill down the front of Guilford's cassock. When it slowed to a trickle, when the priest's head had slumped to the side and the last breath had foamed between his lips, Odo spat noisily on the ground and turned to Rolf.

"Fetch that pike. We will leave the good priest spitted here as a warning to God Himself that nothing and no one will stand in my way."

Chapter Five

The second time Amaranth woke up, when her head was clear and not clouded by pain, it was easier. Someone had hung a kettle of broth to simmer over the fire, and the contents filled the air with the heady scent of stewing beef and onions. There was still an element of fear of the unknown—Where was she? Who were these men?—but it was tempered by the knowledge that she was not strapped to a subjugator's table, nor were there hot irons and pincers waiting to tear at her flesh. She was no longer stretched out on a table, for that matter; she had been moved to a bed, placed on a mattress stuffed thick with fresh, sweet-smelling rushes. And there was light. A great deal of light, most of it streaming from a large mullioned window recessed in the wall beside the bed.

Amie lifted her head. There were no shelves, no rows upon rows of bottles. The walls of this chamber were bare but for a few wooden pegs and several iron sconces. There was a stone fireplace set into the far wall, the opening as tall as a man and as wide as would require three long strides to cross from one side to the other. A log the size of a small tree trunk burned inside, heating the contents of the iron pot that hung suspended on a tripod.

Amie tipped her chin down. Her injured shoulder ached, but at least the pain did not tear the breath from her body when she moved. Beneath the pile of warm furs that covered her, she was no longer naked either. A plain white sheath covered her, the sleeves long and the neckline high beneath her chin. Her hair had been combed out of the plait and washed; it spread over the feather-stuffed bolster like a soft russet fan.

Amie's hand rose to pluck a few strands from her temple and draw them tentatively forward.

Definitely russet. The concoction of stains and pastes Friar Guilford had used to camouflage the true color of her hair were half as dark as they had been when he had applied them.

She heard a sound at the door and lay quickly back. Closing her eyes, she tried to relax her face, but the temptation, after she heard soft footsteps pass by the bed without stopping, was too great and she raised her lashes a slit.

It was a woman. She was slight of frame and dark-skinned, wearing long, flowing layers of silk that shimmered where the light caught each rippled step. Her head was covered with a veil that trailed over her shoulders, the edges embroidered with gold thread. Following close on her heels, one eye warily fixed on the bed, was a small boy no more than three or four years old. Huge brown eyes filled his face, and as he walked, he kept one hand on the woman's robe, the other clutched around a carved wooden horse.

The woman bent over the fire and stirred the broth. She murmured something in a strange language to the boy, who released her robe and ran over to the window embrasure. He scrambled up onto the stone lip and, because the ledge was deep, disappeared for the few moments it took him to close and latch the wooden shutters.

Amie was puzzled enough to forget that she was supposed to be feigning sleep, and when the woman straightened, their eyes met. That alone was startling, but when Amie saw the ugly, ragged scar that marred the woman's right cheek, her lips parted over an involuntary gasp. The whole cheek was caved in, the flesh puckered in such a grizzled knot that one corner of her mouth had been stretched to the side in a distorted grin.

The shutters closed, locking out the sunlight at the same time the woman hastily lifted a corner of her veil and turned her head to the side.

Amie was momentarily stripped of speech. Her reaction to the woman's deformity had been cruel and obvious, and she was in no position to make more enemies.

"Please . . ."

The woman again spoke to the little boy, who scrambled instantly to her side and ran so quickly to the door that he dropped his wooden horse.

"Please wait!"

Amie pushed herself up onto her elbows, but it was too late. The woman and child were gone, and in their place, moving through the open door like a hooded wraith, was the tall thin seneschal, Marak.

"You are with us again, then, are you?"

"That woman . . ."

The hood shifted slightly as if he had turned his head within its shadowy confines. "Inaya? She has been tending to you these past few days."

"I—I may have startled her."

"She startles very easily around strangers—take no offense."

"But I am afraid I reacted very badly when I saw . . ."

"Her face? Ah, yes. A terrible misfortune. The wound was full of poison by the time she was brought to me. I did what I could, but"—his shoulders lifted in an apologetic shrug—"I cannot work miracles, despite what you may hear. I am not even a good magician, though I am often credited with raising spirits and changing good, god-fearing Christians into toads."

He came closer to the bed, close enough that Amie could see the point of his chin taking shape under the shadowy hood.

"How are you feeling today?" A cool white hand came forward and rested on her cheek a moment. "No fever. That is excellent. And the shoulder? You are able to move it without too much pain?"

Amie looked down. She had pushed herself up onto her elbows without thinking about the action, and only realized now that the arm was holding her weight. The skin felt as though it was stretched tight and the muscles protested from disuse, but in truth, there was little more discomfort beyond a dull thrumming to remind her of the injury.

"It still hurts," she admitted with no small amount of wonder, "but it is nothing that cannot be borne."

"Excellent. In a week or two, you will hardly flinch when you lift a sack of flour—something I will start having you do on the morrow. Just a small sack at first, to rouse the muscles that have grown lax this past week. Then we will add more and more flour to the sack each day as you gain your strength back. Before we can begin that, however, we must make more blood. And to do that, you need something with more substance than wine and honey."

Amie's stomach gave off an audible rumble in response to the suggestion. The sound must have carried farther than the bed, for she heard Marak give a low chuckle, and a moment later, he was beside the fire, ladling some of the contents of the steaming pot into a small wooden bowl. When he returned to the bedside, she was lying down again, the furs pulled up to her chin.

"Come now. My cooking is not that dreadful. What can one do to spoil broth, anyway? Some beef bones, some onions, some garlic, a little mustard and salt . . ." He tipped the spoon to his lips and slurped up a noisy mouthful. "Mmm, yes. I forgot to add the nightshade and the belladonna, but if luck should have it that you survive another day, certes I will remember it on the morrow."

The smile she could see reshaping his mouth belied

the gentle sarcasm and invited a small one of her own, for had she not had the same thought already?

He filled the spoon again, bringing it slowly to Amie's lips.

The broth was delicious. It flowed from her throat straight down into her toes, curling them under with pleasure. Marak used a scrap of linen to catch any dribbles that ran down her chin, but there were not many that were squandered so needlessly.

When the bowl was emptied, refilled, and emptied for the second time, she looked hopefully for more, but he wagged a cautious finger and set the empty vessel aside. "Wait, Little One. Too much too soon can be more painful than the lack. If you suffer no ill effects, you can have as much as you like—and bread and cheese besides—for there was not much flesh on your bones to begin with. After such a long fast, I began to fear we would lose you in the bedding."

"Little One," she whispered. She leaned back against the bolster, and her gaze rose to the ceiling beams crossing overhead in the gloom. "I have not been called that since I was a child."

"I would call you by your name, but alas, I do not know it."

Tell too many lies, a voice echoed in her ear, *and you begin to forget the truth.* "Amaranth," she said. "My father called me Amaranth."

"The flower that never fades," Marak said, smiling.

"He hoped I would grow into a likeness of my mother."

"And did you?"

"I do not know. Mother died when I was two and Father when I was twelve. He told me yes, but he might have been saying that through a father's eyes."

"You have no other family?"

Her jaw clenched. "No. No other family."

"Save for your uncle, of course."

She frowned. "My—" She remembered, then, telling the knight with the green eyes that she had been living with her uncle in the village. *Tell too many lies* . . . "Yes, save for my uncle," she said in a whisper.

Hopefully he would assume her stumbled words stemmed from the loss of her home and family, although there was something in the way the shadowed shape of his mouth moved that suggested he knew more of the truth than she suspected.

"If it please, may I ask where I am? How far are we from the village?"

"You are inside the stone walls of Taniere Castle. The vill lies along the easternmost border of Lord Tamberlane's land. Luckily for you, he was out hunting when he was alerted to the raid."

"Yes," she mirrored. "Luckily for me."

"They counted a score of crossbowmen enjoined in the ambush . . . an uncommonly strong force to lead a raid on a simple farming village."

"I . . . did not stop to count. I was too busy running for my life."

"And your . . . uncle?"

She glanced up. "My uncle?"

"He did not run into the woods with you?"

"He . . . stayed behind. To try to help the others, the other women and—and the children."

Her voice trailed away again, and this time the horror was real. She had been looked after by a pretty, dark-haired woman with three small children and if, as Marak had said, there were no survivors . . .

"You had no children of your own?"

She looked up. "No. No, I had none of my own."

That much, at least, was the absolute truth.

"Lord Tamberlane said the men who attacked your village were no common thieves and outlaws."

"Yes," she murmured. "The one who chased me rode a destrier and carried a sword wrought with a fine silvered hilt. But . . . how did Lord Tamberlane know this?"

"The man he saved you from was a knight."

"He slew him?"

The gray hood shifted again. "Lord Tamberlane is not a man to be trifled with when his temper is roused."

Said casually, Amie wondered if it was a warning or a threat. *And these knights who were slain—did any of them have hair the color of hell's own flames?*

"The scar on your shoulder will be ugly," Marak said, abruptly changing the subject, "but alas there was no help for it. The greater concern was for you to be able to use it as freely as before. It will be stiff for a while and will likely ache to beat the devil, but with care, full use of it should be restored."

Amie slid her arm out from beneath the covers and

tested how far she could lift her hand without gasping from the pain.

"Perhaps it would be easier if you sit up first," he suggested.

Since he kept his hands tucked inside his long sleeves and made no move to assist, Amie sucked in a small mouthful of air and rolled herself onto her right elbow, using it to inch and wriggle her way up the bolster. Her own determination fueled her past the pain, and half an eternity later, she was propped against the wooden backboard, her face glistening with sweat, her injured arm cradled across her chest. Straggled lengths of hair fell over her brow, and when she shoved it back, she could sense Marak watching her every move and gesture.

Her brow pleated with a frown. "Why do you keep your face always hooded?"

He hesitated for a moment before answering. "It is an affliction. Too much light causes me great pain."

"Light?" Her frown deepened, and she remembered how dark the chamber had been where she had wakened the first time, and how the child had been ordered to close the heavy shutters before Marak would enter this one.

"It also spares good men and women the need to run from me, screaming. If you found Inaya's scars discomfiting . . . you would likely find my appearance harrowing."

"You judge my entire character on one sorry lapse?"

He chuckled softly. "I judge it on many things, Amaranth. The whiteness of your skin, the manner of your speech, the softness of your hands . . . the stain of burned walnut shells in the water that was used to darken your hair. Even the admission that you were too busy running into the woods to count your attackers reveals more to me than you seem willing to share." At her puzzled stare, he added by way of explanation, "Only one peasant in a thousand knows how to count, and I doubt that one would be a woman.

"My guess is that you were not born in that village," he continued quietly. "Nor in any village like it."

Amie curled her lower lip slowly between her teeth, unable to stop the flow of heat that rose in her cheeks.

"You expressed shock that there were no other survivors, yet you asked no further questions, blurted no other names, asked after no close friend. No neighbor. Nor did you show any sign of recognizing Lord Tamberlane's name, which you surely would have done had you been in the village for any length of time."

"It is small and isolated . . ."

"Yet must still pay tithes and give homage to the Dragon Slayer."

"Dragon Slayer?" she whispered.

The broth that had tasted so delicious only moments ago roiled in her stomach, threatening the back of her throat. She could tell more lies, of course, add more half-truths to the bevy she had gathered about her already, but she suspected they would not stand the test of those unseen eyes. More lies, more shameful falsehoods would only make her appear more of a coward than she was already.

She pushed an errant lock of hair behind her ear, conscious again of just how much of the dye had washed away. It had only been meant as a temporary measure, a means of spiriting her away from her husband's demesne and allowing her to travel in the guise of a peasant. Now it seemed it had only contributed to her being uncloaked for the charlatan she was.

"I cannot help you, Amaranth, if you do not tell me the truth," he said quietly.

She felt the hot sting of tears building behind her eyes. "Why would you want to help me at all?"

Instead of answering, he made a general observation. "People say many things when they are burning with fever. Things they fear, cruelties they have suffered, horrors they have endured . . . even crimes they have committed." He paused and watched a slow, fat tear slide down her cheek. "The men who attacked the village," he asked gently. "Is it possible they were looking for you?"

She closed her eyes and nodded faintly. "It is possible, yes."

"You . . . have been running away from someone?"

She nodded again. "M-my husband."

"Your husband?"

"Wed less than a day, but long enough to know he was a vile and brutal animal." She shivered through the words. "A man who would not have had a moment's pause in ordering the death of so many innocent people in his quest to catch me and put me in my grave."

"Where were you running to, child? Surely you were not attempting such a thing on your own?"

"No. No, I was . . . with someone else. I was with my confessor. A sweet and gentle man whose life, I fear, must have been forfeited as well in his efforts to protect me."

"He helped you escape?"

She nodded. "But we were caught out in the rain one night, and I came down with a chill. I was too weak to walk, and the cart we had was smashed in the storm. He brought me to the village and begged the good people to keep me there while he went back to fetch what few belongings we had. He was taking me to a convent, you see. A convent in the south of England where he thought I would be safe." Her voice trailed away, and she squeezed her eyes tight against a stronger flood of tears. "And now all those good people are dead. All dead because of me. They did nothing. They were guilty of nothing but trying to help the friar and me."

She covered her face with her hands and turned away from Marak as the sobs began to wrack her body. Once set free, she could not stop them, and he was left standing there, unable to do anything but watch while her grief and anger ran its course.

He had suspected, from the moment he saw her, that she was no ordinary peasant girl. Uncalloused hands, flawless skin unblemished by sun and weather, the dulled stiffness of her hair . . . and the

fact that the plaited length on her head did not match
the soft yellow down at the juncture of her thighs.
She had been raised in wealth and luxury, with servants to tend her every need, a fact that had been
oddly contradicted by, among other things, evidence
of faint white lines tracing across her back and buttocks. She had been beaten, lashed until the skin split
and bled in places where it would not show to the
casual eye.

The many hours he had sat beside her, bathing her
flaming skin in cool water, he had listened to disjointed ramblings, bits and pieces of a story he was
unable to stitch together fully, but one that hinted at
a far broader tapestry of evil and brutality than one
day of marriage would explain.

Even so, the laws of the land declared a wife to be
nothing more than chattel, able to be beaten within
a breath of life if she was disobedient or rebellious,
killed if she raised her hand against her lord, even
in self-defense. As chattel, she was also bound by
law to be returned to her rightful owner if she was
discovered hiding in another man's house.

Marak steepled his hands under his chin.

Tamberlane would be obliged to send her back if
he discovered her secret. As a knight, a warrior, and
a monk, he knew there were lines of battle that could
not be crossed, and interfering with a husband and
wife was nothing he could concern himself with save,
possibly, to demand compensation for the village and
its tenants.

Perhaps if the girl had been a virgin there might
have been some grounds to annul the marriage and

spare her from the fates of the court. But she was not a virgin. Marak had enlisted Inaya's help in examining her to ensure the blood between her legs had come only from external cuts, and the lack of a maidenhead was discovered.

Playing devil's advocate against himself, Marak also knew that Tamberlane's interaction with women was severely limited. He had never had dealings with a wife or a mistress, never gone through the ordeal of flirtations or courtship where what a woman said was often the complete opposite of what proved to be the truth. Naive in every sense where women were concerned, Ciaran would have no reason to suspect Amaranth was anything other than what she appeared to be . . . the victim of terrible circumstances. If anything, he might even be driven to feel more protective of her, since she was found on his land and was now, to the extent of his current knowledge, *his* chattel.

Not to be discounted was the fact that she was a beauty. Beneath the pallor, her cheeks were high and smooth, her face a perfect oval with enormous, long-lashed eyes and a delicate nose. Her mouth was well formed with a full lower lip and a sweet upper bow that would rouse warmth in the most frozen of hearts. She was fine-boned and slender. He suspected that her hair, when all the stain was washed out, would be the same silvery yellow as her thatch, although, even in its present state of reddish-blond, it was striking. Similarly, she was all skin and bone now, but with a few healthy meals in her belly and a resplendent tunic of silk molded to her curves, Marak guessed she would turn many a man's head in passing.

A husband should have willingly gone to any lengths to keep such a beauty by his side, yet this one had sent hunters out to kill her.

Marak clasped his hands together under the shield of his long sleeves. He was no frothing Samaritan, yet during these past eight days he had formed an admitted attachment. She had been all but dead when Tamberlane had brought her to his chambers, and in truth he had given her one in one thousandth of a chance of surviving.

Yet she had. She had fought through fevers and corruption of the wound. He had drained the poison half a dozen times and filled the wound repeatedly with maggots only to discover a sliver of the arrow embedded in her flesh that had to be cut away before the process of healing could begin all over again.

A faint sound intruded on his thoughts and prompted Marak to glance behind him. Tamberlane stood on the threshold, one hand on the latch of the door, the other pressed against the wall.

Amaranth was still sobbing, still rolled into a fetal ball, and was not aware of the knight's arrival. The pale green eyes searched the bed a moment, then sought Marak's with a questioning frown. The seneschal, in turn, raised a bony finger and touched it to his lips.

"She needs to do this," he whispered. "She needs to weep for more than just the pain of her wound."

Tamberlane lowered his voice. "Her uncle?"

"Among others, yes," Marak said slowly.

The knight nodded and glanced back at the bed. It was clear he was discomfited by the sight of the girl weeping, and Marak would almost have smiled at the awkward, stricken look on the warrior monk's face had he not just then realized he had seen that look several times over the past eight days.

Each of those occasions Tamberlane had come quietly into Marak's tower room to stand in the shadows and observe, usually under the guise of seeing if she had wakened again. Marak had done nothing to discourage him, for the brooding knight had not shown that much interest in anything over the past three years. While it was true that he had barely looked at the girl when she was naked, turning his head away like a chaste altar boy, it was also true that Tamberlane was first and foremost a man. On more than one occasion, Marak had caught him staring down at Amaranth's face, his gaze lingering on the sweet curve of her lips or the smooth line of her cheek.

Now, by God's own curious grace, there was concern . . . yes, *concern* in the iridescent green eyes as they glared at Marak and silently commanded him to heal whatever was making her sob so inconsolably.

"A posset," Marak murmured thoughtfully. "A posset might help ease her mind. Will you stay with her until I return?"

Before the knight could answer yea or nay, Marak retreated to the door, pausing before he pulled it closed behind him.

"By the by, her name, should the need arise to use it, is Amaranth. And do try not to scowl as if you have just come away from kicking the dogs."

Tamberlane stared at the banded oak planks long after the door had been shut, then turned back to stare at the bed. Amaranth had stopped sobbing, but her face was still averted, and he could see the tremors shaking her fingers as she tried to erase the wetness from her cheeks. She knew he was there. She had not yet looked directly at him, but he knew that she was aware of his presence.

He glanced at the fire, at the pot hanging over the tripod . . . and frowned slightly when he saw the wooden horse lying on its side before the hearth. With one eye fixed guardedly on the bed, he walked over and picked up the carving, turning it over in his big hands.

"Jibril never lets this out of his sight," he said quietly. "I vow he sleeps with it."

Amie exhaled over a large shudder and looked up. "I—I think I frightened him."

"He is a timid boy and frightens easily."

"Is he your son?"

"My son?" The knight looked up sharply. "No. No, he is not my son. He is my"—a pause produced a small, wry smile at the corners of his mouth—"my gift from Allah."

Amie sniffled and rubbed her eyes again to dry them. "Your gift?"

"I saved his mother's life. Her husband was dead, and her family did not want to be indebted to a

Christian, and so they gave her to me. Her and her son. Had I refused to take them, they would have been stoned to death for bringing shame on the family."

"Stoned because you saved their lives? That makes no sense."

Tamberlane shrugged. "In truth, the whole idea of a Holy War—men fighting over the right to claim their God is superior to another—makes no sense. Just as the notion of any God sanctioning murder and slaughter in His name makes little sense either."

"You question God's judgment?" she asked in a whisper.

He could see that he had shocked her. Hearing such words said by another a few short years ago would have prompted him to draw his sword and defend his faith unto the death.

"I question my own judgment more often," he said quietly. Remembering Marak's parting words, he attempted a faint smile. "How are you feeling, Amaranth?"

That he used her name startled her for a moment, but she managed a weak smile to show her gratitude. "Much better, thank you. The healer said I owe you thanks for saving my life, for slaying the man who would have otherwise killed me."

Tamberlane was equally discomfited by compliments and moved in front of the fire. He was dressed in a plain tunic and doeskin leggings, with little to camouflage the fact that his shoulders were bulked by muscle, his waist solid and flat, his legs well hewn from the years of commanding a raging warhorse.

He presented the silhouette of a powerful knight, a prime specimen of a man who one might believe could, indeed, slay dragons.

He picked up an iron rod and pushed at the burning log, sending a fan of red sparks crackling up into the air.

He had not expected to see her sitting up when he came inside the room, and certainly not weeping. The sight had caused a strange tightness in his belly, for he had always felt awkward and clumsy around women. He had no experience whatsoever with weeping females who looked so small and crumpled and helpless. Add to that the clever wit of his tongue, wherein he had undoubtedly succeeded in convincing her he was a heretic and a blasphemer. Certes, she would run screaming from the room if she knew the full extent of his disgrace in the eyes of man and God.

Why that should suddenly matter to him was anyone's guess.

Yet it did.

He heard a faint shuffling and turned in time to see Amaranth struggling to push the covers aside and swing her legs over the side of the bed.

"What are you doing?"

She sat on the edge of the bed, gasping slightly through a wave of dizziness. Her limbs felt like candles left too long in the hot sun, and she was not altogether certain they would hold her if she stood, but she was determined. She had to leave Taniere Castle as soon as possible, and she could not do that if she was too weak to even get out of the bed.

Swallowing hard, she pushed herself up and was valiantly able to wobble there for a full two heartbeats before the room began to spin and the floor took a sudden lurch and swooped from under her feet.

She started to pitch forward, but in a heartbeat, there were strong, muscular arms reaching out to catch her.

Amie tipped her head up and saw bold green eyes staring back down at her. He was holding her tight against a chest that was as solid as a wall of rock, supporting her with arms so strong and steady that part of her shivered from the sensation. She remembered being held in them before. She remembered being lifted off the forest floor and cradled against his chest during the long and painful ride to Taniere Castle. She remembered the smell of his skin, earthy with the masculine scents of leather and sweat, and she remembered pressing her face into the crook of his neck where it had been warm and comforting . . . and safe.

For Tamberlane, reaching for her had been but a reflex. Holding her was something else entirely, for the breath stilled in his chest and the blood began to throb sluggishly through his body. Inaya had bathed her, gently washing away the stink of Marak's poultices and mustard pastes. She smelled fresh and clean. Her hair was soft as silk where it spilled over his hands; her face was a sweet oval; her eyes as blue and clear as a summer sky. And her mouth . . .

He blinked and quickly guided her back onto the bed. "You try to do too much. Marak will not thank you if you fall and crush your head against the stone wall, not after all he has done to keep you alive."

Amie sat on the edge of the bed, shaking so badly the linen of her sheath trembled. Tamberlane snatched up the top covering of fur and wrapped it around her shoulders, then spied an ewer of water and tipped some into a cup.

"Drink this."

She focused intently on the cup a moment before raising her hands to try to take it.

Tamberlane crouched down and closed his bigger hand over hers, steadying the vessel, helping to guide it to her lips. She kept her lashes lowered, refusing to look into his face again, but that only made him notice the soft, downy spirals that grew at her temples and the way the firelight wove threads of red and purest gold through her hair. Her tunic had become rucked up at the knee, and his gaze strayed unwittingly to the slender length of her calf, the delicate turn of her ankle, the small white feet and pretty pink toes. The faint red scratch where the mercenary's sword had cut her was still visible, and that made him recall the sight of her sprawled on the ground, her thighs kicked apart, the point of the blade poised over her womanhood.

"Drink it all," he urged, conscious of her eyes rising to his face. She obeyed without question, and when the cup was emptied, a small bead of the clear liquid clung to her lower lip. He watched her capture it with the tip of her tongue, and the action caused him to lick his own lip before he shook himself and set the cup on the table.

It was when he was turning back that he noticed Marak standing quietly in the doorway.

"Ah. Here is the Venetian with your posset. More effective than water, I am sure."

Marak came into the room, followed closely by Inaya and the boy, Jibril.

"Plaguing her with your questions again, are you?" Marak asked, beckoning to Inaya to set the board she was carrying on the table.

"I have inquired after nothing but her health," Tamberlane said.

He stood up, relinquishing his place to the Arab woman, who now wore a veil across her face, leaving only her huge kohl-rimmed eyes visible. The boy moved with her, his fist clenched tightly to the folds of her sari, but when he spied the carved wooden horse where Tamberlane had left it by the hearth, he let out a small squeak of joy and ran to retrieve it.

Inaya murmured something under her breath that Amie could not understand, but she gathered by the flurry of scolding fingers that she was being ordered back beneath the bedcovers. This she did willingly, for Tamberlane was still close, and her body still echoed with the shivers caused by his embrace.

When Tamberlane stood, he glanced down at the steaming bowl in Marak's hand. "I thought perhaps, with her mind free of your possets, old man, she might remember something more. My foresters tell me there is a large encampment of men just beyond the border of my land. The camp is heavily guarded, and they could not get close enough to see, apart from one among them having red hair, any markings or colors on their tunics."

The hood shifted slightly as the shadowy figure looked at Amie. She sat very still and quiet on the edge of the bed, her hands clutched so tightly on her lap that her nails gouged into her flesh. She kept her eyes lowered and what little color she had gained back into her cheeks drained away like blood from an opened vein.

She could feel Marak's shuttered gaze watching her.

Waiting.

Was he searching for signs that she recognized the camp from Tamberlane's description? Was he leaving the choice to her as to whether or not to tell Lord Tamberlane about her husband? Or was he testing her, testing her character, seeing if she was desperate enough to lie to the man who had saved her life? And if so, if she lied, would he reveal her for the coward and charlatan that she was?

In a household full of secretive strangers . . . whom did she dare trust?

Chapter Six

In the end, Amaranth took the cowardly way out and lay back on the pillows, her eyes fluttering closed as if collapsing in a weak faint. Marak did not hasten to her side to attend upon her, but neither did he betray her. The hooded figure had remained silent save for a whispered comment that came some few moments later, suggesting that he and Tamberlane should leave the chamber and allow Amie to sleep. He did not make any further references to her husband or her plight, although the very act of him treating her deception so casually only made her more uncomfortable.

Inaya assumed the bulk of her care now that her shoulder was on the mend. Initially wary of Amie, the tiny dark-eyed woman conducted all of her duties in utter silence, moving on small, soundless feet, seemingly able to anticipate any request Amie might make before she even thought of it. The faintest rumble of hunger was met by steaming bowls of stew and broth. A licking of the lips brought forth an ewer of water or wine. A hand raised restlessly to push a stray hair out of the way resulted in the appearance of a horsehair brush and a strip of colored ribbon to bind it into a long plait.

The boy, Jibril, shadowed his mother, running instantly to crouch in a corner farthest away from where Amie happened to be. His constant companion was the carved wooden horse, which he clutched to his breast and whispered to as if it were a live pet.

By the next day, Amie could stand without the floor sliding out from beneath her. By the day after that, she could walk the length and breadth of her chamber several times a day, and could feel herself growing stronger each time. She forced herself to eat whatever Inaya put in front of her, knowing that each mouthful made her stronger. Marak still came to check on her several times each day, beginning early in the morning when he brought a mulled brew of honey, wine, and herbs that sent the blood surging through her veins like liquid fire.

On the fourth day, when Marak arrived with her morning libation, Amie was already out of bed and restless. A plain tunic covered the linen sheath, and her hair had been brushed into a soft, wavy curtain that fell halfway down her back. She was standing by the window embrasure, her injured arm cradled gently in her right hand, her face turned to the outside even though Jibril had hopped up and closed the wooden shutters moments before. A single, muted thread of sunlight filtered through a crack in the panel, the stream dancing with motes of dust, the light touching on her face, revealing a strength of determination Marak had not seen before.

"I have to leave this place," she said, not even turning to look at him when she heard the telltale rustle of his robes dragging across the floor. "I have imposed on Lord Tamberlane's hospitality far too long as it is."

"To my knowledge, he has not remarked on any imposition."

"Nevertheless"—she turned her face slightly—"you know why I must leave."

"You are afraid your husband will come here looking for you."

"He will not stop searching. He will have discovered that I did not die in the village, and he will send more hunters to find me, more killers. Eventually, yes, after they have searched the forests and villages, they will come here."

"You give him a deal of credit."

"He does not give up easily. Especially not when . . ." Her voice faltered, and Marak waited, a shadow among shadows.

Amie shook her head, dismissing whatever she might have said. "He wants me dead. He will succeed at any cost. I—I only wish I had killed him when I had the chance."

"Murder is a heavy sin to bear, and you would have carried that burden with you the rest of your days."

"Nay, the burden would have been a small one," she assured him with yet another surprising show of intensity. "Easily discarded."

Marak approached the window. The same thread of light touched on the shadows inside his hood, and for a moment, Amie caught a glimpse of pale gray-white flesh, colorless lips, pink-rimmed eyes that grew no lashes or brows. Waves of snow-white hair trailed to his shoulders, yet Amie sensed the healer was not much above the age of the knight. The revelation was fleeting, gone an instant after he noted her inspection, but from what she had seen, she thought he also had a kind face with eyes that had seen and known much sorrow.

"I have to leave this place," she said again, turning to the window.

"If your new husband is as determined as you say, where would you go that he would not simply follow and find you?"

"Friar Guilford was taking me to a convent—the Holy Sisters of Mary Magdalene. He deemed it far enough away that I would be safe, where even *my lord husband*"—she spat the words out like pits from a melon—"would not dare violate the holy laws of sanctuary."

"I strongly doubt he would dare violate the walls of Taniere Castle . . . if, indeed, he could reach them." At her frown he smiled. "The castle sits upon an island, surrounded entirely by deep water. The only access is by a narrow draw that can be raised or lowered at a moment's notice."

Amie shook her head. "Walls do not deter him, neither do narrow draws or—or locked and bolted doors. If he suspected I was here, he would find a way inside, then he would burn the castle down and slaughter everyone within it."

"That would seem excessive even for a man smitten through the heart with love for his new bride— a condition I suspect your groom did not suffer?"

She chewed a moment on her lip before looking up. "He was smitten with the promises my uncle made—promises of influence and wealth. But . . ." She hesitated and drew a deep breath. "I was not entirely truthful with you the other day. I did not simply run away from my husband. I . . . beat him soundly with a candlestick first. Hard enough, in fact, that I was convinced I had killed him."

"Ahh."

The single sound bore neither condemnation nor revulsion. A faint hint of curiosity, perhaps, and Amie bit her lip until she tasted blood.

"He was not the first, you see," she whispered. "My uncle had sold me once before in marriage to a man as old as England itself and twice as foul smelling. Lord Eglund was a fat, stinking oaf who expected me to—to see to his every disgusting pleasure, and when I would not obey upon the instant, he punished me. He whipped me and beat me and took what he wanted in the end, and when I saw the same look of lust and depravity in Odo's eyes"—her voice had risen in a crescendo of despair but faded again under Marak's steady gaze—"I could not bear it. I simply could not have endured another moment. Nay, I would have drawn a blade across my wrists had the candlestick not been handier. It was in my fist before I knew it, and in the next instant, he was lying in a pool of blood beside me. He will not forgive the insult to his pride or to his person. He will keep hunting me. Stone walls and battlements will not stay his hand."

Marak smiled easily. "And now you do not give Lord Tamberlane the credit he deserves."

"I am but a mere peasant wench in his eyes. Certes, he would not risk losing his castle, his life to protect me."

At that, Marak laughed softly. "You might be surprised to know what he has risked and lost for far less." After a moment, he added, "Come. Your doubts rankle, and if you are feeling strong enough, perhaps you would care to venture outside your room and see for yourself what lies beyond these dreary four walls?"

Amie glanced at the door. The notion was tempting, for she was beginning to feel like a prisoner. On the other hand, she felt safe here. For the first time in more than a year, since her uncle's greed and avarice had set her on a long, dark path into hell, she almost felt safe.

Safe. With perfect strangers. One an albino who did not even react to the confession that she had tried to murder her husband; the other an enigmatic knight who slew dragons and blushed at the sight of a woman weeping.

"Come," Marak said again, shifting to one side and stretching out his arm by way of further invitation.

Steeling herself, Amaranth moved slowly ahead of the robed Marak and walked toward the door. It opened onto a stone landing, which led down a cork-screw staircase to the floor below. Her feet were bare, as would befit a peasant girl, for only noble ladies were accorded shoes, and the stone was rough beneath her soles, not to mention cold. There was only one way to exit the tower, and she followed the narrow corridor until it led through a stone arch that opened into the great hall. The latter was an enormous, cavernous chamber, fully a hundred broad paces long and fifty wide. The ceiling rose three stories above and disappeared into a gloomy realm of crossbeams and stone arches, misted gray from the fires that smoldered in two large iron braziers positioned at either end of the room.

Black iron cressets were hung on the walls at regular intervals, but where one torch was lit, the flame crackling and snapping up the stone wall, the three between that and the next were dark, adding to the thickness of the shadows. Tall multibranched candelabra stood at either end of the dais, their crowns of tallow candles almost succeeding in overpowering the earthy stench of a century's worth of dampness and smoke embedded in the stone walls.

The only windows were hardly more than cross-hair slits, carved high up on the walls and useful only as watching posts for the sentries who must, at one time, have stood high on the narrow wooden walk that surrounded the room.

The rushes scattered on the floor looked and smelled as though they had not been changed in months. Chickens pecked around in the debris searching for crumbs while two enormous wolfhounds sprawled below the dais crunching on well-cleaned bones.

Seated there, alone at the table, his head leaning against the tall back of the chair, was Lord Tamberlane. He had his eyes closed and one leg hooked over a wooden arm of the chair. He looked asleep . . . or drunk . . . and his dark hair had fallen over his brow like strokes of black paint. Amie would gladly have turned around and gone back to her room if Marak's hand had not been firm on her elbow steering her down the short flight of steps.

Amie's borrowed gown snagged on the stone lip of the step . . . a sound she thought only she could hear . . . yet no sooner had the first threads torn than Tamberlane's eyes opened and his head came upright.

His first reaction was a scowl. It stayed in place for several moments until his eyes widened with recognition of who it was who walked beside the seneschal.

"See who I have brought with me this morning?" Marak said casually. His hand dropped away from Amie's elbow and retreated into his long sleeve as they drew near the front of the dais. "Amaranth expressed a wish to explore her new surroundings, and to thank you for your generous hospitality."

Tamberlane unhooked his leg from the chair and straightened. The creases on his brow deepened to retrench the scowl, and he raked his long fingers through his hair, pushing it back in blue-black waves and scratching the scalp on their return. "There is no need to thank me," he mumbled.

Amie stared at the knight. She judged that she had been right with her second guess, for his eyes were underscored and puffy, the whites marred by spidery veins, the lids red and polished. His voice was rusty, and there were questionable stains spotting the front of his dark tunic, as if he had spilled more wine on his chest than he had managed to pour into his mouth.

In his favor, however, he almost looked uncomfortable beneath Amie's scrutiny. She had no idea why he should feel thus. He was the overlord, the master. He could do as he wished when he wished, where he wished, and . . . to whom he wished.

"Good my lord," she began, speaking softly and keeping her eyes lowered, "it is indeed necessary for me to thank you once again. You saved my life. You have given me shelter, you—"

"More wine!" Tamberlane said abruptly, beckoning behind him to where a lackey stood in attendance.

A subtle lift of Marak's hand stopped the young man from coming forward.

"Amaranth would also beg to demonstrate her gratitude in other ways," he said, nudging Amie gently on the arm. When she looked askance, a thin finger crooked in the direction of the flagon sitting across the board from Tamberlane. "She has recovered much of her strength and would beg to make herself useful in the household."

Amie realized at once what Marak was doing. If she proved herself capable of blending in with the regular castle servants, Tamberlane would be less

likely to regard her as a burden or an intruder, and
the urgent need she felt to leave might not weigh so
heavily on her mind. It was generous of Marak, and
kind, but to judge by the seeming dearth of serving
wenches in the master's proximity, she doubted she
could become entirely invisible.

Even so, the pressure of Marak's hand on her
elbow was firm. Gathering her wits and the hem of
her tunic in her good hand, she stepped up onto the
dais to retrieve the pewter flagon of wine. It was
heavy, and as she filled the knight's cup, the ewer
trembled and the wine poured in a less than steady
stream. When some threatened to splash over the rim
of the cup, Amie glanced at the knight, and the shock
of gazing directly into those eerie green eyes rippled
disconcertingly down her spine.

There had been moments, even in her weakened
state, she had thought him handsome. But here, with
his chin stubbled with unshaven beard, his shirt un-
laced and gaping open over a chest that was composed of band upon band of hard muscle . . . a
heated sensation washed through her, catching her
by surprise and making her tremble enough to set
the ewer down before she dropped it.

Tamberlane scowled at a drop of splashed wine
and glanced over at Marak. "Are you certain she is
strong enough to assume household tasks?"

"I grow stronger every day, my lord," Amaranth
replied, preempting an answer from the seneschal.
"My wound is nearly healed and I would sooner
pour wine and"—she paused to cast hastily along
the board, littered as it was with the remnants of

meals long passed—"and see to the condition of my lord's table than lift the sacks of flour Marak has promised to burden me with."

A dark eyebrow arched. "Sacks of flour?"

"To strengthen the arm and shoulder," Marak explained easily. "She must begin to use them again if she is to recover fully. She requires good, solid food as well. Broths and possets can fortify the blood, but she needs meat and bread and pottage to fill out her tunic again."

Tamberlane's gaze turned unwittingly to Amie's bodice and remained there longer than was necessary, held hostage by the way her breasts swelled against the cloth. When he recovered and looked quickly up into her face, he saw that she, in turn, was staring at a particularly succulent slab of roasted venison sitting in a puddle of its own juices.

"There is more than enough here to tempt any appetite," he said. "Roland, slice a fresh trencher and bring a chair . . ."

Amie was startled. "Oh, no, my lord, I—"

"Roland!" He held up a hand to silence her protest, then crooked two fingers to bring the squire forward. "A chair, if you please. A trencher and a clean cup, as well, if you can find one."

Amie glanced sidelong at Marak, but the hooded figure remained impassive. She was appallingly aware of the strict proprieties adhered to in a nobleman's house wherein the seating arrangements were dictated by the worth of one's blood. Servants and those of lower stations in life sat well below the salt and barely above almoners and beggars. Tamberlane's tongue should have changed to stone in his mouth before issuing such an invitation to a peasant wench, yet he had done so without a thought.

Nor did anyone else in the great hall seem to pay much heed. There were two long trestle tables flanking the room and a third stretched across the far end, but of the three or four dozen men scattered here and there about the room, most were more intent on their food than on their overlord's table manners.

The other singular oddity was that no one shared Tamberlane's table. No priest, no favored knights, no chatelaine or hostess, no silk-clad ladies whispering their disapproval from behind raised hands.

It was as if the lord of the keep chose to isolate himself even within the walls of his own castle.

Amaranth's gaze was caught and held again, this time by the large wooden carving that loomed above the massive central fireplace. A full thirty feet high and twenty wide, Amie had first mistaken it for a tree, possibly with coats of arms suspended at the end of every branch. But now, with her eyes accustomed to the gloom, she could see that the branches were in fact fashioned into dragons, their scaled bodies twined to form the thick trunk, their heads and forearms writhing outward to form the branches.

Marak tipped his head.

"The dragon tree," he said. "You will find smaller depictions of it throughout the castle. The largest of all graces the outer gates and is iron, with each dragon holding a bell in one claw. It was made, so the story goes, long ago in an enchanted forge, and according to legend, when a pure heart rings the magical bells, the dragons will awake to fly in six directions. The dragon of the nether region will flee from despair and bring hope. The dragon of heaven will return with the gift of true love. And from the four corners of the earth will come peace, health, wisdom, and happiness."

The soft echo of Marak's words held Amie's attention until the squire brought forth a heavy X-chair and placed it before the board. He offered her a shy smile, then took up a dagger and sliced a thick round of hard brown bread, setting it on the table to use as a plate.

"Sit," Tamberlane insisted. "Marak? You will join us?"

"My thanks, but no. I have already broken my fast and there is a mare in some distress down at the stables. I was on my way there to attend the foaling now."

Amie scarcely heard his excuses for her focus was now fixed squarely on the haunch of venison, the platter of cheese and apples beside it, and a tantalizing bowl nearby filled with sugared almonds. From somewhere, her appetite had returned with a vengeance, and she could feel the anxious spurts of hunger flooding her mouth.

Tamberlane carved off several thick slices of the venison after stabbing the roast to locate the tenderest pieces. He cut wedges of cheese and set all before her along with his own eating knife, which he graciously wiped first on the back of his sleeve.

"Eat," he ordered. "As much as your belly can hold."

Amie needed no further prompting. She began with delicate enough intentions, cutting the chunks of meat into smaller cubes and slices before transporting them to her mouth. But the delicacy vanished after the first few heavenly mouthfuls, and soon she was using her fingers, her teeth to tear at the viands, blissfully ignorant of the runnels of grease that dripped down her chin.

Tamberlane watched, half amused. While compliments and expressions of gratitude unsettled him, hunger was something he understood, and each time her trencher showed the lack, he passed more venison, more roasted onions, more chunks of cheese.

When the frenzy slowed and there was some sign of her belly rebelling, Amie set her knife aside and leaned back, horrified to feel a belch rising up the back of her throat. She contained it as best she could within the cup of her hand, then glanced across to see if Tamberlane had noticed.

He had. The faint crinkle at the corners of his eyes suggested he was as amused by the belch as he had been by the ravenous display of feeding. He was the only one who showed a reaction, however, for Marak was nowhere in sight and the squire, Roland, had again retreated a respectful distance behind the dais.

Amaranth did the only thing she could do: she smiled. It began as a faint mirror image of his own response, but then it spread and her lips trembled apart enough to show a row of small, even teeth. More than merely altering her face, the smile also hinted at a longing for days past when gaiety and laughter were as common to her as light to the sun.

To cover her embarrassment, and to do something to distract her from looking too deeply into the shuttered green eyes, she took up a cloth and wiped the knife before placing it back in front of her host. She then stood and began sweeping the crumbs and scraps off the board. The two huge wolfhounds pounced before the first morsels hit the rushes and growled happily as they snapped the air on each forward brush of her hand.

When she had cleared the board in front of her seat, she widened the circle to include the area in front of Lord Tamberlane, at which point he again looked discomfited.

"You should not trouble yourself. Despite evidence to the contrary, there are lackeys to do such things."

"All dust-gatherers, from the look of it." The unveiled criticism in her remark, more worthy of a chatelaine than a peasant wench, brought Tamberlane shifting forward in his chair.

Amie, having been the recipient on more than one occasion of a sharp cuff to curb her tongue, flinched instinctively back, but he was only reaching for the ewer of wine.

"You have a keen eye, Amaranth, although we have not had much need in recent months for clean linens and impeccable table manners."

"I—I should not have spoken thus, my lord. It was rude and petty of me to do so, even in jest."

"Ofttimes it is the jest that carries the greater weight of truth. More wine?"

Amie sank down onto the chair again, uncertain what to make of this enigmatic knight. On the one

hand, he was no fool to be trifled with if he had
fought and slain the mercenaries who had attacked
the village. On the other, he kept a marked distance
between himself and the other men in the castle—
women as well. He dressed plainly, yet his cup was
gold, his knife encrusted with jewels. Despite signs
of apparent wealth, there were no visible coats of
arms on the walls, no pennants bearing his colors,
no tournament banners hung behind the dais. The
vast belly of the great hall was empty, the rushes
crackled and stank from neglect, and he seemed to
see nothing untoward in inviting a lowly peasant
wench to break bread beside him . . . not only bread,
as it happened, but venison, a meat reserved by royal
decree for those of noble blood.

He claimed there were servants, but she had seen
few. For a household this size, there should have
been half a hundred or more maids and lackeys mill-
ing about, each with specific chores and tasks. Marak
had insisted that she was well protected here, inside
Taniere Castle, yet to the casual eye, there was not
enough protection to safeguard the remnants of the
venison haunch from the two wrestling wolfhounds.

Tamberlane had taken her silence for assent and
refilled her cup. While he poured, he stole a moment
to study the comely blush in her cheeks, the soft
spirals of fine new hairs that grew at her temples.
He had not noticed Marak's departure either and that
disturbed him almost as much as the pleasure he had
discovered of having someone other than Roland or
the brooding seneschal for company at the board.

That pleasure had increased measurably when Amaranth had begun to tidy the table, for the sweeping action of her arm had brought the clean scent of her skin tantalizingly close. She smelled like almonds and honey . . . cleaner than anyone or anything in recent memory, and it had made him aware of the tawdry stains marking the front of his own shirt and tunic.

He could not recall any time since reaching the age of majority when he had been seated alone beside a beautiful woman. His years of study and training for the priesthood had kept him away from any possible temptations, and after taking his vows, he had presumed he was safely immune to such worldly distractions.

Distracted he was, however. By the smell of her skin and the shine of her hair. By the whiteness of her skin and the movement of her fingers when they had disappeared between her lips to be sucked free of grease and gravy. His own calloused hands had experienced a strange tingling in the fingertips. And after one particularly long and vigorous suckling venture, his whole body had grown so tense and sensitive to the smallest movement that he could not have torn his gaze away from her mouth had the castle exploded around him. Each time she pulled her finger from between her lips, the tip wet and pink, a rush of icy prickles poured down his spine. Each time she thrust it in again to lick it clean, his head felt light enough to float away.

He fared only slightly better now that she had finished, and it was his thought to discuss more mundane matters before his skin turned to solid gooseflesh.

"Marak says you have grown weary of the patterns on the walls of your tower room."

"I do miss having the sun on my face."

"Roland?" Tamberlane half turned to address the squire. "Is the sun out today?"

"Aye, my lord. 'Tis as fine as a midsummer's day."

"There you have it then." Tamberlane stood and, to Amie's further surprise, extended his hand and arm, inviting her to accompany him to the staircase. "I was about to venture to the stables myself, and if it please, you may keep me company as far as your yearning for sunlight allows. Roland will follow, and if you tire, he will see you safely back to your room."

Amie weighed the merits of remaining in Tamberlane's presence any longer than necessary against a curiosity to see what lay beyond the doors of the shadowy hall. In the end, curiosity won out, for she would need to know her way out the castle gates and off the island when the time came to leave.

Chapter Seven

Amaranth followed the knight up the stairs and across the landing to the arched doorway, careful to avoid walking too close. The opening was cut low in the stone, and Tamberlane had to duck to clear the lintel. Another set of covered stairs led down the outer wall of one of the corner towers, the space narrow and lit only by cross-shaped arrow slits cut into the stone blocks. The knight had to keep his head bowed forward the whole way down. Moreover there was barely enough width to the stairs to keep his shoulders from brushing against the stone, a defensive design meant to hinder any swordsmen who sought to gain entry to the keep uninvited.

At the bottom of this covered pentice, another thick, heavily banded door opened into the main courtyard, and there Amie was met by the first warming rays of sunshine she had felt for nearly two weeks. Bright and hot, they forced her to raise her arm to shield her eyes, and it was thusly, through

the spacings of her sunlit fingers, that she inspected
the inner ward of Taniere Castle.

There was not much out of the ordinary to see.
The area in front of the keep was cobbled in stone,
bordered by a ring of outbuildings. The yard was
crowded, by Taniere's standards, with several
women gathered around the common well winding
up buckets of water. Men pushed small carts filled
with wood and hay; even a baker crossed the ward
balancing a large wooden tray stacked with bread
rounds. She saw two pairs of guardsmen talking by
the arched bridge in the curtain wall that let to the
outer ward, and two more strolling leisurely along
the parapet that surrounded the main battlements.

Behind her, the gray stone walls of the castle rose
steeply into the sky, and she had to tip her head well
back to see the tops of the crenellated towers. The
uppermost branches of trees were visible where they
swayed above the south and eastern facings of the
battlements, and on the far side of the arched bridge,
she could just catch a glimpse of the long stretch of
grass that comprised the outer bailey. The equivalent
of a small village was contained within the towering
stone walls, including a smithy, tannery, abattoir,
even a weaver's cottage.

Her uncle's household had been strict, and she had
grown up accustomed to seeing everyone come to a
complete, utter standstill until an imperious wave of
his arm set them free to go about their tasks again.
Both Sir Eglund and Odo de Langois kept a full garrison of men-at-arms, most of them rough, crude men
who raised fists to their breasts like Roman centuri-

ons and tipped their heads with respect in the presence of their overlords. Every one of them, from man to child, stopped and either nodded or bowed and few dared to ever raise their eyes.

By sharp contrast, when Tamberlane had stepped out into the sunlight, the men who saw him tugged on a forelock, and some of the younger women offered up a smile. The children scrambling in the dust continued to chase the chickens, and the older women who were gathered around the central well did not skip a word of their gossiping. Most of the curious looks were directed at Amaranth. They wanted to see who was keeping company with the vaunted Dragon Slayer as he crossed the courtyard.

Amaranth took pleasure in wriggling her bare toes on the sunbaked stones, for her feet had not lost their chill in all the time she had been at Taniere Castle. A low whistle brought the two wolfhounds bounding past her skirt, and with the dogs leading the way, Amie and Tamberlane crossed the bailey and walked beneath the strip of shade that marked the arched bridge.

The outer bailey was a wide and flat grassy common. For everyday use, it was an archery field, practice run, and exercise yard. Two straw butts leaned against the far wall, their fronts painted with rings in three colors. Farther along, dividing the field in two was a disreputable line of broken posts and bars used for a mock jousting run.

At the moment, two lads were waging a battle against one of the quintains, their shouts echoing off the walls, their wooden swords bashing and stabbing at the swinging balls of hay-filled canvas. Several younger children hung on the bars watching, cheering when an obvious strike against the Huns was made. Amie recognized Jibril among them, his small wooden horse clutched under his arm.

When she ventured a small wave, he looked down at his little brown toes and did not look up again until Tamberlane came close enough to issue a soft rebuke. It was delivered in a language Amie did not understand, although when she glanced sidelong at the knight, he switched immediately back to English, the language both he and Marak had used to converse with her from the outset. Neither would have assumed a common village girl could speak Norman French, although now that her brain had been fattened on venison, she recalled the conversation she'd had with Marak when he suggested she was not from the village had been conducted entirely in French, the language of the nobility.

Oh, he was a clever one! She had not even noticed him tripping her up on her own tongue.

"Practice your words, Jibril," Tamberlane was saying. "Bid good morning to the lady and ask how she is faring."

The boy murmured a shy greeting, heard only by the carved wooden head of the horse that jutted from under his arm. The instant he was finished, he turned and ran away as fast as his legs would carry him.

"Do you always have that effect on children?" Amie asked.

"Only those who know me."

The fleeting smile appeared again, gone in an instant, sent back to that place where he appeared to hoard all of his deepest secrets. His was a face that gave nothing away, whether by training or desire, and was near impossible to read insofar as what mood or thoughts were upon him. Such deliberate blankness might be unsettling to some, but for Amie, in whose experience a man's unpleasant tempers and lecherous notions were as clear as script in a book, it was a strangely appealing change.

Against the far wall of the bailey was a long row of covered stalls, most filled with drays and rouncies, the workhorses of the castle. Several of the stalls had been enclosed with wooden planks to protect the more valuable beasts against the elements of weather. One warhorse would be worth fifty drays, a hundred if it was battle-trained, and a knight would sooner sleep out in the open himself than subject his destrier to rain or sleet.

It was to this end of the ward that Tamberlane walked. As they drew closer, the air grew thick with the pungent scent of horseflesh and fresh manure, a combination that gave Amaranth a strong reminder that she was barely a day out of her sickbed.

Her face must have reflected the gentle wave of nausea that flowed through her body, for a moment later, she felt the strong grip of a hand cradling her elbow.

"There is a bench over by the wall where you can sit. Or Roland can take you back, if you prefer."

Amie managed a weak smile of gratitude. "I would prefer to sit a moment, if it please my lord."

Tamberlane led her to the low stone bench set

against the base of the castle wall. A swath of fragrant blue wisteria grew halfway up the stonework, and a small blot of shade was provided by a scrawny beech tree. She sank gratefully onto the seat, taking a moment to catch her breath and settle her stomach. Tamberlane beckoned his squire to her side and offered a brief, polite bow.

"Roland will remain with you, and when you have rested enough, he will escort you back to the keep."

"My thanks, my lord, for your kindness."

Tamberlane emitted what might have been a soft grunt of acknowledgment before he backed up two steps, turned, and carried on down toward the stables.

Amaranth released a slow, deep breath and leaned back against the hard stone. Her shoulder was burning, her head was pounding, and she was not entirely confident of her ability to walk all the way back to the keep.

She kept her gaze fixed absently on Tamberlane's broad back as he walked across the stretch of open sunlight. His strides were long and confident, his shoulders were squared, and where the snug fit of his leggings molded his thighs, it invited the eye to roam higher where the tight muscles in his flanks moved with every step.

"Amaranth?"

She blinked and looked up.

"That is your name, is it not?" Roland asked.

"Yes. Yes, it is."

"Then that is what I shall call you."

He smiled and tipped his head in a way that Amaranth suspected had sent many a maid's heart fluttering within her breast. Young and handsome and earnest, with a full set of teeth that flashed whitely in a smooth, chiseled jaw, Roland was already well bulked across the chest and shoulders. His eyes were blue and sparkled with mischief as he gave her bosom a thorough and obvious inspection.

"You are only a small wisp of a thing, are you not? I warrant I could carry you back to the castle with ease if your legs lack the strength."

Amie smiled tightly. Doubtless he had carried more than his fair share of wenches when their knees were too weak to support them.

"My thanks, sir squire, but I only require a moment or two to catch my breath."

He rested the flat of his hand on the tree trunk. "For a beauty like you, I would happily rob you of breath every time I had the chance. Nor would you regret it," he promised with a crooked smile.

"I am certain I would not," she said dryly, returning her gaze to the stables.

He followed her glance and gave off a low chuckle. "If you were hoping to win a better offer elsewhere, you will only be wasting your saucy glances. My lord Tamberlane has no interest in pretty little minxs with round eyes and soft bosoms."

Amie looked up, astonished by the accusation. "I assure you, I am not—"

"Many before you have tried, to be sure, but not a one has succeeded. You are aware, are you not, that he has taken his vows."

The rest of her interrupted protest died in her throat. "Vows?"

Roland nodded. "Taken before he left for the Cru-
sades. Lord Tamberlane was trained and schooled
since boyhood for the Order of the Knights Templar.
Grant you, he no longer bends a knee with consent
of the church, but he is still a monk in his own mind.
One who has taken his vow of celibacy, among other
things, serious unto death."

"No longer bends a knee . . ."

Roland leaned in with a conspiratorial whisper.
"Defrocked. Excommunicated. Cast out of the Order
in disgrace. He bides here only by his uncle's good
will and generosity—some of which I wish had been
accorded to me before I was bound into his service."
He held up a hand. "Nay, read nothing untoward
behind my words, for he is an excellent master and
teacher with unparalleled skills. A warrior the likes
of which I have never seen before. But alas, what do
we wage war against? Squirrels and deer, ferrets and
boars? We could have such glory, such riches! But
he has not ventured more than a few leagues beyond
the gates in more than three years, will not even seek
out a tourney where the mere name of the Dragon
Slayer would cause men to bash their heads against
their own shields in a panic."

"Perhaps he seeks something other than glory or
riches."

Her words caused him to puff out his chest with
indignation. "There is no greater glory for a knight
than to win battles and bring honor to his name."

Amie's gaze flicked back to the stables. An excommunicated Templar, defrocked and disgraced? She

could only guess at what ghastly sin he had committed to earn him an exile to such an isolated place as Taniere Castle. It would, however, explain the distance he maintained between the other castle residents, as well as his disregard for precedent and rank. As a monk and a Crusader, he would have been seated well below the salt to show humility. He would have been more comfortable in the presence of peasants and commoners despite being of noble blood himself.

"What of Marak?" she asked. "He seems an odd choice of companion for a monk."

"I am not privy to the entire history of their friendship, though I know it has existed for more than two decades. They met in Venice as boys, where Lord Tamberlane was training for the monkhood and Marak was learning the secrets of alchemy and"—he lowered his voice as if the birds might carry his words to other ears—"sorcery."

"Sorcery?" This made Amaranth smile, for what impressionable young maid would not have instantly thrown herself into the squire's waiting arms seeking protection?

When she did not, he frowned.

"Mock me if you wish, but I have seen the wizard work his magic and conjure things with mine own eyes. A ball of common lead was transformed to pure gold. A noisome child was turned into a toad for a full afternoon. A blind man was made to see again." The squire's voice dropped even lower. "What is more, he is neither a man nor a woman beneath those robes. He lacks that which makes the one, and has no pouch for the other. Not a eunuch proper, but not an epicene either.

"So you see," he added by way of conclusion, "if you had hopes of finding yourself invited into either bed, consider yourself well advised not to wait too long for the hellfires to freeze over."

"The notion never once crossed my mind," she said evenly. "I have had enough of men to last me this lifetime and the next. Moreover, that would include *you*, sirrah, so if *you* had a hope of luring me behind a haystack, you may regard it as being dashed here and now."

Roland only grinned. "We shall see about that, minx. We shall see about that."

Amaranth expelled a sigh and pushed to her feet. She had taken but a step or two back out into the sunlight when a high-pitched scream rent the air. Roland froze as he was leaning over to grasp her arm. With a muttered apology and an order to remain on the bench, he broke into a run and headed for the stables, leaving Amie staring after him. She considered sitting back down, for she had been given a good deal of information about her host and his seneschal and could well use the time to digest it. But she found herself walking instead toward the sheltered end of the stables where yet another pitiful scream echoed hollowly off the stone walls.

The inside of the stable was gloomy, the floor littered with sticks of straw that bit into the soles of Amie's feet as she walked in out of the sunlight. She saw Roland and another man—a hostler by the look of him—standing in front of one of the open stalls. Inside, a large mare lay on her side, her belly heaving, her head jerking and thrashing with the pain of birth. Amie crept silently forward, passing three empty stalls before stopping alongside one that held a whining ass. She knew asses were often used to calm the bigger warhorses, but to all appearances, it seemed the ass was the one in need of a reassuring hand now.

She placed a hand on its rump and moved up to the wooden bar that separated the two stalls.

The screaming had stopped.

Marak was there on his knees, his sleeves pulled back, his arms buried to the elbows inside the mare's womb. Tamberlane sat with the animal's head cradled in his lap, his hands stroking the velvety snout, his mouth bent close to her ear murmuring words meant to calm and reassure her.

There was a good deal of blood and slime in the straw beneath the mare's rump, and at first Amie did not see the newborn foal. But it was there, covered in birthing fluids, its legs still curled against its body. Marak pulled out the sac containing the afterbirth then swore softly when he saw the gush of bright red blood that followed. The mare's body seemed to collapse in on itself with a mixture of relief and exhaustion, her belly heaving with long, loud pants.

Amie had seen enough animal husbandry to know there was a deal more blood in the straw than there should have been. Marak had already started packing the womb with fistfuls of herbs and moss. His hood was pulled back and his expression was grim, although when he spoke to the mare, his words were laden with the same gentle encouragement Amaranth had heard over the past sennight.

Amie tipped her head slightly, trying to see with more than one eye around the thick post. It was the first time she had seen Marak without his hood drawn well forward, and her gaze was momentarily fixed to his face—a face that was smooth and un-lined, pale as chalk, and as delicately beautiful as a statue head carved in marble. His hair was as thick as her own and gathered hastily back into a fat white braid, the end of which was lost somewhere beneath his robe.

"The foal needs attending," he said, lifting his head and looking directly at Amaranth. His eyes were large and devoid of all but the faintest hint of blue. Lashes and eyebrows were white, as fine as those of a woman, sweeping above a nose that was long and thin, a mouth that was colorless but well formed, as if shaped by the hand of a master sculptor. " 'Twould be a shame to lose it now after all this pain."

Amaranth ducked beneath the wooden bar and sank down on her knees beside the struggling foal. Its eyes were sealed shut; its nostrils clogged with mucus. She grabbed a handful of straw and began wiping the slippery mess away, and within a few strokes, the creature was breathing easier and had one large brown eye opened, rolling with confusion as he inspected his new world.

Amie continued to wipe him down, using fresh

handfuls of hay. There was a bucket of water nearby, and she dampened the tips of her fingers, using them to clean around the eyes and nose. The colt was a bundle of shivers and soft, weak cries, and Amie tried to soothe it with soft words and softer strokes of her hand.

It was when she tried to move it closer, to perhaps take the snout onto her lap, that the little creature startled her by unfolding its legs and kicking out with its first attempt to stand. She flinched back, hitting the water bucket with her arm, splashing some of the contents over the side. Almost as an afterthought she noticed an oddity: the floor she was sitting on was not dirt, but wooden planks covered in straw. The water ran through a crack in the boards and made a distinct dripping sound, suggesting there was a hollow space beneath.

No one else seemed to pay heed, and after a moment, even Amaranth forgot it.

Marak had managed to stop the mare's bleeding. Tamberlane's steady murmurs and long, stroking fingers had soothed her enough that her eyes lost the look of wide, glazed panic, and she was actually trying to lift her head, to see behind her where the foal continued to bleat and squeak.

"There, you see?" Tamberlane's voice was so low, it barely carried beyond the mare's ears. "You have a son, my beautiful Isolde. A son who will grow to be as fine and strong and proud as his sire. Look you how he struggles to put his legs beneath him, how his eyes gleam with wonderment. Look at the breadth of his shoulders—the shoulders that caused you so much distress—look at the power they show already. He will be a champion, just like his sire."

He glanced up and saw Amaranth watching. His voice faded as their gazes locked, and Amaranth felt such a strong wave of heat pass through her that she could swear it left part of her melted. His eyes were rife with emotion, and in that single glance, she saw the full, haunting depths of a self-imposed loneliness that allowed him to hold nothing close to him. This she saw and recognized because the same fears were present in her own breast. A dog, a horse . . . these were safe because they loved unconditionally and asked nothing in return. They did not know how to deceive, how to hurt, how to lie or cause pain. They did not know how to take something that had been full of hope and beauty, and twist it into ugliness, fear, and pain.

Amie forced herself to look away the same instant as Tamberlane, an act performed in embarrassed unison that none but Marak noticed. To conceal his smile, he examined the foal, running his long fingers gently over the trembling body, down each of the spindly legs.

"He'll be big, like Tristan, with the same piebald coloring."

"What of Isolde?" Tamberlane asked.

Marak glanced back at the mare. "Let her lie quiet until the herbs take hold. In an hour or so, if she tries to stand . . . let her. If she makes no effort . . ." He offered up a slight shrug. "But she is strong and has a brave heart. I expect she will be nipping your ears before the sun sets on this day. As for you, Little One," he said, frowning sternly at Amaranth, "if you do not wish to undo all my good work, you will return to your solar at once, find your bed, and remain there until I give you leave to rise again. Roland, your arms will do. Carry Amaranth back to the keep and make no stops along the way."

The squire grinned. "Aye, my lord, as you command."

Before Roland's eagerness could push Marak out of the way, Tamberlane stood and reached down to help Amie to her feet. She put her much smaller hand into his, and when he pulled her up, she was aware of an energy, an underlying power that rushed through her fingertips all the way into her toes. She could well imagine that power exploding. The thought, the feeling, the stirrings it caused made her waver when she stood.

In the next instant, Roland was by her side, lifting her with an easy swing of his thickly muscled shoulders. Her hand slipped out of Tamberlane's, and she did not have to glance at him to know that he had already turned away. The realization that he could dismiss her so easily should not have troubled her, should not even have caused a second thought.

And yet it did. She knew this because her cheeks burned and her flesh ached with regret that it was not Tamberlane's hands instead of Roland's that were holding her so close.

Chapter Eight

Roland had been most diligent in carrying her to her room. He had ignored her protests when they arrived back at the keep, and merely crooked an officious eyebrow when she said she could walk the rest of the way herself. He had carried her up the pentice, through the great hall, and all the way up to the narrow landing outside her chamber. There, the look in her eye and the set of her jaw had finally stopped him. That and the silent presence of Inaya, who stood on the threshold guarding it like a silk-clad barbican.

Roland had set Amie down gently, if reluctantly, and retreated before the glowering, kohl-rimmed eyes. Inaya took one frowning look at the strain showing on Amaranth's face and shooed her into bed, filling her with hot broth and a posset that had her sleeping soundly before the liquid had dried on her lips. She slept through the rest of the afternoon and evening and well into the night, waking only slightly when Inaya came to add more wood to the fire.

She had an odd, disjointed dream wherein she was holding the newborn foal in her arms. She was stroking its neck, the soft fuzz on its snout, when a larger, more calloused hand covered hers. The hand raised her fingers and carried them up to a mouth that was warm and exquisitely tender as it kissed her fingertips one by one. The eyes above the mouth were green, and they were filled with such unspeakable longing that the shock of it brought Amaranth sitting upright in the bed. Her body was flushed, her nipples peaked tight. Between her thighs, where she had not felt anything for longer than she could remember, there were unnervingly warm, moist quiverings.

The image of those green eyes lingered a long, dreamlike moment before fading away in the harsh reality of stone walls and a smoldering fire. The candle that marked the nocturnal vigil was burned down to the bottom line scored in the wax, indicating it was but an hour before Prime.

Amie swung her legs over the side of the bed and walked on slightly tender feet to the garderobe. Inaya had frowned and scolded her in her own strange language over the cuts and scrapes on the soles of her feet, and Amie noticed that a pair of soft leather slippers had appeared magically by the side of the bed.

She returned to the warm nest of linens and furs, but in the end, removed the top blanket and draped it around her shoulders. Her hair had been brushed out of its tight braid for sleeping, and it fell in a thick cloud of russet waves to below her knees. The absolute stillness of the hour before dawn was her favorite—a time for gathering thoughts and courage to face the day ahead. Tucking her feet into the leather slippers, she walked toward the long woven tapestry that hung in the corner of the solar.

Amaranth had discovered there was a staircase behind the tapestry purely by accident. During one of her many pacings back and forth across her room she had paused to rest and nearly tumbled on her arse when she leaned against what she thought was a solid wall. Recovering her wits, she had inched the tapestry aside and found the concealed steps that led up to the roof.

With the blanket around her shoulders and stray hairs snagging on the close stone walls as she climbed the spiral, she made her way up through the darkness and emerged onto the roof through a low arched portal. The sky above was still black as a sinner's heart, but lying low on the eastern horizon was a thin, watery line of palest blue. The roof itself was smothered in darkness, for the moon was long gone and the stars were fleeing before the dawn. It seemed vast and flat, the stone crenellations sticking up like pale, square teeth along the parapets.

There was no wind, no breeze to rustle the tops of the trees. A layer of morning mist hung thick over the surface of the lake, and as the light grew stronger in the eastern sky, it turned the shifting mass grayish-blue. Somewhere on shore, night birds called to one another before retreating to their niches for the day.

The smallest sound of a frog plopping into the lake came to Amie as if it happened a foot away. Her tower faced out over the lake, and she was content with the view for as long as it took to turn her head and gain her bearings. When the light allowed, she followed the parapet along to the section of roof that overlooked the baileys and draw.

From there she could see the sleeping village, the thatched roofs of the cottages nosing up a darker shade of gray through the mist. She wondered that there were no lights to be seen in any of the windows, for surely the farmers would be awake long before now and heading out to till their fields. It was still too dark to see any manner of road or path leading up to Taniere Castle. It seemed, in fact, as if the forest stretched out vast and unbroken for miles in all directions. The only cleared acreage was behind the village, and she could well imagine that every foot gained was hard fought to keep against the continuously encroaching wall of saplings and bramble.

There were lights twinkling in both of the barbicans, likely for the guards who had spent the night as most guards did everywhere: dicing or pitching stones. There was a soft, pale glow coming from the sheltered end of the stables as well, suggesting that someone had ordered a watch to be kept over the dam and her new colt. If Amie hopped up slightly and leaned far over the stone ledge between the merlons, she could gaze straight down and·see torch lights flickering in the courtyard below as well.

It was while she was in this ungainly position, with her rump hoisted and her toes dangling inches above the parapet, that she became aware of someone else on the roof. She heard the drag of his robes first before a soft footfall placed him directly behind her. With a sigh she pushed back from the lip of stone and touched her feet flat again, anticipating the look of disapproval on Marak's face well before she saw it.

"If you are looking to fling yourself off the wall, I suggest you do it over there," he said, pointing to the diagonally opposite corner of the roof. "Below are jagged rocks and boulders piled up at the base, which will ensure the task is done properly. The villagers tell a tale of a man who leaped from here and fell on a lackey. He broke nothing but his wrist." Marak leaned forward to peer over the embrasure. "Mind you, he killed the lackey, so the act did not go entirely without notice."

Amie smiled. In the growing bloom of dawn, their faces were painted the same blue-gray of the mist, as the stones, as the silvery tops of the trees. She guessed that he liked this time of day as well, when he could bare his face to the wind and raise his eyes to the sky.

"Roland told me Lord Tamberlane was a Templar."

"Roland wags his tongue overmuch, especially in the presence of a lovely young woman."

"Is it true?"

"That he wags his tongue, that you are a beautiful young woman, or that Tamberlane was ordained a priest? Nay, do not distress yourself over my early morning wit"—he held up his hand—"for the answer to all three is yes. I will assume, however, that it is the last one that interests you most?"

"It does not interest me, good sir, beyond a vague curiosity. I have not heard of many priests who were excommunicated, much less a Templar, for surely those good men are committed to God unto death."

"You envision them as being holier than most?"

"Most Templar knights believe they were born to wear the cloth, do they not? Whereas most priests decide to take their vows only after they have squandered their inheritances or witnessed their first miracle."

Marak laughed. "And here I thought you would be the one to take me to task for my heresy."

"You mock me."

"No, my lady. I enjoy your candor. It grows proportionately with the return of your strength."

"My uncle often locked me in my room in an attempt to curb my tongue."

"Did his efforts succeed?"

"Not all the time."

Marak laughed again, and she realized that the sound, much like the man himself, hinted at a longing to be set free more often.

"Your eyes burn with questions, Little One. While it is not my place to answer them all, I can try to ease the burden of a few."

"What sin was so grievous that Lord Tamberlane was cast out of the Order?"

"Starting at the top of the mountain, are you? Very well . . . he committed the sin of compassion. He

walked away when there was slaughter to be had,
and he hacked off the arm of a Brother Templar
rather than surrender an innocent woman and her
child to the sword. To further compound his crime,
he did not blame his lapse on battle fever or sun-
stroke. Nor did he repent, or offer recompense to the
knight whose arm was left behind in the desert sand.
Some attempted to brand him a coward, but they
were quickly silenced by the steel in his eyes and in
his hands. He was trained to fight and to kill enemies
of God, and if one were to stand before him, he
would do so gladly without a second thought. He
was not, however, trained to disembowel a wounded
man for sport or cut off his manhood and feed it to
the dogs. Nor was he trained to take newborn babies
and smash them up against a wall. All these things
and more were done in King Richard's name, a fact
that Tamberlane was not hesitant to mention in a
private audience with his liege."

"He took the king to task?" she asked in an
awed voice.

"And then some. Luckily, Richard admires courage
in a man, both in deed and word, and while some
of the Brothers may have questioned the Dragon
Slayer's actions, not one man stepped forward to
question his courage. Indeed, so many knights and
soldiers stood behind him to show their loyalty, there
was a genuine risk of revolt within the ranks of the
king's army. Richard wisely sent him home, while
his holy Brothers unwisely cast him from the Order
and declared him *in excommunicato*.

"He sailed by way of Crete and Brindisi, where I

heard of his presence and joined him there. We traveled overland and arrived in England some four months later only to find another scion of royal breeding disabusing his powers, waging a war of taxes and greed upon peasants and children who paid in blood that which they could not pay in coin. When Tamberlane's uncle offered Taniere—a castle in the middle of a forest so vast a man could live out the rest of his days in relative obscurity—Ciaran took it gladly, yet while he will say to anyone who asks that he does not miss the clashing of swords and horseflesh, there are days when he trains as if the demon is in his own soul."

"Yet he does not leave this place? Certes, there are demons aplenty beyond these walls that he could throw himself upon and put his sword to good use."

Marak smiled. "He has lost his taste for politics and intrigues. And now that the king's ransom has been paid and the Lionheart is returning to England, perhaps the demon will flee of his own accord and take his league of disciples with him."

"Prince John? Flee?" She scoffed at the notion. "A scant fortnight ago he was at Belmane for my wedding. He did not look overly concerned at the notion that he might be forced to return the crown to its rightful owner."

"The prince regent was a guest at your wedding?"

Amaranth nodded and could have cursed out loud at the looseness of her tongue. Instead, she bent over to scoop a stone off the rooftop, hoping the action would buy her a moment's delay to think of a sound reason why John Plantagenet, regent of England, would visit Belmane. "I was there a week before the wedding ceremony actually took place. Servants gossip, especially if they are trying to impress a new mistress. I was informed that the prince was a frequent visitor, most often in secret."

"Lackland is a sly, secretive fellow," Marak remarked dryly.

"He gathers carrion-eaters around him like dung gathers flies, and long before I was sold to Odo de Langois I knew of my intended husband's greed and ambitions. There is no doubt in my mind where his loyalties lie."

"With the prince." It was not a question and did not require an answer, yet Amie gave one anyway.

"He allied himself with Prince John the day King Richard left to go on Crusade. Marrying me was only adding one more feather to his cap."

Her voice faltered and fell low, but the dam was breached, and the flood could not be held back.

"My uncle, who was never one to count his pennies wisely, was unable to pay the scutage demanded by the prince to help raise the ransom for King Richard. Sir Eglund d'Avignon heard of this and offered a handsome sum in exchange for my presence in his bedchamber. Naturally, my uncle did not use the gold to placate the prince; he spent it on women and feasts and frivolities. A year later, when my 'protector' died from eating a poisonous toadstool, the prince sent another demand for taxes owing, plus a sizable fine for the delay."

"This time it was Odo de Langois who came sniffing like a bloodhound?"

She turned away so that Marak found himself staring at a cloud of coppery red hair. "If my uncle had refused the marriage, everything he owned—his home, his land—would have been stripped from him, his family cast out and beggared. My marriage to Odo ensured that the Three Benches would remain under my uncle's control and passed into the hands of his two greedy sons."

It was Marak's turn to be grateful that her face was turned away, and she could not see how the name of the Three Benches startled him. The castle was the seat of Lord James Alderbury, and if he was Amaranth's uncle, that made her the daughter of Peter FitzWalter. She said her father had died when she was a child, and that certainly matched the years that had gone by since the monarchy had been embroiled in the bitter feuding between old King Henry and his three sons. And if she *was* FitzWalter's daughter, it was no wonder Odo de Langois had pressed for the marriage. FitzWalter was the bastard son of Geoffrey Plantagenet—father of Henry Secund—and uncle to Richard the Lionheart. It must have spun de Langois's head in a circle to bind himself to a wife whose blood flowed in the veins of kings.

"So you were pressed to accept the terms of the marriage?"

"I was given no choice. Not the first time, nor the second. For the second, however, I did try to convince myself that Odo was a handsome man, young and vigorous—a much better fate than the old, foul-smelling baron with black teeth and sagging skin. How foolish I was. How wrong. One man is no different from the next. As long as their beds are warm and their bodies are eased, a woman need be nothing more than a pawn traded back and forth among them."

"You make a harsh and bitter judgment of all mankind," Marak said, "painting us all with the same tarred brush."

She turned and looked Marak squarely in the eyes. "The day before the wedding was to take place, Odo's brother Rolf tried to rape me. When Odo came upon us, Rolf insisted that it was me who lifted my skirts and lured him into the woods. Since I was neither an innocent nor an altogether willing bride, Odo chose to believe him. When he came into the bridal chamber that night, I knew he meant to punish me. Just as I knew he would punish me every single day and night thereafter. I knew I could not endure it. Death would have been far sweeter and"—she paused and clenched her teeth a moment to stop her chin from trembling—"it was something I would have borne alone. Now—now the good people of that village have paid for my weakness, and there is every good chance that you will too, all of you. For even if you are able to defend your gates against an attack, a word to the prince regent and Lord Tamberlane's quiet existence will be at an end."

"I suspect part of him would welcome it, if that were true. Another three years of living this half-life he has chosen and he may well be the one dashing himself onto the rocks below." Marak's mouth softened with genuine concern. "Do not judge all men based on the few you have encountered. Some live with nightmares as terrible as your own."

The pale eyes shifted away from hers and for a long moment remained fixed and staring at some distant point on shore.

When Amaranth turned instinctively to see what had brought such a stillness to his features, she saw that the dawn light was streaking across the sky, giving the shadows and shapes on shore more substance.

Close to the water's edge were six mounted knights. They were perhaps a hundred long paces from the gatehouse and drawbridge, seemingly intent upon studying the island on which Taniere stood. The horses were well-trained beasts and did not twitch so much as a muscle. Judging by the undisturbed threads of mist clinging to their fetlocks, they had been there for some time, unobserved by the guards in either barbican.

The knights were sworded and fully armored, with shields slung across their backs; the largest of the six wore a surcoat emblazoned with a red boar rampant against a dark green field.

"Dear sweet Jesu," Amaranth whispered. "He has found me."

Chapter Nine

Tamberlane's eyes narrowed against a flare of sunlight. He had been in the stable when the guard brought news of men on the far shore. He had taken the stone stairs to the top of the parapet two by two, joining the rest of the guardsmen in staring out over the battlements. The six knights had not moved from their original position on shore. The sky was the color of pewter, the mist still thick over the water, the moss so green beneath the horses' hooves, it looked like a velvet carpet.

"It would appear as though we have visitors," Tamberlane murmured to no one in particular.

One of the foresters who had been with the hunting party when they came upon the marauders raiding the village scowled. "An odd way for visitors to approach. Shall I trumpet forth the rest of the guard, my lord?"

Tamberlane shook his head. "Do it quietly, without fanfare. Thus far we have no reason to believe they are anything but weary travelers seeking nothing more than a place to rest their heads, fill their bellies, and share a jug of ale before moving on."

"Do you believe that, sire?"

"No." Tamberlane smiled tightly. "But we should give them the appearance that we believe it is at least possible."

The forester left to pass the order but had to stand aside as Marak and Amaranth approached along the parapet. The haste with which they had descended the roof of the keep and hurried through the wards was reflected in the two bright spots of color on Amie's cheeks. The rest of her face was gray, her lips completely bloodless, making her eyes stand out as two prominent circles of clearest blue.

"We saw from the roof," Marak said by way of answering the frown that appeared on Tamberlane's face. "None of the sentries saw or heard them? What of the men in the gatehouse?"

"There has been no movement from within," the knight said slowly. His frown deepened and he looked at Amaranth. "Why have you come out into the chill? You should have remained back at the keep."

Amaranth glanced down. She and Marak had left the roof via her chamber, and she had barely paused there long enough to trade the woolen blanket for a proper cloak—one that was several sizes too large and engulfed her like folded moth wings. Her hair fanned out around her shoulders in thick russet waves that undoubtedly gave her the appearance of a wild woman.

"The men outside the gates," she said, her breath

rasping in her throat, "they have come for something and will not leave without it."

The knight held her gaze for a full count of three. "Explain. You know who they are?"

Amaranth returned his stare steadfastly. "The one wearing green with the red boar on his chest is Odo de Langois and beside him, on his right hand, his brother Rolf."

"How do you know this?"

The faintest hint of a tremor shivered on Amaranth's lips. "Odo de Langois is my husband. He has been hunting me these past two weeks. May God forgive me, but it is because of me the village was attacked, and because of me the peasants were slain."

Tamberlane was silent for so long Amie could actually feel the blood chilling, thickening, and being pushed sluggishly through her veins.

"Why did you not tell me this before now?"

Amie searched for an explanation that would sound even somewhat reasonable, but all she could do in the end was part her lips to speak . . . then close them again.

The pale green eyes flicked sharply to Marak. "You knew about this?"

The robed shoulders gave a shrug. "I knew there were lash marks and whipping scars on the child's back, across her buttocks and legs. I knew she was frightened beyond words, yet had she the strength to do so, she would have left here the instant upon waking in order to spare you any further inconvenience."

"Inconvenience? Is that what you call this?"

"Verily," Marak said wanly. "For we are ill equipped to hold off a siege by six men."

Tamberlane's eyes narrowed. "Look you again, Venetian, how the loaves have divided and the fishes multiplied."

Marak stepped to the top of the wall walk and looked through the square stone teeth of the parapet. On the verge of the woods, forming a wide semicircle behind the six knights, were a score or more of men-at-arms, most carrying crossbows, all wearing mail and breast armor of molded bullhide. While their weapons were not strung or quarrelled, the threat was implied, for the ominous line they formed skirted the edge of forest and enclosed the quiet, sleepy village in such a way as none could have escaped without notice.

"He would use the villagers as hostages," Marak murmured thoughtfully.

Amaranth's lashes shuddered as she closed her eyes. "I would have no more deaths on my shoulders, my lord. I could not bear it."

"Then it is just as well we had the foresight to bring all of the villagers inside the castle walls."

Amaranth was slow to open her eyes, even slower to raise them and focus on the handsome face.

"Two days hence," Tamberlane said matter-of-factly. "I have had men watching your husband's encampment, and although I was half convinced he was someone else, here for another purpose, I anticipated his coming to Taniere sooner or later. Only a fool leaves his sheep untended twice when he knows there are wolves in the woods."

The knight brushed past Amaranth and hastened down the steps. She stood there a moment, swaying under the weight of her own indecision, but then she turned and followed him down the stairs, the hem of her gown snagging on the rough stones. She followed him into the shadow of the barbican, where Roland was waiting to buckle him into a hauberk of polished iron links.

Her voice, strained to the point of cracking, came out barely above a whisper. "I am grateful for all you have done for me, Lord Tamberlane, but I do not want to jeopardize the peace or safety of your holding any longer. My husband is without conscience or mercy. He will not stop until he gets what he has come for, even if it means killing every man woman and child within these walls."

"He must consider you a prize of great value." Ciaran lowered his arms and adjusted the weight of the heavy link tunic. He made a long, measured study of her face, her hair, even the gathered wings of the cloak before nodding at Roland to bring forth his helm. "What would you have me do?"

"The only thing you can do, my lord. Return me to him."

The words so softly spoken cut through Tamberlane's anger like a knife. Had she pleaded for his help, wept her excuses, thrown herself at his feet and begged his mercy, he might have done just that—returned her to her husband and God's riddance to her. He knew the law of the land. He knew he had no jurisdiction over another man's wife and indeed, could be held to account for her presence at Taniere.

De Langois, if he knew of her presence, could attack the castle with impunity. He could also appeal to the king and the courts, and the ruling would not only go against Tamberlane but likely cause him to suffer a heavy fine for his interference.

"How long has he been your husband?"

"H-how long? Less than a day, my lord."

His hands hesitated again in the act of donning his mail hood. "Less than a *day*, did you say?"

"We were wed midmorning, and I struck him with a candlestick well before midnight of the same day . . . so, yes. A day, give thee, take thee grace."

He continued to study her face while he brusquely fastened the pennyplate camail, and his eyes, as was their habit of late, chose some small detail to focus upon—in this instance, a tiny white scar at the corner of her mouth. With unaccustomed distraction, he wondered how it had come to be there and why he had not noticed its presence before now.

"You struck him with a candlestick?"

"Yes, my lord. Several times."

"The marks on your back and flanks . . . how did you get them?"

Amie's eyes burned, but she did not look down or away. "Odo de Langois was not my first husband, though he will most assuredly be my last."

Tamberlane stretched out his arm, and Roland was quick to smack the hilt of a sword into the gloved hand. Ciaran studied the blade a moment, his keen eyes gauging the sharpness of the edge before flickering over to Amie again. "If I were to give you back, would you run away again?"

"No, my lord. I would accept my fate as God's will."

"God's will?" Tamberlane's voice was laced with soft scorn. "A fickle constancy at best."

"Ciaran—" Marak stepped forward to interrupt, but Tamberlane held up a hand, the palm flat, the look in his eyes gone well beyond a mere warning.

"I will hear it all before the day is through. For now, there are hunters in my woods, and I have not granted them permission to trespass."

The surcoat that went over his mail hauberk was black with no markings. The hilt of his sword lacked ornamentation of any kind, yet the blade was exquisitely wrought and of such a length as to suggest it had been specially made for his taller frame.

He tucked a much smaller, thinner blade into the span of his belt, and as Amie watched, she was almost able to imagine the sweet sharpness of the edge slicing across her wrist. How many times had the thought haunted her mind before? Each and every day for a year, at the least. Now, it would be an easy matter to reach out, take the knife, and end it. God would surely forgive her. Regardless if canon law decreed that she be buried unshriven, He would forgive her. He could not possibly expect her to walk calmly back into her husband's arms to endure whatever manner of agonizing death awaited her.

Hesitation cost her dearly, for before she could act on the thought, Tamberlane's enormous piebald stallion was being led out of the stables. Behind it came Roland and three other knights, their mail glinting in the early morning light, helms pushed low over their brows, visages concealed by the wide iron nasals. Each wore swords and had their shields slung over their shoulders in a subtle show of strength. There were more serjeants lining the walls as well, and among them were several foresters who held their longbows low and out of sight.

"Close the gates behind us," Tamberlane ordered. "Have men standing by the windlass, and if I give the signal, be ready to drop the portcullis."

"What are you going to do?" Marak asked. Before answering, Tamberlane climbed the low wooden steps that aided a knight in mounting a horse when he wore a hundred extra pounds of armor.

"I am going to go and see who stares so rudely at my walls."

"Is that wise?"

"Likely not as wise as it would be for you take the girl into the shadows with you. Her wing may be damaged, but her head is clear enough to know that if she is seen, I will be obliged to acknowledge her presence."

He wheeled the piebald around. With the pair of wolfhounds trotting on ahead and Roland and two other guardsmen riding on his flank, he passed between the enormous barbican towers and rode across the draw.

Amie stood as still as stone, listening to the horses' hooves cross the wooden planks.

"I warrant if I tried to send you back to the keep with a lackey, you would clout him and return the instant my back was turned?"

Amie said nothing as she looked up at the hooded face, but the set of her jaw gave an adequate answer.

"Very well, come with me. But at the first sign of trouble, you will do exactly as I instruct . . . agreed?"

"Agreed."

A soft, dubious grunt accepted her promise for what it was before Marak tipped his head to indicate that she should follow him through the small portal at the base of the closest barbican tower.

The square, crenellated structure had been built for the main purpose of protecting the castle's entrance from direct attack. Constructed entirely of stone, the towers were composed of three landings connected by a narrow block staircase. Each landing housed several arrow slits that presented nearly impossible targets for anyone firing from shore but gave defenders inside an excellent view and ample room to draw and fire a bow.

What little light these meurtriers admitted was washed gray by the depth of the wall and by the lacy veil of ivy that grew up the outer face of stone. The uppermost landing was further shaded by the machicolations—murder holes—that jutted out from the roof above through which boiling water, pitch, or burning faggots could be thrown down upon the heads of attackers.

The light was muted enough to allow Marak to slide the thick wool of his hood back. Amie's gaze was once again drawn to the crystalline clarity of his eyes, the unearthly beauty of a face that could have been shaped by the hand of a master sculptor.

"I would have thought you would be more curious about the events taking place on shore," he murmured quietly.

Blinking, Amie turned away and moved in front of the middle arrow slit. She felt Marak's eyes stray toward her for a brief moment before he too concentrated on the scene unfolding on the opposite green.

Tamberlane crossed the draw and led his small group at a dignified walk toward the waiting party of knights. Odo de Langois had wheeled his steed about and was watching their approach with undisguised interest. Glittering dark eyes showed on either side of his nasal as he noted that their swords were sheathed but within easy grasp.

Tamberlane rode close enough for a hail then stopped.

"I would know who it is who comes bearing arms and armor to threaten a peaceful village."

"Threaten?" Odo's chin came up. "I have made no threat, sir. I come in peace, I assure you."

"What manner of peaceful business brings you to Taniere Castle with knights and bowmen standing at the ready?"

"These are dangerous woods, my lord, and we have heard of outlaws who build their nests in the trees and stop a traveler with arrows rather than questions."

"These are dangerous times. The tax men bleed the peasants dry, and if there are outlaws in the trees, it is because they have no other place to live."

"The taxes have gone toward the ransoming of our king, held like a common prisoner by Leopold of Austria. You grudge the regent his right to save his brother, our liege and king?"

"I grudge him nothing, except when the fires, unprovoked, come upon my land."

De Langois's eyes narrowed. "Aye, we did pass a vill that looked charred. But I am not come from Prince John. Nor do I have a taste for blood or burnings this fine day. Rather, I go about my own business and come only to appeal to your hospitality, Lord Tamberlane, and to perhaps beg a hot meal for myself and my men."

"Your own business?"

"A personal matter of some delicacy, more easily discussed over a stoup of ale." He saw Tamberlane's eye slant across to the silent ring of crossbowmen again, and he added with a faint smile, "My guardsmen will remain without, if it please you more, with your leave to build a fire and draw water from your lake."

"The water is free and plentiful," Tamberlane said. "They may draw their fill. Send a man up to the cookhouse, and he can carry them back bread as well, and viands. As for you and your knightly companions, I can provide hot food and fodder for your horses. Our fare is plain and our accommodations humble, but I offer them freely."

"A crust and a jacket of ale will suffice," de Langois said expansively. "Though I must say it surprises me to hear that the Dragon Slayer of Hattin lives within such modest means."

"I have modest needs. My lord . . . ?"

"Odo de Langois. My holding is Belmane, to the south. On my right stands my brother Rolf, on the left our cousin Sigurd."

The latter lowered his eyelids in a lazy acknowledgment of the introduction, but Rolf's gaze was fixed on the magnificent piebald destrier Ciaran rode, his dark eyes kindling with recognition, knowing there could not be two such champion beasts within hailing distance of the destroyed village.

"You are welcome at Taniere, my lords," Tamberlane said and touched the reins to his horse, turning the piebald around.

The leather of de Langois's saddle creaked as he turned to murmur a few words of instruction in his squire's direction. When he was done and the younger man had trotted away, he put a spur to his horse's flank and moved closer to Tamberlane. The other knights followed behind Tamberlane and Odo de Langois. Tamberlane's men were the last to wheel their animals about and fall into line, a delay noted by two of the burly knights, who swiveled their heads to look back over their shoulders.

De Langois himself seemed nonplussed as they rode toward the drawbridge. The planks were wide and thick, producing a solid thud beneath each hoofbeat. The knight's slitted eyes moved constantly, assessing the height of the barbicans, the looming shadow of the walls, the number of heads he counted peering through the embrasures. As they passed under the portcullis, his attention was held by two things. Firstly, that the iron teeth gave less than a hand's width of clearance to a mounted man and the cables were wound so tightly in the winch that the bars hummed with the tension.

The second thing that caught his eye was the carving on the massive wooden gates. The doors were embossed with dragons—their bodies wound in a thick coil that spread open at the top like branches of a tree. The tree was split down the middle, joined when the banded halves were closed and bolted shut.

The carving was so intricate and lifelike that his head turned as he rode past, his gaze fixed on one of the massive heads that overlapped the gate and seemed to be watching them as they entered. Once beneath the portcullis bridge, they rode directly across the outer ward and through the arch to the inner bailey, where hostlers were waiting to take the reins of the horses.

"This castle is far from the Roman road. I scarcely knew of its existence," Odo said when he dismounted.

"The solitude suits my needs."

Odo de Langois removed his gauntlets, tugging one finger free at a time. He then folded them and tucked them into his belt, offering up a smile as he did so. "Ah, yes. As I recall, the life of a monk must needs be full of quiet and solitude. All the better for praying."

He watched Tamberlane's face for a reaction as he loosened his camail and pushed the mail hood back off his head, revealing a shock of thick red hair stuck close to his head from the weight of the hood. A quick raking with his fingers eased the tightness on his scalp and left some of the greasy strands sticking straight up like spikes. His eyes, the color of oiled iron, still looked to the defenses of the keep and the inner ward, while his nose, thin and hooked at the tip, sniffed the air as if he were a bloodhound trying to catch any scent of his prey.

"I confess I have not felt hot water on my skin in nearly a fortnight," he said, slapping a thigh to dislodge some clinging mud. "If your hospitality might extend that far, my lord, my men and I would be most appreciative."

Tamberlane signaled to a lackey. "Have water boiled and fill the barrels. We will have that stoup of ale, my lord, then Derwint here will provide you with hot baths."

"Excellent, excellent! My tongue is dry enough to sand a plank."

Tamberlane, with Roland at his back, walked up the stairs and led the way into the keep. Word of visitors had reached the hall well ahead of the men, and there were already flagons of ale and wine on the tables set beside loaves of coarse barley bread. All of the knights, with the exception of Odo, Rolf, and Sigurd took seats at one of the lower tables. Tamberlane invited the three to join him on the dais, where there were varlets waiting with bowls of water that they might wash their hands before breaking into the loaves of bread.

Just as Rolf's gaze had narrowed with recognition outside the castle walls when he saw the piebald that Tamberlane rode, Ciaran's glittered to acknowledge the limp in Rolf de Langois's stride, recalling the arrow that had jutted from the thigh of one of the attackers.

Instead of cleaning his hands, Odo pushed one of the young serving boys aside, causing him to stumble and slosh water down the front of his tunic. The knight then drew his knife and stabbed into a loaf of bread, tearing away a huge chunk, which he proceeded to stuff into his mouth and wash down with a full jacket of ale.

"Our victuals over the past two weeks would make even a mendicant weep," he said, the crumbs spitting from his lips, the ale glistening on his chin. "God's wrath, man, but I have craved a mouthful of anything that did not have to be soaked and softened beforehand."

"This 'business' that brings you to Taniere Castle," Tamberlane said, "you said it was of a personal nature?"

"Mmm." Odo nodded even as he curled his lip and spat a hard knot of unground barley onto the table. "It concerns the fickle nature of my bride, Elizabeth de Langois. Despite my bowing to her every whim and pleasure, despite my ability and desire to lavish her with wealth and comforts beyond anything she could imagine, the sulky ingrate has taken it upon herself to run away."

Tamberlane's face remained blank, and he was able to say with complete honesty, "I am not familiar with any lady by that name, my lord, nor have any errant wives come knocking on my gates."

"I only mention this as a matter of course, but you are aware, naturally, that by law you would be required to surrender her to me if she had."

Tamberlane's long fingers stroked the side of his pewter mug, gathering beads of condensation. "If I knew of Lady Elizabeth de Langois's presence here at Taniere, I would most certainly surrender her forthwith."

Odo continued to chew thoughtfully, trying to gauge the expression in the cool, steady green graze, which struck him now as being remarkably similar to the gaze of the dragons that watched as they passed through the gates.

"Perhaps she was seen in the village? She would be a difficult trick to overlook. A tall young woman, slender as a wisp, with long flaxen hair and a bold mouth?"

Tamberlane pursed his lips. "On my honor, I have not seen any woman hereabouts who meets that description. The villagers hereabout are mostly Saxon, with dark hair and darker eyes. A noblewoman, especially one so fair as you describe, would surely draw attention in a village of barley growers and cabbage farmers. Roland?"

The squire stepped forward at once.

"Have there been any strangers seen in the village lately? Any noblewomen, tall and slender with long yellow hair, traveling alone or"—he consulted with Odo through a glance—"with a companion, perhaps?"

"She had an accomplice, a priest, but he left her off somewhere down the road."

"Surely you questioned him as to her whereabouts?"

"He was questioned most thoroughly," Odo said, his thin smile leaving no doubt as to the degree of persuasion used. "But he gave up nothing. He claimed no knowledge of her whereabouts."

"Why would you think to look for her here? Taniere is hardly a sanctuary for wayward wives."

"I have been following the trail of whispers these past two weeks and more, some faint, some loud," Odo said, his eyes narrowing. "I thought I had found her a sennight ago, but if you say you have no knowledge of her, then it would appear as though she may have slipped through my fingers again."

"It would appear so. For rest assured, I have no use for rebellious women here and would happily be relieved of so troublesome a burden whither it were a dictate of the law or no. In the meantime, rest and eat your fill. And while you do, pray catch me up on all the news from the outside world. We have few visitors, and a stray plover that wanders into the ward is cause for rejoicing."

"Not only visitors, I dare swear, for I noticed the village outside your gates was oddly lacking in villagers."

Tamberlane smiled. "Merely a precaution until we can determine who it was who attacked my vill. I would do the same if it were the regent himself come to my gates. Neither they nor I have any wish to wake up of a morning and find ourselves held hostage by wolves."

After a calculated pause, Odo returned the smile. "Wise, then, since the woods would seem to be full of all manner of creatures these days. Wolves, outlaws . . ."

"Thieves and tax collectors, though I would argue the two are one and the same. Of late, they have been as thick as flies on a corpse and just as eager to pick the bones clean."

"Of late, there has been need of extra scutage to

pay for the king's own folly. Richard has emptied the treasury many times over to pay for his holy Crusade. Did you not find it to be one of the finer ironies that such a vaunted warrior should have been caught trying to sneak through his enemy's lands disguised as a stableboy? An even greater irony that his people—his Englishry, who have had the pleasure of his presence a mere smattering of months since his reign began—should have had to unearth their coppers and deniers to pay his ransom?"

"The last news we heard was that the ransom had fallen well short of the mark despite the prince's best efforts, and the dowager queen was being pressed to sell the Aquitaine to Leopold to win the king's release."

Odo de Langois hesitated a moment longer, the sarcasm bristling down his spine. "Your news is weeks old, friend, and sprinkled with faery dust. The dowager would see all her sons dead before bartering away her precious Aquitaine. Nay, the treasure train is on its way to Austria as we speak. Five tons of silver, a weighty matter."

"It departed England safely?"

"And why should it not? The prince has been just as eager as his mother to see the release of the king."

The words sounded ludicrous, even to a man who was loyal to Prince John, for it had taken nearly two years to raise the sum demanded by the Emperor Leopold for King Richard's release. During those two years, John Lackland had done nothing to aid either his mother, Eleanor, or the newly appointed Archbishop of Canterbury, Hubert Walter, in collecting the ransom. Indeed, he had done everything he could, including theft and murder, to prevent the silver ever reaching Austria.

His actions had plunged all of England into a period of treachery and violence, where greed outweighed loyalty and neighboring barons turned against each other to the point of open rebellion. Those who sided with the prince were promised great wealth, land, and power in return for their support. Those who upheld their allegiance to Richard found themselves arrested on imagined charges, their property seized, their sons outlawed, their families cast from the gates like peasants. Even the Archbishop of York, Richard's bastard brother, had been thrown into prison. William Longchamp, his chancellor, had fled to Europe days before an assassin's knife could silence his dissent.

Prince John had assumed the throne in all but name and had grown so fat and comfortable in the position, he would do everything in his power to keep his brother prisoner at Durnstein. Nobles were kidnaped and murdered, their deaths blamed on the roving bands of outlaws who filled the forests—outlaws who were, for the most part, men who had spoken out against Prince John and chose the forest over being drawn and quartered. One such band was led by the nephew of William the Marshal—Henry de Clare—and it was he, working in concert with Canterbury and the queen, who had robbed the prince's thieves and tax men and eventually helped raise the bulk of the ransom.

Odo de Langois was the prince's man. His loyalties

were as plain as the scarlet boar emblazoned across his surcoat. The iron-gray eyes did not look to the walls and defenses of Taniere merely to search for his errant wife. He looked with a greedy eye and an ambitious desire to add to his holding of Belmane.

Moreover, he had already assessed the vaunted Dragon Slayer as a threat and found him sadly wanting. Despite the breadth of his shoulders and the overbold contempt in his voice, Tamberlane's mail was poorly made, the links showed rust, and the plain caste of his surcoat showed he was not inclined to boast his identity to the world. Nor was he likely to want attention drawn down upon himself by openly declaring against the prince.

It was equally unlikely that such a man would break the king's laws over something so paltry as a runaway wife.

The castle itself seemed unkempt, disordered. The walls were poorly defended—Odo had counted less than three dozen guardsmen on the walls. The villagers and inhabitants, if indeed they were all of Saxon blood, would be a surly and filthy lot, not ones to risk their necks for the sake of an errant noblewoman. There did not appear to be a handsome wench among them, which only prompted Odo to remember that his host was a monk and would have monkish ways and monkish tastes.

And yet . . . there was something not right. All castle walls had ears; gossip traveled from one end of the keep to the other before the breath had dried on the speaker's lips. Every shadowy corner had eyes as well, and while Odo's skin had reacted badly the first time he had fallen under the scrutiny of his host's eerie green gaze, the sensation of being watched and studied had not left him. The hall was large but sparsely furnished, the tables deserted but for his own men and a handful of varlets who served them. There was a minstrel's gallery high on the far wall, but the beams and pilasters were spun with veils of cobwebs so thick and loosely hung they were like curtains; any movement there would stir them.

He stared up into the blackness for a long moment, wondering at the cold prickles that rose across his nape. The source was not resolved until a finger of smoke, climbing up from one of the brazier fires, led his gaze to the wall above the hearth. There he saw the same dragon tree as had been depicted on the front gates, the same entwined creatures with their jaws open and their tongues curling outward with ominously chilling realism. The carving was in polished oak this time, breathtakingly lifelike, from the scaled and twisted heads of the dragons to the six pairs of sightless eyes that seemed to be staring right into the skull of Odo de Langois.

They were the kind of eyes that would follow a man whether he sat in the front of the hall or the rear, whether he walked or stood perfectly still.

They were also, he resolved, the first thing he would dismantle and burn as soon as possession of Taniere Castle fell into his hands.

Chapter Ten

Marak, who had been a friend of Tamberlane's for nigh on two decades and a constant companion for the past three years, was fairly certain the knight would not betray Amaranth's presence at Taniere Castle. Not, at least, until he'd had a chance to speak to her further.

He was not so certain, however, that Amaranth would not betray herself.

They had watched together from the gloom of the barbican as her husband and Tamberlane had met on the shore. They were too far away for any words to carry across the distance, but it seemed to be a surprisingly amiable exchange. At the end of it, when Tamberlane had led the knights back across the draw, Marak had been more intent upon watching Amie's face than studying the men as they filed past, and the changes he saw there surprised him more than Tamberlane's civility with Odo de Langois. The look of the lost, fragile waif was gone, and in its place was loathing in its purest form.

She did not take her eyes off her husband, trans-
fixed by the presence of the man she had sought to
kill. Amie was able to follow de Langois's progress,
moving from arrow slit to arrow slit, studying him
as long as she could before changing quickly to gain
an unbroken view through another slot cut in the
stone. When the horses and riders passed beneath
the portcullis, she stood over a murder hole and
stared down at the tops of their heads, and Marak
actually felt the hairs across his nape rise.

He had been on a ship once, in the still moments
before a storm struck, and had witnessed the light-
ninglike bursts of energy that danced across the
yards and mast. He felt as though he were in the
presence of that same crackling tension, that same
excruciating stillness—and had either one of them
moved so much as a fingertip, Amaranth's rage
would have charged the air with sparks.

A man with a long arm could lie on his belly and
reach through the machicolation to snatch a helmet
off the head of someone riding below. Marak was
certain he saw Amie's nostrils flare, as if she could
smell her husband's clothes, his hair, his body stench
as he passed beneath. He suspected that if she had
a pot of scalding oil at hand, she would have emptied
it over his head without a qualm.

When the last rider had passed beneath, she
crossed to the opposite side of the tower and peered
once again through the arrow slits, watching the men
ride across the outer bailey. Because of the flat, open
ground between the battlements and inside curtain
wall, this inner ward was also referred to as the kill-

ing field—an appropriate name, to judge by the look in Amaranth's eyes.

"Are you still so willing to offer yourself up in sacrifice?"

Her head gave a slight turn, and he could tell that she had been so absorbed in her hatred that she had forgotten he was even there.

"There must be another way out of this castle," she said quietly. "Castles are not built to trap the residents inside. There is always a way out when the last defense has been breached."

"The first has not even been assaulted yet. Will you not bide and put a small measure of faith in Ciaran?"

"Ciaran?"

Marak smiled. "Even a Dragon Slayer is given a human name at birth. His is Ciaran Richard Edward Tamberlane. And yours, I vow, is not Amaranth." The question was met with instant suspicion, and his hand waved to dismiss it. "A small talent I possess for reading words on lips when distance prevents me from hearing them."

"Elizabeth," she admitted on a soft sigh. "It is Elizabeth, but my father did indeed call me Amaranth. That much was not a lie."

"Then I shall continue to call you Amaranth. And it is just as well you did not use your given name. For all his self-righteous skepticism, Tamberlane would sooner pierce his own tongue with a wooden spike than twist it around a lie. 'Tis a flaw that has cost him dearly many times in the past."

Whatever strength she had mustered to stare at

her husband began to wane, and the slope of Amie's shoulders grew more pronounced. The color that had burnished her cheeks was faded again, and her eyes looked so huge and dark they brought to mind the foal he had recently pulled out of the mare's belly. The legs had been wobbly, the head unsteady as if it was too heavy for the neck; the eyes had been wide, glazed with fear and uncertainty.

"You are safe so long as you stay out of sight," he assured her quietly.

"You do not know him. If he suspects I am here— and why else would he have come to the gates?—he will find a way to search every room in the castle."

"Having seen the man, I am inclined to agree. Unfortunately, I also agree that you should be away from this place—far away—as soon as possible."

She looked at him with the first signs of relief, acknowledging that at least one argument had drawn to a conclusion. "Then there *is* another way off the island?"

Marak smiled again. "There are catacombs where you could remain hidden for years and not be found, but I think you would suffer for not having daylight on your face. And, as we speak of it, while daylight is full upon us, we shall have to find the means to make you invisible."

"Invisible? You have that power?" she asked in a whisper that was partly unbelieving, partly hopeful.

Marak laughed. "Would that I did, Little One— then we could all go safely about our business. Alas, my powers extend only to making people see what they wish to see."

"I do not understand."

"Do you trust me?"

It was the first time he had asked the question outright, and Amie hesitated only a moment before nodding her head.

"Then wait here. I need to fetch some things from the stables but will return upon the instant. Will you do this much for me?"

She nodded again.

He pulled his hood back up over his head and, with the usual whispering drag of his robes, was gone, leaving Amie quite alone in the silence. The fishy smell of the lake water combined with the earthy scent of perpetually damp stone was suddenly oppressive, and she sat on an overturned bucket before her legs gave way beneath her. Her heart was still pounding like a drum, and her wounded shoulder was throbbing. She felt physically ill, her stomach roiling even though it was empty enough to rub on her backbone. Leaning forward, she cradled her head in her hands, breathing slow and deep until the nausea passed.

This would not do. It would not do at all to turn into a quivering heap of fear now. From somewhere, nourished on tears and whiplashes, she had found the courage to survive a year of hell as a whoremonger's plaything. Surely she could survive this.

Ciaran Richard Edward Tamberlane. The name popped into her mind unbidden as did his face. His expression had looked utterly unforgiving when she had confessed her duplicity, and she did not expect it to improve over the next few hours. She suspected that he would be more than anxious himself to see her leave Taniere Castle.

Admittedly, it had come as a shock to hear that he was a priest, for he was as dark and brooding as the devil himself. Roland's cautions had been unnecessary; he had a look about him that would have warned her against appealing to his softer side anyway . . . if he even had one.

Yet she had seen that harsh, chiseled face falter out of its arrogance over something so trivial as returning a wooden horse to a child. At some time he must have been capable of vast measures of tenderness, something he had been hardened against through prayer, discipline, and warfare.

They were, she reasoned, not so very different in some respects.

Marak reappeared on the stone landing. He carried a thick bundle under his arm and in his hand a pair of doeskin boots still warm from their previous owner.

"Your husband and his men will be keeping a keen eye on the gates, the wards, the outbuildings for a slender young woman with"—he crooked an eyebrow in askance, his glance traveling along the scattered length of thick russet curls—"pale yellow hair? The priest who helped you was a clever fellow, altering the color, but we will need to alter the rest of you."

He unwrapped the bundle, and she watched as he produced a shirt, jerkin, and leggings. None were particularly clean, and to judge by the size, she suspected there was likely a young boy running about in stables with naught against his skin but a horse blanket.

" 'Twas the best I could do without needle and thread," Marak said, catching the dubious look in her eye.

She shook her head to dismiss his concerns and unfastened her cloak, letting it fall to the floor. She was still dressed only in the straight, shapeless sheath she had slept in and, at Marak's suggestion, left it on to add more bulk beneath the clothing. He helped her into the coarse woolen shirt and gave instructions for the leggings—a garment she had never worn before and one that required a thin leather belt to go about the waist to keep the crutch from sagging down to her knees. The boots fit the best of the lot thus far, but required several scowling attempts before the rawhide straps were wound and crisscrossed properly to her knees. When the jerkin was added, Marak stood back to inspect and was satisfied with all but her hair, still a great and glorious cloud of long rippling waves.

She saw where his concern was focused and reached up, grimacing with the pain in her arm. There was too much, and it was too heavy for her to drag it all forward. Once again Marak assisted, watching her divide the glossy mass into three equal parts and begin to weave them into a plait, using her fingers to free the tangles as best she could.

When she was finished, it was an improvement, and he said as much. She could see the hesitation tainting his praise and knew she would not deceive anyone into believing she was a lad wearing a braid down to her knees.

"Do you have a knife?"

The Venetian produced one from somewhere inside a voluminous sleeve. Thinking she meant only to sever the end of the braid, he was startled to see her grab it at its thickest point near the nape of her neck and saw the sharply honed edge of the blade back and forth. The skein was severed and in her hand before he could question the merit of the act, for a woman's hair was her pride, a symbol of her station in life. Many a noblewoman went her entire adult life without ever cutting an inch.

"Well!" he said. And then again, "Well."

She held out the braid and the knife, her lower lip held firmly between her teeth. He set the one aside, but took the knife and, after seeking permission with a silent gesture of his hands, tried to give her impulsiveness a more evenly trimmed appearance.

This time, when he stood back to make his inspection, he was blatantly shocked at the transformation. Her face was now surrounded by a scruffy mop of reddish waves, some already curling in the dampness against her neck. Her breasts were camouflaged by the layers of sheath, shirt, and jerkin, the latter long enough to hide the slimness of her hips. She looked much like the fourteen-year-old lad he had borrowed the clothing from, and he dared to swear she could stand within ten paces of her own husband and he would not recognize her. If she kept her face and her eyes lowered, that is. The former was far too pale and smooth, the latter seemed to be twice the size as before, the lashes—which had not been overly noticeable before—long and honey-colored.

Nodding to himself over his own foresight, he unwrapped a final small parcel of cloth he had brought from the stable.

"For this I do heartily apologize," he said, "but the smell should turn the most belligerent head away."

Amie held her breath as he smeared a clod of fresh horse dung down the front of her jerkin. It was ripe enough to make her eyes water, but she did not protest, not even when he cleaned his fingers on her sleeves and bent over again, carrying dirt up to spread on her cheeks, forehead, and throat.

"Not perfect, of course, but certes good enough to gainsay an eye looking for a fair maid."

Before Amie could release the breath she had been holding, they heard the sound of footsteps running up the stairs behind them. Marak raised a warning finger to his lips.

It was Roland, his cheeks flushed from running.

"My lord Tamberlane requests your presence in the hall," he said to Marak. "He also said—and quite specifically, as he made me repeat the words twice—that you were to deal with the matter at hand as you saw fit, but to deal with it swiftly, for if he remains alone in Lord Odo's company overlong, he may be tempted to test the edge of his blade on the bastard's throat. Those were my lord's very specific words."

"Relishing the role of pleasant host, is he?"

"He also told me to advise you to be on your guard. That Lord Odo's men have positioned themselves in such a way as to see, count, and mark every face that comes and goes."

Marak's expression sobered. "Did he also mention the business that brings Lord Odo to our gates?"

Roland shook his head. "But I overheard enough to know that de Langois has come to Taniere in search of his wife. He suspects she may have sought sanctuary here."

"A nobleman's errant wife? Here at Taniere?"

Roland shrugged. "God spare me if I would see the sense in it either. She is, according to his men, young and sweet and comely. A rare beauty with hair the color of sunlight and eyes like circles of the sky."

Marak pursed his lips. "I have not seen anyone who would resemble that description, have you?"

Roland frowned. "No. Not in the least. And I am certain a woman of genteel birth would have made herself known at once."

"At once," Marak agreed. "I had best hasten back to the keep." He turned to address Amie. "You may return to the stables, boy, and sit with the foal."

Amaranth started to walk past, but Roland reached out and grabbed her by a handful of the jerkin. "Nay, you'll come with me. They are in need of more pages to carry food and water."

"In the hall? Oh, no. No, I think I should stay here—"

Her protest was cut short on a brusque clout from the squire's hand. "Puling cur! How dare you question an order from me! Lord Marak should turn you into a toad for your insolence! If I say you are to go to the hall, you are to go to the hall, though by the look and stench of you, I'd not want you carrying any platter of food that might touch my lips."

Marak's eyes narrowed. "You may be right about that, Roland. Aye, perhaps he should go up to the keep. The foal is fine; the mare is looking after it well enough. The boy can help by tending the fires and turning the spits, where the smoke is thickest and will disguise the odor."

Amie was in the process of tipping her head up to question the wisdom of Marak's suggestion when Roland gave her another clout for good measure. This time it landed squarely over the tenderly healing wound. A cry broke from her lips, and she half flinched, half spun away to protect the shoulder from another blow, but the pain took hold of her breath and left her doubled over.

Marak was instantly by her side. The look on his face rivaled that on Roland's, who was staring down near his feet at the cut braid of hair that lay like a glossy snake coiled on the stone. He looked from the braid to Amie, back to the braid, and finally, with a slowly opening mouth, to Marak.

Roland's mouth gaped wider. "My lord, I—I had no idea . . ."

Marak raised an angry hand to silence him. His arm went around Amaranth's waist, and it was thus he supported her until the waves of pain subsided and she could straighten again.

"Amaranth, I had no idea . . ."

"Since you are not as thick in the skull as you might appear to be," Marak interjected quietly, "I have no doubt you would have discovered the charade in short order anyway."

Roland's mouth gaped wider. "But why?" He looked down at the severed braid again and comprehension flushed hotly—if slowly—into his cheeks. "Of course. Yes, of course, and . . . oh, dear God, your shoulder! My most humble apologies. All I saw was a boy standing there. I had no idea . . ."

"All you were supposed to see was a boy," she said, smiling weakly. "And if I were a boy, you would have had every right to clout me. I hold no ill will."

Roland was still staring at her hair, at the dirt on her face, the dung streaking her jerkin. He started to smile, but even as Marak watched and counted off the seconds in his head that would bring Roland into a further dawning of the light, the squire's expression changed; his eyes grew rounder and slowly flicked from one conspirator to the other. "The one they search for is named Elizabeth. Lady Elizabeth de Langois."

"Amaranth is a pet name," she explained softly. "Given me by my father."

"He claims his wife ran away to spite him. That she ran away with a lover."

"There was a priest who helped me escape."

"He showed a wound on his head, where she tried to murder him in his sleep."

She saw no point in denying it.

"He raided . . . and *slew* an entire village to get you back."

"As I know him—he would not hesitate to slay

everyone within these walls if he knew I was here," she said evenly.

"Lord Tamberlane . . ." Roland chose his words carefully. "He knows all of this?"

"He does," Marak said. "He also knows, as do you if you take a moment of thought, that the men who attacked the village were not sent there merely to find Lady Amaranth, but to hunt her down and kill her. And to do it in a most brutal, painful way."

Roland looked once again at Amaranth. His memory of the raid was clear and vivid, and in the end he offered up a slow nod. "What can I do to help?"

"Take her to the keep, as you intended," Marak said. "De Langois and his men will be sniffing for someone who keeps to the corners and endeavors not to be seen. Thus far, only three of us know who she is, and only two know she is now . . . Tom, son of Herne, yeoman of the dale of Sherwood. Set her to turning the spits, where she will be in plain view, yet invisible. My lady, does this sit well with you? Can you do it?"

She hesitated long enough for Roland to offer up a rueful smile through the dark mottlement of red that flushed into his cheeks. "In truth, my lady, I did not glance at you twice and would not have suspected you were ought but what you appear to be."

"Then you must not err in addressing me as my lady," she said softly. "Either one of you. Thenceforth I am Tom, son of Herne, yeoman of the dale of Sherwood."

Chapter Eleven

Amaranth experienced several harrowing moments through the long, seemingly endless afternoon and evening. The first came the instant she set foot inside the gloomy vault of the great hall. The addition of Odo de Langois and the other five knights did little to alleviate the sense of emptiness, and she was certain all eyes in the room would turn to stare at her as she followed Roland down the stairs and along the length of the room. A step, two at the most, and she would hear the shout that would bring her husband raging toward her, his hand on the hilt of his sword, the promise of all black things in hell gleaming in his eyes.

To her surprise and infinite relief, not one single glance was squandered in her direction. At intervals as they walked toward the rear screen, Roland pretended to cuff her, as if she had been caught shirking her duties. But true to Marak's prediction, no one gave a thought to a scruffy, ill-smelling stable boy. Even the rotund trio of women who were skewering hens and setting them to roast over the cooking fires did little more than grunt and point at the nearest spit that wanted turning.

From her vantage point at the rear of the hall—when she could see through the smoke—she had a clear view of the dais. Odo's bright red hair stood out against the stone blocks that composed the wall behind him. He was eating, drinking, talking, laughing with Lord Tamberlane who, by contrast, sat quietly and observed, his smiles as scarce as snow in summer. Odo's cousin, Sigurd the Oaf, ate with both hands, getting greasy to the wrists. He pinched the maids who brought fresh platters and drank with such gusto the ale splashed over the rim each time he slammed his tankard on the table.

By contrast, Rolf de Langois picked at morsels of food here and there with the point of his knife, trying to make it appear casual as he studied the faces of everyone in the hall.

Amaranth kept her head bowed whenever Rolf's dark eyes roved the room. Odo was a brute with his contempt and his fists, but Rolf was sly, cunning, and dangerous. He had neatly twisted the story of his attempted rape to place the blame squarely on Amie's shoulders, convincing Odo with his protestations and, at the same time, letting his gaze promise her he would finish what he started.

The rear of the long hall was where the lowest of the classes sat, the working men, the peasants, the almoners. The men who had accompanied de Langois into the keep sat above the salt but still much closer to where Amaranth worked over the spit than was comfortable. Once, when she looked up, two of them were nowhere to be seen. A moment later, her eye was caught by movement through the haze of smoke, and she saw them walking around the great hall, pausing here and there to exchange a word with someone seated at the board. They were hardly being discreet with their purpose or their questions, moving on when they won a grunt or a shake of the head.

Amaranth's blood turned as cold as ice. Every step that brought the knights closer sent another rush of chilling flutters scratching down her spine. She bowed over the handle of the wooden spit and concentrated on turning it in the forks of the metal brackets, aware by the fanning of hairs across her nape when the knights had reached the end of one long table and were crossing the width of the hall to stroll along the other.

Heavy, wooden-soled bootsteps stopped not two feet from where Amie stood. She bowed her head and scratched furiously at an armpit, punishing some imaginary vermin. One of the knights—a man she had seen at Belmane countless times—reached out and plucked a crispy curl of roasted chicken off the nearest hen; he was so close she could hear the crunch of the skin between his teeth before he grunted and moved along.

When they completed their circuit of the great hall, Amaranth saw one of them give a barely perceptible shake of his head in Odo's direction. De Langois, in turn, tipped his head to indicate the towers. They too were about to be thoroughly searched without regard for their host's privacy or troubling to obtain his permission first.

Watching them, Amie's gaze settled briefly on the hooded figure seated beside Tamberlane on the dais. Marak's face was completely enveloped in shadow, but she sensed he had seen both exchanges between Odo and his men. She felt, suddenly, as if her belly were full of butterflies crashing against one another to find a way out. If they searched her solar . . . would they find anything that might give her away? No, how could they? She had come to Taniere with nothing but a borrowed peasant dress and . . .

Her hand went up to her throat. She had meant to ask Marak about the crucifix. It had belonged to her father's mother . . . a gift presented by her lover, the father of a king. Amie vaguely recalled that the knight who had pursued her into the forest had parted her bodice with the tip of his sword and for a moment had smiled at the glint of silver resting over her breasts, as if he had needed to see it to confirm her identity. But then the pain had blurred what happened next; she knew only that the sword had moved lower, and she had felt the edge of the blade cutting a sliver in her flesh up the length of her thigh. Had he taken the cross from her? Or had she somehow lost it between the village and Taniere Castle?

She had no time to ponder the question further, as a hamlike hand slammed down on her shoulder and she was asked by one of the gnarly-faced cooks if she meant to spin the hens right off the spit and set them flying onto the tables. Ruefully, she went back to the job of slowly turning the birds over the grate, but it took several minutes for her heart to leave her throat and pound its way back down into her chest.

The meal lasted fully two hours or more. As soon as a haunch was cooked, a stew brought to the boil, a fowl scraped sizzling onto a wooden platter, it was whisked away and devoured. When Amie's turn at the spit ended, she was given a shovel and told to haul away ashes, then to bring more wood to keep the fires stoked, for preparations for supper started immediately upon casting aside the bones from the noon meal.

She was surprised, yet not surprised, to see Odo linger at the board so long Tamberlane had no choice but to invite him to remain the night. Only then did the trio of knights excuse themselves to indulge in hot baths and, Amie was certain, the opportunity to search the outbuildings.

Marak had been right. No one even gave her a second glance. She was out in the open, hidden better than any of Odo de Langois's ferrets could imagine.

By the end of the long day, however, her shoulder ached so badly she could hardly see straight. She was light-headed from the smoke and the worry, and felt as if she was moving in a daze. When, at length, there were no more tasks being assigned by a stern finger, no more frowns dispatched by a disapproving brow, she found a quiet place by the fire and curled up on the stone floor, too tired to contemplate more than the flames rippling along the logs.

She was not even aware of falling asleep until she

felt another hand on her shoulder. Groaning, she tried to bat it away, but the fingers were gentle, and they waited for her to open her eyes rather than shake her roughly awake.

It was Inaya, her dark eyes cautioning Amie not to make noise. All around her were the snores and curled-up bodies of the lackeys, peasants, retainers who, having finished their days' work, simply found an empty spot near the fire to make their bed. Inaya tipped her head to indicate that Amaranth should follow her, and with a swish of silken robes, she moved away as quietly as she had approached.

Amaranth tasted blood on her tongue from the effort it took to push up on an elbow, then struggle painfully to her feet. Her hip was stiff from lying on the unforgiving floor and her shoulder ached, so that when she moved, she was slightly twisted and hunched forward.

Inaya led her into the deeper shadows that hugged the wall, stopping only once when she was on the landing that led up into the north tower. Amie limped as best she could behind her, fighting the tears that were stinging at the back of her eyes, her breath hot and dry in her throat.

The tower was much like her own, only larger. Marak had pointed it out earlier as being where Tamberlane's chambers were located, and she felt a small clutch of fear growing as she mounted each step. Men were unpredictable, volatile, and—in her limited experience anyway—indifferent to tender mercies. She knew she had surprised and angered him that morning. She knew also that he was taking

an enormous risk upon himself by concealing her
from Odo de Langois. He would likely demand answers, explanations . . . perhaps even repayment for
his largesse.

That last thought made her footsteps falter. Luckily
they had reached the upper landing, and she could
lean her shoulder on the wall for a moment's respite.
Inaya had already disappeared inside the open doorway. It was arched, the door made up of thick oak
planks banded with straps of iron. Here again, there
was a carving of the dragon tree, smaller and even
more exquisitely detailed.

Gathering her courage in hand, Amaranth walked
into the chamber. First glance told her it was perhaps
twice the size of her own, yet no more lavishly furnished. The bed was plain and set against the far
wall, hung all around with curtains to ward off
drafts. There were three window embrasures set into
the walls at intervals that would give him a complete
view of the surrounding shore and land. A fire crackled in the hearth. Candles flickered in sconces, on the
top of a large writing table, and in a prayer niche
that contained a small altar and reliquary.

It was the first visible indication of Tamberlane's
past association with the Templars. Marak had said
there was a chapel in one of the other towers, but
there was no regular priest to hold services, and
Tamberlane had not set foot inside it since his arrival.

Yet here, in the privacy of his own chamber, there
was evidence of his past devotion. The reliquary would
contain some fragment of the cross Christ bore on his
shoulders; the triptych behind it was solid gold and

obviously brought with great care from the Holy Land.
Hung on one wall inside the niche was a white Crusader's mantle emblazoned with the scarlet cross, on the
other a sword that so shockingly made up for the plainness of the one he had worn that morning that it nearly
took Amie's breath away. The hilt was solidly crusted
in jewels; the guard was wrought in silver with gold
inlay. The blade was easily four feet long, the surface
polished to a mirror gloss.

Inaya moved on soundless feet to stoke the fire and
set a small wooden tray laden with bread, cheese, and
slices of cold mutton closer to the warmth. She curled
her fingers to beckon Amie forward and pointed to a
low, three-legged stool she placed beside it. Amie was
not especially hungry, having worked close to the smell
of grease and roasting animal flesh all day, but her legs
were trembling, close to buckling, and she was grateful
for the excuse to sit. Wine was poured into a small
silver goblet. A small frown and fluttering of hands
halted Amie before she could quench the dryness in
her throat, and a moment later, a basin of warmed
water appeared on the hearth.

Despite Amaranth's protests, Inaya used a scrap of
soft linen to bathe her face, her hands, and forearms.
The filthy jerkin, the appearance of which had not
improved overmuch throughout the day, was ordered removed with a Saracen epithet, an emission
that brought forth a low chuckle from the shadows
beside the fireplace.

Amaranth gasped, for she had truly not seen
Tamberlane standing there. Granted, the wall dipped
and the shadows were too thick for the candlelight

to penetrate, but he was a large man and, to her mind, one not easily rendered invisible.

He said something to Inaya in her own language then laughed again when the woman scurried away, the silken wings of her sari belling out behind in her haste. Amaranth heard a click and knew the door had been closed. Had there been the strength in her legs to do so, she might have shot to her feet and bolted out of the chamber as well.

For the longest time, Tamberlane did nothing. He had one shoulder propped against the wall, and his arms were folded over his chest. Now and then she caught a faint glint of light reflected in his eyes, and she knew he must be watching her, studying her, wondering what to do about her.

"Inaya will be back in a few moments with some buckets of hot water and"— he paused and made a poor attempt to conceal the wrinkle in his nose— "clean clothes."

She looked down, having almost grown immune to the sour, vinegary smell of dung and wood smoke.

"Marak's idea, no doubt," he surmised. "And effective . . . to a point. But what in God's name did he do to your hair, and why did you let him do it?"

The question startled her. "It was not Marak who cut it. I did. It was a nuisance and a hindrance and would have been sheared when I reached the convent at any rate, so the loss is not lamentable."

Tamberlane tilted his head to the side. "You look like a faery elf . . . or, at least, what my impression of a faery elf would be."

Amaranth's hand crept self-consciously upward,

her fingertips reaching for the familiar wealth of hair that was not there. She had almost forgotten that too, although in truth, the lack of weight was a welcomed change, as was the freedom to turn her head this way or that without the burden of heavy braids or cumbersome coils.

Her fingers danced across the ends of the reddish curls, and her gaze instinctively sought a mirror. There were only bare, utilitarian walls, of course, no luxuries of any kind save for the soft glint of precious metal from the prayer niche.

"I see you did not rid yourself of the hindrance of vanity," he murmured. The casual jest, made from the shadows, concealed the fact that he was all but frozen in place where he stood. The flames bathed her face and tarnished her curls with threads of bright light. He had been mind-numbingly unable to move or speak when she first entered the room. Her features, softly feminine before, were rendered dangerously beautiful when framed in the coppery nimbus. Marak had not warned him. He had merely indicated that all was well in hand.

Now, watching Amaranth's slender fingers comb lightly through the sheared waves, Tamberlane felt his body growing strangely tight and heavy. Even dressed like an urchin, streaked with grim and soot, her beauty shone through like a flame that burned hot and bright. However, he dared not reach a hand too near for fear of singeing himself in the heat.

Marak said she bore lash marks. Whip marks. Thinking of how those marks got there, the tightness in his body changed, unexpectedly, to cold anger.

"Tell me about the lash marks," he said quietly.

Amaranth glanced up from the fire. Her gaze met his and held for the span of a heartbeat, and he could see that she was not startled by the question, merely caught in a debate over how to answer it.

"The first husband my uncle sold me to . . . he thought I needed disciplining to curb my tongue and make me more amenable to his wishes."

Tamberlane reached down and took her wrist in his hand, raising it and angling it to the light so that the faint shine from ages-old rope burns showed.

"There were times he had to tie me down," she stated flatly. "Although I believe he enjoyed that even more."

Tamberlane continued to hold her wrist, and Amie continued to look up at him. She was aware of the heat from his touch rising up her arm, flowing through her body.

"What happened to him? How did he die?"

"He enjoyed a meal of mutton and toadstools and . . . one can only suppose there was an error made in picking the latter."

There was the smallest change in the pressure of his fingertips before they released her wrist, but if the question was on his tongue, he kept it between his teeth.

"I was widowed less than a month before his grown sons sent me back to my uncle, and free barely another month before Odo de Langois appeared at the gates bearing a purse full of coins and a writ from Prince John sanctioning the marriage."

"Tell me more about him."

"What would you like to know?"

"Something more than what I know already. He is the prince's man, that much is as obvious as his lack of concern in showing it. His ambitions are etched clearly in his contempt when he speaks of King Richard."

"He was ever Prince John's lickspittle," Amie said, clasping her hands together around her knees. "They have been friends since boyhood, and I know the regent has promised him a barony as well as several estates in the Marches in exchange for his support."

"That would explain why Lackland would sanction a marriage between such a brute and his own blood relation, however distilled that blood might be."

Amie tilted her head. "You knew?"

"Marak saw the two points on the map and connected them. The first came to him when you mentioned your uncle's estate, the Three Benches. It was named for the three sons of Eleanor and Henry Secund, but it was deeded to the king's illegitimate brother, who was a favored uncle to the royal scions. He in turn bore a daughter . . . Elizabeth . . . who provided the second point on the map, as it were. For myself, I am not so well versed in the Plantagenet family tree. My own is enough to keep untangled. And what did you mean a moment ago when you said you were on your way to the convent? What convent?"

"The Holy Sisters of Mary Magdalene. 'Twas where I was bound before I took ill and had to seek shelter in the village. Father Guilford knows the prioress there—they are brother and sister. He assured me she would welcome me and guard my anonymity with her dying breath."

"A family trait, it would seem," he murmured. To answer her frown, he added, "It happened to fall, in the tedium of conversations I had with your husband today, that the priest who had helped his wife escape . . . held up well right to the end."

"To the end? Oh, dear God," she whispered in horror, hastily making the sign of the cross from forehead to breast, shoulder to shoulder. "I did not think he would dare kill a holy father."

"I am under the clear impression he would dare a good deal more to have you back."

"Have me back?" She stood, the weakness in her limbs dissipating with her anger. "Is that what you think? That he is so stricken by affection for me that he wants me back by his side, wife to his needs, chatelaine of his castle, mother to his children? Even if a man could ever love a woman as much as that, Odo de Langois would not be that man. He wants me back, aye. He wants me back so he can kill me, punish me, humiliate me for what I have done. No one . . . surely no one who still walks this earth . . . has ever defied him and lived."

She turned slightly, staring down into the fire, hoping to shield the gleam of tears that flooded her eyes.

Her voice had gone so low that it left Tamberlane with no choice but to lean closer to hear. He could only guess that she was telling him all of this because he was a priest, and priests were supposed to be immune to the sins of the flesh and carnal thoughts of the mind. And somewhere inside him, he was certain he could remain impartial and understanding.

The difficulty came in telling that to his body, which seemed to surge to life every time he came within close proximity to Amaranth. It was a surge he had no control over, nor any explanation for its presence. He had felt it the first time he knelt beside her in the forest, and he felt it now, raw and powerful, as elemental as breathing, thinking . . . needing.

He had prided himself on not needing anything or anyone in his life these past three years of self-imposed exile . . . not even the God to whom he had once vowed his life in service. He had turned his back on that God, just as God had turned His back on the innocents who screamed the name of their God when swords were being hacked and slashed into their flesh.

Perhaps that was what he had seen in Amaranth's eyes that day in the forest. She had forsaken her God too, begging Tamberlane to end it, end the pain, end the misery. How many times had he walked the ramparts willing up the courage to do exactly the same thing?

She tipped her face up, and for a moment, the full measure of her despair and loneliness was suddenly, painfully revealed in her eyes. Watching the firelight play havoc with her hair, her skin, even the soft gleam of her eyes, Tamberlane felt the knot in his gut twisting tighter. He had consumed a vast quantity of ale and wine through the day, trying to temper his dislike of Odo de Langois, and he blamed this for the almost involuntary way his hand trembled and might even have reached out to brush a lock of hair back from Amie's cheek had not a noise from the doorway diverted his attention.

Inaya was back, leading two lackeys burdened under heavy buckets of hot water. A third rolled a hewn barrel into the room and, at the command of a pointed finger, settled it in front of the fire.

"Since even your husband's boldness would not extend to searching my chambers for his errant wife," Tamberlane explained, "Marak thought it safest if you remain sequestered here for the night and, indeed, until our guests depart on the morrow. Inaya will help you bathe, and if there is anything you need or require for your comfort ... ."

"You have been more than overly generous already, my lord. I would have been content with my crust of bread and a bed on the rushes."

Tamberlane was obviously discomfited by the praise and turned away with an unintelligible murmur. He was halfway to the door when the sound of boots on the landing outside stopped him. He could hear Roland's voice protesting over the heavy clumping, and in the split second before he whirled and met Amie's horrified gaze, he heard Odo de Langois's unmistakable bark of laughter.

"Unless your master is wenching, I see no reason why he would not take a last sup of wine with me."

"Good my lord—"

"Out of the way, pup." The door was shoved open and Odo strode into the chamber, his one fist clutched around the neck of an ewer, the other holding two richly tooled silver goblets.

"There you are, Dragon Slayer! My oaf of a squire was finally able to locate the ass that carried my personal service, and look you here . . . a small token of my appreciation for your hospitality."

He brandished the goblets before setting them down, the glare from the fire sending pinpoints of light off the silverwork. As he did, his eyes swept around the chamber, probing into every shadowed corner, lingering longest on the bed.

"I am not interrupting anything, I trust?"

Tamberlane looked behind him, seeing nothing but the fire, the empty bed with its undisturbed coverings, the barrel of water steaming lazily before the fire. His hand uncurled from the hilt of the dagger he wore at his waist, but it did not stray far.

"I was just about to bathe."

"Ah, yes. I'd heard you monks were adamant about cleanliness and godliness. Do not let me disturb you," he added, waving the hand with the ewer. "Partake while the water is hot. I will sit here and regale you with tales of my errant boyhood while your squire stands over me with a sword to ensure I do not stare too long or hard at your bare buttocks."

The crude jest was punctuated with another coarse bark of laughter as Odo spied a chair and indicated by gestures that Roland should drag it closer to the fire. He then filled both goblets to the brim and passed one to Tamberlane. "Your continued good health, sirrah."

Tamberlane accepted the goblet, raised it to his lips, but did not do more than moisten the tip of his tongue with the bold Rhenish plonk. He doubted the wine itself would be tainted with anything, but there was always the possibility of the goblet itself having been rubbed with some tincture. Unwarranted suspicions? Perhaps. But Tamberlane's instincts leaned always toward caution and had rarely led him astray.

Odo de Langois, conversely, emptied his goblet with gusto and indicated the barrel of water with another wave of his hand. "Waste of good hot water, that."

Tamberlane smiled wanly. "I am pleased to share a sup of wine with you, my lord, but I prefer to do my bathing in private."

Odo grunted. "I'll not keep you, then." He poured another measure of wine from the ewer, not troubling to disguise the fact that he was looking with a keen eye into every nook and corner of the large chamber. "Rather plainly furnished for a lion of the desert."

"As I said before, my needs are few."

Odo pursed his lips and strolled casually past the foot of the bed, his eyes searching where the shadows were darkest. He was on the verge of turning back when he spied the two heavy panels of brocade that concealed the prayer niche. As he watched . . . and as Tamberlane noted with a small grinding of his teeth . . . one of the panels shifted slightly, a jerky movement not caused by any draft in the still air of the room.

"I have known some Templars over the years," Odo said, taking a step toward the niche. "They drape themselves in the mantle of poverty yet those

mantles are of the finest silk. They drink from gold
vessels, and their walls are adorned with trophies
from the glorious battles they have fought in the
name of their God. They are bigger moneylenders
than the Jews and do so with full impunity, paying
no scutage to the crown, believing they are bound
only to the church to answer for their actions."

"If you are attempting to convince me to make my
penance and rejoin the Order, my lord, your argu-
ments are poorly vested."

There was the faintest hint of a warning threaded
through Tamberlane's words, and de Langois crooked
his head slightly by way of acknowledging it.

"I am merely pointing out that flying in the face
of the king's law might become second nature to a
man accustomed to answering only to God. The laws
pertaining to chattel and marriage, for instance,
might be set aside in exchange for a tear and a mew-
ling plea for *sanctuary*."

As he said the word *sanctuary*, he reached out and
yanked one of the brocade panels aside. He was
broad enough across the shoulders to block the inside
of the niche from Tamberlane's view, but there was
no mistaking the shock in his voice as he stared at
the figure huddled against the wall.

"What manner of devilry is this?"

Tamberlane glanced over at the far wall where his
sword belt hung from a wooden peg. Ten long paces
would carry him there—nine too many if Odo de
Langois reached up and snatched the jeweled sword
out of the prayer niche.

Ciaran's long fingers caressed the dagger again, and he slipped it out of the sheath, concealing the hilt in his palm and the steel against his forearm.

"Come out of there, woman," Odo said with a snarl, his back to Tamberlane. "Come out into the light."

Tamberlane was halfway confident that Amaranth, with her hair sheared and darkened and wearing urchin's clothes, could fool a guardsman at twenty paces. But up close, with those searing blue eyes and soft, bow-shaped lips, she would not deceive a blood-hawk like Odo de Langois longer than it took him to blink.

"All the way into the light, damn you. By God, Tamberlane, you're a sly bustard." Odo turned at the same moment Inaya stepped out from behind the shadow of his broad frame, her sari loosened and draped half off one shoulder. Her head was bowed, and her black hair spilled unbound over the side of her face that bore the scar, covering it.

Odo glared across the room at the excommunicated Knight Templar and gave out a bark of crude laughter. "Acquired a taste for Saracen nectar while you were on Crusade, did you, my lord?"

He threw his head back and laughed, the sound continuing as he walked back across the room. After draining his goblet, he slammed it down on the small table and gave one last resounding roar of laughter before he walked out the door and descended the spiral stairs.

For a full minute, no one moved. Roland, the last to arrive, stood staring, his gaze flicking between his master and Inaya. Inaya began to slowly restore her clothing and gather her hair back into the sleek knot she wore at the nape of her neck. Tamberlane crossed to the prayer niche and brushed the second panel aside, but there was no sign of Amaranth. Nor would he have thought to look down until he heard a faint scuffling sound from beneath the draped altar cloth.

Lifting a corner, he saw a pale russet curl, then a large blue eye peering up at him. How she had folded herself so impossibly small as to fit under the altar was beyond his comprehension at the moment, but he lifted the cloth higher and moved to one side as she painstakingly inched her way out and stood trembling before him.

In the next instant, she was leaning forward, almost crumpling, her arms reaching out, circling his waist. Her head was buried against his chest, and soft gasps that were trying desperately not to be sobs were muffled by his tunic.

Tamberlane's arms remained awkwardly by his sides. Inaya was busy twisting and knotting her hair and would not meet his eye. Roland had been dispatched out the door to ensure that Odo was not hovering on the landing.

Ciaran's hands flexed, the fingers curling and uncurling with an unsteadiness that was as foreign to him as the slender warmth of a woman in his arms. Those selfsame instincts that had always leaned toward caution now brought his arms slowly forward, sent his head bowing down, and bade him press his cheek into the tousled mop of soft curls, holding her with all the tenderness at his command.

Chapter Twelve

Amie lay in the dark, listening to the sound of her heart beating in her ears. It was a very distinct *thud*, now slow, now fast, dependant upon which memory of the day's events was spinning through her mind. The fastest *thud*s, those over which she had no control, occurred when she thought of how close she had come to being discovered in the prayer niche. The cloth draped over the stone pillars had been sheer enough that she had seen Odo de Langois's splayed legs and the firelight shining between them. She had expected at any moment to see the linen snatched away and her arm grabbed, to be hauled out into the open and thrown halfway across the floor.

The thumping of her heart slowed measurably when she remembered the look of surprise on Tamberlane's face. He had stood in the same place as Odo, only when he lifted the cloth, he did so gingerly, the disbelief and surprise etched clearly on his face. Amie could not have said what had sent her tumbling into his arms afterward, but it was this memory, this unaccustomed sense of feeling safe in his embrace, that periodically slowed her heart to soft, curiously mellow *thuds*.

She lifted her head and searched the shadowy expanse of the chamber. The night candle was burning excruciatingly slow. She could swear the wax had not melted at all the last few times she had checked, and there were still several lines to burn through before the hour of Prime. She was lying in Tamberlane's bed. Inaya was sleeping on a pallet beside the bed, and the warrior monk was seated in a wide X-chair placed before the fire, one long leg stretched out, the other bent at the knee. He had been there the last time Amie had looked, and the time before that . . . He had his head cradled in his hand, and were it not for the glitter of the flames reflecting pinpoints of light in his eyes, she might have thought he was fast asleep.

Beside him, within arm's reach, was his sword. Roland, she knew, was keeping vigil in the small antechamber outside the door. Tamberlane had assured her she would be safe here for the night, and she had no reason to disbelieve him.

"You should be trying to sleep, my lady."

His voice came out of nowhere, causing a pulse to jump in her throat. He hadn't turned, hadn't looked, and the movement she made had been minuscule at best.

Amie sighed and sat up. She wrapped her arms around her knees and hugged them to her chest, her gaze drawn to the bright orange flames licking across the fire log. "How can I sleep knowing he is under the same roof?"

Tamberlane shifted just enough to slant a glance down the length of the bed. "He would not dare intrude upon my chamber again. Once, he could blame on the amount of wine he consumed; twice, he knows I would run him through."

"Do you think he believes I am not here?"

"We will know come morning. If he bids farewell and leaves without turning back to look over his shoulder, then he is leaving to search elsewhere for you. If he looks back, it will mean he thinks you are here somewhere—he simply has not been able to find you yet."

"Either way, I—I must leave this place, Lord Tamberlane. I must. Certes, you can understand that now."

"He does seem quite determined to find you."

Amie stared into the fire and clasped her arms tighter to her knees. Earlier, while Tamberlane had waited out on the landing, she had bathed the dirt and lingering stench from her skin. The mud had been washed out of her hair and with the ends turning naturally upward as they dried, her face was now surrounded with a soft cloud of glossy curls. She was not used to the absence of weight yet and ran her fingers frequently through the waves, a recurring gesture that sent spikes and whorls standing upright on one side of her face or the other.

"You have not yet asked me if I was out picking toadstools the day my first husband died."

"It is not my place to ask, nor is it necessary for me to know."

She was silent for a long moment . . . a moment in which he turned his head to look directly at her. "But if you wish to tell me, do so with the knowledge that nothing you say to me is safeguarded by the sanctity of the church. I am more man than monk and no longer have the power to cleanse any sins that may burden your soul. Indeed, my own sins have yet to be fully expunged in the eyes of the Holy See. In short, Amaranth, if it is the solace and affirmation of a confessor you seek, you would do best to seek it elsewhere."

He had used her name without conscious thought, and by all sense of logic and common sense it should not have sent such a strong flutter down Amie's spine. But it did. He spoke with a faint tilt to some of his words, one that suggested he had spent many years in foreign lands exposed to the heat of the sun and the dust of a hundred deserts. Amie had heard him speak to Inaya in her own language, and to Marak in yet another. He had addressed her in Saxon English when he thought she was a peasant girl but had recently reverted to the Norman French that was spoken by the nobility.

There was something else in his voice tonight—a blurred, mildly bitter edge to the words that made Amie glance to the hearth beside him where a stone crock of wine caught the flickering light from the fire. In his far hand was one of the goblets Odo de Langois had presented him as a gift. It was held carelessly in limp fingers, the stem hanging down at an angle, the bowl tipped enough to allow that it was empty.

Amie felt the chill of a fist tightening inside her chest. Her first husband, Lord Eglund, had always been cruelest when drinking. The wine sharpened his tongue, turned his words to daggers. It hardened his body and made her own go tense with apprehension.

Yet she saw nothing of the beast in Tamberlane. His dark hair was fallen over his brow in a silky wave, and his face looked somehow softer, as if a decade of deeply etched lines and angles had been erased. There was no threat in the way he held his body. It was slumped in the chair like a doll made of knotted rags, arms and legs gingerly propped by good intentions, the head slightly canted to one side, the hard green gaze gentled by the shadows.

"I do not seek to make my confession," she said carefully. "Not for the sin of murdering husbands, at any rate, for it seemed that I was not the only one Lord Eglund sought to favor with his filthy appetites. A week before he died of poison, the cook's daughter—only eleven years of age—bled to death from a brutal rape.

"As to my other sins," she added with a heartfelt sigh, "I fear they are still ongoing."

He arched the black wing of an eyebrow. "Other sins?"

"Vanity, pride, foolishness, recklessness . . ."

"Ah, yes. All punishable by several score of paternosters and a solid regiment of seeking forgiveness on bended knees."

"You speak lightly of such things," she said softly. "But I saw—"

When she bit her tongue to halt the words, he looked directly at her. "Yes, you saw . . . What did you see?"

She assumed he was expecting her to recount some horror she remembered from the attack on the village. But she was thinking of earlier, when she had been in his arms, her face buried against his throat. Her hand had been spread flat on his chest, and her fingertips had detected an unmistakable prickle under his tunic. She recognized the scratchy bulk of it at once, having seen poor Friar Guilford's expression of quiet agony one hot afternoon when he had worn a horsehair shirt beneath his robes to atone for some petty sin he had committed.

It seemed at once unwise to mention it to Tamberlane, and so she glanced instead at the prayer niche. "You keep an altar in your room. You display your Crusader's mantle and sword, the reliquary with the precious fragment of Christ's cross."

The crooked smile that had been playing across his lips faded. "It serves as a reminder, nothing more."

He turned away and exhaled a full lungful of air, then, as if his gaze had just now fallen on it, he spied the crock of wine and struggled to straighten himself in an effort to reach it.

Amie cast aside the heavy blankets and swung her legs over the edge of the bed. She was modestly clothed, having donned a shapeless garment that Inaya had given her for sleeping. The sleeves were bell-shaped and overlong, and the hem dragged behind her on the floor as she hastened to the hearth, but the bodice was high and loose enough to conceal all that lay beneath.

She stooped down to pick up the jug and held it in both hands for the ten full seconds it took for Tamberlane to hold out his goblet. She poured slowly, carefully, the stream of red wine catching the light from the fire and rippling amber. When the goblet was nearly full, she straightened, set the jug aside again, and, wanting to cover her further nervousness, fetched a new log from the iron bib and set it carefully on the flaming embers.

Tamberlane raised the goblet and touched the rim to his lower lip as Amaranth stood and brushed the bits of wood and dirt from her hands. She was standing between the fire and the chair, and as the bark on the dry wood caught and flamed, the light glowed through her sheath, reducing the cloth to gauze. She stood with her legs slightly apart, and there was no mistaking the distinct, soft shape of her thighs. Her waist dipped above slender hips, then flared again where her breasts swelled round and young and full above.

His gaze climbed higher, to a face that was half turned into the light. As he had so many times before, he found himself holding his breath, not daring to acknowledge even through his own inner voice how sweet a face she had, how delicate the shape of her chin, her nose. The cropped hair only added to the cherubic quality, and he surrendered, howsoever involuntarily, to the most unholy thought of wondering how it would feel to run his fingertips along her cheek, across the shape of her mouth.

In his mind's eye, he lowered his lips to hers and explored those same contours. He caught her about the waist and pulled her up hard against him, tasting her, feeling her, drinking in the sweetness of her womanhood.

A cinder snapped in the fire.

He took a deep swallow of the wine and set the goblet aside. Pushing to his feet, he mumbled something about the heat becoming oppressive and started across the room toward the stairs that led up to the roof.

"Oh, please," she said at his back, "may I come with you? I would take a breath of fresh air as well."

"There was rain earlier. It will be damp."

"A moment only," she pleaded.

Tamberlane paused just inside the shadowy stairwell. He watched her return to the bed to peel away the top blanket, and while she did so, he leaned his forehead against the cold stone. His chest and back were a mass of raw, abraded nerve endings from wearing the coarse horsehair shirt all blessed day long. His hands trembled if he did not keep them clenched into fists, and his mind had wandered to the bed more often than he thought possible during the night, regardless how much wine he consumed.

He needed air.

The heat and smoke from the fire were smothering him.

Without waiting for Amie to join him, he took the

narrow stairs two at a time and flung himself out into the night with an audible gasp. The wind was gusting strong over the parapets and snatched at his hair, pushing it back off his brow. The smell of dampness was thick in the air; the rain had stopped, but the roof was dotted with puddles that reflected light from the emerging moon.

Tamberlane walked over to the wall and pressed his hands flat on the wet stone. There were more sentries than usual patrolling the outer walls, more torches burning in the inner and outer wards. The brightest blots of light were around the stables and main gate. The portcullis had not been lowered—to do so would have been an insult de Langois could not have ignored. But there was a strong presence of Taniere guardsmen walking back and forth across the draw, sworded and armored, watched by more men in the barbicans.

Taniere Castle was no fortress by any measure, but it was defendable. The only real vulnerability was the drawbridge and gate when both were open, and that weakness could be sealed with a moment's notice.

Not that he thought for a moment that Odo de Langois would order an assault of any kind while he was within the walls and his men were outside. Tamberlane had been around fighting men most of his adult life, and he recognized a dangerous adversary in the red-haired baron . . . one who would wait, bide his time until all the advantages were in his favor. Doubtless he would know by now the exact fighting strength of the meager garrison. He would have charted the walls, the baileys, the approaches in his mind. He would have already ruled out a frontal attack of any kind and would be curious to know if there was any other way in or out of the castle.

Amie came up behind him as Ciaran was looking out through one of the merlons. She had the blanket drawn close around her shoulders and snatches of the wind made the bottom bell out around her legs. She looked out over the same view as Tamberlane, but she was seeing the endless stretch of black forest that surrounded them, the glittering water of the lake that hemmed them in on three sides. Above them, the last lacy shreds of cloud were scudding toward the southern horizon, and the moon had broken through, the sky around it pale blue leading to deeper shades of darkest indigo and purple. The light was faint but gave shape to the village on the far bank. Odo's men had made use of the empty cottages to stay out of the rain, but she could see the occasional pale gray blur moving around the perimeter.

"There was a storm soon after we escaped from Belmane," she said softly. "It plagued us for a full day, and the next morning, I woke with a fever. God's way, perhaps, of telling me I should have stayed and taken my fair punishment. If I had, all of those innocent people would not have died. Friar Guilford himself would not have died."

"Innocent people die every day to feed the greed and the blind ignorance of others. You cannot let what happened at the village weigh you down, for the guilt is not yours to bear. Your actions were not dictated by rashness but by fear for your own life."

"And that justifies it?"

"No. But it allows you room to forgive yourself."

She shook her head. "I will never forgive myself. Never."

"People are burdened by far more guilt than you bear, Amaranth, and they cannot believe the pain will ever fade. Yet it does. They find a way to bear it."

"By wearing a horsehair shirt?"

Tamberlane's head turned slowly, and his eyes were painstakingly slow in rising to meet hers.

"I felt it," she said quietly. "Earlier."

He smiled faintly, almost sadly. "My sins would make yours seem petty by comparison."

"Is that why you have cloistered yourself away in this castle like a—a . . ." She waved her hand, searching for an appropriate word.

"Like a monk?"

She sighed as she looked at him. "You said yourself you were more man now than monk. You should set aside your monkish ways."

Was it deliberate? he wondered. Was she deliberately testing his limits? The image of her set against the firelight was still scorched on his mind—now she was adding the soft tease of moonlight.

Her mouth kept drawing his stare like a magnet. Moreover, it seemed indecent that hair should curl so softly over such a sweet brow or that eyes should possess such a shine as to render a man bereft of speech. Nay, bereft of the ability to even form speech. His heart began to pound strangely. The palms of his hands grew damp, and he held them in fists . . .

but that was no help. Nor did the pain caused by pressing the knuckles into the stone leave him feeling any less desirous of gathering her into his arms and kissing her until neither of them had the sense or wit left to fight it.

Amie was not entirely aware of what had caused the sudden tension in the air between them, she only knew it was not there one moment, and in the next, it was. The night sky, the forest, the moonlight . . . they all seemed to fade, to withdraw far into the background. It was as if she and this dark brooding knight stood at the end of a tunnel and there was nothing to distract them. Her mouth went dry but another part of her body reacted the opposite way, and she gasped softly into the night air, wanting desperately to press her thighs tightly together.

"You are shivering," he said. "You should go back inside."

But the shiver went far deeper than he could see. It began on the outside, with her skin tightening as thousands of tiny pinpricks of icy mist poured down her spine. Once there, it formed a shimmering pool of sensations that flooded her limbs, her belly. It rippled the length and breadth of her body, causing her knees to tremble from the strength of the rushing heat.

She turned and managed to take a halting step back toward the portal before Tamberlane's arm stretched out to block her path. He stopped just short of touching her, and it was Amie who leaned forward with a soundless sigh and welcomed the contact. His hand curved around her waist, and as long as it took him to look away from the battlements and focus on her face, it took Amie twice as long to send her gaze climbing slowly up his arm to his shoulder . . . then up from his shoulder to the square ridge of his jaw. By that time, he had bent his head lower, had pulled her closer so that their breaths mingled in soft white puffs on the cooler air.

"Go inside," he murmured, his lips brushing against her hair. "Before I am tempted to commit a sin that neither one of us could scrub away with mere horsehair."

Amie shivered again. The throbbing between her thighs was very real, commanding every thought that was not already held hostage by his voice, the feel of his hand on her waist. Each pulse beat was so strong it verged on pain, the ache so near to pleasure she knew the smallest touch of his lips would have her melting onto her knees.

Throughout the long months of her marriage to Sir Eglund, she had never once experienced desire or passion. She had endured. She had suffered his gropings and thrustings, but she had turned her mind into a blank wall that nothing could break through, not even the pain of the lashings.

But this . . . this overwhelming tenderness was shockingly new to her. As new as the longings, the tension, the knowledge that she was not dead inside. That she was indeed capable of responding to a man's hunger.

"If you wish it, my lord," she whispered. "I shall return."

Ciaran's lips parted. He made a sound, deep in his

throat, and from whence he found the will to move away he would never know. But he did. He turned his broad back to her and stared out over the parapets, closing his eyes against the sound of her blanket dragging across the roof as she moved away.

Chapter Thirteen

Tamberlane did not come back down into the solar that night, and Amaranth surprised herself by falling fast asleep. When she awakened, Inaya was already gone and the pallet hidden away under the bed. Amie climbed gingerly out from beneath the heavy covers and padded barefoot to the garderobe; when she was finished using the privy, she stood by the fire a long moment, rubbing her hands in the heat of the flames.

She was still not altogether certain what had happened last night. Had Lord Tamberlane been about to kiss her? Had he wanted to? Had she wanted him to? The thought was as foreign as the notion that she might actually crave the touch and warmth of another man. A monk, no less. A priest. Defrocked or not—and here her gaze stole toward the prayer niche that seemed to blaze white from the purity of the crusader's mantle—he was still a man who had devoted most of his life to God.

A sound from the outer landing startled her back

toward the bed, but it was only Inaya with little Jibril in tow, his huge eyes peering out from behind his mother's skirts. His hand was clutched tightly around a fistful of the silk as if he had no intention of ever letting go again. Before Amie could wonder where the little boy had spent the night, Marak was coming through the doorway bearing a stoneware bowl steaming with one of his infernal possets.

"You might be relieved to know that Lord Tamberlane is escorting your husband and his men to the outer bailey. They are fed and refreshed, profuse in their thanks for our hospitality, and vowing to remove themselves from our forest within the hour."

"He is leaving? Odo is leaving?"

"So it would seem."

Amie whirled around and ran up the steps to the rooftop. She sought out the same merlon where she and Tamberlane had stood during the night and was peering anxiously through the gap in the wide stone teeth when Marak moved up beside her.

"You wished to wave a fond farewell?" he asked dryly.

"I want to see if he looks back."

"If . . . he looks back?"

She shook her head, too intent on peering below to offer explanations. The ground was covered by a thin blanket of mist, a milky haze that rose no more than knee-deep and swirled apart in creamy waves wherever someone cut through it. There were still puddles in the courtyard below, mud on the path that led across the outer bailey to the enormous barbican gates. She saw Lord Tamberlane at once, his

broad shoulders encased in hunters green. Odo de
Langois stood by his side waiting for the hostlers to
bring their horses from the stables. He held his
gauntlets in one hand, slapping the leather fingers
on the palm of the other, seeming to be chatting
about things of little or no consequence. His brother
Rolf stood slightly behind, his eyes still roving the
walls, the arched bridge in the curtain wall, the well
where half a dozen women were already gathered
and squabbling like geese.

The other four men, including Odo's cousin, were
standing at ease behind her husband, one digging for
something in his nose, another adjusting a buckle on
his chain mail hauberk.

With the exception of Rolf, who seemed incapable
of looking relaxed, the others appeared not to have
a concern in the world. There were no furtive
glances, no knowing exchanges. Odo's laughter was
genuine as he clapped a hand to Tamberlane's shoulder and thanked him once again for his generosity.
While the knights mounted their horses, Tamberlane
stood to one side, the weak morning light making
his hair gleam blue-black. Odo's was fiery red by
contrast, and since he rode away without troubling
to don his helm, he was easy to follow through the
inner ward, beneath the arch, and across the outer
ward to the gates. There was only a brief span
wherein he was not visible as they rode across the
draw.

Once on shore, the six horsemen were joined by
the crossbowmen and men-at-arms who had been
waiting and fell easily into step behind them,

marching down the muddy lane. Two by two they disappeared into the darker mists that blurred the forest, and not once did Odo turn to look back. Not a single sparing glance was wasted on the tranquil beauty of the lake or the sheer gray stone of the castle walls behind him.

When the last crossbowman tramped out of sight, Amaranth breathed a long, slow sigh of relief. He had not looked back. If Tamberlane's quiet assurances were to be believed, it meant that Odo was convinced his errant wife was not within the walls of Taniere Castle.

Marak was watching her face with interest. "Is that a smile I see?"

She turned to look at him. Was she smiling? She couldn't tell. Her whole body felt at once numb and weightless. The tightness was gone from her chest. The sense of dread that had hung over her since waking on a table in Marak's chamber was gone, howsoever briefly, and she felt as if she could breathe deep again and fill her lungs to bursting with the damp crisp air.

Yes, she was smiling, and the change it wrought in her face was almost as startling as the prolonged growl that came from her stomach.

Marak laughed. "Methinks the lady has found her appetite again. Indeed, I believe there are still some scraps of food left on the boards if you would care to partake. The posset first, of course. I left it back in the solar, not wanting to hinder my hands if you had taken the thought to leap from the walls."

Amie smiled again. "Your possets taste like the

stewed underbellies of garden slugs, good sir, but I shall tip it happily."

"And . . . you would be acquainted with the taste of stewed underbellies?"

"My uncle's table was notoriously ill prepared."

Marak laughed again and extended an arm. After staring at it a moment, her smile took on a wistful tilt, and she delicately placed her fingertips upon his wrist, allowing herself to be escorted back through the low-slung portal.

Under the healer's stern eye, she drank the horrid posset as quickly as her throat would allow, then stood lacking all patience while Inaya drew a tunic over her head and laced it at the waist and throat. It felt odd not having to sit and have her hair brushed and plaited, but she was happy being able to join Marak out on the landing and accompany him down the winding stairs. The great hall looked much as it had the previous day, with few men seated at the boards and smoke rising from the cooking fires at the far end. There was no one seated at the dais; Tamberlane had not yet returned from the bailey.

When Marak pointed to one of the seats beside the lord's enormous chair, Amie hesitated a moment then gave her head a little shake and chose to sit instead at one of the trestle tables. She was careful not to sit too close to the dais and deliberately took a seat on the bench well below the saltcellar.

Some of the men gave her glances, but she assumed it was because Marak took a seat beside her. Lackeys rushed up at once bearing platters of food for the castle seneschal—hard cheese, bread, a whole roasted fowl sitting on a bed of boiled onions. Amaranth was ravenous and did not stand on ceremony, reaching with bare fingers to tear the meat from the bone and break off thick chunks of the yellow cheese. Marak ate sparingly, more amused to watch her eat than to interrupt her with conversation.

"The shoulder seems to be mending well," he remarked at one point.

She glanced ruefully at the breast of fowl she had just torn from the carcass. It was true. Her strength was returning hour by hour, it seemed. There was still a painful tug in the muscles to remind her they had been recently torn asunder, but the moment she had watched her husband ride away into the mist, the pain had become of little consequence. She could even, when she caught sight of Tamberlane entering the great hall, look upon him without remembering the feelings that had rippled through her after leaving him on the rooftop—or at least, she could regard him with a calmer eye.

He stood on the stone landing for several moments, and as his gaze scanned the enormous chamber, Amie was again struck by the quiet authority of his presence. Even if she had not been told who he was or how he had earned his reputation, she would have known he was a slayer of dragons, a man equal to fight at the right-hand side of Richard, Coeur de Lion.

At the moment, he looked like he wanted to slay more than just dragons, for his expression was as black as his hair. He spied Marak first, then his eyes shifted next to him on the bench and held Amie's.

She sat frozen for the few moments it took for his long legs to carry him down the stairs, and when she realized he was walking to where she sat, she pushed to her feet and stepped quickly out from behind the bench.

"You insult yourself and me by sitting here," he said softly, without ado. "Your idea, Marak?"

"I merely followed where she led, and as it happens, I thought she chose wisely." Marak tipped his head and glanced pointedly at the dais.

Tamberlane followed his glance. The clusters of candles, wall sconces, and tall, spidery iron candelabra were concentrated to shed the brightest light on the dais, presenting it like an altar. With the rest of the chamber in heavier shadow, anyone sitting there would have drawn the eye, especially if that someone had short coppery hair and the face of a cherub. While Odo de Langois may have ridden away from Taniere Castle, he had drawn his own fair share of attention in the court by announcing a reward of one hundred gold sovereigns to anyone bringing him news of his wife's whereabouts.

One hundred gold sovereigns was ten lifetimes' fortune to common villagers and soldiers, and it was doubtful that even their fear of the Dragon Slayer and his wizard would temper their greed.

"We have matters of some importance to discuss," Tamberlane murmured, smiling for the benefit of anyone who was showing interest. "But not here. You are right, there are too many ears about. Nor should the three of us depart together, for eyes would surely follow, and curiosity would be roused."

Marak wiped his hands unhurriedly and stood. "I will take Amaranth to my solar and await you there."

Tamberlane nodded, but instead of walking directly back to the dais, he paused further on to engage another pair of knights in amiable conversation.

When he judged enough time had passed, Marak led Amaranth toward the far end of the great hall and the narrow stone corridor that led to his tower rooms. Once inside the musty, dark chamber, he left her standing by the door while he lit a taper and touched it to several candles. Over each of these, he placed a long glass tube that was tinted in such a way as to allow the light to shine through but softened the piercing yellow eye of the flame.

Amie had not been back to the chamber since being moved to the west tower. She looked around, her gaze touching on the shelves with their bottles and pots, the long oaken bink littered with the implements of an alchemist—strange objects for which she could not even guess the function. A mortar and pestle she recognized, but little else. When her curiosity flickered across to the room, she noted that the table upon which she had lain for so many pain-filled days now held books and papers, assorted quills, brushes, and pots of ink.

Walking closer, she caught sight of writing on the top of one page, the Latin words set down in bold black ink: PRAXIS MAGICA.

Beneath this was an illuminated, ornate drawing of a circle with four arrows pointing outward to four strange symbols. Between each symbol was another, and the whole was encased in a ring that held other symbols and odd lettering around the circumference. Below the drawing were words unfamiliar to Amaranth, though she supposed they might be in any language other than Latin. The first letter of each word was highly stylized and illuminated in inks of gold and red and blue.

Her eye was caught by the dull gleam of metal, and Amie nudged aside a sheet of parchment to run her fingertips over a round medallion. The depiction on the front was the same as the one on the paper—identical, in fact, and she was tipping it to the light to examine it more closely when Marak came up beside her.

"Peasants are simple people," he said. "They wish to believe in magic, and therefore are willing—nay, even eager—to attribute all manner of wondrous things to amulets, medallions . . . even vials containing water scraped from the nearest pond and proclaimed to be the bile of Christ. That particular medallion, for instance, when worn over the breast, gives the owner immunity from all manner of ferocious animals. It also gives the one who possesses it knowledge of their secret language, and, when certain words are invoked, drives maddened beasts away in terrible fear. To ensure proper potency, it must be fastened about the neck on a ribbon of red silk and worn in conjunction with this—" He leaned over and picked up a ring, the head flat and square, engraved with a pattern of double Xs. "I made it for the village smithy, a man of copious strength and body size who freezes and turns as gray as ash when he comes upon a squirrel in the forest.

"And then there is this one," he continued, turning the pages in the large volume until he came across another beautifully illuminated depiction of a talisman. "It has the power to call down hail and thunder from the skies, to occasion storms, high winds, and so forth. Or this—" He turned to a random page and tapped it thoughtfully with a forefinger. The picture was of an elongated octagon with the head of a unicorn in the center ring, surrounded by more symbols and mystic lettering. "Ah, yes . . . this one claims to make the most taciturn man unburden his soul to the one who possesses it. By laying one's hand flat over the talisman and encompassing it in the palm thus"— he took Amaranth's hand and placed it over the drawing—"and pronouncing the words *noctar . . .*"

He looked at her expectantly and tipped his head, waiting until she whispered, "Noctar."

"*Rathban . . .*"

"Rathban."

"And *sunandam . . .*"

She started to pull her hand away with a small shake of her head, but Marak held it fast. When her gaze lifted to his, the light from one of the hooded candles was reflected as a tiny, bright point in each eye, the effect unnerving enough to make it impossible for her to look away.

"*Sunandam,*" he repeated quietly.

"Sunandam."

Whether it was her imagination or the effect of his eyes burning into her, Amie felt the parchment grow warm beneath the palm of her hand. The heat spread up her arm and prickled across her chest, rising even up the back of her neck and making her lips part with surprise.

He smiled, and the grip on her hand eased. "Now, even the most stubborn man in your acquaintance will be compelled to unveil his secret thoughts and longings to you."

"But it is only a picture of the charm, not the talisman itself."

Marak's hand, which had also seemed to grow inordinately warm, lifted off hers. "Nine tenths of what may be perceived as magic is dependent upon what is in the mind, not the hand."

"I prefer to believe what I can feel and touch." She hesitated and looked up into his eyes again. "Which leads me to wonder, however, if you have a charm for finding lost things?"

"You have lost something?"

Her hand crept up to her throat. "I have no idea where I may have lost it. I remember having it in the village, but . . ."

A different kind of light came into Marak's eyes, and he held up a hand. "Of course, how thoughtless of me."

He went back to the long worktable and opened a small carved box. Amie caught the glint of metal, and when he returned, he carried a crucifix, the face clean and polished like newly minted silver. He placed it in her hand. The edges were delicately filigreed, the cross itself thick and of a substantial weight. Far more weighty than her own thin crucifix.

"It is beautiful," she said, "but it is not mine."

Marak took the cross out of her hand, flicked a small, hidden catch with a thumbnail, and opened the outer casing to reveal a second cross encapsulated within.

"The one you wore bears the device of the Plantagenets," he explained. "You could run as far as the land of elephants and saffron, yet one glance at the cross would betray your royal lineage."

"The cross belonged to my grandfather. 'Twas the only thing passed to my father upon his birth, and in turn to me, and I value it above all else."

"Even your life?"

"If need be, yes."

Marak moved his hand over hers and closed the front of the outer casing again. "Then look upon it whenever you feel the need, my lady, but while you wear it, wear it safely."

The worn leather thong that had held the cross around her neck had been replaced by a fine chain of metal links. They felt cold against her neck, as did the heavy crucifix when she slipped it beneath her bodice. It slid down between her breasts, the metal warming in short order from contact with her skin.

"You have been very kind to me," she said, chewing pensively on her lower lip. "You and Lord Tamberlane both."

"We are not nearly as fearsome as the rumors would make us out to be. Not unless provoked, of course. Then I would but say a few words, scatter my wrath upon the flames, and—" He extended his hand in a quick motion, passing it over one of the hooded candles. Almost instantly the flame shot up above the glass rim with a great *whoosh* and flares of sparks, giving off a great white cloud of smoke.

Amie jumped back, landing squarely against the solid wall of Tamberlane's chest. He put up his hands to catch her upper arms and steady her, but that only startled her more, making her twist away and scramble to one side.

Their eyes met and held. Long enough for both of them to recall a more deliberate touch made under the moonlight.

"Pay no heed to the Venetian's tricks," Ciaran murmured. "Show fear or awe and you only encourage him."

"Tricks?" Marak protested. "You offend me."

"You would be offended, old friend, by nothing less than a truncheon."

Marak waved a hand as if casting an insouciant spell over the knight. "You said there were matters of importance to discuss?"

Tamberlane looked at Amie again. "I am come reluctantly to your way of thinking, my lady. Your husband will not be easily dissuaded from his search. He is convinced you were in the village, is certain you live still, and is determined to recapture you if only to have the pleasure of killing you by his own hand."

Amaranth paled somewhat at the bluntness, but it was Marak who offered comment.

"Ciaran, you might have softened your words a measure or two."

"Why? She knows he does not want her back in order to lavish her with kindness."

"Even so—"

"No," Amie said. "My lord Tamberlane has not said anything contrary to what I know to be the truth."

Tamberlane nodded, quietly admiring her candor. "This convent to which you were bound?"

"The Holy Sisters of Mary Magdalene."

"Tell me again why your Friar Guilford thought it would be the safest place to hide you?"

Amie clasped her hands together in front, lacing her fingers tightly. "The prioress is his sister—his natural sister. He claimed that no meaner shrew walks the face of the earth but that her devotion to God and her adherence to the laws of sanctuary are inviolate. Even the prince regent has no power over her, for she is adamant in her loyalty to King Richard. He also said . . . though it was but a whispered rumor and I think it mortified him to repeat it . . . that she took the vows herself in order to remain loyal in body and spirit to the king's bishop, Hubert Walter. That she had a great love for him and would sooner take the veil than enter into a marriage with another man.

"What is more," she added, "the convent itself is on the coast with easy access to the Channel and escape to Brittany if it became a necessity."

"And is it still your wish to go there?"

Amaranth hesitated for the first time since leaving Belmane Castle. It was not so much that she was suddenly adverse to the idea of spending her remaining days cloistered behind the cold stone walls of an abbey—a month ago she could not have envisioned a more perfect refuge. She could not even say, or think, what made her hesitate now, but she squeezed her fingers tighter and nodded.

"I can see no other choice readily at hand."

Tamberlane seemed to stare at her mouth a long time before he finally nodded. "Then that is where you shall go. I will take you there myself." He glanced at Marak. "If you have any spells or talismans to ensure a safe journey, I suggest you chant your words now, for we leave tonight, before moonrise. No doubt Odo de Langois has left someone behind to keep a keen eye on the gates, so we will leave by way of the catacombs. Be ready," he said to Amie. "Take only what you can comfortably carry. I have already given Roland instructions to select four of our finest foresters to accompany us. Their talents as huntsmen and trackers should hold us in better stead than amulets and spells for making our way halfway across the forests of England."

Chapter Fourteen

Amaranth paced a good many hours away waiting for midnight to arrive. She prowled a path from the door to the bed to the window to the hearth and back to the door. Each time she neared the door, she stopped and listened, hoping to hear the scrape of footsteps on the landing. Each time she passed the window, she paused to listen to the rush of the wind outside. At the hearth she stood a moment to contemplate the glowing embers, wondering if she should add another log or let it die out completely.

She had been alone for more than three hours . . . nearer four by the lines on the candle. Tamberlane had said they would be leaving before moonrise, but he had neglected to add anything beyond a vague mention of midnight. He had also given her orders to sleep, but that was impossible. Marak had sent one of his possets, but for once, she had taken a sip then spilled the rest down the garderobe. Her stomach was roiling enough without adding the taste of slug underbellies.

At one point, and with much hesitation beforehand, she knelt beside the bed and clasped her hands beneath her chin. She had no idea if God listened to the pleas of disobedient wives and would-be murderesses, but she thought it could do no harm to try. The prayers, said by rote for nigh on eighteen years, stuck at the back of her throat and would not come forth. Words, phrases she knew by heart failed her, and she squeezed her hands so tightly around the silver crucifix that the edges left imprinted patterns on her fingers.

The attempt to gain solace failed, and the next time she paced the room, she did not stop at the door but went out and stood on the landing, her heart pounding at the base of her throat. The stairs were in darkness but for a pale bloom of light showing around the lower curve of the spiral. It was enough to give her feet surety as she hastened down the stairs, and once at the bottom, she was guided along the corridor by the torches that flickered in their wall sconces high on the walls.

She approached the end of the corridor on softly set feet and peered around the stone block corner with one wary eye. The great hall seemed even gloomier than ever, with the candles unlit behind the dais and no one seated at the boards eating or drinking.

Amie curled her lower lip between her teeth and inched forward until she had the entire room in sight. There were men rolled in blankets sleeping on the floor in front of the fire. Dogs were still active, rooting around in the rushes for scraps of meat or bone that might have fallen under the boards. It was quiet but for the snores and the occasional snap of a bone clenched in a canine jaw.

Amaranth edged farther around the corner, keeping her back pressed to the cold blocks. Her eyes were as wide and round as they could be, flicking warily side to side as she tried to watch all corners of the vast room for any signs of movement. Slowly she moved on soundless feet across the breadth of the dais, then down the far stairs. She was not sure why she knew Marak would be in his tower rooms; she only knew she could not spend one additional minute on her own, just waiting.

Keeping to the heaviest shadows, she hurried along the length of the great hall. She had her head down, her gaze turned to the sleeping bodies, and thus did not see the guardsman until he stepped out of a darkened niche so close in front of her that she nearly slammed into him.

"Frothing Jesus, boy, watch where you put your feet!"

Amaranth started to splutter an apology, but the words faded to horror-struck silence. There was just enough light from the hearth and from a solitary torch burning in its cresset for her to recognize the scarred and surly face that belonged to one of Odo de Langois's men. It made perfect sense that her husband would have left someone behind, yet the shock of actually coming face-to-face with the ferret was such that she stared and could not find the wits to form words.

"Well, then, move along," he growled harshly.

"Move along unless ye want to feel the heel of my boot up yer arse."

He belched loudly, sending a hot stream of ale-scented vapors into Amie's face. With a flush of relief she realized he was staggeringly drunk—a condition common to most of Odo's men—and that whatever light there was was behind her, doubtlessly keeping her face a dark blot. Muttering another apology, she bowed her head and dashed quickly past, her heart still stuck in her throat, dreading at any moment to hear a curse of recognition and the pounding of boots chasing after her.

All she heard, however, was the sound of blood rushing through her ears as she hastened along the corridor that led to Marak's tower. Only when she was in the blackest of shadow did she turn and look behind her, but the guardsman had already weaved his way across the breadth of the great hall and was kicking himself a space between two sleeping bodies to get closer to the fire.

Amaranth sagged against the wall for a moment. He was drunk; the shadows were heavy. She reached up and ran grateful fingers through her short-cropped hair, doubting he would have recognized her even if the light had been full. She would have to mention it to Marak anyway, perhaps even point the man out so that he might be detained somewhere in the bowels of the castle until they were well and safely away.

Pushing away from the wall, she hurried along the utterly black corridor. There were no torches to throw down their light, but she did not expect there to be. She groped her way to the opening at the bottom of the stairs, then climbed them with one hand dragging on the stone wall. At the top, she again slid her hands across the surface of the wall until she found the door, and then the cold iron of the latch that opened it.

With the darkness almost smothering her, she did not spare a thought to calling out or even rattling the latch before she lifted it and swung the heavy door open. The hinges were well oiled and moved without a sound, and Amie was fully inside the room and starting to close the door behind her when she heard noises coming from across the chamber.

All but two weak candles had been snuffed, and from those the light was barely strong enough to reach the corner where Marak stood, his body pale against the darker gloom that enveloped the table. She could see that he was bent forward, his arms braced straight out, his head bowed. Something was wrapped around his waist, and it took a long moment for her to realize it was another pair of legs and that his hips were moving back and forth in the rhythmic strokes of intercourse. The noises she heard were soft grunts of passion being matched by softer cries of pleasure, and as Amie watched, a pair of hands stole around his hips, the fingers gouging deep in the thrusting flesh of his buttocks in an effort to pull him even closer.

For the second time in what seemed like as many minutes, Amie was shocked into breathlessness. She had already started to close the door behind her but stood frozen in place now, afraid to move lest her presence be discovered. She knew she should look away or turn her head at the very least, but try as she might, she could not, and her gaze remained fixed on the two lovers. The woman was writhing, twisting with the intensity of her pleasure, her cries and whispered pleas caused waves of gooseflesh to rise along Amaranth's arms in cool, tingling sprays.

All of the times Lord Eglund had stiffened and expended himself between her thighs, Amie had never once shared his trembling gratification. She knew there were women who gained enormous amounts of pleasure from their couplings, but in her own experiences it was usually the man who bleated and shook in the grips of some mindless, unshared ecstasy.

A particularly low, ragged moan left Amie's ears scalding, and she took a step back, intent upon sneaking out the door before she was caught spying. But she was neither quick enough nor quiet enough, for a soft scraping of leather on stone made enough noise to bring Marak's head jerking up and around.

Quicker than Amie would have thought possible, he was away from the table and across the room. The point of a dagger was thrust beneath her throat, the sharp bite of the blade forcing her back against the door, slamming it shut in the same motion.

A split second and a soft curse later, he recognized her. "*Amaranth?* What, by all the Brothers of the Left Hand, are you doing here?"

She tried to swallow, to get her tongue working again, but the pressure of the cold steel on her throat prevented it. With another curse, Marak moved it to one side and jabbed the tip angrily into the wooden plank of the door.

"Now. Answer me."

"I could not bear to be alone any longer. I know Lord Tamberlane ordered me to remain in the solar . . ."

"For good reason. You should not be wandering the halls of the castle on your own."

Amie thought of the guardsman and grew even paler against the shadows.

"What?" Marak frowned. "What is it?"

"In the great hall. I bumped into a guardsman. One of Odo's men. I recognized him . . . from a scar over his eye . . . here," she said, tracing a finger across her brow. "It causes the eye to be always half closed."

Although the question seemed redundant in light of the fact that Amaranth was standing before him and not being dragged to the gates, Marak asked, "Did he recognize you?"

She shook her head. "He was drunk. He kicked me out of the way then stumbled to find a bed by the fire."

"A man with a scar over his eye," Marak murmured, nodding. "We shall find him in the morning and introduce him to the cold waters of the lake. Put him from your mind, Little One. Concentrate on what is before you."

At the sound of his words, and the order implied therein, Marak took a self-conscious step back. The light from the two candles made his body glow like white marble, drawing attention to the lean musculature of his chest and arms, the tautness of his belly and thighs, and the impressive display of manhood that as yet stood straight out from his body, gleaming wet with proof that the woman's cries had not been feigned.

Another soft sound made both Marak and Amie glance to the shadows behind him, where Inaya was in the process of covering her nudity beneath the voluminous folds of silk that she wore. She was not quite fast enough to conceal the swollen shape of her belly or the fact she was several months along with child.

Marak studied Amie's face for a moment, then turned and held his hand out to Inaya. After only the smallest hesitation, the Saracen woman came forward and slipped her fingers into his, allowing him to draw her with the utmost gentleness into the protective circle of his arm.

"I resisted her beauty as long as I could," he said softly. "But the heart is not often willing to listen to the head, is it?"

It was not Amie's place to judge nor to criticize, but her embarrassment could not have been more acute had she stumbled upon Lord Tamberlane naked and tumescent.

An astonishingly vivid image of just that flooded her mind and rendered her speechless for another full minute while Marak fetched his robes and covered himself.

"Certes," she said a little breathlessly, "I would not have intruded had I held the smallest inclination, my lord . . ."

Marak waved her apology into silence.

"In truth, my lady, you have likely saved us from Tamberlane's wrath, for we were to have fetched you from your solar an hour or more ago. Doubtless he will be stomping his way through that same door at any moment, expecting us to be ready and waiting. To that end, we have procured new clothing for you to wear. Your imitation of a squire was so convincing we thought we would uphold it—for safety's sake—until we reach the convent. Have you any objections to this?"

Amie shook her head. "No, none."

"Good. Inaya will help you dress. I shall wait without," he said, heading toward the door.

As if struck by a sudden thought, he stopped and retraced his steps to where Inaya was standing. He tucked a hand under her chin and tipped her head up, smiling into her dark eyes for a long moment before kissing her soft and full on the mouth.

"My desire for you," he murmured, "is and always shall be as pure as the tears of lovers in thrall."

The small, dark Saracen closed her eyes briefly and smiled. Marak gave her another small peck then walked out the door, pulling it closed behind him.

With her eyes downcast, moving on silent bare feet, Inaya brought forth a bundle of clothing from somewhere in the shadows and beckoned Amie forward. Inside the bundle were woolen hose, a belt with points and eyelets for keeping them secure, an undertunic and linens, an overtunic, a leather jerkin, and a Phrygian cap with a narrow brim that hugged her cheeks and ended below her chin.

Apart from the baggy leggings and loose shirt Marak had borrowed from the stable boy, Amie had never worn men's garments before, and some were curious enough to win a small frown as Inaya helped her dress. The eyelet belt with its fifty leather points was a fascination until Inaya was finished tying the last thong through a corresponding loop at the tops of the hose and Amie saw that the wool was held smooth and tight to her limbs. Over these, wrapped from knee to ankle, were leg bandages, for it would be uncommon to see a squire wearing tall boots even if the knight he served was the vaunted Dragon Slayer.

The bundle itself had been wrapped in a mantle, a plain gray cloak woven thick enough to keep out all but the heaviest rain and dampness.

After she was finished, bade to turn slowly around, and inspected by the narrowed, dark eyes, the door was opened again, and Marak was ushered back inside. He nodded approvingly then fetched his own heavy cloak off a peg by the door.

"Shall we?"

Amie followed him out onto the dark landing and had only the faintest outline of his shoulders to guide her down the stairs. At the bottom, instead of turning right toward the great hall, they turned left and, after Marak paused to light them each a small stub of candle, startled Amie by stepping behind a screen that appeared to be covering little more than a shallow niche in the stone wall. He probed a moment with his long, slender fingers, then pushed on one of the blocks, sliding it back with a low scraping sound and exposing an opening just wide enough and tall enough to duck through. The light he carried outlined the portal and showed there was a passage on the other side, one which Amie entered with enough trepidation to cause a flutter of weakness in her belly.

Inaya came through behind her, and when she was clear of the opening, Marak leaned his weight against the stone to push it back into place. Amie was already holding her candle stub high, gazing at the long and narrow passage that seemed at once airless, completely soundless but for their own breaths and heartbeats, and wont to crush them between the two high, sheer walls of massive stone blocks. What looked at first like a haze of dust turned out to be draped blankets of spun cobwebs, thick as wool overhead, clouding the spaces where nothing shy of a lance or pike would ever disturb.

Marak again took the lead, following the curve of the tower, walking into black shadows ahead and leaving blacker shadows behind. His strides were long and sure, and Amie stayed close, cupping her hand around the sputtering flame and praying that the light did not go out. She had no love of small, dark places and wondered, in the utter silence, how far a scream would carry within these stone walls. Visions of being trapped, sealed in a silent tomb, flooded her mind and kept her feet scuffling in the dust in an effort to remain apace.

They walked what must have been the entire circumference of the tower before Marak stopped again and signaled for caution. Ahead were steps that led steeply down into the disappearing gloom, and Amie saw the flame on his candle shiver in the first hints of a draft sweeping up from somewhere below. Something tickled Amie's neck, and she batted anxiously at a trailing strand of cobwebbing that had trailed down from above.

"Come," Marak said. "Stay close on my heels and watch where you place your feet, for the blocks are crumbled in places."

The whisper barely carried beyond her ears, and Amie nodded. By holding her candle stub higher over her head, she could better distinguish the rough-hewn walls and wide but steep stairs that started to descend down, down, still in a circular direction. The air became progressively cooler, damper, the smell of stone and earthworks nearly overpowering. The walls oozed moisture, and the constant dripping grew louder with every passing moment.

If not for Marak's shoulders ahead of her and Inaya's soft footsteps behind her, Amie might have faltered and run back the way they came. Even so, the chances of her finding the hidden doorway again would have been slender at best.

The passage took a sharp turn to the right then suddenly grew wider. The air was so cold there was gooseflesh on Amie's arms despite the bulky layers of clothing. It was obvious they had left the castle behind, for they were in a tunnel of sorts now, with bare earth underfoot and chiseled rock forming the walls and ceiling. Marak's pace increased noticeably, as if Amaranth was not the only one glad to put the stifling closeness of the passage behind her, yet the tunnel through which they walked now was hardly more inviting.

"The island, indeed the lake bed itself and the hills hereabout, are riddled with catacombs and caves," Marak explained. "The original owner of Taniere must have discovered them when laying the foundation and decided to cleverly make use of them both as a defense and a means of smuggling people or foodstuffs in and out of the castle in the event of a siege. There are," he added, raising his candle as they arrived at a junction where the tunnel branched off in three directions, "dozens of arteries leading off each passage, and if one did not know the way, he could wander aimlessly for days without finding the way out."

If that was meant to be reassuring, it failed miserably, as did the flame on Amie's candle a few paces later when they passed by another gaping hole in the wall. Inaya paused with her to relight it, and as the two wicks flared together, the shadows were lifted enough for them to see two pairs of eyes glowing red at them from just inside the mouth of the tunnel that branched off beside them. Amie screamed and jumped back; Inaya babbled something in her native language and shrank with her against the far wall of the tunnel.

Marak came running back. He had drawn a sword from somewhere beneath his robes, but lowered it with a curse when he held his candle to the opening.

Tamberlane's two wolfhounds, Maude and Hugo,

came bounding out and ran off down the tunnel, leaving the minor chaos of two shaking women and the still cursing seneschal in their wake.

"Bloody hounds, as truculent as their master." He turned and made long strides into the darkness ahead. Cupping their hands more securely around their candles, the women nearly ran in their haste to catch up.

After two more turns, and just when Amie was about to forsake any hope of seeing the sky again, they saw a faint bloom of light ahead. It grew brighter with each pounding heartbeat and soon the smudges turned into bright yellow blots from a dozen pitch-soaked torches that flickered in a circle around a large natural chamber formed in the rock. Standing there, clad in mail with their swords buckled about their waists, were Tamberlane and two other knights. Roland was the only squire present, but waiting patiently off to one side were four foresters wearing hunters-green leggings, tunics, and brown leather jerkins. Each carried a quiver full of arrows slung over one shoulder, a longbow over the other. The two dogs were there, tongues hanging out, but most amazing of all was the sight of nearly a dozen horses stomping warily from one foot to the next, their eyes rounded, nostrils flared, ears moving constantly to follow every sound.

"How on earth?"

Marak followed Amie's gaze to the nervous beasts. "You recall the wooden floor in the stable?"

Amie nodded slowly. It had been covered thickly with straw, which she had thought odd at the time, but she had felt the planking beneath her, and when the water had spilled, it had fallen through cracks in the boards and made a dripping sound.

Tamberlane had turned at the sound of their voices. He opened his mouth to say something to Marak . . . something that would likely have been accompanied by a frown . . . but then his eyes slid back to Amie, widening as he recognized the face beneath the Phrygian cap. He took in every small detail . . . the fringe of reddish curls across her brow, the bulky layers of shirt and tunic that concealed the shape of her breasts, the smooth tautness of her hose and the rounds of bandaging that could not quite disguise the slenderness of her calves. When his gaze arrived at her feet, it started to make a slow climb back up again, and every place it lingered, every wrinkle or fold that fell victim to his minute inspection, brought forth a wash of heat that fluttered through her loins.

"It will do," he murmured, nodding with approval. "We were about to send men to the keep to look for you. The horses grow restless in such a confined space."

Amie wanted to say that she understood exactly how they felt, but her tongue was stuck fast to the roof of her mouth. Her belly had turned to liquid heat, and her knees felt as if they were knocking together.

It was Marak who said, "Then you had best be on your way."

He produced a small canvas sack from somewhere inside his voluminous robes and held it out to Amie.

"I have taken the liberty of blending the proper herbs and nostrums together in small packets for you to steep into your favorite posset each morning. As well, there is a vial of aumosniere to be taken a few drops at time only should the pain in your shoulder cause you undue discomfort. Take no more than a few drops, however; any more and you will fall into a deep, deep sleep."

"You are not coming with us?" The thought that he would not had not even occurred to Amie.

"Alas, I do not travel well, and under certain circumstances, I am afraid, could even become a liability."

She was at a loss for words. "I do not know how to thank you, kindest sir, for all you have done."

Before she could attempt to say more, he held up a hand. "Your smile, Little One, is thanks enough. That"—he leaned closer and lowered his voice—"and perhaps a kind word in the mother abbess's ear when you reach the convent, for I am told the sweetest French wines can be found along the coast where the smugglers ply their wares.

"Between then and now, however," he added, straightening, "I have faith that you will be in very good hands. The two knights you see standing with Lord Tamberlane rode by his side in Jaffa and were among the first to seek him out here at Taniere and offer their swords in service. Anyone approaching you would have to do so over their slaughtered corpses, and considering that neither Lord Boethius nor Lord Geoffrey de Ville have met defeat in the lists or in battle, I would think the possibility of that happening is slender. The four bowmen are culled from the finest outlaws in all the king's forests, and each can shoot the eye out of one of Prince John's tax collectors at two hundred paces."

A soft clearing of the throat brought Marak's head tipping around. "Ah, yes, and not the least of the surly lot is Roland. As the One Chivalric Deed to be completed before entering into knighthood, he has been charged with delivering you safely into the hands of the abbess at the convent of the Sisters of Mary Magdalene. The charge is sacred and binding and to fail would mean he would never wear the spurs of a knight."

The squire stepped forth and offered up a small, courteous bow. "From this moment forth, your comfort and safety are my utmost concern, my lady. To that end, might I inquire . . . do you ride?"

She thought the question a little absurd under the circumstances, until she followed the squire's glance to the four palfreys who stood trembling in the company of the much larger beasts meant for the knights and foresters. Two were packhorses, burdened under supplies; the other two were saddled without thought to a woman's comfort or style of riding. In keeping with her guise as a squire, she would be expected to ride as one, enduring the aches and discomforts for a much longer journey than she had experienced before. There would be no covered chairs if it rained, no frequent stops to ease a tired back. Moreover, she would be expected to sleep on the open ground and do her fair share of duties should they attract the attention of other travelers.

"Yes, I can ride," she assured him. "I can also fire an arrow with a modicum of skill, hunt and skin a hare, then cook it over an open fire. But you, Roland, must not address me as my lady, nor even as Amaranth. You must call me simply 'boy,' or 'you there,' and I shall answer."

Roland grinned. "I doubt I could address you by either byname, my lady, but perhaps we will settle on an amiable sobriquet ere we travel too far."

"So long as it is not Oaf," she said with a slight smile. "For I feel very much like one already."

"Never that, my lady. I think you are brave and courageous, and your plight touches upon the very meaning of chivalry. To that end, I pledge my sword unto my last drawn breath."

They had kept their voices low throughout the exchange, but at the last declaration, it seemed to Amie as though Tamberlane's head had turned slightly to better catch the words. It turned back just as quickly though, when he thought she noticed, and with no further delay, the men were ordered to each take up a torch and lead their animals into one of the gaping tunnels. The knights went first, led by the Dragon Slayer himself. Two of the foresters followed after, then Roland leading his palfrey and holding his torch high. Amaranth was next, with the last two foresters bringing up the rear.

Her last glimpse of Marak, before the catacombs swallowed her into their depths, showed him standing with Inaya, one arm around her shoulder, the other raised in a soft salute.

Chapter Fifteen

By the time dawn broke gray over the horizon, the small party of knights and foresters were miles away from Taniere Castle. The tunnel had taken them below the man-made moat and beneath the village, leading them into the deepest heart of the forest. There, where the river spilled over a sharp incline of rocks, they exited the catacombs behind the wall of sheeting waters.

Amaranth was in complete thrall. The long walk through the twisting, musty tunnels had been half terrifying, half thrilling; it was exiting beneath the waterfall, and seeing the light from the torches reflected off the undersurface of the roaring water was breathtaking.

Once they were out in the open, Tamberlane ordered the torches doused. The moon was full and bright, bathing the forest floor with streamers of bluish light that cut through the high treetops. It was bright enough to see their way through the stands of oak and ash, and they rode while they could see, walked the beasts where they could not. The foresters took turns running on ahead to scout the way, and it was a credit to their outlaw ways that none of the rest of the party saw or heard them return until they dropped down from a tree limb or stepped out into their path.

Amaranth's excitement kept her fueled through the first few hours, but then the long anxious day, the evening spent pacing, the harrowing walk through the catacombs began to creep up upon her, and her shoulders started to sag, her legs to ache. The novelty of riding astride wore off long before the moonlight faded and was replaced by the watery dawn sky. Although Roland inquired periodically after her welfare and she always replied with a smile and a nod, her inner thighs ached like the devil and her shoulders—both of them—were throbbing. She kept glancing at the small canvas pouch she had tied to her saddle and wondered how she could discreetly add a drop of Marak's tincture to her skin of drinking water. She could not, would not show signs of weakness, not when all of these men were putting their lives at risk to see her safely to the convent.

Happily, when he estimated the hour of Prime was upon them, Tamberlane called a halt to the little troop. Amaranth dismounted with care, not wanting to betray how stiff and sore she was, and managed to smile warmly at Roland when he produced large portions of cheese, bread, and dried herring to break the night's fast. The food, as well as the ale that was consumed along with it, helped restore Amie's spirits somewhat, and she was able to hold her saddle until noon when another halt was called. This time, she did manage to put a single drop of the tincture into her pannikin, which worked remarkably well in easing the cramps in her back and legs throughout the long afternoon that followed.

The good weather did not hold. Clouds moved in midafternoon and turned the sky overhead a sullen gray. The trees were thick enough that when it did start to drizzle, the leaves buffered the raindrops, splitting them in half, then half again, so that when they reached the ground, they were more of a heavy mist than a rainfall. The light turned eerie as well, transforming the carpets of ferns into a sea of emerald green.

Still they slogged forward, following no path, no road that Amie could see. When the sky grew even more ominous and no amount of leaves overhead could diffuse the pellets of rain, one of the foresters was dispatched ahead to find a safe place to shelter for the night.

Amie, hunched beneath her cloak, took another surreptitious drop of Marak's potion, washing the bitterness down with a mouthful of water. Her shoulder was aching continuously now, and she was cold enough to feel her bones rattling together with each jostling step the palfrey took. Her fingers were locked into claws around the reins, and she suspected the dripping from her nose was not all due to the rain.

Eric the Fox, one of the foresters, appeared before them through a break in the trees and declared that he had found a place to shelter for the night, if his lordship thought the risk worth taking. Tamberlane veered his horse in Eric's direction, leading the small party down a gully and along a spongy tract of ground that ended, abruptly, on the upper slope of a shallow valley. Stretched out below them was a meadow dotted with small clusters of huddled, rain-soaked sheep. A river flowed through the lowest part of the valley, bridged by a narrow wooden structure with a gatehouse on the opposite side. Beyond that was a monastery with its two long wings comprising the pilgrim's hall and almonry, separated by an iron gate and cobbled yard. Behind that lay the cloisters and refectory, and to the north a small priory church.

There was a line of pilgrims waiting at the gate-house, seeking refuge from the stormy night. Men would be taken to the hall, women to the cloisters; the horses would be stabled and meals provided in the rectory hall. Accommodations could be improved if there were coins shown to the gatekeeper, for many lords and ladies preferred lodging at a monastery if it was convenient rather than seeking shelter at a disreputable inn. It was left to Tamberlane to weigh the risk of paying that coin and possibly drawing attention to themselves. Certes, Odo de Langois would have eyes watching every possible place where his wife might seek refuge.

While Amie's disguise might get her past the gate-keeper's nose, the horses were another matter entirely. The Dragon Slayer's piebald was as mighty as his master's reputation, and no absence of silks or saw-toothed caparisons could disguise the beast's calling as a warhorse. Likewise, the animals belonging to the two knights betrayed their lack of penury as did the richness in the coats of the palfreys. The rain would be in their favor. With hoods pulled low over their brows and their knightly trappings hidden beneath the wings of their cloaks, there was a good chance they might be taken merely as a party of Crusaders returning from the Holy Land.

As if to aide in making the decision, the skies cracked open with a jagged fork of lightning. The rain increased to slanting sheets that forced everyone in the small group to turn their heads to the side. Ciaran caught sight of Amaranth's face and was appalled to see that her lips were blue, her eyes glazed and smudged with dark circles beneath from the pain.

"We cannot stay here," he said. He raised a gloved hand to signal them forward, cautioning the men needlessly to pull their cloaks tight about them. It was not uncommon for monasteries to insist that all weapons be left at the gatehouse, but a knight without a sword was as naked as a forester without his bow and quiver, and so he ordered that daggers and swords be well concealed.

Amie did not care. She was cold, wet. The rain had penetrated the tightest weavings on her cloak and was running down the back of her neck. This was, she recalled, as cold and wretched as she had felt the night before Friar Guilford had sought refuge for her in the village. She was thinner and weaker now despite a fortnight of Marak's potions and possets, and the chills swept through her in waves. Reaching beneath her tunic, her icy fingers groped for and found the small vial that contained the aumosniere. She did not think it would warm her, but perhaps another drop on her tongue would numb the aches.

Two of the foresters volunteered to remain behind and watch the approaches to the monastery. As Tamberlane led the remaining group across the meadow, the rain beat down on their heads and shoulders and did not let up until they were across the wooden bridge and awaiting the nod of the gate-keeper. The latter looked as sodden and as sullen as the pilgrims. He was as broad around as he was tall, with a round, fat face shielded under the brim of a hat that collected water and spilled it over his eyes each time he tipped his head to or fro.

"God's greetings to you, my son, and in His name, I bid you welcome to St. Albans."

"God's greetings to you, good Friar. We come seeking shelter from the storm."

"As do all His sheep, my son," he replied wearily. "How many, anon?"

"There are seven of us. Hungry, weary, and wet enough to beg a humble roof over our heads for the night."

"Humble, eh?" The friar eyed the two wolfhounds, who sat and calmly returned his stare.

Tamberlane produced a small handful of copper coins. "Not so humble as to prefer the common hall over a bit of privacy," he said quietly.

"Ah." The pudgy hand reached out for the coins and weighed them without looking, then the friar glanced up from beneath the brim of his hat. "I perceive ye have horses that will want shelter too, and fodder as well."

Tamberlane dropped another coin into the cupped palm.

"Ye'll be wanting to leave your swords here with me, being as how ye be resting on hallowed ground and all."

Several more coins joined the first ones as Tamberlane said, "We come in peace, Brother."

"Peace? Is there such a thing in mother England these days?" He made the sign of the cross as a blessing, and when he was done, the coins had vanished somewhere inside his robes. "Ye'll find yer lodgings on the left—seek out Brother Ignatius. Meals at matins and midday in the rectory hall. God go with you."

"And with you, good Friar."

A nod and a long trickle of water flowing off the brim of the hat sent them on their way through the iron gates. Inside the cobbled courtyard, the men rode directly to the stables. Tamberlane dismounted and handed the reins to a waiting stableboy. He looked around, clapping his hands on his arms, and on each clap a spray of water droplets exploded into the air. Amie was the last to dismount and did so with enough care to put the hint of a frown on Ciaran's face.

She looked up, and his sense of alarm increased. Her eyes were huge, the centers as dark as two holes burned into her skull. She seemed unable to hold his gaze for any length of time, and when he approached, he saw the small vial of blue liquid she was clutching.

"How much of that have you taken?" he asked softly.

"Only a drop or two," she murmured, narrowing her eyes to concentrate on the movement of his hands as he reached out and gently uncurled her fingers to extricate the vial. She smiled suddenly. A huge, wide smile that plumped her cheeks and betrayed the existence of a dimple. "But I feel quite fine, my lord. I trust you have not sought refuge at this foul-smelling inn on my account, for I could ride another half day at least without discomfort."

"Yes, I can see that," he murmured.

While she stood staring down at her empty hand, he passed the reins of her horse to Roland. "The 'lad' needs fire and hot food. You, Quill, and Fletcher see to the animals—buy each an extra rasher of oats, then come and find us in the pilgrim's hall."

Amie giggled. "Quill and Fletcher . . . not dreadfully fearsome names for outlaws, are they? I should think Gut-Eater or Throat-Slitter would be more convincing and, indeed, that is what I shall call them henceforth."

Tamberlane cast a wary glance about the stable, but there was no one within hearing distance. The newly christened Gut-Eater and Throat-Slitter gave off little grins, which faded when they saw the scowl darken the Dragon Slayer's brow. He took hold of Amie's arm and turned her around, but when she saw the heavy sheets of rain still bouncing off the cobblestones, she balked and drew back against him.

It was an innocent enough reaction; doubtless she was not even aware of pressing back against his body. Yet Tamberlane felt the impact like a jolt of lightning through his veins. Last night, in the catacombs, he had again experienced the loss of the ability to breathe when he saw her emerge from the shadowy tunnel and step into the torchlight. Not even the plainest of plain men's clothing could conceal her slender form, nor could the most ridiculous hat take away from the smoothness of her face, the sweet ripeness of her lips, the haunting vulnerability of her eyes. His arms had actually ached from the memory of holding her on the rooftop, his fingertips had tingled recalling the softness of her cheek. Desires that had lain dormant for so many years had taken nearly every scrap of his considerable willpower to crush back down into submission.

He felt them stirring again now. Blood rushed hot through his veins, and the instinct to protect, to hold, to keep her safe and warm within his embrace rose with a guilty flush into his throat and cheeks.

Taking a subtle step back and to the side, he tucked his hand more firmly under her elbow and pulled her forward, welcoming the beat of the rain on his head. Flanked by Lord Boethius and Lord Geoffrey de Ville, they crossed the courtyard and entered the pilgrim's hall through a low, arched doorway. Here was the common chamber, where travelers and pilgrims sought to lay their heads on a dry pallet of straw for the night. There were two fires blazing, one at each end of the hall. What few benches there were had been dragged in front of the heat and were occupied by a dozen or so men who would likely sit there all night in order not to lose the choice positioning to the scores of other bedraggled, wet, and stinking masses who filled every open space on the floor.

A monk approached, his face round and serene. "I bid you God's welcome. In His name, we bless His generosity . . . *pater, filius, spiritus sanctus* . . ."

Tamberlane and the two knights went down on one knee to receive the blessing; Amie followed an instant later, responding somewhat mulishly to a hard tug on her sleeve. When Tamberlane rose again, he left it to Lord Boethius to lift her back to her feet, which the knight did by grabbing a fistful of cape at the scruff of her neck.

"We were told at the gate to seek Brother Ignatius."

"You have found him, my son."

"We seek more private accommodations than a common hall."

"Ahh." He shook his head solemnly. "Alas, my son, the foul weather brings many a man and beast to our door, as you can see—" He spread a hand to indicate the crowded floor. "We are but a small monastery, and the cells were filled quickly."

Tamberlane held up a gloved hand holding a shiny gold coin. "We require four."

The monk's eyes grew as round as the coin. "Four? Gracious goodness, you seek the miracle of loaves and fishes where we have not even one loaf or fish."

A second gold coin joined the first.

The friar stared at the coin a moment and sucked on his lower lip. "One. I could perhaps arrange for one chamber. My own, by happenstance, and smaller than a mouse hole."

Tamberlane dropped the coin in his hand. Leaving the two knights to grumble and kick their way toward the heat of the fire, he and Amie followed Friar Ignatius along the length of the pilgrim's hall and out a rear doorway to an adjoining corridor. There they found themselves walking along a covered breezeway that was flanked on the left by arched doorways and on the right by a low half wall that opened out onto a cobbled courtyard.

They followed the breezeway to the end and ducked through another portal, pausing to bow their heads before a statue of the Virgin Mary before carrying on down a longer, darker passageway broken every few paces by the doors that housed the monks' sleeping quarters.

Once again, they were led to the very end before the friar stopped and opened one of the cell doors. Inside was a narrow cot, a stand containing a jug of water, a candle stub, and a small three-legged stool. On the wall hung a wooden crucifix, on another a black robe. Covering the single small window was a wooden shutter that rattled against the stone and let in enough rainwater to stain the wall and form a small puddle on the floor.

"It is colder than Satan's heart in here," Tamberlane said. "We need heat. The lad here is cold and wet right through and needs to be warmed."

Friar Ignatius glanced at Amie, who stood swaying by Tamberlane's side, her eyes closed, her shoulders drooping. "Unfortunately, the only chamber with a fire is the common hall."

"Is there not even a brazier? A pan where we might burn some pine knots?"

The friar glanced at the coin in Tamberlane's hand and sucked violently on his lip again before nodding. "Of course, I could perhaps arrange for a brazier."

"And a supply of wood."

The coin was plucked from his fingers and vanished under the friar's robes. "And a supply of wood, of course."

When the monk was gone, Tamberlane closed the door and stripped off his gloves. The leather was wet, and he had to struggle with each finger, which did little to improve his disposition.

He glanced up. Amaranth was standing where he had left her, her eyes closed, her head bowed. Water *drip-drip-dripped* off her cloak, forming a wet circle around her feet, and she looked like a bedraggled waif, far too young to have been the object of lust for two men.

Three, he amended inwardly, though the last was a fool and his misguided yearnings did not warrant consideration.

After shrugging out of his own sodden cloak, Tamberlane approached Amie.

"Amaranth?"

Her chin tipped up in response to his voice, but her eyes remained closed.

"I am going to leave for a few minutes. You must

get out of those wet clothes—look you here is a spare robe belonging to the good friar. Put it on, and when you have done so, call to me. I shall wait right outside the door and will take your wet garments out to the fire where they can be properly dried. Amaranth? Do you hear me?"

"So tired," she whispered. She swayed forward and turned her head so that her brow was pressed tight to his neck. When she spoke, her lips were touching the pulse that beat in his throat. "So tired and so c-cold."

Tamberlane stared over her shoulder at the wall behind them. The candle threw their shadows on the stone blocks; although the embrace was innocent, in dark relief it looked intimate as well as passionate.

Sparing a soft curse for Marak's potion, he slid his hands up her arms and held her away from his body. He unfastened the toggle holding her cloak closed at the neck and removed it, then tossed the sodden garment over the stool with his own. Her tunic was soaked through, darkened by the rain, and he drew a deep breath before he unbuckled her belt and lifted the hem over her head. Working quickly, not pausing to either think or look, he removed her undertunic and dropped down onto one knee to unwind the linen bandaging around her calves. Her shoes were soaked, her stockings sagging heavily with the water; her legs, when he unfastened the points and peeled the wool leggings down, were white as ice, her feet pink, the toes a chilly red.

He snatched the shapeless black robe off the wall peg and pulled it over her head, feeding her arms into the long bell-shaped sleeves as if he was dressing a child. Without debating the wisdom of touching her so intimately, he wrapped her in a blanket and bade her sit on the edge of the cot while he used the coarse wool to chafe some warmth into her legs and arms.

When he looked up again, her eyes were open. They were still huge and round, the centers still dilated, but she had found his face and was focusing intently on it while he continued to rub her feet with the blanket. Her lips were a faint blue, but at least her teeth had stopped chattering enough for her to speak.

"Your name is Ciaran," she said.

He smiled. "Yes. It is."

" 'Tis an unusual name. I do not know it."

"My mother is a Celt."

"A Celt." She nodded sagely. "And thus the black hair and green eyes. Brothers? Sisters?"

"Two brothers, both dead."

"You have my sorrow, good knight."

He shrugged the gift aside. "I barely knew them. One was fostered at a young age to a knight who traveled to Rome where both of them died of the pox. The other was gored by a boar while out hunting when I not yet five years old."

"Yet there is longing in your voice when you speak of them."

Tamberlane released her foot. "The longing you hear is for dry clothes and a stoup of mulled wine."

"Yes . . ." Her eyes roved across the breadth of

his shoulders. "You are wet, my lord. You should rid yourself of your own garments before you catch the fever. Come, let me help."

"No!" He sat quickly back on his heels, placing himself out of reach as she stretched her arms forward. When the frown creased her brow, he covered his bluntness with a hasty chuckle. "I mean to say, I am quite capable of managing on my own."

She sighed extravagantly and settled her hands back onto her lap. She had removed the mawkish hat, and the reddish-gold curls framed her face in a soft halo that required very little light to create a glow. The robe did not close tight at the throat, and thus the entire length of her neck was exposed as well as an alarmingly deep vee that reached almost between her breasts. It did not look as though it would take much of a shifting of an arm or shoulder to have the garment slip right off, and for that Ciaran found himself willing her not to move, if for no other reason than the sake of his own well-being.

Her modesty was safeguarded by a thin linen bluet underneath, for he had not been half so bold as to strip her completely to bare skin, but the cloth was wet and had left little to the imagination. It molded to her breasts and showed the darker circles where her nipples peaked against the wet linen. Her waist had looked incredibly tiny, and where the bluet molded itself to her thighs, he had seen the faint outline of her mound at the junction.

"Why are you doing this?"

His gaze jerked up to her face. "My lady?"

"This," she said, waving her hand abstractly. "Why are you doing this? Why are you taking me to the convent?"

He frowned. "Is that not where you want to go?"

"Well, yes, but . . . you could have sent me in the care of your squire or Sir Boethius or Sir Geoffrey. You did not have to escort me yourself. Indeed," she added, bowing her head, "I thought you would have wanted rid of me as soon as possible."

Tamberlane reached up and tucked a finger under her chin, forcing her to look at him. She was right, of course. He should have wanted to be rid of her, rid of the temptation, rid of her eyes that haunted him, enchanted him. Rid of her smile teasing him, rid of the sound of her voice and the way it traveled down his spine like a soft echo. He should have wanted that and yet . . .

His thumb stroked softly across the rounded point of her chin. "To my shame, my lady, I did not want rid of you at all."

She expelled a small puff of air and grew so still the air seemed to tremble between them. It trembled more as he drew slowly closer, rising on his knees again and closing the gap between them. For some known-only-to-God reason, he pushed his hands into her hair and leaned forward, covering her mouth with his own. She tasted like some exotic, rare delicacy, and his eyes closed under the weight of such unexpected pleasure.

He had kissed before—kisses of a youth eager to prove his manliness. But that was long before God had placed a sword in his hand. The memory of those kisses were dim, but he knew they had been nothing like this. Nothing that made him want to invade and explore and devour.

His fingers tightened in her hair and his tongue traced across her lips, winning a gasp from Amaranth and a shocked gust from his own lungs that forced him to release her.

She was blinking, staring at him, her mouth round and shaped in a soft O of surprise.

"Forgive me," he said hoarsely, pulling his hands quickly away. "Forgive me, Amaranth. That was . . . it was . . ."

Before he could even begin to find the right words, she reached up and pressed three cool fingers over his lips, silencing him.

He met her eyes without evasion. Her fingertips were cool against his lips—a sharp contrast to the heat raging through his blood. When she slid her fingers down to his chin, then let them trail along his neck to his shoulder . . . he felt a shudder, then another as the subtle pressure from her hand pulled him forward again.

She put her mouth to his, touching, holding, breathing in the soft oath he whispered against her lips. Brazenly, the tip of her tongue flicked at him, and he responded with a husky groan that brought his hands up to her shoulders, then to the sides of her neck.

He sent his tongue lashing between her lips, sliding deep into her mouth like a starved man who had craved the sustenance of human contact too long. His fingers thrust up into the short, damp locks of her hair again, holding her as the kiss grew bolder and deeper with each ragged breath.

Where the heat, the magnificent desire came from, he knew not; he was only aware of the hunger that kept him plundering, ravaging the sweetest recesses of her mouth. Images came and went, broken and unrelated, of the hours spent droning the prayers meant to rid his mind and body of unchaste thoughts. And with each new thought, each new echo of a sonorous voice charging him to rid his soul of the devil . . . he kissed Amie harder, deeper, even started to pull her down beside him on the cold stone floor.

Something stopped him. The sudden stiffness in her body or the pressure of balled fists against his shoulders.

He stopped and tore his mouth away, and for the longest ten seconds of his life, he stared into Amaranth's eyes, not even knowing where or how to find the words this time.

Amie sat very still. Her lips throbbed and the inside of her mouth was hot, seared by the unexpected violence of his need. Clear thought was still hampered by Marak's little blue drops, but her mind was suddenly spinning at a frenzied pace, for she had tasted the violence of lust before. She had suffered mightily from it, been punished by it, been forced to endure it so much she had thought she would never be able to bear a man's touch, a man's hunger again.

Yet there was something in the way Tamberlane's hands trembled, something in the way he had cursed softly into her mouth the instant before he broke away.

For an instant, no more, the impenetrable green eyes had been naked and exposed; he had made no effort to conceal the depth of his loneliness and despair.

Now they contained only shame and self-disgust.

In a welter of confused emotions, she watched him rake his hands through his hair then rise quickly to his feet and begin to gather up the wet clothing.

"You are leaving me?"

"A simple brazier will not dry these things," he muttered. "They must be hung in front of the fire in the hall. You will not be alone, my lady. I will leave Maude and Hugo to protect you, and I will send Lord Boethius to stand guard outside the door. No one will get past them."

She bowed her head, closing her eyes through a visible shudder.

He stopped fumbling with the wet clothes and frowned at her. "Get you gone under the blankets before you shiver all your teeth loose from your head. Where is that blasted monk with the brazier? I will find Roland and have him bring some hot broth to warm you."

Amaranth did not protest when he swung her legs up onto the narrow cot and covered her to the chin with blankets. Her eyes never left his face, but even with the heat of his kiss still tingling on her lips, there was little that could have prevented her lashes from drifting down. Within moments, her breathing was deep and even, and with a harshly whispered command to the two wolfhounds, Tamberlane gathered up the bundled clothing and quietly exited the cell.

Chapter Sixteen

Amaranth woke up several hours later, totally disorientated for nearly a full minute before the pounding in her chest slowed and she recognized the wooden crucifix hanging on the wall. The monk's cell. She was safe at St. Albans. A glance down confirmed that she was wearing the black robe and there was a small mountain of dry, warm blankets piled on her.

The soft hiss and crack she heard came from a small iron brazier that sat in the corner of the chamber. The rain must have stopped, for the shutters were not rattling and water no longer streamed down the inner wall. The two wolfhounds were asleep on the floor, sprawled out at right angles to each other, Maude's blond head propped on Hugo's belly.

Amie relaxed, whispering words that were not flattering to her sense of perception. She stretched and shook off the remnants of sleep, pleased to find no new aches. The old ones were all still there, but at least she could move her arms and legs, and her hips were not seized up like rusted links of armor.

She pushed aside the blankets and cautiously sat upright. Her head felt fuzzy, and she recognized the familiar light-headedness brought on by one of Marak's herbals. Her feet, touching on the rough planking, were instantly chilled, and she curled her toes under in response. The heat coming off the brazier was minimal. Most of it was sucked upward with the thin threads of smoke and lured out the window.

She looked at the dogs again, surprised they had not jumped to attention at the first sign of movement from the bed. But then—she rationalized—they had traveled just as far but with naught but their own legs to carry them.

Looking at their sleek bodies reminded her of their master. Riding behind him she'd had little else to look at but the breadth of his shoulders, the straightness of his back. The doeskin leggings he wore did little to conceal the shape of his thighs and were so close-fitting she could see the flex and ripple of the muscles beneath. She knew he was hard and muscular elsewhere, his arms like oak, his waist trim and lean. She guessed he would be imposing everywhere, though the mere thought of where her mind was wandering made her blush.

She moistened her lips unself-consciously. The memory of his kiss was still there. The feel of his hands raking up into her hair, the fingers spreading to hold her while his lips ravished her was as real now as it had been at the time. Her scalp tingled and her skin flushed hotly. Her nipples hardened against the confining fabric of her bluet, and when she parted her lips, a sigh came forth.

She was still vastly unsettled by her response to Tamberlane's kiss. She had thought any such showings of desire or lust—and it was lust, she could not deceive herself into believing it was anything else—were long gone.

Without knowingly doing so, she ran her fingers across her lower lip.

It had been a new and unique experience to feel herself wanting more. More of the taste of his lips, more of the feel of his hands holding her, more of the heat of his body pressing against her. In truth, she had not stiffened out of fear for what he might do to her if he bore her down onto the floor beneath him. Her apprehension was more to do with what her own reactions would be.

To that end, it had been almost as shocking and unique an experience to pull back and have a man like Ciaran Tamberlane actually stop. Not only stop but be apologetic and shamed for even touching her in the first place.

Amie realized she was still staring at the dogs. She felt a creeping sense of alarm rise up the back of her neck and did not understand the cause of it until she realized that in all the time she had been watching them, neither Maude nor Hugo had moved. Their bodies were perfectly still. Their chests did not even rise or fall to draw a breath.

The feeling of dread increased as she stretched a toe out and gently prodded Hugo's flank.

Nothing.

The wolfhound's limbs were already stiff.

Something glinted on the floor beside them, and Amie identified the vial that had once held the potent drops Marak had given her. It was empty now. The floor was stained blue where the contents had spilled, possibly to be sniffed and licked by the two wolfhounds.

"Jesu," she whispered, "Mother Mary, and Joseph."

Gathering up the loose folds of the black cassock, she rose gingerly off the bed and, stepping quickly to one side, kept her back pressed flat against the wall as she scraped her way sideways to the door. She had seen enough of Tamberlane and the hounds together to know there was great affection shared between the three. The notion that she might, inadvertently, have caused their deaths made her stomach rise up and burn sourly at the back of her throat.

At the door, she fumbled with the latch for several seconds before she was finally able to pull it open. It was dark in the corridor. The clouds were low, and there was no moon to flood the courtyard. The only light came from the very far end of the long walk, where the statue of the Virgin stood guard over the breezeway leading to the pilgrim's hall.

Amie took a step and bumped into something lying at her feet. It threw her off balance, and she tottered forward, only saving herself from a bad fall by sticking her hands out in front of her. The fingers of her left hand sank into something horribly wet and spongy while those on her right brushed against the large jeweled salamander broach she had last seen pinning to the top of Lord Boethius's woolen cloak. The mush beneath her left hand was acknowledged with a hoarse cry as being where his face should have been.

He was dead! The dogs were dead, and Lord Boethius was dead! They had been left to guard and protect her, and now they were dead!

Amie shot to her feet and scrambled several terrified steps along the darkened corridor, using her hands to scrape her way along the rough stone wall.

"Lord Tamberlane!" The cry echoed hollowly through the empty silence. "Sweet Jesu, is anyone there?"

She paused beside the cold marble statue of the Virgin, then started running along the breezeway toward the glowing light. Her cassock tangled around her ankles, and she fell heavily to her knees, skinning both through the rough wool, but she was up and on her feet running again before the pain could deter her.

"Lord Tamberlane!"

A door swung open just ahead, and before she could stop or veer to miss it, the brilliant flare of a torch cast its light in her eyes, blinding her. Odo de Langois stepped out behind it and stood glaring down at her, his eyes gleaming red, his hair a fiery frame around his face.

"Elizabeth." Her name was snarled with more venom than Satan himself could have mustered. "Elizabeth, my lovely bride. Did you think you could run away from me? Did you not think I would find you regardless of where you ran or who you played whore for to buy his protection?"

"No," she gasped, staggering back. "No!"

He roared an ugly laugh and took an ominous step toward her. He reached out to snatch at her arm, but Amie was too quick. Fear drove her forward, and she darted beneath the hand that held the torch aloft, fleeing as fast as her legs would carry her.

Odo's laughter followed, punctuated by the ominous *thud* of his boots and the erratic patterns of her own shadow thrown ahead of her by the torchlight.

At the end of the breezeway she risked a glance over her shoulder. He was a large man with long legs that ate as much in a single enraged stride as three of her smaller ones. He was gaining quickly, fueled by his rage and hunger for revenge, and Amie whirled around and ran again, straight into the pilgrim's hall, into the center of the huge chamber where she was again brought to a skidding halt.

There were no men sleeping on the floor, no men huddled on benches in front of the fire. Instead, they were all standing about the circumference of the room, their bodies touching shoulder to shoulder to form a solid ring of humanity around her. She recognized no one. Tamberlane should have stood a head and shoulders above the others, but she did not see him.

Whirling in a slow, desperate circle, the hem of the black cassock fanning out around her feet, she searched for Roland, for the foresters Fletcher and Quill, for Lord Geoffrey de Ville.

She spun again, even more frantically, for the circle was closing, sealing off the corridor to the monks' cells and trapping her within. Odo was inside the ring with her as well, the torch still held high, the flame crackling and snapping over his head.

"No," she gasped. "No!"

"Amaranth!"

She turned, her panicked gaze searching the dark, sullen faces for the one who had whispered her name.

"Elizabeth . . . come to me. Come willingly, and I vow it will go easier on you."

She looked at her husband, at the false smile on his face, at the torch with its dripping globs of hot pitch . . .

"Amaranth!"

She spun around again, a sob caught in her throat, for it was *him*. It was Tamberlane's voice, but she could not see him, could not find him even as the ring of wooden-faced men began to move inward, forcing her toward the center of the room where Odo stood waiting.

"Amaranth! Can you hear me?"

She gasped as someone reached out and grabbed her. She tried to bat his hands away, to shove her fists against his chest, to lunge and twist and break his hold, but he was too strong. His arms went around her, and his hand quickly covered her mouth when she opened it to scream.

"Amaranth! It is me, Lord Tamberlane. It is Ciaran. Hush. Hush now. You are safe. All is well—you are safe."

Safe? Her mind latched on to the word as if it were the end of a rope and she was hanging over a cliff. Safe?

She opened her eyes and looked wildly around. She was not in the pilgrim's hall; she was in the monk's tiny cell. She was not standing inside a shrinking ring of spectrelike figures; she was sitting up on the bed, the blankets in disarray. Ciaran sat on the bed beside her, his arm holding her close against his chest, his hand clamped gently—if firmly—over her mouth to prevent her from screaming. Standing beside the bed, their ears pricked upright, were Maude and Hugo, very much alive and looking for intruders to maul.

Amie blinked once as her eyes grew watery with tears.

Maude and Hugo were alive! Tamberlane was alive! He was here and he was alive and that meant . . .

"You were having a bad dream," he said gently. "It is over now. Gone. I am going to take my hand away from your mouth . . ."

Slowly, almost finger by finger, he did so, wary lest she start to scream or cry out again. Amaranth shivered and looked around the room, her gaze touching on the dogs, on the open door and the concerned face of Lord Boethius—very much alive and perplexed—watching from the entrance to the cell.

Finally, she looked up into Ciaran's eyes and felt such a flooding of relief that she crumpled forward against his chest.

"It was so real," she whispered. "I woke up and

the dogs had been poisoned, Lord Boethius was dead, you were gone and—and—Odo was here. I ran to look for you but . . ."

Tamberlane raised a hand and stroked her hair with gentle firmness. "The dogs are quite alive, as you can see, as is Boethius. De Langois is a half hundred leagues away from here and likely crouched in some rat hole to wait out the weather. You are completely safe, Amaranth. I vow it to be so."

Her face pressed tight to his throat, she gave her head a little shake. "I will not be safe until he is dead."

Even before the whispered words left her lips, she knew it to be the truth. She had known it the instant she had seen the look on Friar Guilford's face when he told her Odo was still alive. She knew it when they fled the castle that night, and she knew it when she ran into the woods with an arrow buried in her shoulder.

Tamberlane became aware of something hot and wet sliding down his neck, and he felt the tremors in her body as she wept quietly against him. He glanced over and signaled Lord Boethius to remove himself and close the door, then lifted his hand away from her hair long enough to point a silent command at the dogs to retreat and lie in the corner.

Amaranth remained cozened in the warmth of his arms long after her tears had ceased. She felt so safe, so protected by the shield of his body that she did not want to leave it.

Eventually, however, she knew she had to extricate herself and did so with a soft, embarrassed smile.

Tamberlane straightened as well, admittedly relieved to be able to draw a breath without taking in the scent of her hair, her skin.

"Better?"

She nodded and bit down lightly on her lower lip.

"You should try to sleep some more. There are still several hours to go before dawn, and we have a long day's journey ahead of us."

Hearing the soft whimper that escaped her lips, Tamberlane knew that the mere thought of closing her eyes again terrified her.

And how well he knew that feeling! How many hours, nights had he spent pacing the rooftops of Taniere dreading the notion of sleep. Sleep brought the dreams, the sound of screaming men and women, the sweat of the desert heat, the smell of blood and scorched flesh.

"Look you here," he said, rising from the bedside. "Roland brought a cup of broth earlier. We can warm it over the brazier. There is bread and cheese also," he added, unwrapping the folds of a square cloth. "And two handsome slices of mutton."

"I am not very hungry."

"You need to eat. If the rain lets up, we will have a very long day of riding ahead of us."

Amie glanced at the window, surprised to see and hear the rain beating a faint tattoo on the shutters. Her dream had all been silence and shadows.

"And if it does not let up?"

Tamberlane shrugged and carried the cup of broth over to the brazier. After balancing it carefully over the glowing coals, he straightened, and Amie could see where his shirt was still dark with dampness and clinging in patches to his skin. She was happy to see he had forsaken the horsehair shirt, but . . . perhaps he was thinking he had done so a day too early.

"There was not enough heat in all of Christendom to dry all of our clothes in the meager space we fought to procure in front of the fire," he was saying. "Not even the shine of a new coin could budge some arses from their warm perches. I left my cloak and surcoat with Lord Geoffrey, but I do not hold much hope for the state of either. Eat," he ordered brusquely, noting that she had not touched anything in the opened cloth yet. "All of it, to the last morsel."

"Only if you will share it, my lord."

"I have already enjoyed the mutton," he said with a wry arching of an eyebrow. "But the goat cheese is quite excellent."

Amie smiled and broke off a small piece. It was indeed delicious, and she ended up devouring all but the generous wedge she held out to Tamberlane. The mutton was tough and stringy, boiled out of all hope of flavor from a beast who had likely been well past its prime for growing a worthy coat of fleece.

The brown bread was palatable but best of all was the broth when Tamberlane deemed it sufficiently warm. It was strong and steamy and took the last of the chills out of Amie's body.

She kept one of the blankets wrapped around her knees but insisted that Tamberlane take the other and put it around his shoulders to act as a buffer where he sat and leaned against the damp stone wall.

He looked exhausted. She could not even begin to

reason when he might have slept last, for he had been making their travel arrangements the afternoon and evening before their journey began. They had ridden most of the night and all day, then he had seen to her wet clothing when he should have been trying to rest himself.

Marak had said that the Dragon Slayer never slept, but she thought it was an exaggeration. Now she was not so sure. There was bruising under his eyes and a heaviness in his shoulders that suggested he was fighting the urge to lay his head down.

"My lord, I will not be able to close my eyes again this night, but there is no need to waste a perfectly good cot. You need sleep more than I, and you will not do so with your back stiff and your boots squeaking with water."

Before he could offer up a protest, she was out of the bed and kneeling before him, her hands starting to tug at his wet boots.

"No, stop," he said, scraping his foot to the side. "I am perfectly able to rest right here."

"Indeed." She caught his foot again and set it back in front of her with a firm *thud*. "And by morning there will be rot on your skin, your toes will fester and begin to fall off, and then we shall have to drag you the rest of the way to Maidstone in a litter, with your brain in a fever and your eyes rolled to the back of your head."

He stared at her, unblinking, for the length of several heartbeats before the iron that formed his jaw began to melt. By degrees it softened as a grin crept across his lips, and at the end, he actually laughed.

He laughed so long and hard that Amaranth was able to lift both unresisting feet and slide off his boots.

When she had inverted them and set them by the brazier to dry, she stood and pointed sternly to the bed.

"If you give me further grief, my lord, I will summon Lord Boethius to assist me in lifting you onto the bed and tying you down."

"My dear lady, I—"

She brought her face closer to his. "I will allow you to retain the rest of your clothing, sirrah, wet as it is, but only if you do as I say and get into the bed."

The green eyes stared back calmly. "The guise of a shrew does not become you, my lady."

"Nor does the guise of a pillock do aught for your appeal as a guardian and fearsome protector, my lord."

Tamberlane's gaze kindled a moment while he pondered if there was any wisdom or benefit to be gained by arguing. In the end, he simply sighed and heaved himself to his feet, swaying as the rush of blood hit his head. He was beyond tired; there was no denying that fact. Lord Boethius was outside the door. The dogs were alert. An hour, no more, with his eyes closed was all he needed.

He crossed over to the narrow cot and, after unbuckling the wide leather belt from his waist, eased himself onto the mattress and lay back, resting one arm across his forehead and keeping one stockinged foot on the floor.

Amaranth watched him for the few seconds it took

for his breathing to become deep and slow. She went to where he had been sitting and gathered the wings of the blanket tightly around her shoulders before sliding down to sit on the floor. The wolfhounds lay down beside her, one across her feet, the other at her side, and added the comfort of their warm bodies to that of the meager fire. She did not take her eyes away from Tamberlane's sleeping form, thinking it was odd that even though he was asleep she still felt completely safe in his presence.

Chapter Seventeen

A quiet tapping on the door roused Tamberlane out of a surprisingly deep sleep several hours later. He glanced quickly toward the corner, but saw Amaranth cocooned in her blanket, her head tipped to one side and cushioned by Hugo's body. Maude was already on her feet, standing poised at the door. Her growl was barely audible, indicating it was most likely Roland on the other side of the door. She had bitten him once for stepping on her tail and was not a forgiving bitch.

Ciaran swung his legs over the side of the bed and raked his hands through his hair. The scored marks on the night candle told him—and he had to look twice—that he had been asleep for five dreamless hours. If so, no wonder Roland had come to wake him. If it was past dawn, they should be well on their way by now.

It also occurred to him that Roland was showing unusual discretion by knocking first before entering. A second glance at Amaranth gave him more than enough of an explanation for the squire's sudden show of manners, and he could feel his cheeks staining red despite the complete propriety of their sleeping arrangements.

It was not Roland, however. It was Lord Boethius standing out in the misty corridor, and behind him Brother Ignatius and another, much older monk.

The latter had the half-squinted eyes of a man who had spent many an hour toiling over illuminated manuscripts in poorly lit scriptoriums. His tonsured head wore a fringe of gray hair, and his skin bore such deep wrinkles in places that he could have held his brushes and quills in the folds.

"I endeavored to tell them 'twas not a good idea to wake you, m'lord," said the burly knight, "but they were determined."

The wizened blue eyes of the older monk glanced down at the naked sword in Tamberlane's hand. "I can see the warning was not delivered without due cause. We shall have to instruct Brother Dominick to have more care with regards to relieving our guests of their weaponry at the gates. This is a house where peace and prayer rules above all."

Tamberlane lowered the tip of the blade. "I seek only to defend what is mine. I mean no insult to your peace or your prayers."

"Spoken in such a cold tone," the old priest said, "and from one who has put his sword to such infamous good use defending the Word of God."

The Dragon Slayer's green eyes narrowed with curiosity, then flicked to Brother Ignatius.

"Yes," the monk said. "It was I who informed Father Michaelus of your presence here. No doubt you would scarce remember one humble face out of the thousands who cheered your victories in Palestine, my lord Tamberlane, but yours was a visage not easily forgotten."

The green eyes flicked again, this time to the night candle that guttered in the drafts blowing through the open door. "An unusual time to be reminiscing, good friar."

"The choice of hour was mine," Father Michaelus said. "The decision to send you here was God's."

"No one sent me here," Tamberlane said, frowning. "I am but a weary traveler seeking respite from the storm."

Father Michaelus smiled and stepped across the threshold. "God's ways are indeed a mystery to some."

He cast around the room, his inspection touching first on the rumpled bed, then on the huddled figure of Amaranth where she sat flanked now by both alert wolfhounds. The voices had wakened her, and she sat rubbing her fists in her eyes to clear them.

"I confess I was intrigued to hear that the mighty Dragon Slayer had come knocking upon our gates. And only a scant day after another mighty lord had come banging his fists and clanking his armor, demanding he be allowed to search the buildings and grounds for his errant wife."

Amaranth ceased her rubbing and could not prevent her eyes from flinching swiftly upward and meeting Tamberlane's—an exchange that was noted by Father Michaelus before he too turned and looked at Ciaran.

"It might be of some interest to you to know that had you arrived in our valley an hour earlier, you would have seen that selfsame lord riding away with his entire host, having been found here himself by one of Prince John's couriers and summarily ordered to abandon his quest. Indeed, all of the regent's most loyal henchmen have been summoned to attend upon him at once. It seems he has recently been in receipt of some discomfiting news."

When Tamberlane showed no interest in inquiring what this news might be, the monk tipped his head at Brother Ignatius, who nodded solemnly and backed out of the cell, pulling the door closed behind him.

"You are aware, are you not, that the ransom for King Richard has been paid to Leopold of Austria? The gracious dowager queen, Eleanor of Aquitaine, saw to its safe arrival herself, sending her own champion, Lord Randwulf de la Seyne Sur Mer, to meet the treasure train once it arrived in France."

Tamberlane nodded, not exactly sure where the revelation fit into the order of things. "I had heard the ransom was collected and departed London. I have also heard of la Seyne Sur Mer—the Black Wolf. A formidable defender in and out of the lists."

"One of the few men feared by Prince John and one not likely to be challenged by any misguided attempts to waylay the treasure train before it was delivered into Leopold's hands. As I further understand it, the Black Wolf will also be acting as escort to the king as far as the Channel, thereby ensuring no further accidents befall our liege lord on his journey home."

"I am pleased to hear it, good Father, but curious as to how you know all of this and, further, why you should be telling me."

The monk pursed his lips. "My purpose is twofold. Firstly, your reputation for accepting strays and outcasts is well-known, my lord. So is your inclination to remain locked behind the walls of Taniere Castle. To be seen outside those walls, and in the company of a—a rather fair-skinned squire . . . might draw a curious eye."

Tamberlane weighed the warning against the value of denying it, and ended up acknowledging Father Michaelus with a scant nod. "I thank you for your concerns, but any man showing too curious an eye will have it cut out."

The pronouncement was made with such confidence, the priest was driven to smile.

"My true concerns lie in another direction, my son. And for it, you may credit Hubert Walter's vast web of spies and couriers, for it rivals even that of the prince himself. He knew the instant the ransom was delivered, knew when Leopold held up the first silver coin to test its weight, and knew the moment the gates to the castle at Durnstein were thrown open and the Lionheart was set free. He also knows that every assassin and dog at the prince's command will be sent to the English coast to watch for the arrival of the king on these shores, and that they will have

orders to stop him at all costs from setting foot off
that beach alive."

"Are you suggesting the prince would order the
death of his own brother?"

"It would not be the first time our greedy regent
has contemplated the deed. He has grown fat and
comfortable on the throne and will not be pleased to
remove his arse too quickly.

"He had fond hopes that two years in prison
would accomplish what war with the Saracens could
not, but alas the Lionheart merely scoffed at his con-
finement. Lackland even tried to ally himself with
Philip of France and buy the king's release into his
enemy's hands, but that too failed. He was quite
vexed to discover that Leopold had some scruples
after all."

"I would ask again, why do you tell me this? The
king's homecoming is to be celebrated, to be sure,
but beyond my gratitude and thanks for his continuing good health, I fail to see . . ."

"He will have no health at all if Prince John has
his way. He will be assassinated the instant he steps
foot in England. I tell you this that you may go forth
and prevent it."

"Me?" Tamberlane was genuinely taken aback.
"Why the devil would I embark on such a thing?"

"You are still Richard's man, are you not? He is
your liege lord, to whom you have sworn loyalty
and obedience, whom you have sworn to serve and
protect with your life, second only to God. Moreover,
he is . . . was . . . your friend and comrade in arms.
He defended your honor when others would have

spat upon it and shunned you as a coward. Are you so eager to turn your back on him now?"

Tamberlane drew a deep breath to control his anger. "Surely he does not make the crossing alone. What of la Seyne Sur Mer? The sword of the Black Wolf should be enough protection for ten kings."

"The Black Wolf has no love for England and would not soil his feet walking upon this ground. He holds even less affection for Prince John, with whom he has crossed swords before. And then, of course, there is Richard's pride. Having been caught in a snare once by two prancing fools, he will not be pleased to be treated like a child who needs his hand held to cross a stream."

"I am bound for Maidstone," Tamberlane said. "My business there is somewhat pressing."

"More pressing than safeguarding the life of your king?" Michaelus's white eyebrows bristled upward, and he looked at Amaranth again. "You would rather he guard your passage to a convent rather than guard the life of the king, your own cousin?"

Amaranth's eyes grew as round as coins, and her hand rose instinctively to clutch the crucifix that hung around her neck. She could see Tamberlane stiffen and she pushed herself to her feet, using the stone wall for support. For a full minute the three stood in total silence, the solitary candle melting just enough of the shadows to show their faces and the glint of Tamberlane's sword.

"I would not begin to presume to tell Lord Tamberlane where his services are required," she insisted. "Indeed, I had no right to presume upon his intentions at all, least of all to break the laws of the church and the throne to hide me away from my husband. He is and always was free to go where he will, and I would, of course, release him freely from any tenders he may have made in haste."

"I rarely do anything in haste," Tamberlane said quietly. "As for loyalty and friendship—I warrant the king was not defending my honor so much as he was protecting his right to keep killing in the name of God, for up to then I had been one of his finest murderers. I give thanks to God that he is free. I am pleased to hear he is coming home. But if God wills that he dies on the shores of England rather than in the land of the holy sepulcher . . . who am I to interfere with the irony?"

Father Michaelus bowed his head and pursed his lips thoughtfully. He had been standing with his hands clasped behind his back, but at Tamberlane's bitter words, he brought them forward and funneled one hand into the opposite bell-shaped sleeve so that they rested on his forearms.

"A man can lose his way in this world so easily," he said softly. "He can see horrors that make him question his sense of worth, his sense of well-being, his sense of what is right and wrong. He can be overcome by greed, by lust, by the lure of another man's possessions. He can have everything he owns, even his name and his reputation taken away from him in the blink of an eye. But the one thing, the *only* thing a man cannot have taken away from him is his honor. That, he has to give away."

With a small nod in Amaranth's direction, Father

Michaelus turned and walked to the door. He paused there a scant moment as if he contemplated saying more, but one look at the Dragon Slayer's wooden features and he reconsidered.

"*Pax Domini.* Peace go with you, my son."

Amaranth heard the door open and close, but she did not look away from Tamberlane's face. It was terrible to behold in the flickering candlelight, all ridges and angles and deeply carved shadows. Even the dogs could sense the rage smoldering just beneath the surface, for they stood and made a low rumbling sound deep in their throats.

"I meant what I said, my lord. About releasing you from your tender."

He looked at her. "We leave at first light. Be ready."

Tamberlane strode along the darkened, vaulted corridor, his boots ringing off the stone floor as he made his way to the pilgrim's hall at the far end. It was still raining, still driving down in sheets, and by the time he reached the arched portal, his face was gleaming wet from the fine needles of mist. Inside the hall, fires were blazing at each end and in between were sprawled the forms of men sleeping, rolled in blankets. Ciaran had left Lord Geoffrey de Ville in charge of the cloaks and garments they were trying to dry, and the knight was there, seated in front of the blaze, his arms folded over his chest and his chin resting comfortably low.

He looked to be fast asleep, but at Tamberlane's approach, his chin came up off his chest and his hand edged briefly toward the hilt of the dagger lying not very well hidden beneath his surcoat. It fell away again as he recognized the knight, replaced by a yawn then another settling down of his chin on his chest.

Tamberlane stood with a hand leaning against the top of the brick opening. The fireplace was enormous, easily accommodating the ten-foot tree trunk that burned hotly within. The stone lip was inches above Tamberlane's head, darkened by years of soot and smoke.

He stood there, his face a mask, his thoughts in too fearsome a tangle to try to sort one from the other. The monk was right, he owed the king his allegiance and his sword, yet it was a commitment he was not certain he could make. Indeed, he resented the old monk for even asking, for putting him in a position where he had to choose. He wished he had never set foot outside Taniere Castle, for no one would have come seeking his aid there. He wished, further, that he had never gone hunting in the woods that day, never interfered with the attack on the village, never taken Amaranth back to the castle for Marak to bring back to life.

He wished he had never looked into her eyes, never touched her, never kissed her. The latter, especially, for the remembered touch and taste of her assaulted him each time he forgot he was a monk and was reminded he was a man.

Yet he was neither. He was not a man; he was not a priest. He was some aberration between, unable to take up the cloth again because of all he had seen and done; unable to completely cast it aside for that would leave him naked and vulnerable and, he feared, inadequate to the task of being a man. Amaranth terrified him. His feelings for her terrified him. He could still taste her lips, could still feel the warmth of her body pressed against him.

Leave her to her fate merely to save the life of a king?

Perhaps that was exactly what he needed to do. Leave her. Walk away from her. Forget her eyes and the way they looked at him. Forget that ridiculous cloud of russet hair and the way the candlelight shone through every curl. Forget the softness of her cheek, the slight tilt to her smile, the small catch in her voice when she spoke to him.

It could never be. She was a married woman, bound for a convent. He was an excommunicated priest, bound for hell.

He slammed the flat of his hand on the stone and offered up a vile epithet that caused Lord Geoffrey de Ville to open one eye and peer up.

It caused someone else to look over as well, one of the men not privileged to find a place close to the fire. His face was long and pointed, his eyes narrowed and crusted by sleep. A curse was on his lips from having his slumber disturbed, but as he stared at the figure outlined so boldly by the blazing log, his mouth went slack and his eyes widened. He started to push himself upright, but it took two attempts for him to roll and pull himself out of the twisted blanket. By then Tamberlane had turned away from the fire and was kicking drying clothes out of the way to take a seat beside the other dozing knight.

But there could be no mistaking that profile. No two men had such an eerie shade of green eyes, such black hair, such a square chin.

Hugh de Bergerette felt a sudden, violent flare of pain in the right hand and wrist that was no longer there. He reached across and rubbed the stump where his elbow should have been, and in his mind's eye he saw the flash of a sword biting into his flesh, tearing it away, and leaving his hand and arm lying in a spatter of blood on the hot desert sand.

He had not seen Ciaran Tamberlane for nigh on three years and while he, a man loyal to his king and his God, had been reduced to a one-armed pauper, it was evident by the cut of his tunic, the healthy breadth to his chest that the defrocked Templar had barely suffered at all for his disgrace.

Bitterness, as fresh and hot as the blood that roared through his temples, caused the knight to clench his remaining fist in outrage.

He would not let such an insult go unanswered a second time.

Chapter Eighteen

As much as Tamberlane wanted to leave the monastery, the weather did not favor it. The rain had obscured the dawn, falling through the night in waves of heavy, slanting lancets that flooded the meadows and ran down the slopes, swelling the little stream until it overflowed its banks and threatened to wash the bridge away.

Tamberlane spent the morning in the pilgrim's hall and, at midday, with no relief in sight, joined Lord Boethius, who was standing beside the statue of the Virgin Mary and watching the driving torrents.

"Stupid creatures," the knight said, tipping an unshaven chin to indicate the corpses of several dead chickens in the courtyard. "Turn their heads up to watch the rain and they drown."

Tamberlane glanced down the long walkway and could just make out the distant figure of Lord Geoffrey—who had offered Boethius relief from his watch—where he now sat wrapped in a blanket with his back against the door to the monk's cell.

Boethius grunted. "We would not manage a mile in this downpour."

"No," Tamberlane said, sighing to express his resignation. "I warrant we would not."

He started off down the breezeway, forced to keep close to the wall to avoid the spray that came through the many arched openings. De Ville heard him long before he reached the last door and was on his feet, his expression as stony as always, though his eyes betrayed some mild curiosity.

Tamberlane shook his head. "We would be like the chickens if we tried to ride out in this today. Go and warm yourself by the fire. Put a toe in Roland's ribs and ask him to fetch you bread and cheese and ale from the rectory."

Lord Geoffrey accepted his orders with a casual nod. He looked out across the courtyard, his eyes scanning the mist and rain, before he set off down the passage in the direction from whence Tamberlane had come.

Ciaran drew a deep breath and released it slowly through puffed cheeks. He turned and stared at the iron latch for a long moment before carefully raising it and pushing the door quietly open.

Both dogs were on their feet and standing to attention as he ducked and crossed the threshold. Amaranth was hunched over and cursing, a scattering of leather points flung to the floor around her.

She whirled around with a startled look and sent another point flying out of her fingers.

"If you are come to fetch me, my lord, I am more than ready to leave this place. Certes, I will be, if I can but learn the proper way of binding these wretched things."

She was standing in the middle of the tiny room, clad in the now dry, long, shapeless white shirt and stockings Roland had delivered earlier. She appeared to be having some difficulty tying the leather points, for at the sound of the door opening, her hands came up from under the hem of the shirt and the top of the hose sagged down to her knees.

"I vow I watched Inaya do it," she said, holding up one of the short leather thongs. "But I confess I must be stupid, for I cannot grasp how she tied the blessed things. Twice I have thought I found success only to move and have everything fall down about my ankles."

By way of demonstration, she took a step, and Tamberlane heard several soft but audible popping noises as the points slipped out of the corresponding loops on the belt, and the left stocking rippled down her leg and puddled around her knee to match the one on the right.

After some consideration—including whether to smile or not at the perplexed look on her face—he walked forward and took the thong out of her fingers.

"There is a knack," he said. While she watched, he folded the point in half. "Thread this through the hole in the belt first, then bring it down and through the eye in the top of the stocking and tie it . . . like so." A twist and snap of his fingers produced a fine, tight knot.

She had him show her again then tied one herself.

"But . . . and forgive me again for asking . . . how do you manage the ones in back?"

Tamberlane hesitated again. Normally there was a squire or page present to assist a lord in dressing. Roland was in the pilgrim's hall, but he doubted he would trust the young squire to the task of helping Amaranth truss her points. Likewise, he was certain either of the two knights would most happily oblige, but he was equally aware that neither possessed the faintest blush of monkish restraint.

Quicker than his better judgment would allow, he went down on one knee behind Amaranth and reached up beneath the hem of the shirt, excruciatingly careful not to come in contact with her skin as he raised the stocking and located the lower edge of the belt.

Amaranth stood as still as a statue, barely daring to breathe. She had not expected him to assist her himself, and while she knew he tried to work swiftly and with as detached a manner as possible, she could not help but be aware of the heat of his hands and the shifting hem of her shirt. Staring at a fixed point on the far wall did not help. Neither did staring at Hugo, who chose that unlucky moment to affectionately lick the back of Maude's ear.

A soft, near-soundless whimper escaped her throat, one that abruptly halted the movement of Ciaran's hands.

The movement ceased, but the warmth of his fingers remained resting against the silky flesh of her upper thigh.

He was midway through tying off one of the

points. The backs of his fingers were tucked between the top of the hose and her leg, and at the sound of her softly expelled breath, his gaze shifted to the visible tremors that shook the folds of her shirt. He tried, slowly, to extricate his hand, but that only served to send another shiver rippling through the linen.

The leather point fell slack in his fingers; the unknotted end slipped slowly free of the loop. His right hand opened and spread flat over the top of her leg, the fingers shaping to the curve of her thigh. The left hand did the same, holding still for but a moment before his thumbs stroked softly up and brushed against the lush curve of her bottom.

Too late he noticed the linen breeks on the chair and realized she had also dressed in the wrong order, leaving nothing but bare skin to tease the pads of his thumbs.

Tamberlane groaned and closed his eyes. He brought his head forward and rested it on the thin scrap of linen that was the only barrier standing between him and a lust so shameful it burned through his body and sent a shudder through his arms.

Amaranth felt it. She felt it in his hands, and she felt it in the heat at the small of her back where his brow rested. A year of being forced to suffer every intimacy a woman could share with a man bade her move instinctively to part her legs wider, to lean her hands forward and grip the back of the chair, for she knew that fighting a man's lust only brought greater pain. Some of her tremblings came from the fear that this knight would be no different from either of her husbands, from Rolf de Langois, from any of the dozens of men who had looked upon her with hunger in their eyes.

Part of it came from her own shocking hope that she would indeed feel his hands, his body move to roughly possess her.

She felt his hands tighten where they gripped her thighs. A ragged sigh brought greater pressure to bear on her hip where he had turned his head and now rested a cheek against her.

"This is wrong," he whispered. "It is wrong and I know it is wrong, and yet . . . I am helpless to stop myself. I see you, and I want to touch you. I touch you, and I long to caress you. I caress you, and . . ."

Startled by the raw emotion in his voice, Amaranth slowly straightened, releasing her grip on the back of the chair. She drew a breath, then another, then turned within the circle of his arms, noting that the pressure from his hands had eased at once but did not drop away completely.

When she looked, she saw that his eyes were closed, his clenched jaw like a ridge of granite.

Amie sank slowly down onto her knees before him so that they faced each other again. She smiled faintly, for he still had not taken his hands away, though they had slid higher and now rested at her waist. She raised her own hands and cradled his face gently between them, causing the pale green eyes to open.

There was nothing in them to fear. She saw only confusion, loneliness, desperation . . . and a silent plea for understanding.

Amie leaned forward and brushed her lips across

his. The touch was light, the kiss fleeting. She did it a second time and a third. On the fourth his hands slid around to the small of her back then crept slowly upward until he was pulling her forward. His mouth captured hers on a rush of breath that might have been her name, or it might have been a curse—she could not tell. She cared only to know the heat of his lips when they covered hers, to feel the thunder of her heart, beating within her chest like some wild, caged thing that longed to be set free.

Both of his hands pushed up into her hair, holding her while his mouth opened and the kiss became bolder, deeper. His tongue was there to taste her, to probe between her lips, lashing and swirling and matching his hunger with her own.

Amaranth shuddered with every heated thrust. The shaking in his arms grew more pronounced, but there was no need to conquer, to abase, to prove possession. Tamberlane's lips were warm and roughly tender—they pressed against hers with a need to know, to taste, to feel, as if, above all, he was astonished by the simple passion found in the act of two mouths clinging together.

But as suddenly as he had invaded her mouth, he abandoned it again, leaving her bereft, gasping. His fingers remained tense where they were tangled in her curls, but he bent his head and touched his brow to hers, shaking it slowly side to side.

"I am lost," he whispered. "God knows . . . I am floundering."

She did not know how to respond, not with her body melting and her blood rushing through her veins like liquid fire. She knew how she *wanted* to respond. She wanted to take his face in her hands and drag his mouth back to hers. She wanted him to kiss her again . . . and again . . . and by all that was holy and unholy . . . she wanted to kiss him in return.

"God is not here," she said, her voice no more than a broken whisper. "There is only you and me, my lord, and in truth, I am as lost as you."

He sighed again, and his hands slipped down to cradle her neck. "Amaranth . . . you know nothing about me."

"I know all I need to know, good sir. It is there in your eyes when you look at me."

He shook his head and startled her somewhat by laughing. "No. I think my true dilemma would surprise even you."

Amaranth's heart stumbled inside her chest. It was, of course, a polite way of telling her he still thought as a monk, behaved as a monk.

"Forgive me, my lord. 'Twas my fault. I am to blame. I should simply have found a way to tie the knots and not imposed upon you to—"

A low growl in his throat preceded a tightening of his hands, and he silenced her stammered apology with a kiss so deep and passionate it stripped the breath from her body.

When her lips were pink and throbbing, he found the pulse that beat below her ear and followed it down the length of her throat. While she knelt before him, blinded and quaking, he unfastened the laces that bound the front of her shirt and pushed the cloth aside, trailing the heat of his tongue across her bared shoulder. His hands continued to ease the shirt down until it was crumpled about her hips, clinging by the merest thread of modesty. Her breasts gleamed pale as marble in the scant light that bled through the closed shutters. The nipples were hard and tight, an irresistible lure for calloused fingers and starving lips.

He kissed, he licked, he suckled. He caught a nipple between his teeth, and when she flinched from the pleasure, he razed it gently with his teeth then took as much of the soft, succulent flesh into his mouth as he could, groaning at the taste and feel of her.

Amie's arms went around his broad shoulders. Her hands came together at the back of his head, and she held his mouth against her flesh. The heat of his breath, the swirling of his tongue, the strong greedy suckling that seemed to want to pull her soul from her chest—they combined to send her head arching back and sent a cry shivering into the cool air.

He heard the cry and stopped again, lifting his mouth away with a harsh gasp for air and reason.

"Amaranth, I . . . did not mean to . . ."

She kissed him, hard and full on the mouth. Her fingers twisted in the long black waves of his hair as if she knew that to hear another word, another apology, the spell might be broken, the magic would end.

He accepted this as meaning he had not hurt her in his eagerness. Further, he accepted it as meaning he could send his hands down and unfasten the belt from around her waist, peeling it away and sending it down to her knees with the shirt and the half-bound hose. His fingers stroked their way back up to her breasts, and this time when his mouth was free, he leaned back and let his eyes drink their fill.

"You are so . . . beautiful," he whispered. "As beautiful as the flower that bears your name."

She started to raise a hand to cover the angry red scar on her shoulder, but he caught her wrist and lowered his mouth to tenderly kiss the edges of the wound.

"Sweet Jesu, sirrah, you melt me."

He moved his lips so that they were pressed against the curve of her neck. "You deserve better."

"Nay. No better."

"I can offer you nothing. I *have* nothing to offer."

Amaranth combed her fingers gently through the waves of his hair. "You have already given me more than any man before you, my lord, and I fear that any who would come after you would suffer as fools."

"Be that as it may . . ." He looked at her, his tormented face ever more the image of a fallen archangel. "Tomorrow we leave this place. You must go on to Maidstone, and I must see you safely there. I have shattered too many of God's laws already."

Her hands drifted down and hung limp by her sides. "Then . . . you do not want me?"

"Not want you? Is that what you think?" His eyes narrowed, and he tucked a finger beneath her chin, forcing her to look at him again. "Amaranth . . . never think it for a moment. I want you. I want all of you in every way imaginable. I am just . . . afraid of disappointing you. I have . . . I have never . . ."

He bowed his head a moment and cursed softly. "I have never lain with a woman before and am at a fool's loss how to do so."

The look on his face, the tension in his body was raw and poignant, and it filled Amaranth with more of a sense of relief than surprise. Marak had hinted at as much, and she should have known that he would honor his vows as a monk despite being cast from the Order and banned from the church.

The relief—for she had feared something much more dreadful—flooded through her in a soft, lush wave and brought the veriest hint of a smile to her lips.

"You have done nothing in error yet, my lord. In truth, there is no great secret to the act itself and, certes, no fools present here this day. If you wish"— she paused and moistened her lips, suddenly the driest place on her body—"I could . . . perhaps . . . guide you . . ."

He raised his head slowly, and she caught her breath again, for he was looking at her in a way that made her insides flutter, her limbs go molten, and her fingers tremble where they had begun to unfasten the wide leather belt at his waist.

Tamberlane did not move. Nor did his eyes stray from hers for one tenth of one hundredth of a heartbeat. He was aware of the belt falling away, then of her hands gathering up the hem of his tunic and raising it. He had to release her for as long as it took to aid her in tugging it up and over his head, but they lowered quickly again and drew her closer than before.

"I am told," she whispered, her cheeks scalded

red, "that for a man the act is instinctive. It comes . . . quite naturally."

"And for a woman?"

Amie ran the tips of her fingers up his bared arms, tracing the contours of each bulging muscle as she went. "It is responsive."

"I want to know what gives you pleasure."

"We will have to discover that together, my lord," she said, "for you have already given me more than I would have dreamed was possible."

His mouth captured hers again, and together they sank slowly down until they were lying on the floor. Tamberlane made some attempt at providing softness by dragging the blanket off the cot and tucking it beneath her, but he was back in her arms before she knew he had gone. His lips covered her breasts; they trailed down to her belly and chased after the visible tremors that caused her flesh to shudder and her limbs to shiver uncontrollably.

He slid a hand between her thighs and groaned when he felt the wetness on his fingers. A moment of tugging at laces and fumbling with leggings and his weight was replacing his hand, the solid heat of him causing her limbs to flare wider apart and her hands to clutch at his shoulders.

His flesh was hard and thick and slipped along her nether lips twice, thrice, bringing her arching up beneath him. He groaned, lifted himself, and probed again with no better success. Amaranth caught her breath, slid her hand down between their bodies, and curled her fingers around his shaft, guiding him into her heat.

She was wet enough that he plunged easily, deeply within her. So powerful was that first thrust that Amie cried out. Her head tipped back and her body tightened around him; her limbs rose of their own accord and wrapped around him, holding him, clinging to him as his hips rose and fell in the hard, pounding rhythm of his need. It was pleasure, pure and exquisite. And as the ecstasy shook her, she heard his ragged gasps against her throat. She felt his hands, his arms, his body grow tense and rigid, and when a second wave of bright-hot sensations rose and burst within her, she felt the liquid heat of his own release, strong and pulsing, flooding her with joy.

They remained locked together and continued to rock with the pleasure, seeking every last flutter and spasm. His thrusts gradually slowed, the shivers faded, and when their strength was drained, utterly depleted, they collapsed in a warm, panting heap on the blanket.

Amie lay beneath him, stunned. Her hands were splayed flat on his buttocks, her fingers gripping the taut flesh in a shameless plea for him to remain inside her. He was still a throbbing, formidable presence, though most of the urgency had been expended. His head was resting on her shoulder, his breaths shallow and warm against her neck, and she wanted to savor these few minutes of tender intimacy, fearing she might never know them again.

Tamberlane had neither the wit nor the desire to deny her. He lay there torn between a need to lift his head and shout for joy . . . or to remain where he was until such time as he could crawl away and find some dark corner to hide in. He knew he had been clumsy and oafish. He had heard her cry out but too late. Too late to stop himself from thrusting deeper and deeper, from exploding into that sweet, clenching oblivion.

His sin was greed, and he acknowledged it readily. He had been greedy to know the secrets of a woman's body, greedy to know why his own ached and burned each time Amaranth cast a glance his way. There had been instances in the past when his flesh had grown thick and hard, swelling beneath his tunic when the fury and bloodlust of battle had sent the thrill of victory pounding through his veins.

There were bishops who kept mistresses and priests who regularly frequented nunneries seeking mutual satisfaction from their cloistered lives. But Knights Templar were conditioned through prayer and constant piety to be above even the use of their own hands for surcease.

He turned his head and kissed the side of her neck. Her skin was warm, smooth as silk, and he could feel the sudden jump in the pulse that beat softly just below her ear.

There would be no crawling away to repent his sins.

He lifted his head and found her eyes there waiting for him, filled with questions, fears, anxiety. He set all three to rest with a kiss as gentle as it was within his power to make it, and long before he lifted his mouth away he could feel his body stirring, stretching, furrowing into the sleek, tight heat again.

Her fingers dug into his buttocks, and she started to move beneath him, making slow undulating motions with her hips that lured him deeper . . . deeper . . .

Maude's first growl went unnoticed.

The two wolfhounds had retreated to a corner and watched the writhing humans with mildly quizzical expression. When the groans and harsh, guttural whispers had stopped and the silence had become as thick as woolen fleece, it was Maude whose head had turned toward the door. Her ears pricked up sharply, and she gave a warning rumble in her throat. Hugo pushed himself upright beside her and curled his lip back over a snarl, stalking over to the door as he did so.

Tamberlane heard it then too—the soft scrape of a footstep outside on the breezeway.

Pressing a finger to Amaranth's lips to signal caution, he gently extricated himself from between her thighs and rolled to his feet. His leggings had been pushed down to his knees, hampering his movements, but he had his sword in his hand before he had finished yanking them back up around his waist.

Another silent signal sent Amie scrambling noiselessly to the far side of the cot. A tilt of his head dispatched the two dogs to stand guard over her while he took up a stance beside the door and reached out to grasp the iron latch.

Chapter Nineteen

Hugh de Bergerette had watched Tamberlane leave the pilgrim's hall and had followed at a sly distance. He kept to the shadows, and hunched his chin to his chest if anyone glanced his way. Twice it had been necessary to retreat from the portal and wait until curious eyes turned elsewhere, but with the weather so abysmal, there were a number of restless movements in the hall, and no one noticed him when he did slip out the door.

The courtyard was deserted, washed in a steady drizzle that had started to thicken with the added bleakness of mist. The breezeway was long and wet and devoid of anyone foolish enough to chill themselves to the bone. He paused beside the statue of the Virgin and felt for the hilt of the long poniard concealed under his tunic. With a last glance behind him, he crabbed sideways along the walk, keeping his back to the wall and ducking furtively into every niche that marked a doorway.

Tamberlane's was the last one, and if nothing else,

de Bergerette knew he had distance and surprise in his favor. Even if someone should hear a hue and cry, he would have more than enough time to deal with his nemesis before help could arrive.

Silent as a ferret, the one-armed knight approached the door. He pressed his ear to the wood to listen for sounds of movement within. Catching the Dragon Slayer asleep was too much to hope for, but . . .

He lifted his ear from the door and stared at the planking for a moment. The muffled sounds he had heard were familiar enough to set the nape of his neck tingling and send a surge of hot blood into his loins.

The Dragon Slayer had a woman with him. A woman who was whimpering and snuffling like a bitch in heat.

How far the pious and mighty had fallen, indeed!

Excommunicated, cast out of the Brotherhood, and now fornicating with a whore of Satan under God's own roof!

With renewed rage burning like acid through his veins, de Bergerette had to force himself to move slowly and calmly. He tested the iron latch on the door and found that it moved easily enough.

After scanning the walk and courtyard, he raised the hem of his tunic and started to unsheathe the wickedly sharp poniard, but then he stopped again.

A final shivered cry had brought silence on the other side of the door. It was the ideal moment to burst in upon the room, yet there were two now, not one. While de Bergerette had worked with single-minded fervor to retrain his left arm in the use of a sword and knife, he was not so blinded by hatred as to be unaware of his shortcomings.

There was something else. He had been at the monastery four days, and the thought prickling at the edge of his memory was of a tall red-haired knight scouring the halls and cells in search of his errant wife.

There was absolutely no reason for de Bergerette to believe the woman rutting with Ciaran Tamberlane was that same woman, yet he did not believe in coincidences either. If it was her, and if Tamberlane was helping her escape her husband's clutches, Hugh might only have to stand by the side of the road and watch the slaughter happen.

Not only that, but the Red Boar had offered one hundred gold sovereigns to any man who could bring him information concerning his wife's whereabouts. One hundred pieces of gold was more than enough to relieve Hugh's pride of the burden of revenge.

The filthy knight melted back a pace, examining this new thought from all angles. Something snapped under the heel of his boot, and he looked down. An acorn shell. It had sounded like the crack of a whip and abruptly ended the debate on what to do.

With a curse and a promise, he turned and leaped over the low half wall, vanishing around the corner and into the obscuring mists.

Tamberlane jerked the door open. His sword was raised, his teeth set to answer a challenge, but there was no one there to issue it.

The breezeway was empty. There were frogs burping in the courtyard, and water was dripping steadily from the overhanging roof, but other than faint sworls in the encroaching mist, there were no sounds, no signs of movement anywhere nearby.

He stuck his head out beyond the niche and looked both ways. Nothing. No one lurking, no one walking past.

Lowering his sword, he was about to withdraw back into the cell when his gaze happened to turn down and he saw the crushed acorn shell. After another wary glance cast about the yard, he bent over and retrieved it, turning it over in his fingertips. The outer shell was wet, soaked by the dampness, but the break was clean and dry.

Someone *had* been standing outside the door. That same someone had tried the latch but thought better of coming inside the room.

Roland or either of the two knights would not have approached with any attempt at stealth, knowing the two dogs were inside. Moreover, it had been less than a minute since Maude had growled a warning. Any or all three would have to run like the blazes back down the breezeway to disappear so fast from view. Roland might have managed it, though for what purpose Tamberlane could not suppose. But not Geoffrey or Boethius. Both carried too much suet around the waist and too much belligerence in their nature to lift their heels and run.

He rubbed the shreds of crushed shell between his fingers and walked slowly back into the room.

Amaranth was still crouched beside the cot, but at his return, she stood, the fingers of one hand resting lightly on the head of one of the wolfhounds. She'd had the presence of mind to snatch up her shirt before she dashed behind the cot, and this she clutched to her breasts now in an embarrassed attempt at modesty—difficult to achieve with her flesh still mottled pink and her inner thighs pearly and glistening.

"I did not mean to frighten you," Tamberlane said, dusting his fingers off on his bare chest. "The blame must needs lie in too many years of tilting at shadows."

"I was not so terribly frightened for myself, my lord," she said faintly, "as I was . . . concerned for your well-being."

"My well-being?" He was startled at the notion. "It has been a good many years since anyone has spared a thought for my being well . . . or otherwise."

"Surely you are wrong, sir."

"Surely I am not. My father disowned me after the shame I brought upon the family. He would not see me when I returned to England. He will not even allow my name to be spoken in his presence. My mother turned her back and walked away when I attempted to see her, but not before she spat on the ground and crushed my heart into the dust."

He curled his fists by his side, not knowing why he had blurted his pain out to her, to this girl he had known less than a month. Perhaps, he tried desperately to reason, it was because she bore enough pain herself to understand the depth of his loneliness and despair. Perhaps it was because they were both wounded souls searching for answers, explanations . . . hope.

"I only know I would give everything I have, everything I am, everything I will be for the two of them to look upon me with a smile again."

"You have made me smile again, my lord. The others will smile too, in time. How can they not for a man whose heart still beats so nobly within?"

He studied her face a moment longer, then let his gaze fall slowly down her body.

Her wounds were physical as well as emotional and it was with a second surge of dawning comprehension that he understood their joining had been a catharsis of sorts for her as well. She may not have been virginal in her body, but the soul he had so clearly seen shining in her eyes had been untouched by any other hand save his.

The knowledge nearly brought him to his knees.

"My lord?"

She had been speaking to him, but his mind had drifted so far he had not heard enough to reply with any intelligence.

A low command, issued to the dogs, brought them to the door, which he opened enough to let them through. He knew they would sit like the statues that guarded the tombs of Egyptian kings until a second command released them.

Tamblerlane walked slowly over to where Amaranth stood. "I am not entirely convinced that we are safe here. There are too many pairs of eyes and ears about, some of which may owe their allegiance to your husband, and some who may simply be greedy for the gold he has offered. I cannot even say for certain that we were not followed away from Taniere, though God knows it would take a tracker with the nose of a bloodhound and eyes of a seer."

Amaranth bowed her head. She clutched the folds of the shirt so tight, her knuckles turned white.

"What is it? What is wrong?"

She gave her head a small shake of self-reproach. "There was one of Odo's men at Taniere. I saw him when I went to Marak's chamber. I am fairly certain he did not recognize me, and Marak assured me he would find the man and—and . . ."

Her voice trailed away, for Tamberlane had moved away from the door and now stood in front of her.

"I—I should have told you sooner, I know, but even though he was close enough for me to smell the foulness of his breath, I did not think he knew me. And Marak said—"

"Marak is a wise man. He says many things."

When she did not look up, he tucked a finger under her chin and forced it gently. "This lout whom you saw . . . was he as close as this?"

"Yes," she whispered, her chin trembling.

"Then he was a stupid man and not worthy of our concern." He smiled and his thumb stroked lightly across her chin. "For I would know you whither it was midnight under a moonless sky and you had wrapped yourself in Marak's robes."

Amaranth swayed, and the hand clasping the shirt to her bosom started to slip downward. "My lord . . ."

He silenced her with a kiss. The hand holding her chin slipped down to curve around her neck and then reached up, his fingers running into her hair as he held the back of her head. He pulled the shirt out of her unresisting grip and tossed it aside.

Her mouth was soft and willing, the gasp unbidden when the heat of his bare chest met the chilled flesh of her breasts. He pressed her back against the wall, his mouth slanting and growing more forceful with every shallow breath. Once the shirt had been cast aside, that hand stayed low, seeking the warmth of her thigh, then the wetness between. His fingers deftly raked through the pale yellow curls and sought the folds that were slick and slippery to the touch. At the sound of her whimper, they curled upward, probing deeper, causing her to rise up on her toes.

His leggings had been hastily pulled up to his waist and fell easily to the will of her hands. He groaned and made as if to pull her forward onto the cot, but Amie held his arms and dragged him back. She lifted one bare leg and curved it around his thigh, whispering short, broken instructions that sent his blood roaring past his ears.

With both hands cradling her bottom, he lifted her and pressed her back against the wall. He was already hard and swollen, and he found his mark on the first thrust, ramming her deep even as he lowered her down over his flesh.

They groaned together. Amie wrapped her legs around his waist and continued to whisper in his ear though the words were shapeless and broken. He thrust and thrust again, driving in and up, and she cried out each time, clutching at his shoulders when the ecstasy threatened to break within her.

Her body was jolted, lifted aggressively up and down, impaled and invaded, and she rode each wave of pleasure as it tore through her, her body a mass of quaking, shivering implosions. He pressed his brow to her shoulder and stroked faster, deeper, his legs starting to tremble, his body tensing, his breath coming in strained pants.

Tamberlane's fingers dug into her rump, and his arms turned to rock. He braced himself for one last thrust and brought her plunging down hard over his flesh. The muscles across his chest bulged, the veins in his neck stood out like ropes, and she could feel the hot spasms burst and pulse deep within her. He gasped and flung his head back and thrust again, and this time Amie shivered in unison with him, her body tightening around him like a fist, holding him until they were both spent.

He held her close, his head coming forward once again to rest on her shoulder, his breath panting in soft warm gusts against her throat. Amie stroked his hair and waited for her own heartbeat to slow. When it did, she thought to ease his burden by unlocking her legs and letting them slip slowly down from around his waist.

He did not acknowledge the movement except to lift his hands from her bottom, circle them around her shoulders and gather her so close against him that they breathed as one.

"I would know you," he whispered softly. "I would know you."

Chapter Twenty

The fog was thick and wet. Spickets of moisture clung to their clothes and faces as they rode out the front gates of St. Albans and crossed over the narrow bridge. Neither the horses nor the riders looked comfortable, for the river was still swollen, rushing past so fast and furious, the peaks of the current brushed the underbellies of the planking. Once on the other side, they turned their beasts in the direction of the forest that they knew was there but could not see. There were some muffled grumblings, some questioning as to the sanity of anyone who would venture out in such soup, but Tamberlane ignored them. It offered protection from the eyes that might be watching and would frustrate anyone trying to follow.

The wolfhounds proved their worth by running silently into the greensward and finding the two forresters Tamberlane had left behind to watch the monastery. The dogs were then dispatched ahead by a series of low whistles to scout the fog and sniff out any potential ambushes.

Ciaran was silent as they picked up their journey where they had left off. They rode through the day and only stopped when it was too dark to go on without risking injury to the horses. A fire was deemed unwise, as the glow would be seen reflecting off the clouds for miles around. The long cold night was spent rolled in blankets, stretched out on the forest floor, and when dawn arrived they were already riding.

It was on the third night away from the monastery that they came across a small mud and wattle cottage set in the middle of an overgrown glade. The roof was gone and the walls half crumbled. It had been abandoned for some time to judge by the number of bird nests built on the crux of every timber or stone.

The heavy weather that had been plaguing them for three days had finally cleared, and there was open sky and starlight above them. They built a small fire and spitted hares the foresters had caught. Eric the Fox supplemented it with a broth made from the wild onions and carrots he had found near the edge of the glade. Fletcher contributed a skin of wine . . . one of four he had come away with from St. Albans.

"Thieving from God's house," Boethius declared. "Ye'll be answering to the devil for that, lad. And pass it here before yer brethren suck it dry."

The forester grinned and handed the wineskin across.

Tamberlane, who had been quiet for the greater

part of the day—for all three days, Amaranth had noted with dismay—began speaking without any manner of introduction or preamble.

"I was visited by one of the monks at the abbey that first night. He advised me that King Richard will be arriving back in England before week's end and that Prince John has called his best assassins into play to prevent the Lionheart from ever reaching London."

Boethius paused midswallow. Lord Geoffrey glanced up from picking a sliver out of his thumb. Roland stopped honing the blade of his knife on a whetstone, and one by one the foresters moved closer to where the knights were seated.

"It was further put to me that I should take my sword to the king's aide and deter those assassins. My first thought was to refuse, for what good would one sword be against forty?"

"Two swords," Boethius said at once.

"Three," said Lord Geoffrey.

"Four," cried Roland.

Five, six, seven, and eight came in rapid succession from the foresters, none of whom showed a moment's hesitation.

"Eight men against forty or more," Tamberlane said quietly. "Poor odds at best."

"One good knight on a fair horse can account for five foot soldiers without breaking into a sweat," Lord Geoffrey said in a dry, flat voice. "Six if he unties his sword arm from behind his back."

"Aye, and we have four o' the finest archers this side o' Sherwood Forest in our company," Boethius growled. "They could cut those odds by a third or more without even coming within hailing distance."

"We would also have surprise on our side," Roland chimed in. "The assassins will be looking ahead, not behind."

"They could well have the greater advantage," Tamberlane said, raking a hand through his hair, "by knowing where to look in the first place. The coast is long, and the monk was vague as to where Richard might come ashore."

"Do any know the lay o' the land?"

"He could land anywhere . . . from Hastings to Dover, a stretch of forty leagues or more."

"Sandwich," Amaranth said quietly. "He will come ashore at Sandwich."

The men turned and looked at her as if most had forgotten she was there.

Boethius frowned. "Why say you that, lass?"

"Because I know . . . some of his habits, from his youth."

"Ye're naught but a youth yourself. How would you know the habits of a king?"

She fingered the crucifix that hung around her neck, then looked at Tamberlane. His face was a blank slate in the firelight, and she moistened her lips first before carefully flicking the tiny metal clasp that opened the outer shell that Marak had made to conceal the smaller cross within.

The two knights recognized the Plantagenet leopards at once.

"I am related by blood, albeit born on the wrong

side of the hedge," she admitted softly. "The king is my cousin."

Boethius was the first to recover his wits and clear his throat. "An' these habits ye speak of?"

"When I was but a child of five or six, I remember my father engaging in a terrible fight with someone I did not know, had never seen before. He was tall and blond and handsome. He looked like a god, and it came as no surprise to hear he was a god of sorts . . . a man destined to be king.

"The gist of the argument was that Richard had been caught in the arms of his lover and that that lover had barely escaped London alive and needed somewhere to stay where King Henry's minions would not think to search.

"Richard turned to his uncle and asked that a sanctuary be provided where there were no steep staircases upon which a foot might accidentally slip or a body might accidentally fall over the parapets and find itself dashed on the rocks below.

"Against his better judgment, my father sent the young prince and his lover to Sandwich, to a small holding he had there that overlooked the sea. That particular lover fell out of Richard's favor in due time, but there were others, and after my parents died, my uncle was only too happy to continue sheltering the king's lovers." She moistened her lips again. "I would think, after two years of being held prisoner in a foreign land, a man might want to see his lover again."

"Do others know of this castle?"

"I'm certain Prince John would make it his duty to know all of his brother's habits—especially habits that might well be used against him at some future date. This would be the case for most brothers," she added with an eloquent intensity. "Would it not?"

She held Tamberlane's gaze far longer than necessary for a simple question. He knew, where the others might not, of the king's penchant for taking lovers that were most definitely unsuited for a prince, a king . . . even a man. It was also obvious to him—for despite rumors and innuendo, there were few who were ready to believe it of their golden Lionheart—that Amaranth was aware of Richard's tastes but was not about to blurt out what else she knew in front of a campfire.

"Come," he said. "Walk with me."

There was an air of authority in his voice she had not heard before, and it sent a shiver through her limbs. She obeyed without question, however, ignoring the stiffness in her limbs and the aches in her back and shoulders. She rose and followed him away from the fire and into the cooler air of the darkness, trusting the blackness of his silhouette not to lead her into a fallen stump or hole.

He walked ahead, his long legs scything through deergrass that grew above the height of his knees. He walked to the center of the clearing before he stopped to see if she had followed. A glance started him walking again, and this time he did not stop until they were at the far edge of the encroaching forest.

"Now then," he said, turning and crossing his arms over his chest. "My lady of many secrets . . . what it is that is stuck in your throat and you are having such difficulty spitting out?"

"I told you, my lord, that Odo de Langois had not

petitioned Prince John for my hand out of any whim or lovelust. What I had not told you was that he saw me the first time when he was on his way to Sandwich in order to retrieve his brother. It happened just after the king was captured by Leopold of Austria, and Odo passed through the Three Benches on his way."

"Rolf de Langois?" Tamberlane thought of the chiseled beauty in the dark, saturnine features, the sensuality of the long-lashed, pale blue eyes. "He was the king's lover?"

"For more than a year, as I understood it. There are few who know, and fewer still whom Odo would have know."

"So he married you to keep you close and quiet?"

Her wry smile was not seen in the darkness. "Make no mistake, he married me, with the prince regent's blessing, because of the blood that flows through my veins. The other was just a boon. And the day Rolf caught me aside in the woods, it was to offer proof in front of his minions that he was a man with a man's lusts and any whispers I might make would be taken as revenge."

"A tangled web," Tamberlane mused.

"Shall I add another knot, sirrah?"

"There are more?"

"Only one. If you are going to make an attempt to avert an ambush at Sandwich, you must take me with you."

"The thought, addled as it is, would not tarry a moment in my mind."

"I know the castle, the grounds, the coastal waters. I know the inlet where a boat from France might put down if its occupant wanted to slip ashore unnoticed. Rolf de Langois will know this too, of course, and likely be there to greet his lover with rose petals and arrow shafts. But you would waste precious hours searching for it."

Ciaran resisted the urge to smile. Standing there under the moonless sky with only starlight to paint a hint of light over her pale hair, she had the pluck to place her hands on her waist and brace her legs wide apart in a stance that challenged as much as it defied.

"Very well." He glared down at her. "What skills do you possess? Can you wield a sword? Toss a pike? Fling an arrow perhaps?"

She stood motionless for a moment, then in a move quicker than his eye could follow, she reached down, snatched the dagger from her belt, flipped it so that she held the blade, and with a quick, lethal snap of her wrist, sent it into the tree trunk behind him, missing his cheek by such a small margin that he felt the lick of air as it passed.

"Admirable," he remarked after glancing over his shoulder. "But not of much use in combat against armored knights."

"You will waste precious time delivering me to Maidstone. Time you cannot make up even if you ride the horses at full gallop."

"I will send you apart with Roland. We will not lose a step."

"Roland will not thank you. And do you think that just because Odo de Langois is preoccupied with assassinating a king, he has not spared his jackals' eyes to watch the roads? How well do you suppose your squire will fare against seasoned mercenaries? Nor can you spare one of the knights, lest those be the next words off your lips."

"You have found your tongue today," he said, frowning, "and it is sharp."

"I owe you my life, my lord. I only wish to repay you in some way."

"There is no need to repay me," he said firmly. "And it was Marak who saved your life, not I. I merely brought you to him."

"And I can bring you to Sandwich."

He lost the battle with his willpower and moved a step closer—close enough that he could raise his hand and draw the backs of his fingers down her cheek. "You said nothing in the room after Father Michaelus left. You offered no argument as to why I should place my sword at the king's command."

" 'Twas not my place to do so."

"Yet you feel strongly enough about it to place yourself at risk."

She closed her eyes against the sensation of his fingers brushing her cheek. "I could ask the same question of you, my lord, for you were more than adamant about not throwing yourself between King Richard and his brother."

"I have been remembering what the good father said . . . in fact, it has been spinning round and round in my head like a wheel. That honor is the only thing that cannot be taken away from us—it is something we have to give away. In truth"—his fingers paused at the bottom of her chin, turned and tucked beneath so he could tilt her face up to his—"I have grown exceedingly weary of giving things away."

Amaranth held her breath. He had not touched her, had not even come this close to her in the three days since they had left the monestary, and she had begun to fear he regretted what had happened between them. She, on the other hand, had not regretted one instant, one kiss, one touch. She still blushed warm to think of how eagerly she had flared her thighs for him, how greedily she had pulled him inside her body . . . how joyously she had ridden the waves of pleasure he had given her.

Pleasure . . . not pain.

From this man, this enigma, this knight and monk and slayer of dragons. This man who would ride out alone and defend his king, redeem his honor in the eyes of those who could not see that he was the embodiment of everything noble and honorable and good.

His lips were there, before the thought had fully ended, and she met them with such fervor and passion he stumbled back a half step. Her arms went up around his neck, and her body crushed up against his. She matched his tongue thrust for thrust, his groans breath for breath, his heartbeat pulse for pulse. She kissed until she did not have the wit or the strength to kiss him further, until her lips were tender and swollen, her cheek abraded by the stubble that grew on his chin.

She did not care. He could have scraped her with a knife and she would not have noticed or cared.

Her legs trembled, her arms shook, and when at last

the kiss ended, she buried her face against his throat and held him tight, introducing him to yet another new rush of feelings that left him no choice but to smile and press his lips into the soft tousle of her hair.

"Please, Ciaran, I beg you: do not leave me behind. Let me come with you, let me help you, let me help the man who is not only my king but my kinsman. Afterward . . . I will go quietly to the convent, but only give me this one last chance to salvage my own honor that I might look back one day and say, 'Yes, I did that and it served a purpose.' "

Ciaran lifted a hand to stroke her hair. He kept his chin buried in the curls and found it discomforting that his heart was pounding like a foolish thing in his chest. He did not want to take her to Sandwich; he did not want to put her in harm's way. Yet he could offer no argument to gainsay her need to feel of some worth. He knew all too well that sense of standing alone in a wilderness, his arms stretched out as he turned and turned, searching for answers.

"You will do exactly, precisely as I command? If I say run behind the nearest rock, you will run?"

She tilted her head up and waited until he met her gaze. "If you command me to run all the way to Maidstone, I will run all the way."

He buried his fingers in her hair and pulled her mouth up to his. This time the kiss was deep and forceful, full of unspoken passions that might never be unleashed, might suffer for what might have been, might have only the memory of this one last embrace to last a lifetime.

Amaranth responded without hesitation, the cry

soft in her throat as his hands descended and cradled her rump, pulling her roughly against him. She could feel his desire rising hard and urgent against her, and she could feel her own stirring with a sharp, needful ache.

They sank down onto the soft deergrass together, their hands fumbling to loosen clothing, to push barriers aside, to melt eagerly together in a coupling that was as swiftly achieved as it was deliciously prolonged.

The initial thrust took Tamberlane where he most wanted to be, and he remained there, sheathed in her heat and wetness, until her cries threatened to draw attention from the ruined cottage.

When, some time later, they did return to the glow of the fire, the eyes that looked up in askance noted the rumpled clothing, the dew-soaked stains, the mottled flushes . . . and looked away again, some startled, some not.

The same response was won on Tamberlane's announcement that Amaranth would be accompanying them to Sandwich, though none were unwise enough to question the hard gleam in the pale green eyes.

The remainder of the night was spent making plans, supplemented by drawings sketched in the moist earth. Since time had suddenly become crucial, and none declared the need to sleep, they doused the fire and moved out of their little camp well before the first streaks of light bloomed in the easterly sky.

Chapter Twenty-one

Fulke Castle took its only glory from its name. More of a manor house than a castle proper, it sat on a small rise of grassy land that ended abruptly at the sea. There were cliffs behind and cliffs on either side, which appeared to isolate it from the rest of the forested countryside. The spindle of land was too narrow to raise battlements, towering stone walls, or a defensive keep. At best, the residents could light a fire on the top of the stone rampart to warn seafarers away from the cliffs in fog.

The seas that crashed against the rocks below offered no hospitable anchorage, nor did the shoreline appear to be unbroken when viewed by a passing ship. If a canny eye knew where to look, however, there was a cove tucked into a horseshoe of rocks where a single small vessel could safely land.

From above, the descent to the sea looked no less harrowing than the cliffs themselves. Odo de Langois ventured as close to the lip as he dared and peered straight down into the calm, sparkling waters of the cove below. His expression, when he looked at his brother Rolf, was openly skeptical.

"Do you expect us to lower ourselves by way of ropes and ladders?"

Rolf smiled lazily. "As tempting as the image might be, no. There is a path. Steep, to be sure, and not for the faint of heart, but smugglers and rogues have used it for scores of years. The horses, unfortunately will not suffer the travail well. It would be best to leave them here."

Odo was not happy to hear this. A knight unhorsed was half the threat he posed mounted—if not less. Most carried between fifty and seventy-five pounds of armor, which made moving with any haste or stealth near impossible. On horseback, with a war-bred destrier between his thighs, a knight was invincible, his power supreme. On foot, he was an oaf.

Odo studied his brother's features—the beautiful long-lashed eyes, the chiseled jaw, the full sensual lips. Once again he damned the beautiful Cyprian for having won the attentions of a king. How many times had he wanted to slay his own brother with his bare hands? How many times had he fought to erase the image of Rolf de Langois on his knees, his legs spread for the rutting pleasures of another man?

It was not natural. It reviled and disgusted Odo each time he saw his brother cast a lascivious eye across the haunches of a passing stableboy. Yet were it not for this depravity, Odo might not have won himself a place in such high favor with Prince John. The regent was a collector and hoarder of secrets, and he rewarded those well who shared their knowledge of the deepest, darkest sins. And this—this beautiful creature, who was also Odo's brother, was the darkest sin of all.

A sin that would have to be eradicated at the same time as the sinner.

Regicide, fratricide . . . Odo would be killing a king, a brother, and when he found her . . . a wife. It was unfortunate their father had died of the pox a dozen years sooner, or he would have tossed in the old bastard for good measure.

He looked out over the choppy blue waters of the Channel, able to see for many miles on such a clear, unclouded day as had finally graced them. The rain and fog that had been dogging them for days was gone at last, leaving not so much as a layer of haze to cloud the distant horizon. The wind was brisk, however, and the waves showed caps of white foam. There were treacherous currents off the lands' end as well, making for tricky seas in fair weather or foul.

The courier who had come to him at St. Albans had impressed upon him the need for speed if they were to intercept the king's ship. Tonight the moon would be full, ideal for navigating between sheets of impregnable cliff.

"Post a keen watch," he murmured. "I want to know the instant a ship appears from any direction. When it arrives, you, brother dearest, will make the descent to greet the passenger it carries. Our knights and archers will bide here, with me, to present a warmer welcome after he has huffed and puffed his way to the top of the goat path."

Rolf's clear blue eyes regarded his brother as a sleepy lion might regard a snake slithering through the long grass nearby. There was no wealth of trust in those eyes. He knew, with a full moon overhead and the glitter of the Channel behind them, that anyone climbing the cliffs would present a clear silhouette to archers and knights alike.

He also knew the way Odo's mind worked. The Red Boar was aptly named for the way he charged full ahead like a wild animal with no attempts at subtlety or deception. Two silhouettes would climb the cliff, and two would be slain.

Rolf was still contemplating the duplicity of his older brother when he caught a glimmer of something out on the water.

At first glance, it could have been just another wave peaking far out in the Channel. But Rolf had spent many a day and night ensconced in the arms of his royal lover, and indeed, before Odo had come to drag him back to Belmane, he had passed whole days staring across the blue void wondering how he might cross over to Austria and rescue his king.

He knew a ship when he saw one.

The initial flush of excitement was halted abruptly when he turned to shout an alert to Odo. The brace of arrows struck with the force of an ax. The first caught him high on the throat, in the soft underside of his chin, severing his windpipe, driving through to scrape the back of his skull. The second pierced his chest, the power behind the iron head punching cleanly through the chain mail armor and shattering his spine as it exited.

Dead already, he slumped heavily onto his knees then pitched facedown on the wet grass, his last glance aimed out toward the sea.

Three days after committing himself and his sword to King Richard's rescue, Tamberlane's small host of defenders had arrived in the town of Sandwich. They made good time by forsaking the forest paths and traveling openly along the main roads. Time had become as much their enemy as Prince John or Odo de Langois, and keeping to the greenwood was neither practical nor beneficial. Caution had been sacrificed to speed as they endeavored to stay ahead of the winds that carried news of their presence to those who would pay dearly to know it.

Those same winds worked to their advantage, for they had known exactly how far they were behind the much larger host of knights and foot soldiers traveling under the pennons and pennoncels of Odo de Langois. The latter could only move as fast as the foot soldiers, and by the time they approached Sandwich, Tamberlane had managed to outflank the Red Boar's men and circle around to come out ahead.

Amaranth's knowledge of the town and the outlying area helped them further, shaving off almost a full day. She had led them to Fulke Castle and unerringly to the ground above the tiny cove, where Tamberlane had immediately discovered even more disadvantages that made it impractical to send men below to lie in wait. The rocks were tumbled and set back from the narrow strip of shore, but anyone walking down the steep, zigzagging path could not help but see men crouched behind them. Moreover, to judge by the lines of seaweed and salt stains, the water level rose sharply at high tide, submerging the only few plausible places of concealment.

The top of the cliff, from the path to the manor house a half mile away, was open meadow, the grasses not long enough to conceal a fieldmouse. They were eight men against forty-eight, and possibly more if Odo's host had been joined by more men than Roland had counted when they circled past. Ten of those men were knights, well mounted and armored. And thirty-eight crossbowmen, while standing even lower in the rank than archers, were not to be discounted as a threat.

Tamberlane had had the night to pace the cliffs and walk the verge of trees. The code of chivalry demanded that he give his enemy a fair chance, to make his presence known before drawing any weapons. But the code of chivalry was not written for men like Odo de Langois, and Ciaran suspected there had been no such warning issued to the peasant's village before the Red Boar's men attacked and slaughtered.

An ambuscade, therefore, would have to be waiting above, from the trees that were more than two hundred long paces from the edge of the cliffs. For it to succeed, he needed his foresters to take up prime killing positions, to fire swift and steady, and to disregard the next highest rule among the legion of rules that shaped the covenant of chivalry: they would have to aim first for the knights.

At dawn, when Amaranth found him, he was still standing on the cliffs pondering his decisions, his choices. She had used the excuse of bringing him bread and ale to break his fast, but when she saw his face dusted by the rising light, saw his eyes so intent upon hers, his hair so dark and ragged where it blew forward on his cheeks . . . her breath caught and her heart pounded within her chest.

He said nothing. Oblivious to the stares they might draw from the trees, he extended his arm and drew her gently against his chest. With a soft sigh, she rested her head on his shoulder and laid her hand flat upon the front of his tunic.

"I have been giving the matter a deal of thought," he said quietly. His gaze scanned the horizon and flicked up to the sky as if he were contemplating the weather. "I think you would not be happy at Maidstone. I have been there. 'Tis a very old nunnery, and the walls reek of dampness. This mother abbess you speak of—I know her as well. A face like a piece of bark, the breath of a dragon, the manners of a fishmonger."

As he spoke, the fingers of one hand stole upward and twined themselves around the tousled curls of her hair.

"I doubt not that she would turn the king himself away from the doors in order to protect that which falls under her dominion. By the same token, I doubt she would take kindly to an excommunicated warrior monk scaling the walls each night to seek out one of her flock."

Amaranth slowly lifted her head off his shoulder.

"Nay—I would not do anything untoward or seek to desecrate the holy grounds of the convent," he continued. "Certes, God showed infinite kindness by overlooking our one indiscretion. But two, three, ten, a thousand . . . I doubt even He would have the tolerance."

Amaranth looked up into his face.

He waited another moment . . . then looked down. "I have made my penance." He spoke softly, looking directly into her eyes. "If I am to die today, I would do so with the knowledge that had I lived, you would be returning with me to Taniere Castle.

"I have nothing to offer, of course. The linens that grace the boards at Taniere are not even mine. I am but a poor man, a lost man who needs finding, but I vow there would be no whips and nothing to fear. I would expect nothing from you that you were not willing to give, yet for the grace of your presence, I would protect you with my life and emerge a far richer man for having done so."

His eyes remained locked to hers, waiting, watching. When she made no sound, no move to respond, the green darkened and faltered slightly, as if a cloud had passed across the sun.

"Naturally," he murmured awkwardly, "if I have made presumptions . . ."

Amaranth's hand lifted from his chest and pressed against his cheek. She turned within the circle of his arm and raised her other hand so that his face was cradled between. Going up on tiptoes, she pressed the softness and warmth of her lips over his, holding fast until a gasp sent her breath, her tongue, the rushed ecstasy of her answer into his mouth.

He gathered her close, crushing her into his embrace, and Amie kissed him with her whole heart and soul, with the passion of lost youth and lost years, the lust of newfound desire and pleasure.

When he eased enough to allow it, she half laughed, half wept, keeping her hands on his face, her brow bent against his lips.

"I will, my lord. I will come back to Taniere with you in whatever capacity you will allow. Mistress, maid, laundress, cook . . ."

"Lover?" he whispered.

She blushed a deep, hot red. "And—and your table is appalling, sir. Do you know the cooks cheat you by sending the plumpest fowl behind the screen? The ale is watered and truly terrible, and the rushes have not been swept from the hall since it was built, I trow."

"Lover," he whispered again, his lips moving down to her temple. "For you still have much to teach me in the ways of courtly love . . . and carnal love . . . and I do swear I would learn both from you and no other."

She looked up, her breath stilled again, but he only laughed and gathered her closer.

"As for my table and my pullets, you have not said anything I did not already know," he assured her. "And it will be my further pleasure to sit back and let you whitewash the entire castle if that is your desire. If it will make you happy. If it will keep you by my side a day longer."

She melted back into his arms, and he held her close, neither wanting to face the true reality of what the day might bring . . . namely, the fact that there might well not be a tomorrow for either of them.

They stood like that until the sun rose above the eastern horizon and sparkled off the surface of the water. Until the seabirds rose and screamed overhead, circling on the currents of the wind.

They stood together until their solitude was interrupted by a soft cough in a cupped hand, whereupon one by one, beginning with the two burly knights, the men had approached the Dragon Slayer and gone down on one knee to pay homage, pledging their loyalty and their swords, their very lives if he should command it of them. The gesture had not been necessary, certainly not foreseen, and Tamberlane found himself swallowing several times during the course. Amaranth stood in silence and watched, unable to move or even raise a hand to wipe the two fat tears that rolled quietly down her cheeks, for here was proof that he was, indeed, a man above all men.

Afterward he had regarded his meager host of comrades-in-arms with humility and a long-unused emotion that verged fearfully close to great affection. Even Roland, who had thrown caution to the wind and brought something totally unexpected away from Taniere, won a hand clap on the shoulder and a soft word of thanks when Ciaran's great jeweled sword was uncovered from its burlap wrapping. Roland had removed it from the prayer niche on a last and fleeting thought, and when he watched his master curl his hand around the hilt with a warrior's pride, he knew he had done the right thing.

It was a motley crew who had departed Taniere a sennight earlier, but it was a band of men who escorted Amie off the meadow that morning and took their positions in the forest. No knight declared precedence by stepping ahead of a squire or forester; they would stand together as equals, and as equals would defend against those who would murder a king.

Once into the trees, the archers melted into the shadows. A good English archer could strike a target easily, dead center, from one hundred fifty paces. Fletcher and Quill were Welshmen and had brought their own unique weapons with them to the south of England. It was rumored to be the weapon of choice for the outlaws who were plaguing the forests of Lincolnshire. Made from five feet of seasoned yew, the bows fired arrows that were twice the length of English shafts, and they could pierce armor and mail, could be fired accurately from three hundred yards with speed and power that were terrifying.

Ciaran, Lord Boethius, and Lord Geoffrey de Ville would be mounted, as would Roland. Although the latter did not yet possess a full suit of armor, enough spares and pieces were found among the packings to add a protective layer of mail to his chest and thighs.

Tamberlane's intent was to let the foresters soften the number of routiers who traveled in Odo de Langois's array, then scatter the foot soldiers in a charge that would, if history bore proof, send the crossbowmen running off the field in a general quest to save their own hides. He was also counting on the fact that more than a few of them might have reservations about killing a king. It was a dirty business, and there would be no looting in it for the foot soldiers, certes no honor in it for the knights. He wished he could spare a man to take another count, for it would lift everyone's spirits to know the numbers had dwindled.

Thus they had waited, patient and sweating in the warm morning air, for two, three, four hours . . . until a glint of sunlight off metal warned them of the approaching host of men.

The brace of arrows that struck Rolf de Langois were fired almost simultaneously from the weapons of Quill and Fletcher. They had waited, their hands steady and heartbeats slowed by many years of stalking and lying in wait for elusive prey. Where an eager fool might have loosed his arrows the instant the impressive body of knights and foot soldiers stepped onto the meadow, the Welshmen were patient . . . anticipating, hoping, and finally smiling inwardly when they saw several of the routiers dismount to stretch their legs and admire the view from atop the cliffs.

They had communicated their targets of choice by a series of hand signals, but at the last moment, Odo de Langois had moved, and the glare from the sun sheeting off the waters of the Channel had caused both men to blink.

When they looked again, not only had both their arrows struck the same man but Odo had heard the distinctive *whoosh thunk thunk* and had leaped instinctively behind his horse. Both foresters nocked and fired twice more in rapid succession but were able to strike only the saddle and notch the ear of the huge destrier.

Immediately, out from cover of the trees, the other archers took up the signal and began to shoot. They nocked and fired as swiftly as a hand could reach into a quiver, and within the first thirty seconds, there were nine men dead, a dozen writhing on the ground, and the rest scattering in search of cover. There were shouts of astonishment from the knights and screams from the horses who found their flanks or withers pierced with arrows.

The foresters, land-bound creatures for the most part, instinctively feared these beasts almost more than the men who rode them, knowing that the great, blooded warhorses were trained to rear and slash a man with iron-clad hooves, or worse, to trample him to bloody mash on the ground. Thus, despite Tamberlane's directive to aim high, a goodly number of arrows were thrown low. Horses dropped and thrashed on the ground; their riders tumbled free only to stand and find themselves the next target.

Behind the veil of trees, Tamberlane dropped the visor of his helm and raised his sword. He glanced both ways to acknowledge his three companions, then touched his spurs to the flanks of his magnificent piebald.

They had carried no fancy silks caparisons away from Taniere, yet the sight of those four horsemen charging out of the woods, their shields and swords raised, their voices calling upon God to aid them in their quest, caused many of the lingering bravehearts to stumble back and reconsider. The four spread apart like the bearers of the apocalypse and galloped straight into the sudden scramble. Swords scythed downward, and blood sprayed through the air. Crossbows were flung aside, some armed yet unfired, their valiant owners thrusting their arms to the sky and screaming for quarter.

The four raked across the meadow and pulled up at the far side. They turned and charged a second time, sweeping through the panicking men and driving them straight into the waiting arrows of the foresters.

Another charge and it was left to the knights to choose specific targets. Tamberlane had noted Odo de Langois tugging furiously on his horse and using a rock to step himself up into the saddle again. He had lost his helm when he dove for cover, and the shock of bright red hair was unmistakable even through the dust and confusion of the melee.

Tamberlane cut through the chaff and made for the edge of the cliff. Twenty feet away from the Red Boar, Tristan responded to the command in his master's knees and drew to a snorting halt.

De Langois was still pulling his shield off his back when he saw the threat and bared his teeth in a snarl.

"What devilry is this? Who are you? And how dare you attack without provocation!"

"Aye, there is devilry in the air. I am come by way of Hubert Walter. He advises England that there is treachery awaiting the homecoming of her king."

Odo clenched his teeth and snarled again. "Who are you, cur? Show yourself so that I may know the face of the man I kill this day."

Tamberlane went one step further. He raised a gauntleted hand and removed his helm, casting it aside with a clank of metal so that the two men were now equal in their defenses.

At first, de Langois's rage clouded his vision, and he saw only the disheveled waves of black hair, the vaguely familiar squareness to the jaw. But then he saw the eyes. The unmistakable, luminous green eyes.

"You!" He blew a breath out from between his teeth. "A one-armed ferret whispered in my ear not two days gone that you had left your lair, but I could scarcely believe it. So . . . you are Hubert Walter's pet, are you? The fox laid low in the chicken coop? In truth, I did not think it possible for a man of your stature to simply hang up your sword and be content to fuck Saracen whores for the rest of your days."

Tamberlane smiled with lethal calm. "Whereas I thought it only too possible for a man of your lowly stature to take up the stinking blade of an assassin. Tell me—what price to spill a king's blood? Two holdings? Three? Perhaps a barony that you might enjoy a taste of that eludes you by birth? I wonder, though, how long you think the prince would let you live? Not long enough, I warrant, to even heal the scar on your head where your wife stove you with a candlestick."

Odo's snarl deepened. "Elizabeth! So it *was* you to whom she fled!"

"Fled . . . and told the tale of how you murdered a village of innocent people. For that alone you shall pay with your life."

Odo roared. He spurred his horse forward, not waiting for Tamberlane to brace himself. His sword was in the air and swinging as Ciaran urged his piebald into the charge. The first pass was met with a resounding clash of steel on steel. Both men were powerfully built, their arms like oak, their blades well blooded in battle. They turned and rode at each other again, this time bashing at shields, striving by sheer force and shock of impact to unhorse the other.

The third pass, Tamberlane's shield was split in two and Odo's sword took a shallow slash out of his arm. He cast the shattered bullhide to the ground and reached for his misericorde—a weapon longer than a dagger but half the length of the battle sword. With blades in both hands, he guided Tristan with his knees, urging the destrier to charge again and again, the turns and circles becoming smaller as the two knights flailed and bashed at each other.

Both were showing blood. Neither showed signs of weakening. There was fighting still going on behind them, but most of the crossbowmen had fled, and those few who remained felt their loyalties draining out of them as the tide clearly turned in the favor of Tamberlane's valiant party of defenders.

Amaranth, lured out of her hiding place by the sound of screams and the clashing of swords, crept closer to the edge of the trees to watch. Her heart was in her throat as she saw Tamberlane take a crushing blow across his back and shoulders, one that surely would have split him in two but for the strength of the Damascene steel used to forge his mail. The blow glanced off, slicing only his gyphon and nicking an ear.

Odo was himself so surprised to see the knight still upright that he paused and stared a moment—a moment that allowed Tamberlane to swing his upper body around in the saddle and drive the pointed tip of his Crusader's sword into the hollow of Odo's armpit and clear through the breadth of his chest. At the same moment, when the shock of feeling the blade punch through his flesh was the greatest, Tamberlane brought the misericorde forward, slashing it across de Langois's throat with enough vehemence to completely sever the head from the shoulders.

The torso remained upright in the saddle for as long as it took for the weight of armor to tip it over and send it crashing to the ground. The head, with its shock of red hair, was sent spinning toward the end of the cliff, where it rolled over the edge and dropped out of sight.

Amaranth had not been aware of holding her breath until she saw Odo's body fall. She released it then on a loud gust and broke from the trees, running at full tilt. Tamberlane's shoulders had taken a decided slump, and she could see that he was struggling with the pain as he leaned forward in the saddle. His head was bowed . . . low enough that he could not possibly have seen the man rise up from the rocks near the edge of the cliff and start running toward him.

"No! No, you bastard, you will not humiliate me again!"

Hugh de Bergerette ran in at full speed, his gyphon, while soiled almost beyond recognition, still showed the red Crusader's cross emblazoned on the breast. He carried his sword in his left hand, windmilling it to gain momentum for the blow that he hoped would earn him his revenge after so many years of dreaming it.

Amie watched in horror, knowing his speed was such that he would reach Tamberlane's side long before her shouts could draw the attention of another defender. She skidded to a halt, judged the distance to be so far out of her range as to verge on impossible, but she reached to her waist and drew her dagger, flipped the blade into her palm, and threw it as hard and straight and true as her heart would carry it.

Tamblerlane heard the shout at the last possible moment and turned in time to see Hugh de Bergerette's filty, bearded face coming at him out of a nightmare. He took in the soiled mantle, the empty sleeve that was folded under, and the screaming epithets, and he watched the brilliant cut of the sword begin to make its final descent.

Fractions of a second before the blade was committed, something struck de Bergerette between the eyes. It was a dagger, and the tip of the blade pierced through the skin and split the bone, sinking in halfway before the guard on the hilt stopped it.

De Bergerette had time to utter one last curse before his eyes rolled slowly up into his skull and his body fell back. The sword flew out of his limp fingers and skidded across the grass moments before pounding footsteps brought Amaranth running up beside Tamberlane's horse.

She saw the knife embedded in the knight's forehead and gasped as she turned, pressing her face into Tristan's warm neck.

Tamberlane swung himself carefully out of the saddle, landing on his feet with an ungracious grunt of expended air. His back still felt like it might be broken, though he knew if it was, he would be on the ground beside de Bergerette.

Frowning, he glanced down at the broken knight. Where the devil he had come from Ciaran could only guess. But he was real, not a fragment of a past nightmare. He had heard the screams of the men and horses dying on the meadow . . . but they had remained part of the meadow. He had not been thrown back to the deserts of Palestine, had not been scorched by the burning sun or tormented by the screams of the innocents being slaughtered. For that, he could only give thanks to God.

To God . . . and to the woman who had saved him from the depths of his despair.

He glanced back once to ensure the field was his. The hail of arrows had slowed to occasional well-placed shots. Lord Geoffrey de Ville and Roland were herding foot soldiers into a circle, with Maude and Hugo hastening any laggards with growls and snapping teeth. Lord Boethius was still engaged with two routiers, but it was plain he was just toying with them, savoring the heady rush of combat again.

Ciaran had felt that same rush of blood through his veins.

He had fought as a whole man again, and as he remembered it now, God's name had been on his lips as he rode out of the forest.

He winced at a sharp pain in his side and felt along his ribs, seeing his hand come away red. He had other cuts and would likely be bruised black and blue come morning.

Amaranth was beside him, her face pale and lovely. He turned his gaze to the brilliant blue of the sky, squinting hard against the glare of the sun and knew that he had come alive again.

Chapter Twenty-two

The ship Rolf de Langois had seen with his dying glimpse sailed steadily toward the landfall and maneuvered unerringly into the small, protected cove. As the sails were furled and the anchor dropped, a longboat was lowered into the water and ten men cloaked in pilgrim's gray boarded and were rowed ashore. All wore conical steel helms with wide, descending nasals. All showed the telltale bulge of swords buckled to their waists and mail links at the wrists and throat.

Nine of the ten, after a small argument on the wet shingle, came up the goat path first, their cloaks swept back over one shoulder to free their sword arms. They had the efficient look of royal guardsmen about them, and proof of that was borne out when the tallest among them saw the carnage that littered the meadow.

He came forward and cast his steely blue-gray gaze down the soiled and bloodied line of defenders. Several were nursing wounds. Boethius had a stained strip of cloth tied on an angle over his forehead, concealing an eye that was split and swollen almost closed.

The leader of the new arrivals was an impressive beast of a man. He stood well above six feet tall, with dark hair and eyebrows; thick lashes shielded eyes that seemed to pierce every man where he stood. His massive torso was made even more so by the jerkin of gleaming black wolf pelts he wore over his mail hauberk. That chest expanded even farther as he insolently placed one hand on his hip and the other on the curved support of the longbow he held casually by his side.

"I am left to surmise some mischief has been wrought here today," he murmured thoughtfully.

Tamberlane stepped forward, a half smile playing across his lips.

"The vaunted Scourge of Mirebeau honors us humblies with his presence this side of the Channel. I had heard he had avowed never to leave his new aerie in Touraine."

The newcomer narrowed his eyes. "I had heard a similar vow with regard to a slayer of dragons, that he had buried himself away in this godforsaken land of noddy-peaks and arse-whistlers, sworn to pluck daisies and count rings on the surface of a lake for the rest of his days."

"Daisies?" Tamberlane paused and rolled the thought across his tongue before speaking. "They were never a favorite flower of mine. Now, speak to me of amaranths, and I would happily count the rings to forever and back."

"Amaranths?"

At the sound of her name, Amie's head came up.

The blue-gray eyes did not miss the slight movement. Nor, after a hastily flickered second glance, did he miss the soft curve of her face, the full lips, the slight shaping of breasts where they pushed against the leather jerkin. The eyes went next to the foresters, Quill and Fletcher among them, both of whom were grinning like buffoons and shifting their weight from one foot to the next.

"You keep strange company, Dragon Slayer. I'faith I recognize these two rogues. But when I last saw them they were throwing arrows at the king's deer in Lincolnshire." The Scourge's pale eyes settled on the two knights. "These brave nobles, I know not, however. Nor the young woman who tries so hard to jut her chin like a man."

Tamberlane conducted the formalities, introducing Lords Boethius and Geoffrey to Lord Randwulf de la Seyne Sur Mer, champion to the dowager Queen Eleanor, Scourge of Mirebeau, and former outlaw known as the Black Wolf of Lincoln.

One of the foresters, hearing the long litany of titles, swayed and crumpled sideways like a windless pennon. The name of la Seyne Sur Mer was dreaded enough, for he was second only to William the Marshal for victories in the tournament lists in Europe. But to be standing in the presence of the Black Wolf was tantamount to standing in the presence of . . .

"By God's blood, what happened here?"

The tenth member of the landing party, obviously grown weary of waiting below, stood at the top of the path, his hood swept back, his golden lion's mane of hair ruffling in the wind.

Upon the instant, Tamberlane and his small group went down on one knee, their heads bowed, their eyes lowered.

"Randwulf, what in God's name—" The Lionheart's gaze had scanned the surfeit of corpses and come to rest on one in particular. Rolf de Langois's chiseled face was turned toward the sea, the eyes were glazed in death and still stared at a fixed point on the horizon.

"What has happened here today?" the king asked in horror. "Rise up, rise up, good men, and tell your liege why this field is red with blood."

"I have not yet heard the explanation myself," said the Black Wolf. "But by the look of it, I would say Hubert Walter's words of caution were well advised."

The king moved slowly to stand over the body of Rolf de Langois. "My brother is greedy and ambitious, but he is also a weakling and a fool. I can believe he would send men to kill me, for he does not have the spine to do it himself."

"His spine has been stiffened these past two years with layers of gold wrung from your people," Tamberlane said. "He taxes them half to death, and the half who cannot pay . . . he simply kills them."

Richard turned his Plantagenet blue eyes on Ciaran. There was a wealth of warnings delivered in that one glance, but in the end, the handsome features softened and looked kindly upon the man he had last seen standing before a tribunal of Templars.

"You have been well, my friend?"

"Well enough," Tamberlane agreed.

"And yet there is a bite to your words."

"No. There is no bite, my liege. It is only weariness you hear and perhaps . . . a lingering disenchantment with the way life spins out its web. I would like nothing more than to live out the rest I have in peace."

The king glanced at the Black Wolf. "Do you hear that, Randwulf? My Dragon Slayer wishes to live in peace."

"An honorable request," la Seyne Sur Mer murmured. "I have turned down that path myself."

Richard laughed. "My two most fearsome swords requesting to be sheathed. You, Randwulf, I have seen your sheath and she fits you well. It was"—he added in an aside to Ciaran—"like drawing teeth with two twigs for my mother to get him to leave his cozy little nest in Touraine." He paused and frowned as if another thought occurred to him. "Do you have a holding?"

Tamberlane shook his head. "I live by my uncle's good grace at Taniere Castle, a demesne of some little worth to the north and east, in Norfolk."

"Taniere . . ." Richard muttered the name aloud, and a moment later another gray-cloaked moth approached to whisper in the royal ear. "Ahh, yes. I know it now. A meager place of stone and dampness, hardly worthy of a man who has saved a kingdom this day."

"I have grown accustomed to those stone walls,"

Tamberlane said quietly. "And the dampness is not so bad with warm fires blazing in the hearth."

Richard laughed. "Then it is yours. I shall speak to Glanville and arrange for him to have some other worthy holding in exchange. Belmane, perhaps. Aye. That should put the beetle up my brother's arse. Unless you would like Belmane for yourself? Its owner seems to have lost his head."

While the king admired his own jest, Tamberlane shook his head. "Taniere suits me well, but if you would wish to grant me a boon, there is one I would ask of you, sire."

Richard looked pleased. "Something has indeed softened your tongue, Ciaran. Ask your boon. If it is within my power to grant it, it is yours."

"A nobleman—especially one with so many strikes against his shield as I bear—requires the permission of his liege to marry another of equal or higher blood."

"Higher blood?" Richard crossed his arms over his chest. "You Templars were never ones to aim low. Well then, out with it. Who is she?"

Ciaran turned and, after a moment's hesitation, held his hand out to Amaranth. With halting steps she moved forward, placing only the chilled tips of her fingers into his palm. The king's eyes raked over her hair, her face, her boyish garb . . . then up to her face again, whereupon his eyes widened with astonishment.

"Elizabeth? My little cousin . . . is it you?"

Amie let her hand fall away from Ciaran's, but only long enough to drop down into a curtsy before the wide-eyed Lionheart.

"It is I, cousin Richard. I bid you welcome home, sire," she said softly. "Your presence has been sorely missed here in England."

Richard nodded. "Indeed, I can see I have missed much. By God, another yellow-haired sheath has stolen away one of my prized swords. Is this your wish, then, as well? To be bound for all eternity to a man such as this?"

"For a man such as this," Amie said, looking over at Ciaran, "I fear eternity will not be long enough."

The journey back to Taniere was a far more comfortable affair than the journey away. For one, they traveled with the king and his guardsmen until they passed close to London. Each day, each league saw barons loyal to Richard stream up the road to join him, their pennons snapping in the wind, their faces grim with determination to support their king should force be needed to oust Prince John from Whitehall.

By the time they reached London, the Great North Road was congested with a solid column of men numbering in the thousands. Word reached them long before they saw the gleaming spires and rooftops of the city that John had hastily boarded a ship in the Thames and fled to France.

Richard reclaimed his city, his throne with much fanfare; the crusading king was home and promising to remain for however long it took to heal the wounds caused by his absence.

Tamberlane stayed only long enough to hear the banns read for his marriage to Amaranth. They continued their way north to the quiet forests of Norfolk, to the still waters of the lake that surrounded Taniere Castle.

They arrived just as the evening mists were drifting up over the shore. There was no fanfare for the returning heroes, although none was expected or needed. Marak's caution had ordered that the massive gates be closed each night, and so it was they stood outside the wooden portal, the six twisting heads of the dragons looking down on them with suspicion and warning carved into their eyes.

"Do you know the legend of the dragon tree?" Tamberlane asked.

Amaranth drew a deep breath and looked up at her lord. She had abandoned her guise as a young lad at Sandwich and had been given a bride present from her cousin—who despaired at her lack of sense in chopping off her hair—that consisted of four wagons groaning under the burden of silks, velvets, and samites woven in every shade of the rainbow. He also presented her with a magnificent white horse bred from his own royal stock, a sweet mare furbished with sky-blue trappings trimmed with tassels and long dragging silks.

Tamberlane—indeed, every member of their group—had not been spared the king's generosity, and they approached Taniere glowing head to toe in new suits of the finest armor, shields painted bright with crests, gyphons and cloaks of the richest weaves and wools. Even Roland rode with his chest puffed out like a peacock, for Richard himself had presented the squire with his spurs and knighted him before the royal court.

"Marak told me," she said softly and quoted: "It was made long ago in an enchanted forge, and according to legend, when a pure heart rings the magical bells, the dragons will awaken to fly in six directions. The dragon of the nether region will flee from despair and bring hope. The dragon of heaven will return with the gift of true love. And from the four corners of the earth will come peace, health, wisdom, and happiness."

Tamberlane smiled. "Then ring the bells, my love. For these lazy dragons have slept long enough."